The Gateway to Imagia
The Tale of Sam Little

JaNine,

Thanks for your support! You are just awesome & I appreciate it. Hope you enjoy it!

Janice J M ____
2014

Written by Jessica Williams
Copyright © 2013

iv

Copyright © 2013 by Jessica Williams

All rights reserved. This book or any portion thereof may not be reproduced or used in any manner whatsoever without the express written permission of the publisher except for the use of brief quotations in a book review or scholarly journal.

This book is a work of fiction. The names, characters, places and incidents are products of the writer's imagination or have been used fictitiously and are not to be construed as real. Any resemblance to persons, living or dead, actual events, locales or organizations is entirely coincidental.

First Printing: 2013

ISBN-13: 978-1494494759
ISBN-10: 1494494752

Author and Illustrator: Jessica Williams
Kansas, United States of America
www.facebook.com/TheGatewaytoImagia

Dedication

To my husband, Josh, for telling me it can be done and to my children Alex, Abby, and Evie for reminding me how wonderful the world can be through imagination.

In loving memory of
My Dad.

Rusty Shaw

Always my biggest fan.
Then, Now...
Forever.

*"Do not neglect to show hospitality to strangers,
for thereby some have entertained angels unawares."*
Hebrews 13:2

Contents

Acknowledgements xi

Chapter One: The Wish 1

Chapter Two: Granted 15

Chapter Three: Detour 24

Chapter Four: Deception 36

Chapter Five: Course Change 46

Chapter Six: Nightmare 57

Chapter Seven: The Guardian 69

Chapter Eight: History Lesson 80

Chapter Nine: Decisions 93

Chapter Ten: The Gateway 105

Chapter Eleven: Theories 118

Chapter Twelve: Lost 131

Chapter Thirteen: Tricks 142

Chapter Fourteen: Preparation 157

Chapter Fifteen: Exile 172

Chapter Sixteen: Southern Shores 189

Chapter Seventeen: The Impossible Way 201

Chapter Eighteen: Wild Ways 214

Chapter Nineteen: False Impressions 229

Chapter Twenty: Trades and Traitors 247

Chapter Twenty-one: Hoodwinked 265

Chapter Twenty-two: Double Crossed 275

Chapter Twenty-three: Connection 286

Chapter Twenty-four: Into the Shadow 303

Chapter Twenty-five: In Between 318

Chapter Twenty-six: Nightmares 330

Chapter Twenty-seven: Unexpected Turn 341

Author's Note 359

Acknowledgements

I'd like to take a moment to give a special thanks to my ever-faithful test audience:
Mom (Brenda Shaw), Aunt Rita (Crawford), Mandy Olson,
Shania Burkhead, John Kraft and Mike Gentry.
You gave me confidence.
Thank you.

Chapter One: The Wish

Two blue eyes were nervously staring out from the bushes. There was an odd combination of fear and excitement hidden in their innocence. Well concealed behind the bushes was a lanky, nine-year old boy. His mouse-brown hair was messy and bits of leaves were littered through it making it look all that much more unkempt. As he hunkered down in the shadows of the bush, he silently thanked his mom for washing his favorite green shirt. It aided in his attempt for camouflage. He sat as quietly as he could while he peered out into the sun of the day. He hadn't moved in at least ten minutes and his knees were starting to ache from kneeling on the dry dirt.

He looked out again. There was no sign of danger from any direction so he slowly crawled further into the line of shrubs. As he quietly crawled along, he placed his palm down on a sharp root that jutted awkwardly out from the ground. It pierced the soft flesh and he let out a quiet, "Ouch!" He looked at his hand and saw the fresh bit of blood oozing from the small wound. He wiped it on the edge of his jean shorts.

As he sat back down, he realized that his presence was no longer unnoticed. He held his breath and listened carefully. He leaned cautiously forward and tried to see what lurked beyond the safety of the bushes. As he leaned in, a twig cracked under his hand. Any hope he had of remaining hidden was gone.

"He's over here!" a deep voice hollered. It came from just a few feet from where the boy was hiding.

No longer relying on his chances for remaining hidden, he risked a closer look. A large scaly, human-like creature with broken horns on his head was beckoning to the others with his gnarled hand. He had a severe under bite that was lined with jagged teeth. His nose was short and stubby and it turned upright at a harsh angle. He stalked closer to where the boy was still doing his best to remain hidden.

But despite all his best efforts, his brief encounter with the root had betrayed his position. For a moment, he considered the odds of outrunning his attacker. Then three others appeared at the first one's side and they all lumbered closer to him. The boy knew his odds of outrunning four was significantly worse than just one. So he puffed out his chest and whispered to himself, "Fine. If you want a fight, then that's what you'll get."

He braced himself for the fight that was sure to come. As his four attackers closed the distance between them, he risked moving to a more strategic position. He started weaving on his knees through the bushes as quick as he could. Unfortunately, he snagged his shirt on a dead twig. "Oh no," he muttered.

Frantically, he tried to reach around and free himself. But it was too late. The creature was already there and without any more warning, two scaled hands reached through the bushes and pulled him out, tearing a hole in his shirt in the process.

"Gotcha!" the biggest one yelled while holding him by his shirt.

The boy kicked out hard in hopes of impacting the creature's shin. It was a successfully aimed kick, but it didn't do much good. It only made the creature angrier and he pushed the boy backwards into the hard ground.

He felt the wind rush out of his lungs as he landed on his back. Trying to get his bearings, he looked up and saw the four creatures silhouetted against the afternoon sun and he knew that there was no way he'd win this fight. Four against one was horrible odds for a boy his size. He decided his best chance was to run, but his decision was two seconds too late. As he started to get up, they already had him by the shirt again.

"Where do you think you're goin'?" the leader asked.

The boy kicked out again and demanded, "Let go of me!"

"Or what? You're barely big enough to make a shadow."

The other three laughed as the boy was dropped on the ground again. He bumped his elbow and he felt the sting of a fresh abrasion. He stood up and backed up against the bushes. He looked for a quick escape but was blocked on all sides. He glared up at them.

The leader glared back and then grabbed him again. "You know what we want, so you might as well just give it up before you get hurt." He smiled devilishly.

"I don't have it, so…so…back off!"

The boy's threatening tone pushed the leader further and he punched him in the belly. "Give it to me, little shrimp!"

As he regained his breath from the jab to his stomach, he started to nod his head. "Okay," he puffed. He reached a small hand into his pocket and slowly fished for something. When he saw that they were gloating in their success, the boy turned heel, ducked under one of their arms, and sprinted off along the line of bushes.

Turning his head, he could see that the four were gaining on him quickly. He came to the end of the bushes and made a sharp left turn. In doing so, he lost his footing and fell, face first, onto the hard ground. There was a blinding pain to his chin as the rocky ground grated across his skin. He tried to ignore the pain and was about to jump to his feet when he looked up and saw a pair of brown dress shoes a foot away from his face. He slowly pushed himself off of his chest and looked up.

The man looked down through his wire-framed glasses at the boy. He had a mixture of anger and confusion on his face. "Sam? What on Earth happened to you?" he asked. He reached a hand down to help the boy to his feet and then looked up suddenly at the four that had just turned the corner and joined them.

Realization swept over the man's face and he barked at the four, "You four, get over here right now!" When they hesitantly approached, he asked harshly, "What is going on here?"

Sam stared down at his tennis shoes while the leader of his four attackers said, "Nothing, sir. We were just messing around. Isn't that right Sam?"

Sam looked up to make eye contact with the one who'd punched him just moments ago. There, where the four scaly creatures would have been, were four very normal looking boys. He nervously glanced between the boys and the man and said nothing.

The Gateway to Imagia: The Tale of Sam Little

The man looked down at Sam and asked more gently, "Did Parker hurt you, Sam?"

Sam managed a small shrug and then said, "No, Mr. Conner."

Mr. Conner squinted while he thought. He looked down at Sam's clenched fist and saw the wad of crumpled dollar bills in his hand. He shook his head and turned back to the four boys. "You four. My office. Now."

Parker glared at Sam. Then he turned to head for the Principal's office. Sam knew that this would only make things worse, but figured that he had other things to deal with at the moment.

Principal Conner was giving him a once over as he clucked his tongue. "Sam, I know this goes without saying, but you really should just give them what they want next time. Three dollars in lunch money is hardly worth all of this," he said as he pulled a handkerchief from his pocket. He dabbed at the blood on Sam's chin. "You can always come and tell me or any other teacher about it later and we would deal with them appropriately. Now, how did all this happen?" he gestured to all of Sam's wounds. "Did those four do *all* of this?"

Sam shook his head. He was suddenly aware of the pains in his chin and elbow. "No, sir. I was hiding in the bushes and…well…mostly I just fell down."

Mr. Conner looked at Sam's elbow and said, "Were you using your imagination again?"

"Yes, sir." Sam felt embarrassed suddenly.

"Well," Mr. Conner sighed, "let's get you over to the nurse's office. But you really do need to keep your head out of the clouds. And next time, just come tell me and I'll take care of things."

Sam followed the Principal. He pocketed his money and rubbed his belly where Parker had punched him. He silently wondered what his mom and dad would say when Mr. Conner called them on his last day of school; especially when they found out he was using his imagination there again.

No one seemed to understand Sam's obsession with imagining. He was always getting into trouble from not paying attention in class or getting himself into sticky situations with his much larger classmates. Being the smallest in his class made him vulnerable as a target. And though he felt stronger and much more comfortable in his imaginary world, it always seemed to get him into trouble one way or another.

As the end of the day came, Sam sat in his class and watched the clock. The sting of his chin had become a dull ache and he itched at the bandage on his elbow. Luckily, Parker and his gang were a grade above him, so they didn't share classes. The worst he had to suffer was hearing a few jokes from the kids who sat closest to him.

Their jeers barely fazed him as he watched the clock hit 3:14. Another minute more and he'd be free for the summer. Free from the bullies and jokes at his expense for three whole months. But most importantly, free to imagine as much as he wanted without the mundane interference of school.

The bell rang and Sam was out the door before the other kids had time to get their footing. His mom agreed to pick him up from school after Principal Conner called and explained the happenings of the morning. He saw their dark blue family car waiting for him at the front of the parking lot. He was about to run to it, but slowed down when he thought about the talk she was sure to have with him about the fight today. When he'd convinced himself that he'd done nothing to get into trouble for, he started to pick up the pace and was opening the door in no time.

As he buckled in, he could hear the irritation in her sigh. "Samuel Isaac Little, I can't stress how frustrated I was to get a phone call from Principal Conner on the *last* day of school. How is it possible that you can't go one week without one of these little incidents?"

Sam shrugged. "I dunno. But this time it wasn't my fault, mom."

As she stared back to him from the rear view mirror, she saw his injured chin and her eyes softened. She sighed again, but this time with compassion. "We'll discuss it later with your dad. Let's just get you home. You have a big day tomorrow and I'll never be able to frost your birthday cake without you." She smiled warmly at him.

He grinned back. Tomorrow was definitely a big day for Sam. His tenth birthday was the reason this day couldn't go fast enough.

* * * * * * * * * *

Sam lived at 1023 Treetop Lane at the edge of a very large forest. Everyone around them came to know Sam as the littlest Little. He was born to George and Sarah Little. He was premature and did not seem to grow as fast as the other children. His mom constantly made it a point to tell him that he wasn't small; he just hadn't grown into his personality yet. Oddly enough, he didn't seem to care too much that he was a couple of inches shorter than the other kids in his class.

In school, he was always picked last by the kids. No one wanted to have him on their team. He always had to sit in the front row so that the teacher could see him when he raised his hand. Which, of course, only gave the kids another reason to make fun of him. In all fairness, Sam was not the shortest person in the world. In fact, if he went to a bigger school in a bigger city, he probably wouldn't be the shortest person there. But to family, neighbors, and everyone else for that matter, he was just plain...well, for lack of a better word...little.

Being regarded as such a small person with even smaller abilities was enough to bother any kid. Size always seemed to be such an issue to people. The bigger the better. The bigger you are, the more things you get to do. The more things you get to do, the more friends you have. More friends meant more fun and more fun is naturally better for any normal kid. Of course, Sam wasn't exactly a normal kid. In his mind, he was a giant among mice. His idea of fun didn't require a group of friends at a pizza place or a sleepover. All he needed to have the adventure of a lifetime was his dog, a bright sunny day, and perhaps an overgrown lawn. Sam may be Little by name and little by stature, but his imagination is bigger than the world.

He was not well liked amongst the kids his age. It never seemed fair to judge him for his size. But, regardless, this made his days rather unpleasant. Between the name-calling and constantly being picked on, the only part of his day that he could honestly look forward to was the part that wasn't real. From the moment he realized he was capable of using his imagination, Sam utilized every opportunity he could to retreat from the doldrums of his life and go to his own special world.

Mr. and Mrs. Little knew that Sam's imagination was always taking him somewhere. He was always trying to tame the wild and vicious neekor cat that stood four feet tall with razor sharp claws, three eyes and saber teeth. Of course, to Mr. and Mrs. Little, it was only their fat, yellow tabby cat, Cooper. He went on countless adventures riding on the shoulders of Yetews, a ten-foot tall, black, hairy creature whose complex language could only be understood by

Sam. When he and his imaginary best friend would go on adventures, Titus, the family dog, was all anyone else could see. And of course, his parents still made him eat his peas, even though he insisted that only the fuzzy-footed migglewumps could eat them without dying a most horrible death.

Yes. Sam definitely marched to the beat of his own drum.

Though frustrated by it, his parents understood why he escaped into his imaginary world, and they felt sorry for their son. They hoped that he would grow out of his awkward phase after he added a few inches to his height. But what they didn't realize was how badly Sam wished it were all real. Yetews, the neekor cat, the fuzzy-footed migglewumps. They were all merely figments of a child's over-developed imagination. But they all seemed to fit into this strange little world he created.

He'd talk of his imaginary friends often, mostly due to the fact that he had no real ones. When dinner came and they would ask Sam about his day, they would rarely hear of happenings at school. Rather, he would go on and on about his imaginary adventures. Though, try as they might to understand him, many times, they ended up shrugging off his strange stories. Over time, they became used to it and chalked it up to the phase he was going through. If they'd have known that on this very day, at their very house, an exceptionally strange phenomenon was about to take place, they may not have put all ten candles on Sam's birthday cake.

Sam had been waiting for this day for what seemed to be a lifetime. It was May 26th. Yesterday had been his last day of school for the year and his big tenth birthday party was now mere moments away. He had convinced himself that turning ten years old was the most important age to become. This idea was solely based on the idea of wishes.

Everyone knows that, short of a four leaf clover or a shooting star, you only get one true wish each year, and it involves flaming candles on a birthday cake. Naturally, a majority of wishes don't come true for most people. Otherwise, everyone would be going around getting whatever they wanted nearly all of the time. So Sam believed that these wishes were granted only in very special circumstances. In fact, he believed this theory so much, that he had been saving up all of his past birthday wishes. It was time to cash in on all of the forfeited wishes of the past. Today was the day.

Each time he would go on an imaginary adventure with Yetews, he would think about how awesome it would be if the adventures were real and if his best friend wasn't really just an ordinary, scraggly dog. Especially when that dog was virtually incapable of letting him ride on his shoulders. Titus was great, but he wasn't Yetews. Yetews was big enough to carry both him and a dog with two arms tied behind his back. After today, he was convinced that things were going to be much different.

His party was to start at 4:00 and it was 3:45 at this very moment. His parents had given him a digital watch for an early birthday present. From the moment he had woken up this morning, he had been asking repetitively 'how much longer until the party?' They let him open the watch early so he could keep an eye on the time himself and stop pestering them. Now he couldn't seem to stop watching the minutes tick by at a snail's pace. He knew that at any moment, relatives would be arriving with presents and 'Happy Birthday' greetings. Sam could barely stand himself. "Why won't they just get here?" he said impatiently.

"My goodness Sam! They will be here in a few minutes. A little patience, please!" his mom hollered from across the house. She had just finished stringing up the last blue balloon. She knew how excited Sam had been for his birthday this year, but she wasn't sure why this birthday seemed so much more important to him than all of his previous birthdays. She shrugged off this thought and went into the kitchen.

He blatantly rolled his eyes at his mom's lack of understanding. She didn't seem to understand the importance of this day. Didn't she realize what turning ten really meant? He sighed and then looked at his watch again. This time it was only 3:46. "Sheesh!" he cried. "Only one minute's gone by!" He grumbled to himself and plopped down dramatically on the couch. After waiting ten years for this day, the next fourteen minutes seemed like an eternity away. For a ten-year-old boy, patience was a great thing to ask for...especially for Sam.

He was lying on his back with his skinny legs dangling over the arm of the couch. The sun was shining brightly outside and it was the first day of his long-awaited summer vacation. The majority of his vacation was spent outside and despite the anticipation of the party, today was no different than the rest. Summer vacation was always the best time of his year. Having no friends actually made things easier because he preferred the company of his imaginary ones anyways.

His mouse-brown hair was messy, despite the fact that his mother had tried to comb it down for the party. There were grass stains on his jean shorts and he was mindlessly picking at a patch of dried mud on his orange t-shirt. He still wore his bandage on his arm from his skirmish at school and the cut on his chin had purpled and left a thick, unsightly scab.

Though his appearance only told him that he'd been having some rather good adventures, his mom was a bit irked that he had already dirtied his new birthday party clothes. He seemed to always be getting into something. Including trouble. His mom was always trying to tell him that his curiosity was going to lead him somewhere dangerous someday. Sam always scoffed at this. He only *wished* that there were something more dangerous than his backyard. He also considered himself to be the bravest kid in the world. So he figured that this was what parents said to keep the good stuff hidden.

As he lay on the couch swinging his legs impatiently, the doorbell rang.

Finally.

It was music to his ears. "Mom!" hollered Sam. "They're here!" He jumped off the couch and bolted to the door. When he opened the door, he saw it was Aunt Josephine holding a rather large box wrapped with lots of elaborate bows.

Grandma Little followed her with a soft package that resembled the same hand-knitted sweater he seemed to get every year. He silently grumbled. He never understood why she always insisted on giving him a sweater at the beginning of summer.

Cousins, aunts, and uncles shortly began to filter their way into the house and soon the house was buzzing with the happenings of the party. The mountain of presents piled higher on the living room floor. But it wasn't nearly enough to stop him from thinking about his wonderful birthday cake. Those ten glorious candles were just waiting to be blown out! He wrinkled his nose at the thought of waiting until all the presents were opened *before* they could have cake.

But as he thought about what might be inside of those carefully wrapped gifts, he figured that it might not be such a bad thing. Maybe he would get that superhero cape he had wanted for so long. It would definitely come in handy on all of his adventures.

When the last guest finally made their way into the house, his mom began to shuffle everyone into the living room to start the festivities. She pulled Sam away from the pile of gifts and herded him into the middle of the room where his cousins were waiting for him.

Being the center of attention was never Sam's idea of a good time. But generally speaking, he was easily overlooked due to his size. So he only had to bear the embarrassment of his cooing aunts for a few moments before he was nearly hidden in the mayhem. It wasn't hard to lose sight of him amongst the rubble of presents and shredded wrapping paper as he tore through each gift at record speed.

He opened the first one from his Grandma Little. He was right about the sweater. Nothing too thrilling, but he thanked her just the same. The next one was a board game he had played once at a cousin's house. They must have thought he enjoyed it enough to buy him the same one.

His mom handed him the next present. She smiled and stood back to watch him open it. He tore through the paper and ripped open the box. He jumped up and held a large red piece of cloth out for everyone to see. "Thanks mom and dad!" He was genuinely excited for this one.

Sam was about to swing it over his shoulder when his least favorite aunt asked in slight disgust, "Isn't he a bit old for a blankie?"

Sam began to get angry and almost replied, but his mom spoke up first. The smile that was on her face was temporarily replaced by annoyance. "It just so happens to be a superhero cape." And as though she meant to frustrate his aunt one-step further, she helped Sam fasten it around his shoulders. Then she knelt down in front of Sam and grinned again. "A perfect hero cape for the world's greatest adventurer." She winked and Sam beamed.

"Thanks mom." Even though they had a hard time understanding his need for his imaginary world, his parents always supported him. It always made things a little easier when it came to his close-minded family.

There were a few more boxes with clothes, a couple of superhero action figures, a baseball bat and glove, and a frog flashlight from his uncle that he added to the pile. He thanked each person as he opened the gifts and then they moved on to the games.

Sam didn't understand why there had to be games. It was frustrating to lose every time at *his* birthday party. His cousins weren't entirely fond of Sam either. A simple game of musical chairs seemed to get rougher than necessary. He was getting tripped far too often and receiving too many suspicious knocks from elbows than he should have. It gave Sam the same feeling of being in school and it was spoiling his good mood.

Sam had lost yet another game. As he sat on the sideline, he could hear the remarks of a few family members as they commented about the fact that there were no kids his age there. One of his aunts was clucking her tongue and shaking her head. "It's a shame he doesn't have any friends. But I suppose he's a bit strange for his age. Maybe with time…" she trailed off when she noticed that Sam was sitting so close.

Sam rolled his eyes. He loved his family, but their lack of understanding him was annoying. Though not soon enough, the games were finally over and his mom whispered into his ear as she passed him, "Get your wish ready kiddo. It's birthday cake time." She grinned at him and his returning smile stretched from ear to ear. The very moment he'd been building up to for ten years was finally upon him. The birthday wish of all birthday wishes was about to be made. His spirits started to rise again.

Sam's mom and dad disappeared into the kitchen.

Everyone squeezed around the dining room table as his mom placed the blue and red iced cake down in front of Sam. It was decorated with a picture of his favorite superhero. "Well," said his dad after carefully lighting each candle, "Do you know what you're going to wish for?"

"Yup!" Sam said.

"Good," said his dad. "Wouldn't want to waste a good wish on something silly, right?"

Sam didn't answer. He just smiled as he watched the tiny flickering flames dance before his eyes.

George and Sarah smiled and everyone broke into a round of 'Happy Birthday'. As the last line was sung, Sam realized that the time had finally come. He closed his eyes tight and wished the only wish he had wanted for as long as he could remember. '*I wish I can make my imagination real!'* He opened his eyes, took a deep breath, and blew with all his might until all ten flames disappeared into smoke. Everyone clapped and his mom started to cut the cake. He didn't want anyone to know about his wish so he'd have to wait until after the party to try it out. It was a secret meant only for him.

"So what did you wish for?" asked his dad as he pat Sam on his back.

He knew better than to answer this question. "Geez, Dad! I can't tell you what I wished for! It won't come true that way." A few chuckles rounded the table after he said this, but he paid no mind to them. They apparently didn't understand the serious nature of birthday wish rules.

It seemed to take an eternity for everyone to eat their cake. And just when he thought that the party was over, all of his relatives managed to sit around and jabber on about things that Sam couldn't care less about.

His mom noticed Sam sulking in the corner and fiddling idly with a few of his new toys. She had been listening intently to Grandma Little. But noticing his deteriorating mood, she decided to begin the process of subtly shooing everyone out the door one by one.

Shortly after his mom's efforts to end the party, there were but a few crumbs of cake left. Empty party cups and plates littered the table and the last guests were shuffling out the front door. Sam impatiently listened to the final 'Happy Birthday!' from Grandma Little and finally the door closed leaving the blissful sound of silence in its wake.

Sam's mood was instantly lightened. He sprinted to the living room, grabbed his most essential presents and took them to his room. He sat down to take a mental inventory of everything he got that was worth making note of. It was actually a pretty good birthday when all said and done.

But time was wasting and he had a wish to get fulfilled. Sitting there on the floor seemed to be the perfect time to test the results. He jumped up and in his haste, nearly slammed his dog's tail in the door. Titus didn't seem to notice and plopped himself down on his favorite spot on the floor. He could hear his parents in the kitchen cleaning up and knew that he was alone for the time.

He thought for only a moment as to what he would imagine first.

It only took him half of that moment to decide. There was only one constant in his imagination and he dearly longed for a chance to meet him. Sam closed his eyes. As clearly as he could, he pictured his hairy best friend, Yetews. As always, he was deep in his imagination instantly. When the image was as real to him as he could imagine it, he took a deep breath. He smiled and readied himself for the awesomeness of his granted wish.

Slowly, Sam opened his eyes. He looked around the room eagerly. But when he saw nothing out of the ordinary, he tried again, concentrating on every detail of Yetews' face – from the emerald green eyes to the way his ears drooped ever so slightly. He pictured every hair on his shaggy body, concentrating on the precise color and sheen.

Still, nothing appeared in front of him. He tried again and again with the same lack of success as each time before, until he realized that Yetews wasn't going to show. Titus, his shabby mutt, would have to continue his role as Yetews. And Cooper was always going to remain nothing but a fat, old, yellow tabby cat that would play the part of an evil Neekor cat. His heart sank.

"How is this possible?" he asked himself. "I saved every single birthday wish for this day! I just don't get it." Disappointment fell over his small face.

His mom knocked and then walked into the room just in time to see Sam kick one of his new action figures across the room. She noticed his sad look and cocked an eyebrow. "Didn't you have a nice birthday?"

He hadn't meant for her to see that. He put on a quick smile. "Yeah, it was nice mom. Thanks for the hero cape," he said with forced excitement in his voice. Noticing her look of doubt, he mustered another smile and she seemed to just shrug off his demeanor as him being tired.

"Did you get everything you wanted this year?"

"Yeah. I guess so."

"Well, I think maybe it's time to get ready for bed." She smiled down at him. "It's been a long day for the birthday boy."

"Alright," he sighed. He trudged past her with his pajamas in tow.

She pat the top of his head lovingly as he passed and said, "Don't forget to brush your teeth."

"K."

He took his bath, brushed his teeth, and slipped on his favorite red and blue pajamas with the cartoon monster on the shirt. His mom and dad tucked him into bed. His mom kissed him lightly on the forehead and said, "G'nite sweetie. Happy birthday."

"Night, kiddo," said his dad as he gave him a quick hug.

"Night, dad." And with that, they shut the door and the late evening glow washed across the room.

The sounds of summer hummed quietly out his slightly open window. Fireflies danced across the back yard and cicadas buzzed in the thick trees of the forest behind their house.

Sam lay there in bed wondering what he had done wrong when he wished his big wish earlier. Did he forget something? Did he miss a candle when he blew them out? He heaved a heavy sigh and gazed out his bedroom window into the dusky evening.

His dog's cold nose bumped his hand on his bed. He panted and then whined briefly in hopes of some extra attention. Even though he wasn't Yetews, Titus was the best friend he had in the real world. He smiled and scratched behind his ears as he said, "Well, Titus. I guess it's still just you and me." He thought for a moment and then wondered aloud, "Maybe it's the eleventh birthday and I wished too soon." Disappointed and confused, he laid there in bed pondering how many more birthday wishes he would of had to save to make his wish come true.

Chapter Two: Granted

A gentle evening breeze blew in the window at about the same time that Sam was thinking he was not sleepy at all. He was counting the stars in the darkening sky as he stroked Titus' head. Something rustled the bushes just outside his window. Their cat Cooper must've been outside wanting in. He was a bit heavy around the middle so his hesitation to come in meant the window wasn't open wide enough. Sam threw the covers back and went to open the window a few more inches so he could fit through. He peeked out the window but didn't see a thing. "Cooper?" he called softly. "Here kitty, kitty."

Nothing.

He called again, "Here kitty, kitty. Cooper? You want in or not?" After no response again, he figured that it must've been the neighbor's pesky calico cat. "Stupid cat," he muttered as he slid the window back to its original position.

He was just about to his bed when he heard the noise again. It stopped him in his tracks and Titus perked his ears up in response. This time the rustling was louder and his heart started to thud a bit faster. "What was that?" Sam muttered into the dark. He was fairly certain that the leaves moved too much for it to be a cat. For a moment, he considered calling for his parents, but then he realized that if it was anything to worry about then Titus would have been barking. So instead, he grabbed his new green frog flashlight that his uncle gave him, switched it on, and shone it out the window into the bushes expecting to see a stray animal. He had hoped that a deer might have come up to the house. He'd heard that they sometimes wandered out of the forest, but had never been lucky enough to see one. If it wasn't that, then it was probably the neighbor's dog from down the street. He was always roaming around at night looking for scraps.

Still nothing.

Was his imagination betraying him now? It had never failed him before.

The beam of the flashlight was surprisingly bright and it shone all the way into the trees of the forest. Regardless of the light, there was still nothing to be seen. He let the light linger on the outskirts of the forest for a few moments longer. As he gazed into the mysterious forest his heart leapt at the idea of what lie in waiting beyond its borders. He had longed to go adventuring in that forest for years. But his mom and dad, as well as the rest of people on Treetop Lane, forbade it. All of the grownups would talk about how dangerous it was. "Especially for little boys like you," he recalled his mom saying. They even tried to scare the children with stories about a little boy that got lost after venturing into the woods alone at night. The stories all turned out the same with the cliché ending of 'he went in but never came back out again.'

The scary stories and constant warnings didn't change anything about Sam's desire to adventure in the unknown of it all. They would say anything to keep kids from going in there. Which could only mean that there was something truly spectacular in its depths. He knew that even though he was small, he was brave. Campfire ghost stories did very little to frighten him.

He squinted his eyes, searching for anything that might be interesting. When he was sure that there was nothing but the slight movements of the gentle breeze on the leaves, he sighed and flicked the power switch.

That was when he saw it.

In the last split second that the light still hit the trees, something moved in the shadows. In his excitement, he dropped the flashlight onto the floor. His heart nearly burst from his chest as he clumsily tried to switch the light back on. His mind raced with possibilities of what it could have been. Whatever it was, it was definitely bigger than the neighbor's dog.

He finally got the light back on just in time to see what looked to be a long tail disappearing into the foliage. It wasn't much, but the important thing was that he saw it.

The logical side of him knew that it was probably just a deer and that his eyes were playing a trick on him in the dark of night. The illogical and much more dominant side of him was sure it was something infinitely more interesting. Regardless of which side was right, he wanted nothing so badly as to follow whatever it was. Even though he could hear his parents' voices over and over again as to just how dangerous the forest was, his curiosity was getting the best of him.

Naturally, his first thought was that it was purely his imagination gone awry, so he tried to consider what it was that he was trying to imagine. After thinking about it, he came to the conclusion that he hadn't tried to imagine anything at the moment and that whatever it was he saw, most certainly had to be real. And there was something more about this particular situation. Whatever the mystery animal was that he saw seemed to be beckoning him forward. Sam's natural sense of adventure convinced him that anything that peculiar was worth getting in trouble for. That was all it took to finalize his decision.

He was going to sneak out and get a closer look.

"Titus?" whispered Sam.

Titus looked up at him, panting, and wagged his big shaggy tail at the sound of his name. I hope you're up for an adventure, buddy." Titus thumped his tail harder on the wood floor. Then talking more to himself than anything, he continued. "If mom and dad catch us outside again, we'll be in big, big trouble. It could be one of the neighbor dogs. Or a deer I guess. Or...." Glancing over at Titus, "...maybe something else." Titus then trotted over to the window to sit by him as any good comrade might. "So what do you think buddy?"

Titus merely leaned a little closer into him and lifted a paw up

The Gateway to Imagia: The Tale of Sam Little

for Sam to take. It was the final push he needed, Sam paused to think of all the things he could imagine might be waiting in the shadows and smiled hugely. Without any more hesitation, he grabbed his frog-light, put on his new superhero cape and tennis shoes, and quietly snuck outside his window.

He was sure to be quiet so his parents didn't know he was outside. This wouldn't be the first time he snuck out after bedtime. The darkness always added more mystery to his ventures. He would get into a lot of trouble when they found out he was outside, but even more trouble if they knew he was thinking of going into the forbidden forest. But he just didn't care. His curiosity was just too much to handle this time. Some strange pull he'd never felt before was leading him to go further than he'd ever gone before. His previous attempts of sneaking out didn't involve such extreme measures. He only hoped that two very angry parents wouldn't thwart him.

Titus was waiting to jump out the window. After Sam was in the clear, he leapt the sill effortlessly and landed gracefully in the grass just beyond the bushes.

Together, they snuck across the back lawn. Sam kept anxiously peeking back to the house in hopes of not seeing the silhouette of his mom in the kitchen window. Luck was with him. His parents' favorite show was on tonight and they were safely out of view in the living room.

By now, they'd reached the chain-link gate to the back and he had it open in no time. He stepped through the gate towards the edge of the forest and stared at the enormous wall of trees in front of him. He'd never been this close before. He'd never made it further than the back gate in his past attempts. This time, something more than the sense of adventure was driving him forward.

It was darker than he had ever believed possible. He tried to use his frog-light to look into the trees, but for some reason, the light just wouldn't penetrate the eerie darkness. For a moment, Sam started to feel something strange. A feeling he wasn't sure about because he had never remembered feeling it before this moment. The feeling made his knees lock tight and seemed to almost glue his feet to the ground. How strange it felt, as though some different part of him wanted to turn back. He pushed through it, stood as tall as he could, and said, "Okay. Here I go." He took a deep breath and took his first step towards the endless black of the forest.

The grass was severely overgrown and was nearly as high as his waist. It had probably never been mowed and was insanely thick. He could feel the cockleburs sticking to his cape as he navigated his way to the awaiting black abyss. Behind him, he heard the familiar sound of padded paws thudding along and he turned to be sure that it was still Titus who was following him.

He stopped and Titus continued to go forward passing him completely. "No Titus! Wait!" He whispered a bit harsher than he meant to. Titus stopped, cocked an ear and then returned to Sam. He sat at his heels and wagged his tail patiently. He was always ready to take his place at Sam's side.

Sam noticed that his long fur was also matted with cockleburs. He couldn't help but smile at his faithful companion's eagerness to follow on yet another crazy adventure. He kneeled and scratched behind the floppy ears. As he knelt, he looked back up into the forest.

That's when something caught his eye. In the residual glow of his light, the same strange tail that he'd seen earlier disappeared once more into the darkness. Sam's stomach did a little flip and his heart began to flutter wildly. He looked down at Titus and something inside of him nagged at his mind. He felt that he had to go the rest of the way without Titus. The funny feeling inside his mind told him that there was only one way he could go forward.

Alone.

He sighed. He'd never left Titus behind before and he wasn't exactly sure how to go about leaving him. He put a hand on each side of his dog's muzzle and looked at him seriously. "I don't think you can come with me this time buddy." He glanced over his shoulder at the darkness. "You need to stay here."

Titus whined at the word 'stay'. He wasn't used to being left behind and Sam wasn't used to leaving him either. That same odd feeling started to lock his knees tight again. "Though, it might be nice to have you there. You know, in case I need..." he paused to think about how to finish that thought as his feet started to glue to the ground again. "I guess in case I need someone to talk to." A nervous laugh escaped. But he once more felt the overwhelming feeling to go alone. He shook his head and used his 'big' voice. "No. Titus you *have* to go home now." He got up and started walking again. Titus was right on his heels, obviously oblivious to the command.

"No Titus. I'm sorry buddy. Not this time." He hesitated for a moment, frowning, because he was sad to have to use a command on his faithful friend. "Titus, *stay*."

The dog whimpered at the command and stopped dead in his tracks. He sat down and started whining more consistently as Sam turned and trudged his way to the very edge of the tree line. He stopped and stared into the darkness. Behind him, Titus barked once. That was all it would take to get his parents' attention. It was now or never. His heart raced as he took one last regretful glance over his shoulder at his reluctant friend.

Titus barked once more as Sam disappeared into the black.

On the twelfth step into the dark, everything around him changed. Daylight shattered through the trees ahead. "No way…" he whispered. He looked behind only to see his house masked in nighttime somewhere beyond the trees. He couldn't hear Titus' whining or barking anymore either. But right there in front of him was daylight! He blinked his eyes in the bright sunlight that filtered its way through the treetops. This was the moment he had been dreaming of all his young days.

He knew at that moment that he had stepped into a strange new world. His wish was granted.

Everything he had ever imagined in his busy mind was right here in front of him just waiting to be discovered. He considered for a fleeting moment that he might really be in his bed at home dreaming of this great, green forest. He reached his hand over to his arm and took a hold of the open skin. He pinched hard. "Ouch!" Sam yelped. "Nope…not dreamin'," he deducted as he rubbed the bright red mark on his arm. It was stinging a bit from the pinch.

Trusting now that it wasn't a dream, he clicked his green froglight off and decided to set off into the wild. He paused only for a moment to look back to see if maybe Titus would barrel his way through the trees. But after one fleeting moment of silent hope, the sandy color of his faithful friend's fur was nowhere to be seen in the trees.

He had stayed. There was a painful twinge of regret for leaving him behind, but that nagging part in the back of his mind knew there was no other way.

Now that he was ready to move forward, he suddenly realized that he wasn't entirely sure which way to go. He took a step forward, but just as quickly stopped again. He looked in every direction and saw the same thing.

Trees. Wild trees that looked strangely unfamiliar to him. Though it was day, he suddenly noticed that the canopy of the trees let far less light in than it seemed to at first. Everything was so new and fascinating that he wasn't sure if he could possibly choose just one direction to go. He wished that he had someone there to share in the wonder of his fulfilled wish.

Sam was starting to question his actions. He regretted leaving Titus more now than before and wondered if he should return for his friend. But in the very moment he'd considered this, a strange noise came from the bushes just ahead of him.

Something was lurking behind a rather large group of bushes in front of him. The bush was massive with wide green leaves and lovely red-orange flowers the size of dinner plates. Sam definitely didn't want to frighten away whatever – or whoever – it could be so he didn't make a sound.

He waited a few seconds to see what was going to happen next. Just when he was about to say something, the bush started to rustle and then it sneezed causing Sam to jerk a little from surprise. At first, Sam thought that perhaps he had missed seeing Titus coming through the trees ahead of him. It had been dark after all. The leaves and flowers from the disturbance of the sneeze fluttered through the air and floated gently to the ground leaving a small hole in the bush just big enough to reveal a hairy snout.

It wasn't Titus. It was something else.

He could see a pale peach nose surrounded by long, shiny, black fur and knew at once exactly what kind of creature was hiding behind the crowd of leaves and flowers. Too many times, he had encountered such a beast. The very tip of the tail he'd seen disappear into the forest earlier was barely sticking out from the bottom of the bush, obviously poorly hidden.

Sam quietly placed his frog-light on the ground so as not to make a sound and tiptoed slyly up to the bush ready to ambush the creature hiding within. A few steps more and he would be in range for the perfect attack. He knew this creature too well and knew what needed to be done to ensure his safety. Much like the safari men he watched on TV, he knew the safest way to approach this creature and what its weakness was.

Just as he was about to make his move, an enormous dark shape leapt from the bushes right over Sam's head and landed directly behind him. The ambush startled him. The strange beast snarled and bared its teeth at him. Sam didn't have time to consider his options. He flipped around without hesitation and ran at the beast with arms wide and roared the best version of a snarl he could make. They circled each other, preparing to battle on the forest floor. The beast tumbled over and lost his guard as it tripped over an exposed tree root. Sam took the opportunity and jumped on its arm, locking onto it as best as his small body knew how and yelled, "Gotcha!"

Sam wrapped his skinny arms and legs around the massive arm, locking them together at his wrists and ankles. Though the size of the hairy arm dwarfed Sam's whole body, it appeared to be unbelievably pinned to the ground. The massive beast made a low moaning sound and grunted in defeat as the rest of its body fell to the ground with a dull thudding sound. Its tongue fell from its mouth and its eyes rolled back in its head.

It was unconscious. The battle was over before it had barely began, Sam knowing himself the victor just as he always did in his mind. He stood proudly above the large hairy lump with his foot placed on its arm and a smile from ear to ear. "Stupid of you to think you could beat me," he boasted. "But I did expect a bit more fight out of you. What a shame." He mocked the creature.

He was too busy bragging about his victory to notice his fallen enemy opening one eye ever so slightly to peer up at him. When Sam least expected it, the beast growled and stood to its full height. It bared its teeth and grabbed him by his feet turning him completely upside down. The beast dangled the powerless boy by his ankles in the air, growling all the while. Sam swung his fists helplessly with a curious frown across his face. Not quite the look one would normally have when being prepared as something's next meal.

Snarling, the beast aimed for its final blow. The two were caught in a deadly stare as the beast opened his mouth to bite Sam's leg. As the creature's mouth was about to close on the scrawny leg, it stopped in mid-bite. Both became quiet. The silence was intimidating.

Neither one could keep their faces serious any longer. They both burst into laughter! The shaggy creature rustled Sam's hair lovingly with a giant ape-like palm. Sam looked up at the now friendly face and said with a smile, "Oh, man!" He sighed and then continued excitedly, "You always fool me with that move! But I almost had ya that time for real."

The only response from the creature was a goofy, half-grin and an eye roll. He dropped Sam gently to the ground and pat him on the head. The huge, shaggy beast was his once imaginary, and now somehow quite real friend, Yetews. It was proof positive that his wish came true. His imagination was *real*. And as Sam and Yetews laughed and played together, he thought for sure that this was way better than his seemingly ordinary old imagination. The fleeting guilt of leaving Titus behind ebbed away as he reached up to throw his arms around Yetews' neck.

Chapter Three: Detour

The bright sun shone through the trees leaving a large spot perfectly sized for Sam and Yetews to lay and rest after a few games of Capture the Beast. Yetews' long black fur glistened in the sun's rays as he rested. He laid on his back propped up on the large, fatty hump that sat above his shoulders. He reminded Sam of his fat cat Cooper when he would lazily sunbathe in the living room window. He was huge compared to Sam, standing around ten feet tall at his hump. His body was covered in long black hair except for his hands, feet and snout. He had large, piercing green, cow-like eyes, big floppy ears, and two twisted horns, one on each side of his head that curved downward into elegant spirals.

Sam leaned up against his hairy friend's side with his arms crossed behind his head. He relaxed while he decided which way their first adventure should take them. He listened to the forest. He heard strange birds flying in and out of the forest canopy as they sang their curious songs. Small grayish rodents of some kind were busily rustling though the grass while an odd looking lizard lazily sunned itself on a large rock. "I wonder how big this world is," he thought aloud. "I bet there are tons of cool places to explore. What do you wanna do first buddy?"

Yetews grunted indecisively and yawned widely showing his large horse-like teeth. He rolled over to his belly making his unsuspecting counterpart fall to his back. "Geez! What did ya have to go and do that for? You could have at least warned me." Sam mustered the best frown he could. This was, of course, hard to do. What with his sheer elation at the granting of his wish, a frown was the least likely of things he could manage right now. Never in his life, had he imagined his wish to become this. It was more than he had hoped for and it was nearly too much to believe possible. His imagination was very creative, but it hadn't ever looked quite like this. His eyes roamed every way to take it all in, always returning his gaze to Yetews.

When he sat on his haunches, Yetews looked much like a dog with short back legs and longer arms. It was easy to see how Titus was his inspiration. His feet and hands resembled that of a chimpanzee and his hair was long and matted in places. There were bits of grass and leaves stuck in his coat from wrestling with Sam and lying around on the forest floor.

Sam stood up when Yetews did and brushed himself off. Yetews shook fiercely all over so that the grass and leaves went everywhere…including onto Sam. "Blech!" griped Sam. "Thanks a lot." Yetews snorted and laughed in his urmph-urmph kind of way. He mockingly grunted something else to Sam and tussled his already messy hair.

"Yeah, Yeah, Yeah. But you could have at least warned me," Sam said with a sideways smile. He could understand each and every grunt, groan, and grumble that Yetews uttered just as easily as if he were talking to a person. There weren't any other people around to see if it was he alone that could understand him, so Sam wasn't sure if this was still going to work in this world. But to him, it was as if he'd been speaking to Yetews his entire life.

He looked himself over now. His hair resembled a bird's nest and his pajamas were spotted with bits of the forest. His cape was already frayed at the edges and had a small tear from catching it on a tree branch. The cockleburs still lingered on it, reminding him of mere moments ago, when he was in his bed at home. He really did look quite dirty for only being gone for…

How long *had* he been gone by now? Sam started to wonder just how long ago he heard Titus' warning bark to his parents. He suddenly remembered that he was still wearing his watch. "Oh yeah! I almost forgot!"

His sudden realization startled Yetews and made him jump

slightly. He glared over at Sam with tightened eyes to express his annoyance.

"Sorry about that. But I think it's only been about an hour. It feels like I've been here a whole day. I wonder if my parents are freaking out. Sorry I scared you but it's just that I remembered something. I was wondering how long I've been here when I remembered I still had my watch on." He tried to explain when Yetews cocked his head in confusion and grumbled a question.

"I guess I mean…er…how long it's been since I crossed over into your world," he answered. But Yetews didn't seem to grasp his meaning of the words 'your world.'

He rumbled another question.

Sam paused for a moment to consider what Yetews asked him and tried to understand. Yetews must have been confused, because to him, there was no other world. Just this one world. A world where they both now stood talking to each other. It was a very peculiar situation, but Sam didn't feel like wasting his precious time here by worrying about the details. He wasn't sure how long he should stay before going back through the trees. Back home.

They were both up now. Rest time was over and adventuring needed to begin. This world was a wild new place with so many things just waiting to be discovered. Sam took a good look around in each direction. He nudged Yetews in the side with a skinny elbow and asked, "How about that way?" He pointed to a break in the trees that seemed to lead to an even deeper part of the woods. "It looks pretty interesting. I betcha there is something cool over there." He looked up at Yetews to see what he thought.

He scratched the hairy hump on his head while thinking about it and finally grunted his agreement. Sam picked up his Frog-light wishing he had brought his backpack to keep it in. Then he wondered if it was even worth bringing at all as it was daytime here. It was kind of heavy and would probably only slow them down in the long run. He couldn't stay for very long so that his parents wouldn't worry too much about him. It was only a matter of time until they figured out where he had gone. Could they even get into this world if it was from his imagination? He'd never considered details like that in his eager wishing. So instead of dragging along the light, he decided that he would put it under a tree close to where he entered the forest. It would be safe there and he could pick it up when he went back home. It would be like a breadcrumb on a trail. He would know exactly where to return through the trees.

As he set the light down, he realized that it wasn't much of a breadcrumb. The light was green and became camouflaged in the grass. So he took off his hero cape and hung it on a branch right above the light. It was bright red, and easy to see. He strained his eyes as he looked through the trees one last time. He was trying to see through the darkness on the other side for some sign that he should go home. He hoped that Titus wouldn't be too angry with him later for being left behind. He silently vowed to bring his faithful dog back with him tomorrow.

Yetews picked Sam up and effortlessly placed him on his shoulders. He fit snuggly between his head and hump, as if it were shaped just for him. He held on firmly by grasping Yetews' hair with both hands and readied himself to go. "Okay Yetews, let's go." They set off down the path into the woods.

Yetews lumbered down the winding path, Sam happily riding along. He walked on all four limbs most of the time. He was able to balance on just his back legs, but because his arms were twice as long and strong as his back legs, it was less awkward and more comfortable for him on all fours. They both looked around as they went on. Sam was trying to take it all in as they traveled. Everything he was seeing made him question the likelihood that he was actually awake. But in spite of what he thought, the reality was that it was more real than anything he'd ever experienced. The colors, the perfect warmth of the air he breathed in and even the smells that were everywhere – it was all too real to deny.

Brightly colored lizards darted across the path occasionally. Rabbit-sized furry creatures scurried into the grass, startled by the sudden disturbance in their forest dwelling. The sun was still high, but the farther into the forest they went, the darker it seemed to get. The path itself, seemed to be melting away the farther they went, as did the busy forest life. It was far from being nighttime, but the tree canopy seemed to be getting thicker, blocking the safety of the sun's light with it.

Sam was humming a tune while Yetews bobbed his head to the music as he walked. They smiled, content. It felt so good to be on a real adventure this time. Sam loved his imagination. But now that it was real, it was so much more interesting. *'Nothing could make this adventure a bad idea,'* Sam thought to himself.

As if the world could read his mind, something's angry roar echoed loudly through the trees ahead of them.

Yetews jolted to a stop nearly causing Sam to fall off his shoulders. Both stood in silence looking around with wide eyes. Sam could feel his friend shudder beneath him. He couldn't blame him. It was a terrible noise. That same odd knee-locking sensation crept up on him again. Whatever this new feeling was, it was starting to get annoying. It was also starting to rattle his nerves a bit. But at the same time, he was curious as to what strange creature could make such a threatening sound. "L-Let's check it out," he partly stuttered. "It sounds like it's coming from that way." He pointed towards where the sounds seemed to originate.

Sam's naïve bravery was not mirrored in his friend for the moment and he whimpered a little at the idea of moving towards the frightful sound. He hesitated going forward hoping that Sam would change his mind and decide to go back the way they came. His little human counterpart was thinking something quite the opposite though.

Sam was becoming anxious to see what was out there. He wondered what the point was of coming here at all if they weren't going to discover new things. But even he could admit that despite this being his imagination at it's finest, many things seemed very unfamiliar to him. It was strange and exhilarating at the same time.

Sam urged him on and Yetews stayed his ground. Going *towards* the terrifying sound was not at all his idea of the wisest course of action. Sam tried to coax him again and gently nudged him forward. "Come on Yetews. What are you waiting for?" he said. He knew he had to say something more convincing. "Whatever it is, I have a good feeling that it isn't gonna hurt us." He bit his lip, hoping he was right.

Yetews noticed the hesitation in Sam's face and defiantly shook his head. He made it perfectly clear that he wasn't about to budge. He sat back on his haunches and folded his arms.

"Okay, fine," Sam muttered. "Be that way. I'll just go over and check it out for myself!" He slid down off of Yetews' shoulders and headed towards where the sound came from, seemingly leaving

Yetews cowering behind him. It roared twice more as he pushed his way through the forest undergrowth. He was getting closer to the sound. He could see a thinning of the trees just over a massive fallen tree. He stopped and wondered if it would be easier to climb over or to fight the branches and go around it. This is where Yetews would have come in handy. He was about to vent his frustration for Yetews not following him, when he felt two strong hands lift him up and place him on the top of the tree.

Sam beamed at him. "I thought you were gonna stay behind?"

Yetews snorted quietly, cocked one eye, and then shook his head while grumbling something low.

Sam just kept smiling and said, "Yeah, well thanks just the same." He slid down from the tree and looked around cautiously. Just ahead of him he could see what appeared to be a deep hole in the ground. He slowly inched closer to the edge until he was on all fours, crawling on the ground. Yetews kept a close distance to him and Sam could occasionally feel a worried hand on his back warning him to be careful.

The hole looked man made like a deep makeshift trap from what he could tell. As he neared the edge of the pit, he could hear what sounded like a woman mumbling to herself. He looked to Yetews who shrugged and then peered cautiously over the edge. He was trying hard not to make a sound just in case it really was something dangerous. There, pacing back and forth like a bored lion, was a familiar sight.

It was a neekor cat. He recognized it right away. It had three brilliant, crystal blue eyes. Two, menacing saber-teeth hung down from its top jaw. It was exactly as he had pictured, right down to the orange striped fur resembling that of his pet cat, Cooper. He had encountered many of these ferocious creatures in his imaginary world back home. There was just one abnormality about this one. He listened close and there was no mistaking it. This neekor cat was actually speaking. In all his time imagining, they'd certainly never done that before.

"I can't believe I'm stuck down here," she said. "This is just absurd! How did I get myself into this predicament? I'm so much smarter than this. And just how am I going to get out of it? Fine mess indeed…" she mumbled to herself. She paced about the bottom of the

The Gateway to Imagia: The Tale of Sam Little

hole shaking her head in frustration. She let out another one of her terrifying roars and then sat down on her haunches in defeat. She seemed to be hanging her head in what Sam thought looked like sadness.

He instantly felt sorry for the poor creature. It didn't seem to be ferocious at all like he had imagined. He decided that if it were really stuck down there then it wouldn't do any harm to draw attention to his presence. He cleared his throat to get her attention.

Startled, the creature's hackles stood up on end and she flipped around to face him. She growled up at Sam and hissed her question, "Who are you? And what do you want? I can tear you to pieces if I have to!"

He cleared his throat again, his mouth suddenly dry as he tried to get the words out. "Don't be scared. My name is Sam Little and this is my friend, Yetews. We were walking when we heard your roar and came to see what you were." He tried to be polite. He didn't want to upset her. Yetews was watching warily as Sam spoke to her.

"Oh?" she said puzzled. "You aren't the creator of this infernal trap then?"

"No. How did you get in there?"

"Well, if you must know, it was covered extremely well. I was tracking something and then fell in. I honestly don't know how I didn't smell this trap. I really am smarter than this."

"Oh. Well..." Sam thought a moment before he finished his sentence. She seemed harmless enough so he continued, "...would you like some help? I think I can get you out of there." He hoped he was doing the right thing.

The Neekor cat looked up at the small boy. She wasn't entirely sure why he would want to help, but it was apparent that she might never get out of the pit herself. "You...want to help me? Aren't you afraid that I'll simply accept your help and then proceed to eat you afterwards?" Though Sam didn't pick up on it, there was a strange sense of sarcasm to her voice as she asked.

A bit hesitantly, he replied, "No. I don't think so." He gulped. "Do...do you want to eat me?"

She snorted. "No, of course not. I don't eat people. Though we have gotten a bad reputation for such things," she told him with disgust. "We only eat tokoo birds and things of that sort. Besides,

30

humans taste terrible." Seeing the look of confusion on the little person's face she added, "Um…so I've heard." Her whiskers turned up in what looked like a smile.

Sam wasn't sure what exactly a tokoo bird looked like, but was quite confident that, unless birds in this world didn't have wings and feathers, then he and Yetews more than likely didn't fit their description. He was convinced that she was not going to harm…or at least eat…either him or Yetews so he looked at her and said, "We're going to go find something to help you out. Be right back. I promise."

He looked around the forest for something that might aid in his rescuing attempt. As he searched for something that would work, he said, "Okay Yetews, we need to find something that can help the neekor cat." Sam furrowed his brow for a moment, considering what he just called the trapped creature. "Well…at least I *think* it's a neekor cat. It can talk, so I don't know for sure. The neekor cats I always saw were scary and wanted to eat me. And they never talked to me. But she doesn't seem mean at all. So we're okay."

Yetews' jaw tightened. He turned around at the pit and grumbled something to Sam.

"No, she's not like that. She's nice. Didn't you hear me talking to her just now? Trust me. She says she only eats some kind of bird." Yetews grumbled something else in reply. And Sam said, "Of course I trust her. She seems plenty nice. Now help me pull some of those big vines down from the trees. I think we can make a rope or something and pull her out."

They looked for the strongest vines and Yetews pulled them down reluctantly. They both headed back towards the hole with the vines in tow, Yetews grumbling the whole way. Sam looked back down into the pit and explained, "We are throwing down some vines. Do you think you will be able to crawl up them?"

"Yes. I think so," she returned.

Yetews held onto one end of the makeshift rope and looked at Sam pleadingly before he tossed down the other end. He didn't get a response so snorted annoyingly and then tossed the vines down. He held on while she climbed up, supporting her massive weight with his full body. He kept a watchful eye on his friend, ready to pull him out of harm's way in a split second's time. Try as he might to discourage Sam, he knew that there was no convincing him otherwise.

The Gateway to Imagia: The Tale of Sam Little

The neekor cat dug her sharp claws into the vine and pulled herself up. Her strong, muscular back legs tore into the earth keeping her from slipping down again. Yetews pulled back on the vines to ease her along. Sam also tried his best to pull. Brave or not, he really wasn't very strong. Yetews was good to have around for such occasions.

The vines groaned menacingly under the weight, as if about to snap at any moment. Sam could hear clods of earth chunking away as she heaved her body closer to the top.

Slowly, between the three of them, she cleared the traps edge and was freed from captivity. She panted fiercely. It was a deep hole and a hard climb. She must have been down there for a while and angry at her situation because she turned back to the trap and hissed viciously at it. Turning back to face her rescuers, she almost purred her gratitude. "Thank you so very much...um...what did you call yourself?" she asked as she sat to catch her breath.

"Sam Little."

"Well then, thank you very much Sam Little. I honestly don't have any idea what I would have done if you hadn't come along. What is a boy of your size doing in such a dark part of the forest anyhow?"

Sam was very impressed with this creature's manners and speech. He had never dreamed he would meet a talking cat. "Oh...well my friend and I were going to go on an adventure. I love to adventure, and that part of the forest over there looked pretty interesting, for as far as adventures go. We really didn't get too far though," he explained to her. "Because we heard you and wanted to see what made the noise. This is the first time I've been in this world. Actually, I just got here." He could hear himself rambling and felt his cheeks going pink.

"*This* world? My dear boy, is there any other world than this? I doubt that. And what is your name again?" she asked Yetews.

He grumbled back and she stared at him blankly.

It became apparent to Sam that even in this world, he was the only one who would be able to understand Yetews. He translated for her. "This is my best friend, Yetews."

She shook her head in disbelief. "You can actually understand him?"

"Yeah."

"How strange." She mumbled something else low but all Sam caught was, "- understand a lorthax…"

He wasn't sure what that word meant. He'd have to ask her about it if he could remember to. But Sam looked back to his doubtful companion and gloated, "See? I told you she was nice."

Yetews shrugged and growled a question to Sam who responded by shrugging. "I can ask her. Er…" Sam paused as he turned to ask her Yetews' question but then realized he didn't know how to address her.

"Is there a problem?" she asked.

"Well, it's just that I don't know what to call you."

As if startled by her rudeness, she jumped right in and said, "Oh! Where are my manners? I," she bowed slightly, "am Keesa. I owe you both my sincerest gratitude. But if you will excuse me, I really must go."

Sam couldn't remember ever meeting someone so polite. He wanted to know more about her. Why she could talk and where she was from for starters. But most importantly, he didn't want to see her leave. "Wait a minute!" he said as she turned to leave. He thought quickly of something to keep her attention. "I-I heard you say that you were looking for something earlier. Can we help you find it?"

"That is most honorable of you, but I don't think you can find them. You see…I've lost my cubs." Remorse shadowed her face. "They were in the forest near our den. I called for them, but they never came. I've looked everywhere for them. I believe it is possible that they may have fallen capture to the same scum that made this trap." Keesa glanced at the trap and bowed her head making a soft cooing sound. "No. Actually, I am sure of this. So naturally, I must go and find them. My poor cubs…they must be terrified."

"Why would someone take them from you?" asked Sam. He was very new to this world. Things really were turning out to be quite different from his imagination. So he thought that asking questions wasn't such a bad idea and perhaps it would keep her around for a bit longer.

Keesa looked at Sam and blinked her three crystal-blue eyes in unison. There was such kindness in them. "My kind are captured so they can be used to do terrible things, Sam Little. They are trapped or

The Gateway to Imagia: The Tale of Sam Little

taken when they are very young. I don't know exactly what is done to them, but I've heard horrifying stories. And, if I don't find my cubs soon, I fear they may be lost to me forever."

She was consumed by sadness as she explained what happened. Sam looked up at Yetews. The concern in his face for the situation they were in had softened by her story. An idea came to Sam suddenly and he said, "We could help you find your babies. I know we can!" Yetews' eyes went wide and his jaw dropped as Sam said this. "After all, six eyes...um...I mean seven eyes, " he corrected himself, "are better than...uh...three." He looked at her hopefully.

Keesa looked moderately surprised at his offer. She glanced at both of them and considered for a moment. With some hesitance she answered him. "I suppose it couldn't hurt. Though I'm really not sure what good it will do. I warn you that it could be a considerable journey. Are you absolutely certain you want to come?"

Sam thought about it. If a gentle creature like her was taken against their will, it didn't seem right to him. He knew, deep down, that he could help her. At the very least, he would try. He looked up at Yetews, knowing that he would certainly object. Just as Sam thought, he had a look of utter disbelief on his face. "Come on Yetews," he pleaded. "Just think about those poor scared babies out there. I betcha they really miss their mom. We can't just let something bad happen to them if there's something we can do to help, right?" It was the perfect guilt trap.

At first he was frowning, but then his face shifted to pity. There was no use in arguing. Sam would win his way. So he put on a noble face, stood tall, and nodded his head as he grunted in agreement. Sam grinned at his friend and scratched behind his ears. "Cool!" he said.

Keesa took a step closer to them as if to examine them better before continuing. "I must warn you," she cocked her head, "I'm not sure where this journey will leave you. I admit that even to me, their scent is not consistent. The variation in their path is what led me to fall into that trap. I have to find it again. But when I do, I cannot promise you that I will not leave you at a moments notice. I'm quite fast, and your pace is likely to disagree with my tracking." Though the look of gratefulness was there in her face, there was also a hint of concern. Whether it was for Sam or her cubs, it was difficult to say.

She continued, "Can you accept that possibility Sam Little?"

He wasn't sure why she seemed so troubled, and whether or not he should be as well. But, he nodded in agreement.

The tawny cat sighed. "Very well, then. I accept your help. May we be successful in our journey."

"Then it's official. Let's go find your babies Keesa." Yetews lifted Sam back onto his shoulders.

Keesa mustered a smile. Or at least it was as close to a smile that a cat could have. "Thank you Sam Little."

He chuckled at her use of both his names. "You can just call me Sam."

She tilted her head questioningly. "Sam. Very well. Off we go now Sam."

Chapter Four: Deception

Sam and Yetews followed their new companion through the forest as they set off on this new course of their journey. Keesa bound gracefully ahead of them as they went forward through the trees, often pausing when she caught a new scent. Sam was perfectly at ease with the situation. Adventuring was all he ever really enjoyed doing at home. The time for his pretend play had come to an end. It felt odd to be doing something so real. To feel the fur clutched under his fingers, tickling his skin. To breathe in the scents of the forest. To feel the sun's warmth on his face. The scene of everything around him was beyond brilliant.

Keesa had led them out of the darker part of the trees. The sun was still high above them. Its warmth filtered through the dense canopy, leaving beams of dusty light to guide their way. He wasn't really sure where exactly they were headed or how long it would take to get there. It didn't really matter. He felt it was his duty to help Keesa in her time of need.

Though this tender creature was nothing like the ones he had imagined, he felt a connection to her. He sensed her desperation. He considered the situation she was in with her lost cubs. He couldn't blame her for wanting to find them so badly. A mother would go to the ends of the world to help her child. Though he was young, this much about life, he understood.

A sudden wave of memories came back to Sam as he walked through the dense forest. One in particular stood out in his mind. When he was eight years old, he remembered a fishing trip at the river. It had just rained and the water was moving fiercely. He had gotten too close to the edge where it was far too steep and muddy and fell in before his mom could grab him. He could still remember the cold water rushing around him as he started to slip further from the bank. But more than anything, he could remember the loud splash near him and the firm, protective grasp of his mother's arms around his body as she pulled him back to dry ground.

As he was thinking of this, he began to think about what his parents would do when they found him missing from his bed. He really hadn't been gone very long. According to his watch, only a few hours had passed. They probably assumed he was outside getting into some kind of mischief. How little they knew. Surely they wouldn't have been too worried already.

But then again, he had spoken so often of his desire to go into the forest. If they had even considered for a moment that he had gone into the forest, would they have already begun to search for him? What would they find when they looked? How much trouble was he already in? He'd probably be grounded for life at this point. Perhaps they would go into the forest and look for themselves or maybe even form a search party.

His thoughts did nothing but make him feel a pang of guilt. The feeling sat like a ton of rocks in his stomach. This was not a particularly good feeling to have and began to damper his good mood. So rather than continue with these upsetting thoughts, he tried to convince himself of another scenario.

He stumbled through his thoughts. The only thing he could come up with was that time couldn't work the same here if it was day already. Luck might just be on his side and his parents would not even know he was missing by the time he returned. It would probably only take a few more hours to find what they were looking for. His adventures never lasted more than a day anyways and by that time, he could sneak back into bed and it would be as though nothing had ever happened. And come to think of it, Titus' warning bark wasn't really that loud. Maybe his parents hadn't even heard it and were still oblivious to his absence.

It was working. He felt better already. The silence was doing nothing good for him, so he opted to start a conversation with his distraught companion.

Sam cleared his throat. "Um...Keesa? Where are we going anyways?" he asked her.

She was ahead of them when Sam spoke. She had to slow down to answer him. "You really shouldn't raise your voice so loudly. I may not be enough to frighten you, but I am certain that there are things out here that could do the trick."

"Oh...sorry." He couldn't help thinking how she reminded him of his mother with her tone of voice. The guilt he had attempted to bury surfaced a moment more before he considered what she had said. If there were frightening things here, then he couldn't have possibly been the one to imagine them. Nothing in his imaginary world was ever really frightening. Mostly when the part called for it, he would simply pretend to be scared. In reality, he wasn't sure he would know what the sensation of fear would be like. He had no memory of that particular feeling which is why he assumed he was so brave.

Keesa interrupted his thoughts, "Nevertheless, I think I've completely lost my children's scent, so I'm leading us to the nearest water source to see if I can pick up anything familiar. I'm not sure where we are headed, but I smell water in that direction." She gestured with her head. "This part of the forest is unfamiliar to me. I've never had a need to venture this way. And though I'm not all too keen on the smell of it, there is definitely a water source close by."

"What do you mean by 'not too keen'?"

"Well, it smells a bit...off. Not quite right to me." She paused to sniff the air.

Sam didn't like the sound of that and he could tell that Yetews wasn't exactly thrilled either. It was a very strange thing to say about water. He didn't really know what could make water smell bad to someone. But this was a strange new world. Maybe here, water was not what he knew water to be. At this point, he believed anything could be possible. If a cat could talk, then water could be mud for all he knew. It was starting to feel more and more unlike his imagined world that was so dear to him.

"I don't think it's dangerous." Keesa seemed to sense their hesitation to continue. "I'm sure it is nothing more than a dead animal. That can easily foul any water."

Yetews stopped so suddenly that Sam nearly flipped straight over his head. He turned his face to look up at Sam and grumbled something as he impatiently pointed in the direction they were headed.

Sam wanted to calm him down, but didn't know what to say. All he could manage in reply was, "I don't know."

They all had stopped now, Keesa sitting on her haunches and facing them. "Is there a problem? I can go on alone from here if you'd rather turn around."

Sam looked at Yetews briefly and translated for her. "Well, it's not that we don't want to help you. It's just that we…I mean…he, doesn't like the idea of the dead thingy." He didn't want to admit it, but he was also a little concerned about the idea of seeing something dead. Death had definitely never been something he had imagined. The strangeness was getting worse.

"Well, logically speaking of course, if it's dead, then whatever it is, it can't really hurt you. Can it?"

"It's not really the dead thing that bothers us…er…him. It's the thing that killed it that makes him scared." As he said the word 'killed', he realized just how serious this situation could be. He was only a few hours into this world, and things had already changed so much. His knowledge and familiarity of this place was beginning to grow faint.

She was shaking her head slowly to reassure them. "I never said anything about something killing something else. Honestly, I'm sure it's nothing. Now we really must continue on. I fear for my young ones. If your choice is to part ways, then please do so now and let me be on my way." She was growing impatient.

It was strange to be following a creature through the forest towards unfamiliar places – especially a creature who seemed so human. Usually, he was the one doing the leading, but he wasn't about to stop now. Even though it was completely unfamiliar, it was still exciting.

He had already made up his mind and tried to nudge Yetews with his knees. But they didn't budge. They seemed to be annoyingly

The Gateway to Imagia: The Tale of Sam Little

locked again. If his knees wouldn't work then he'd just use his voice. "We aren't going to leave you. We want to help. It's just that you surprised us. That's all. Right Yetews?"

Yetews opened his mouth to grumble his opposing side, but blinked twice and then sighed heavily instead.

Keesa was already up and moving by this time. She was a few yards ahead of them when she spoke again. "Good. I think that the water source is just ahead of us in this direction. Not far now."

Sam's attempt at a conversation didn't do anyone any good. It caused nothing but tension. He didn't really feel like dealing with that chance again for now, so they continued on in silence. They went on for about half an hour before anyone spoke again.

By this time he'd finally thought of a question he was eager to know the answer to. He asked Yetews to let him down so that he could be on her level to talk to her. Though Yetews was uncomfortable with Sam so far from his reach, he complied and plucked him off his shoulders. He adjusted his stride to match Sam's.

Keesa heard the boy trotting up to her and glanced over her shoulder. She slowed her pace when she saw him coming to her. "Another problem, Sam?" she asked him.

She didn't seem too upset anymore, so he figured it was safe to talk again. "No. I was just wondering about something. Can I ask you a question?"

"Hmm…what can I ease your mind about this time?"

He smiled at her. "No. It's not like that. I was just wondering why you said something earlier. Before we left, you said it was strange that I can understand Yetews. Then you said a word I didn't understand."

"Which word would that be?"

"Well, I think it sounded something like 'lorthax'."

She looked over to Yetews and smiled. "Well, I suppose that it doesn't necessarily *mean* anything. It is what he is. Or at least what they are commonly called. Strange, that you didn't know that. But I've also never heard of one with a name."

"Yetews! You're a…lorthax? I mean…there are…more?" Sam was completely shocked by this discovery. He wasn't just a single creature that he had imagined up. The idea that there were others like him out there was a possibility that he'd never fathomed.

Yetews didn't say anything. He just shrugged as if he had no idea what she was talking about.

Keesa went on. "Yes, well I've never seen one that looks like him in particular. What I mean is that I've never seen any herds of his type.

Sam was confused. "But I thought you said he is a lorthax and that you'd seen them before."

"Ah. I see where I've confused you. Yes. He is a lorthax. But I suppose lorthax is more of a general term. Lorthaxes are basically large beasts with unintelligible speech. There are countless creatures like him. They're generally a jittery bunch. You'd think something so large, would have a bigger spine." She was smirking.

Yetews frowned back at her and grumbled something low.

Sam chuckled. "I don't think he likes being called stupid. But if I can understand him then he's not a lorthax, right?'

"I suppose."

This was plenty to keep his mind busy now. It opened up a floodgate of questions he wanted to ask, but he didn't even have the slightest clue where to begin. He was overwhelmed now. So instead, he lingered on the idea of multiple creatures that were similar to Yetews. As his mind wandered, they went back to walking on in silence. When Sam started to fall behind, Yetews picked him back up to ride again.

Keesa's sleek body gracefully darted through the trees and undergrowth as she led them towards a clearing in the trees just ahead. It really wasn't very far from where they had stopped earlier. Sam could see the light of the clearing breaking through the canopy. The forest was thinning and he could even see a glimpse of something that shined like glass stretching across a grassy meadow. But it wasn't glass.

It was a pond. Or perhaps even a small lake.

The closer they got to it, the more spectacular it looked. The water was crystal clear. The sun gleamed down on the surface revealing brilliant shades of blues and greens. Sam jumped down from Yetews' shoulders to get a closer look.

Keesa slowed her pace and approached the water cautiously. She sniffed the air around her.

"Look at it!" shouted Sam. "It's amazing!"

The Gateway to Imagia: The Tale of Sam Little

She sniffed the ground around the water's edge. "Yes. Amazing. I've never been to this water before. It appears to be safe. But there is still something strange in the air. I can't place it, but as extraordinary as it seems, I don't think it wise that we linger here." She seemed concerned.

How anyone could smell anything bad here was beyond Sam. He breathed deep. It smelled like the first day of spring when he would get to go outside for the first time after a long winter indoors. The air was fresh and clean. He started to walk to the water's edge to get a better look.

"Please be careful Sam. It doesn't smell like the water holes where I frequent."

He scoffed silently at her. She sounded just like his mother. Always wanting him to be careful. After all, he just wanted to look. Yetews grunted at her with a shrug and followed Sam towards the water. He didn't seem to notice anything out of place either. They both stood at the edge looking eagerly at the water, gazing into its depths. Tiny schools of purple fish darted around playfully between the lush green plants growing on the bottom. The sandy bottom even looked clean. He had been to a beach once and it looked just like the soft white sand he had walked through. The water didn't seem to be too deep around the edges. It was enticing.

They had been walking for a while now and seeing water made Sam realize how thirsty he was. The reflection of the water sparkled in his eyes. In the background he heard Keesa warning them to be wary, but how could she not be as thirsty as he was? And hot. He realized all of a sudden just how warm he was getting. They weren't comforted by the shade of the trees anymore. It made the water inviting in another way now.

Yetews must have been parched because he was licking his lips. Sam's mouth was equally as dry. He heard Keesa asking them to back away from the edge. But he didn't understand why. If she was worried about him falling in then she didn't have to be. He was a good swimmer. He couldn't take his eyes off the water when he answered her. "Just a quick drink. I'm really thirsty." Yetews nodded in agreement. Sam was set on quenching his thirst. It would just take a minute and then they could go.

They both crouched at the edge. Sam cupped his hands and

plunged them into the cool, clear surface while Yetews watched him. He brought the water to his mouth and drank deeply. It tasted perfect. It wasn't enough to refresh him though. He cupped his hands to drink again.

As he swallowed, a peace started to wash through him. He thought he could hear someone in the back of his mind telling him to stop drinking, but he wasn't done yet. He must have been more parched than he realized. It felt wonderful. He could feel the water filling his stomach. Suddenly, he was aware that the cool of the water wasn't only on his inside. He could feel it on his ankles. The water was moving up his legs. He didn't remember walking into the water, but it felt good. It was the perfect temperature.

Then, out of nowhere, the floor of the lake trembled and shifted. Sam could feel the water rising towards his waist. A small voice echoed in his head warning him of the danger he was in. But peace clouded the rational part of his mind. The ground beneath his feet trembled with more ferocity.

As the water started to slosh angrily around him, he could hear Keesa roaring from somewhere behind him and the faint familiar sound of Yetews growling. The water darkened. It's perfect clarity was gone, replaced by a picture he didn't understand. The sky was masked and he was covered in shadow. Replacing the sky was a set of teeth surrounding a large mouth that led to a massive hole that could only be a throat. The water was at his chest before Sam could realize that he was in serious trouble. He wanted to react: to run away. But his mind was too foggy, making it impossible to move his feet. He couldn't shake it off.

Suddenly, Sam felt two strong hands lock onto his shoulders and wrench him backwards out of the water. The same hands shoved him out of danger as he was freed. He landed heavily on the grass, still unable to move. There was a faint cracking sound of glass as his wrist came down hard on a rock. He tried to shake his head to clear his thoughts, not sure what had just happened, but he couldn't even do that. The only parts of him that seemed to work right were his eyes and ears.

Towering above him was a sight that dwarfed anything he had ever imagined. The lake was gone, leaving a gaping crater in the ground. A creature of mind-boggling size was staring down at him

The Gateway to Imagia: The Tale of Sam Little

with glassy black eyes. It had lost its prey and was bellowing in fury. Though he couldn't move, he suddenly felt the weight of a warm, hairy arm shielding him. There, beside him, was Yetews, soaked and trembling, shielding him from the danger at bay. Sam looked up at the creature. Its bottom jaw was like a pelican's that held the water he so eagerly, just moments before, had been drinking. Its eyes were pitch black. It resembled a cross between a monstrous salamander and a menacing crocodile. He didn't know how it was possible, but this creature *was* the lake. It was massive. And just when it couldn't look any more intimidating, the beast roared, causing the ground to quake. A giant, scaled leg unearthed itself from the ground. The creature was moving.

Keesa was in-between the monster and Yetews, crouched defensively. Her growls and hisses were drowned out by the commotion.

Sam was shaking from head to toe; unsure if it was from shock or the cold he now felt from being soaked. Never had he wanted to run so badly as he did now. Yetews continued to use his body as a shield, his eyes wide in terror. For a split second he wondered how Keesa could call him spineless.

The hands that had pulled Sam free just moments ago once again grabbed him and pulled him out from under Yetews' protective arms. He was being pulled away to the trees. Yetews and Keesa followed in retreat. When he reached the safety of the tree line, his rescuer leapt over Sam's head as he laid on the ground staring in shock. The man pulled an arrow from a quiver on his back. In one fluid motion, he shot three separate, but perfectly aimed arrows at one of the beast's great eyes.

They pierced the blackness at the same time as its other leg had unearthed. It shrieked in agony. Or perhaps it was anger. It closed its injured eye and raked at its face with its clawed leg to remove the source of its irritation. It shook its head, raining water down onto the ground. It gave one last echoing roar before settling its body back into the crater. It opened its jaw, revealing the crystal-clear water once again. The head of the lizard shuddered as it faded from view like a mirage turns to heat waves. It once again became camouflaged into the forest background, readying itself for its next unsuspecting prey. The only proof of the turmoil was the residual trembling of the once still water.

Mere yards away, the stranger stood defiantly with his back to the traveling trio. He seemed barely winded from the effort. Sam wanted to know who he was. He wanted to thank him and to see his face. But the shock of everything took over. As his savior turned to face him, everything faded to black.

Chapter Five: Course Change

Flashes of images raced through Sam's unconscious mind. The images started as simple faces. He saw his mom, dad, grandparents, Titus, Cooper. They were merely silent images that were very familiar to him. Then the images morphed. He saw Yetews and Keesa's friendly faces smiling at him from a strange and beautiful world. The forest behind them began to change just as quickly as it had appeared. It darkened and became an eerie sight that swallowed all of the warmth. It enveloped his friends until they were gone. In their place, he saw glowing eyes advancing from the depths of the darkness. As the eyes grew closer, he could see the faces they were attached to. They were individual entities that were almost a part of the darkness itself. The creatures were slowing encroaching on him. Each one was a frightening image that could only be the product of nightmares. Though he was unconscious, he could feel his heart racing. He could hear their growls and snarls as they bore down on him.

Somewhere far away, he could hear a voice. It was warm and full of hope. He searched the darkness for some sign of its source. As the creatures got closer, his heart beat as if he was at a dead run and he could feel a scream building in his chest.

"Sam," He heard the voice, a beacon in the abyss. He couldn't call out to it. His voice was too small and the beasts were nearly on top of him. He could feel their hot breath as they closed the circle on him.

He heard the voice again. "Sam, can you hear me?"

He could think of nothing else to do. He threw his arms over his head, trying to hide from the darkness, and he screamed. The voice heard his cries and he could feel a tender hand shaking his shoulder. "Wake up Sam! Open your eyes!" He didn't want to look, but the voice coaxed him on. "You've got to wake up, Sam. If you can hear me, open your eyes."

He could hear someone screaming as he opened his eyes to the brilliant light of day. The screams he heard were coming from his own mouth. As soon as he realized this, he jerked into a sitting position. He was soaked to the bone and gasping for air. The tender hand he felt in his nightmare was holding him steady as he fought to grasp sight of his situation. That same hopeful voice spoke again, "Are you alright, Sam? You were having a nightmare, but you're safe now."

Turning to look at the source of the voice, Sam half expected to see his father looking down at him while he lay safe in his bed at home. Instead, he looked up into a pair of gentle, brown eyes. His father had blue eyes, just like his, so it couldn't be him. A young man, no older than twenty-five, was kneeling there. One arm was on Sam's back helping steady his position as he stared back up into the stranger's face. The other arm was still on his shoulder for extra support. The stranger had shoulder length, dark brown hair with a slight wave to it. Half of it was tied back with a rough piece of leather string, while shorter stray strands framed parts of his kind face. Though he looked young, his face carried more emotion than one person seemed capable. He had wisdom beyond his time buried in his pale, youthful face.

There was no telling how long he had been unconscious, but from the looks of the three concerned sets of eyes now watching him, Sam could tell that he must look very grim at the moment. It was a strange scene to come by. A small ten year old boy being safely steadied by a young man on the forest floor, surrounded by two very different creatures; all of them donning looks of concern. To a passerby, it would be a sight to see, indeed.

No one seemed to know what to say at the moment. Yetews stared down from over the man's shoulder with a look of worry on his face. His black fur was matted and dripping wet. Drops of water trickled off of him, wetting the forest floor. Keesa paced nervously by

Sam's head. She threw anxious glances at the small boy with each turn of her body. Despite the fact that tracking her cubs had been ceased temporarily, the only looks of concern she wore were for the situation at hand.

The young stranger finally spoke again when Sam's breathing slowed to a fairly normal pace. He seemed confident that Sam wouldn't pass back out, so he took his arms away. "How do you feel? You've been better, I assume." A hint of a smile turned one corner of his mouth up as he spoke to Sam. "You'll feel better shortly though. Are you hurt?"

Sam didn't stop to think how he felt, he quickly answered, "No. I'm fine." But his stomach was answering quite differently. Something was stirring and, though it didn't seem possible, his face grew two shades paler.

"Here it comes," the stranger said taking a half step away from Sam's head. "Don't fight it. You'll feel better afterwards."

At first Sam wasn't sure what he meant, but suddenly a horrific wave of nausea swept over him and he broke out in a cold sweat. Without another thought, he rolled over and vomited fiercely. A sickly dark fluid poured from him, the flavor making him pinch his eyes closed, wishing it was over. Just as quickly as the nausea set on, it subsided. He rolled back over and stared back, slightly breathless from the ordeal, at the suspiciously unsurprised stranger. A bit raspy, Sam said, "That was disgusting."

The stranger couldn't help but grin as he responded. "Well, it may have looked good at the time, but that stuff you just gorged yourself on wasn't exactly water. You were lucky. It came back up fast and didn't linger in your stomach."

Sam wrinkled his nose and rubbed his stomach. "It didn't *feel* very lucky."

The stranger chuckled briefly then replied, "Trust me. You were. See? Your color is already coming back. Feeling better now?"

Sam nodded and realized that he actually did feel better. There was a dull ache somewhere in his back and on his wrist from hitting the ground. He groaned a little as he started to sit up straighter and rubbed his wrist.

The stranger nodded back. "Good. Well I didn't mean to throw you down so hard earlier, but I think you'll understand when faced with the alternative."

The hazy fog that had clouded his thoughts earlier had finally lifted and he was thinking much clearer. He did feel better, overall, than he had felt recently. Parts of him felt sore. He'd probably bruise later. "I'm fine…I think. But…" he could only think of one question for the moment, "How do you know my name?"

The stranger smiled down at him then glanced at Keesa. "Your friend told me while you were unconscious."

It seemed so obvious now, that Sam almost felt stupid for not realizing it. "Oh. That makes sense I guess. Sorry…I guess I wasn't thinking." He felt the tingling sense of embarrassment enter his face.

The stranger shook his head and tried to ease Sam's mind. "You can't really blame yourself for not thinking. You're in shock. It's hard to think clearly after that kind of ordeal. Don't beat yourself up about it." He smiled again.

Yetews was nodding his head in agreement. His expression had finally shifted a bit. He was less worried now that Sam was awake and speaking again. The ordeal was quite a shock to each of their systems. Keesa also began to slow her pacing as the situation normalized.

Sam's mind was definitely returning to full awareness and the questions were forming a line in his mind. He started with his simplest one. "Who are you?"

"I'm Taren," he said as he reached his hand out to take Sam's. They shook hands. Before letting go, Taren asked, "Do you feel like you're steady enough to stand now?" After an answering nod, Taren helped pull Sam up.

Sam was a mess and a half. He gave himself a once over. His pajamas were filthy and soaked straight through. Patches of drying mud covered half of him while leaves and grass stuck to other parts. Now that he was concentrating on what all had taken place, he could feel his bottom lip tingling. Touching it with one finger was enough to realize that it was slightly swollen. There was fresh blood on his fingers from the small cut that he didn't remember getting. He looked down at his sore wrist. His watch had a crack through the middle and didn't have any sign of the time. He remembered hearing the tinkling sound of his watch breaking in the midst of everything. Broken and worthless, he mindlessly unlatched it and tossed it aside. Now there was no way of knowing how long he'd been here.

After taking stock of the situation they had gotten themselves into, Sam realized that he was shivering slightly. Taren noticed and nudged him back towards the sunny meadow. Yetews and Keesa followed and they emerged a good distance from the glassy lake. Sam shuddered when he saw the water and a sinking feeling churned in his stomach. He was realizing the trouble that the creature, now quite invisible again, had caused them all.

Sensing the hesitation of the three companions, Taren felt compelled to ease their worry about the hidden beast. "Don't worry about him," he nodded in the creature's direction. "He isn't about to come storming out of his hole again any time soon. Once they bait the trap, all they can do is wait it out until some poor, unsuspecting soul wanders in. You're lucky I pulled you out when I did. A few moments more and you'd have been lunch, you know?" He wasn't looking at the lake when he spoke, but rather at the other three who were obviously unsettled by being so close to it.

Sam turned away from the concealed monster in surprise at the way Taren spoke of it. "*Him*?" How do you know it's a 'him'? And does that mean there are more of those things?" He was asking the questions through a nerve-cracked voice while Yetews stood next to him, frozen in shock.

"Yeah, there are more. Not a great deal more, but enough. And the reason I know it's a male, is because the females are a lot bigger." He chuckled to himself. "You'd never forget a female once you saw one." He talked about this as though he was entertained by the thought of it all.

"Bigger?!?" Sam squeaked.

Yetews shuddered and Keesa's ears laid back. She hissed her opinion of the monstrosity, "Vile creation."

"Yeah, vile is right, but easily avoidable if you know what you're looking for." Everyone was confused again, so he clarified. "When in your life have you ever seen water that perfectly clear? Or so perfectly calm, for that matter? I'd place my bet on never. There is also the fact that the shoreline and shape of the water is too neat. The key to detection is perfection. If it looks too perfect, then chances are that you are looking at a deceptor. It lures you in. Their drool is poisonous and has a drug-like effect on you when you ingest it."

Sam's eyes went wide with disgust. "You mean that water I drank was actually monster spit?"

"Precisely."

Sam remembered what he threw up and frowned as he rubbed his stomach.

Taren hid a grin and went back to explaining. "But if you can't grasp the finer details, then you can just look for the eye." He pointed up at a spot that would have been easily missed unless you knew precisely what you were looking for.

They all stared where he was pointing. There, in the middle of what looked like an innocent tree line, was a black eye roughly the size of a car tire. It twisted and turned, as it hovered there, appearing to be unattached to anything. The sight of it was the most peculiar thing Sam had ever witnessed. The deceptor's ability to camouflage itself was unmatched to anything. He figured that unless you were expecting to see a random floating eye, it would be next to impossible to spot one floating that high up in such a random spot.

The four of them sat in the grassy meadow, letting the sun dry them. Yetews was hardly about to let Sam out of arm's reach, so sat close by. His wet hair was already half dry after shaking it out like a dog. Keesa never drank or got close enough to the water's edge to get as wet as the other two, so she was already dry and showing signs of her readiness to leave. She didn't speak much, but her pacing seemed to grow more impatient by the minute.

Sam, on the other hand, was finding it very difficult to dry out. He tried to distract himself from the uncomfortable feeling of being so soaked by talking to Taren as they sat there. "What happened to me, anyways? How does the...er...deceptor work? And how did you get me out so fast?" He felt safe now and his curiosity was starting to take hold again. Even though he had just almost been eaten and blacked out, the excitement of it all seemed to overshadow his less than happy moments. Taren appeared to be more than willing to shed light on so many of his unanswered questions.

He sat, cross-legged, adjacent to Sam and Yetews. He, unlike the others, had been barely dampened by the ordeal. He looked up to Sam and thought about something before he responded. "You saw the majesty of that water. That's the bait. They create a mirage of the ideal water source. Clear. Refreshing. But it's just a mirage. They can blend in to nearly any background. No one knows how they do it. All part of the mystery, I suppose. I'm assuming that you understand enough about the water you drank by now. Right?"

"Yeah."

"Well, the water they hold is mixed with their spit which has some kind of pheromone that the deceptor releases. Once the water touches your lips, that's all it really takes. It numbs your mind. The more you drink, the harder it is to move. And I'd say you drank a fair share, because you seemed pretty oblivious to the fact that a gargantuan monster was set on swallowing you whole." He smirked at Sam before going on. "Usually, they wait until larger groups or entire herds drink, so this one must have been pretty hungry to go to the trouble of unearthing itself for a scrawny boy. I heard the commotion from where I was and could tell that someone was over here. I overheard your kupa cat friend yelling for you. I don't generally begrudge something a meal," he looked over at the deceptor, "but seeing as how you were human, I intervened. I ran through the trees to see you being lifted up and your hairy friend here…" He was pointing at Yetews when Sam interrupted him.

"Yetews. His name's Yetews, and her name's Keesa…just so you know." He jabbed a thumb in each of their directions.

"Ah. Noted. Well, anyhow, your friends were putting up quite a fight to get you out, not that it was a fair match. So, I shot an arrow once to distract him. He lowered his jaw enough to grab you and I pulled you out and pushed you back. Sorry about that again. Is your lip still sore? I think you knocked it on one of the deceptor's teeth when I yanked you out."

Sam felt the swollen part with his tongue. "It just hurts a little. No big deal." Regardless of how nerve wracking it was to picture the whole thing, it was nice to know how it happened at least. His bravado was returning as well.

Taren finished recollecting with a few last thoughts. "So, in the end, Deceptors only really have the one vulnerable spot. All it really does is tick them off though. But if you aim for the eye, then they generally realize that the meal isn't worth the fight. They don't like moving. Lazy, you know. Once they settle, they don't leave unless they need new hunting grounds. This one has been here for a while, from the looks of it." He waited for a moment, then said, "So that's that. You blacked out and the kupa cat explained a few things to me. I couldn't understand your bigger friend of course." He pointed at Yetews. "But he conveyed his obvious concern. And there you have it."

As Sam was about to point out Keesa's name again, he suddenly caught what Taren had just called her. He frowned. "Wait a second. What did you just call Keesa?"

With a raised eyebrow, Taren answered, "A kupa cat. Why?"

"But that doesn't make sense. I thought she was a neekor cat."

Taren was about to say something when Keesa spoke instead. "What is a neekor cat?"

Now he was thoroughly confused. "Well, they are cats that look like you, only…kind of different."

Keesa didn't say anything. She merely stared at him, baffled.

Sam bit his lip and wondered how he could explain. He attempted to make more sense without sounding crazy. "Well…when I used to imagine things, I pictured cats that looked like you. I called them neekor cats." The more he explained, the sillier he felt.

Taren stopped him. "I gather that she has some slight differences from the creature you thought she was."

Sam nodded. "Yeah. They couldn't talk and were mean. Weird."

"Well that isn't too uncommon actually." Taren didn't seem even slightly surprised by any of this.

"What do you mean?"

"Now isn't the time to explain that. We should be moving from here for now." It was certain that Taren wasn't about to explain this further for the moment.

It was a lot to take in for Sam. He wasn't sure what to ask next. It had felt like they had been sitting here for a very long time, but it had really only been a short while. He still had so many questions to ask Taren. Most importantly of all, he wanted to know what happened when he had passed out. Amongst the things he wanted to know was how long he was out for and why he had woken up screaming. He asked himself what could cause such a sound to come out of him. The feelings he had were unfamiliar to him for the most part. He had only felt a hint of these knee-locking feelings since his decision to come here. Sam still hadn't quite grasped what it was he was experiencing. What he felt when he dreamt was similar to this sensation, only magnified tenfold. Luckily, the images of what he saw in his unconsciousness were fading quickly from his mind.

As they sat there, Sam silently hoped that Taren knew more about this world than he did. He'd only been here for what he could only guess as half a day, and already he knew only one thing for certain. No matter how powerful his imagination had been before, it was nothing compared to the amazing things unfolding in front of him now. This world couldn't be solely from his mind. It was something much more, and he was intent on finding out what.

* * * * * * * * *

All in all, not an immense amount of time had passed since the ordeal with the deceptor. Each one of them was drier now and it was apparent that they couldn't sit around idly without a purpose to lead them on. While they all basked in the sun's warmth, Taren had discovered a good deal of information about all three of them. He was now aware of the initial purpose of the three's traveling.

Sam had divulged the entire day's happenings. He explained with the same ten-year old gusto that he had when telling people about his imaginary ventures. He explained how he found his way into this world and how he had come from a different place where it was still night. He told of Keesa's escape from, what he now knew to be, a kupa cat trap. He even told of their finding of the perfect water of the deceptor. It turned out that there were some interesting pieces to that particular puzzle.

Yetews never got around to actually taking a drink of the infectious water. That is why he didn't succumb to the lure of the trap as easily. Keesa had apparently been hissing countless warnings to them. When the deceptor shuddered into view she had attempted to distract it by jumping onto its mouth as it raised out of the ground. Sam found that part particularly touching since she barely knew him. He also discovered the reason he lost consciousness was partially due to the pheromones he swallowed.

The only part of his story that Sam had left out intentionally was the wish that he believed brought him to this fascinating place.

Taren had patiently listened to everything and only offered bits of random information here and there. The entire time, the only look on his face was one of total understanding. Nothing came as a surprise to him.

Though he tried to assure them that what they were trying to do was very noble, he was very pessimistic about the entire situation. For some unspoken reason, he was intent on Sam returning back the way he had come from and for Keesa to accept that the finding of her cubs would be highly improbable.

Sam was grateful for his help, but this was the point in which Sam was becoming very impatient with their rescuer. "I don't understand why you don't want Keesa to find her cubs. And I *sure* don't understand why you want me to go home. I just got here!" His voice squeaked on his last word as he scowled at Taren.

Taren just shook his head and tried to give Sam a better reason than the danger of the plan they were all set on following. "You don't seem to understand what you are getting yourself involved in here, Sam. I know, for almost certain, the reason you are here on this very day, doing what you are doing. You think you are merely having some grand and carefree adventure. And as much as I want to explain the finer details of the mistake you are making, I'm not the one you need to talk to."

The scowl he had on his face wiped clean away and was immediately replaced by one of utter confusion. Now he was even more baffled. "What do you mean? Who are you talking about? 'Cuz if there is someone that can explain stuff to me about this place, I wanna meet him...or her...or whatever it is."

As Sam demanded a new course of action, Keesa leapt to her feet and looked at Sam as if his words were a complete betrayal. She was not willing to stray from her initial plan. She still wanted to track her cubs, positive that the situation wasn't as hopeless as Taren had insisted.

With no sign of wavering in his decision, she hung her head and sighed. "You are choosing to follow a much different path than the one I have to follow, Sam. I have not known you long, but have grown fond of your company. I will be eternally grateful for your help, but I must find my children. I can not leave them to torture and famine, if that is indeed where our new friend is sure they will end." Taren had recently enlightened her of a few of the unfortunate uses for kupa cats. She paused to think a moment before continuing.

"Unless this individual you want to seek out can aid in my cubs return, I fear that our time to part ways has already too soon come to pass."

Sam looked eagerly to Taren for an affirmation of this possibility. He didn't want to abandon Keesa. She was the only other thing in this world, so far, that was of any familiarity to him. When Taren didn't answer, he asked, "Can this person help her? Even a little bit?"

Taren closed his eyes and rubbed his temples as if warding away a looming headache. He didn't look at Sam when he spoke. "It's possible."

Sam looked back to Keesa, hopeful for her continued companionship. She glanced over her shoulder in the direction she longed to go, but turned back to him and nodded. With obvious regret she said, "I only have mere guesses as to how I can find them. If this...individual can truly give me better chances then..." she paused for only a moment then finished her thought, "then I go with you."

Yetews, sitting ever protective next to his friend, tousled Sam's messy hair and smiled down at him. Sam didn't even have to ask him to go. It was implied and his goofy smile affirmed it.

"Then what are we waiting for? Take me to..." he smiled as he imagined finishing the sentence with the words 'your leader'. He'd heard that line in about a dozen movies and books. So he was about to opt for something less silly.

Then Taren cocked a smile and finished it for him, only in the form of a question. "Your leader? You have no idea how close you are."

Chapter Six: Nightmare

After what could have only been hours, signs of the seemingly, ever present daylight began to fade into a perfect evening. Without his watch to give him proof of the time he'd been gone, Sam was only half certain that his time here had crossed the limit he had originally set for himself. Of course, this consumed only a fraction of the thoughts he was now riddled with. It was difficult to linger on something so insignificant as time when this had, hands down, been the most amazing thing he had ever experienced or done in his entire life. The amount of creatures that he had already seen combined with the sheer unfathomable size of this world, was enough to keep the attention of anyone.

Four unlikely travelers were now inside what could possibly be the very heart of the forest. Keesa was easily the best at making her way through the constant foliage and obstacles. If the brush became too thick, she would merely climb the nearest tree and delicately balance her way through the branches until she had found an easier path. Yetews' size was his only advantage. Pure brute strength aided his passage, knocking large limbs and heavy vines out of his way for Sam and Taren to pass.

The Gateway to Imagia: The Tale of Sam Little

But it wasn't Keesa's gracefulness or Yetews' notable power that impressed Sam. Now that his rescuer wasn't crouching on the ground or leaning on a tree, Taren was much more remarkable. Sam was small, and used to everyone looking so much taller than him. Taren wasn't only tall, but also very strong. His clothes looked roughly made, like someone Sam might picture stepping out of a *Robin Hood* movie. He carried a quiver of arrows on his back with an elegant bow to match. His shirt was short sleeved displaying his muscular arms. If heroes really existed, he figured that Taren would fit the part. But most amazing of all, was his seemingly intimate knowledge of the world around him. It was as though this was Taren's world and not Sam's world at all. He had some difficulty getting through the thickest spots of the forest, but mastered it, regardless. This was proof of one thing. He had obviously been here before.

Sam, of course, could barely keep up most of the time. He had done so much already today and was starting to get exhausted from the never-ending adventure. He would have normally been atop Yetews' shoulders, but the low hanging branches made it difficult. After bumping his head for the fourth time, Sam opted for walking. It would be much less painful.

He started to drag his feet and found himself tripping over random roots or tightly woven weeds. The longer he drudged on, the more he would even trip over his own feet. His constant strains of 'ow' and 'sheesh' drew the attention of the rest of his traveling party. Keesa would stop and ask frequently if he was okay to go on and Sam would always nod his affirmation, despite the fact that he was dead on his feet. Yetews was now wearing a constant look of concern for his small companion. He obviously preferred that Sam be riding instead of walking.

Taren felt sympathetic towards him. He understood that Sam was young and could see that his energy level was wearing quite thin. He slowed up enough that he could talk to the exhausted boy.

"Hey, kid," he smiled down at Sam. Sam smiled feebly in return, but the tiredness nearly overshadowed his attempt. "You think you have another two hours in you? I really wanted to get to a good clear area of the forest to make camp. It would be much safer there."

The word 'safer' struck some hidden nerve deep inside of Sam, but he was far too tired to let it bother him. The mere idea of walking for another two hours was exhausting, so the act of doing so itself, couldn't possibly be any better. But, regardless of the way he truly felt, he looked up into Taren's kind face and answered him. "Yeah. I think I can make it. I've never been on an adventure this long. I think my feet just need to get used to it." He smiled tiredly once more.

Taren furrowed his brow and thought for a second. He was certain that Sam was putting on a brave face so that they could continue and not appear weak. He understood this more than Sam knew. He saw through Sam's brave facade and called his bluff. "Really? Because you look to me like you're about to pass out again." He cocked an eyebrow and waited for Sam to notice that he wasn't convincing anyone. Then teasingly, he added, "And that could really slow things down a bit, you know?"

Sam took a mental inventory of each face now looking at him. Was he so unconvincing? He really had tried his hardest to keep up, but his small stature was barely able to get through high grass, let alone thick forest underbrush. He suddenly felt defeated and stopped in his tracks. Each of them, as if expecting this, stopped in turn. "Well," he sighed, "I guess I'm getting pretty tired. I really am trying though. Can't we just sit down and rest for a little bit? It might help." He felt himself blushing at his inability to keep pace with the rest of them. It was school all over again. He always had trouble keeping up with the kids in gym and on the playground. His imaginary world was the only place where he could be the fastest and the strongest.

"No one said you weren't trying. We can slow down a bit more, but this isn't exactly the best place to sit idly by. The forest is thinning already, or maybe you haven't noticed. Perhaps Yetews can give you a lift when we break through this last dense area." Taren pointed ahead of them and there was a definite thinning of the masses.

Looking ahead, it still seemed so far away. Sam really was feeling the aches of the day, now that he stopped to think about it.

The look on his face must have betrayed his sense of pride, because Yetews walked up to Sam and started to grumble something to him. The worry in his tone was obvious even to the others. Sam looked up to Yetews and cut him off in mid growl.

"No! You don't need to do that. You need both your hands to get through this mess anyways."

Taren and Keesa asked in unison, "What did he say?"

Sam's face creased with a slight frown and without looking up from his feet again, he translated, "He wants to carry me in his arms until we get to a clearer section of the forest. But he shouldn't have to do that! I can make it, really! If we could just rest for a little bit then we could keep on going." He folded his arms across his chest making him look younger than he wanted to come off.

Taren tried to hide a silent chuckle. He knelt down to Sam's level and tried to reason with the stubborn kid. "It's really not such a bad idea. And if you're worried about the extra burden on him, then you don't need to be. No offense, but you don't look exceptionally heavy. I'm sure he can handle it." When Sam didn't look convinced of his reasoning, he added, "Heck, I could probably carry you myself if I wasn't so sure Yetews could do it easier."

Keesa purred her encouragement of the idea. "You look absolutely exhausted Sam."

Sam interrupted her with a hissing sound of disagreement. "I'm not exhausted. I just need a little break."

Keesa was gazing down to him from the branches above. To Sam's surprise, she clucked her tongue, sounding just like a patronizing adult. "It's been a long day for someone so young. There is no shame in letting him carry you for a short while. You have such strength for a little cub. I wouldn't have expected more from you than I expect from my children and you have already gone so much further. I, too, would carry you myself if it were possible, but I really am no beast of burden."

Sam was touched by her comparison of him to one of her cubs but also a bit offended at the idea of being compared to something so small and helpless. He was too tired to argue this point. He stared at the laces of his tennis shoes as he thought about the suggestion. It was an embarrassing thing to have to be carried like a baby, but the sheer idea of it already sent spasms of hopeful relief to his aching body.

After a moment's hesitation and one triumphant look from Yetews, he nodded stiffly and said, "Fine. But just for a few minutes. This whole trip is my stupid idea anyway, so I shouldn't be complaining about anything." His irritation from the combination of lack of sleep and being ganged up on was starting to show.

Yetews reached out for Sam before he could change his mind and picked him up. He cradled him in one big hairy arm. He lumbered on through the trees in the fading light of evening. It barely slowed him down. Now, what he couldn't move out the way with only one hand, he used his powerful shoulders to shove through.

Sam could see the relief of his friends now, but also noticed a smirk on the edges of Yetews' face when he half-glanced at him. This minuscule look sent Sam into a series of under-the-breath mumblings. More than once he muttered, "This is just stupid."

Eventually his silent ranting ceased.

The sounds of the forest were changing as well as the colors surrounding them. The trees began to fade into cool grays and greens. It was easy to feel that the temperature was no longer a blazing summer heat, but was more comfortable now. There were fireflies twinkling around them while the soft whispers of the forest nightlife began to fill the air. Though Taren's words of warning of the safety of this forest teased the edges of his mind, Sam couldn't see how that was even a glimmer of a possibility. His body began to relax as it swayed to the rhythm of Yetews' gait. He hadn't realized just how incredibly tired he was until this moment. He yawned hugely.

Taren was walking inches from Yetews. Sam could see the triumphant grin when he looked over. As determined as he was to stay awake and not miss a single moment of his time in this world, his eyes were twice as determined to close. He nestled his head deeper into the soft fur and felt his eyes grow heavier. He could smell the familiar earthy scents of the forest in the thick hair and it relaxed him. Try as he might, his mind couldn't master keeping his eyes open another second. He lost the battle and drifted to sleep.

For the second time in this new world, Sam found himself dreaming. It was peaceful. The images that he saw were not familiar to him. At first it was merely the forest that he had just left behind in his consciousness. Then through the trees he saw a boy, much like himself, running next to a strangely beautiful creature that was more human than it appeared at a glance. As they ran, they were almost dancing through the sunny forest. He could hear the boy laughing as he followed the sound. Sam had caught up to them just as he saw the creature swoop the boy up into its arms. Now that they were still, he could see the creature more clearly and could tell that it was a woman. Or as close to a woman as she could be without actually being one. She had soft, glowing, gray eyes and long silver hair. Her gentle face

The Gateway to Imagia: The Tale of Sam Little

was full of nothing but adoration for the small boy as she hugged him tightly. She was obviously too beautiful to be completely human. She shimmered in the sun, as though she were carrying a light inside of her and she wore a long, simple dress of brilliant white. She had elf-like ears that pointed out through her long locks of hair. On her back were two beautiful wings that reminded Sam of an angel.

As he stared at the two, he felt strange. It was as though he were an intruder in someone else's home. He felt like a spy and wondered if they knew he was there watching. She had put the boy down and they were now standing in the sun. As he watched them smile and talk to each other from a distance, he longed to go closer and hear what they were saying. But his innocent intrusion lasted only a moment longer. Just as Sam had made his decision to go to them, the boy suddenly stiffened and turned to stare back at him. The innocent smile washed from his face when he saw Sam staring back. That same peaceful boy now looked disturbed and furious. His face contorted. His eyes were daggers meant only for the person that dared intrude his serenity and they pierced Sam's soul.

Even though he could tell that his naive intrusion had become a dangerous stand off, he still felt compelled to watch the scene unfold. The beautiful creature that had once been smiling for her precious boy was now shrouded in fear. Her face fell and her gray eyes turned to black as she reached out hopelessly for the boy. She was being swallowed by the darkness that now covered everything. Sam blinked, and her inviting white glow was gone, replaced by only the image of the boy who was now becoming one with the darkness. He suddenly broke eye contact and jerked his head to look behind Sam into the looming trees.

Instinct took over and Sam turned around to look too. Something was lurking in the shadows. He could hear the echoing cracks of twigs and branches as some hidden monster advanced on them. He turned his head to see if the boy was feeling the same things he was, only to see that he was gone, leaving nothing but shadows in his absence. He only had a moment to wonder what happened to the boy before he could hear the low rumbling growl of the danger approaching.

The creature was there in front of his very eyes. It was as massive as a rhinoceros. Its fanged teeth were bared and the stench that it emitted was foul, like stale blood and rotted wood. Its sickly, yellow eyes followed Sam's every movement as he slowly backed away. The creature closed the space between them, crouched like a lion hunting its prey. Thick, matted hair, darker than the shadows themselves, covered every inch of its body straight down to its four clawed paws. The creature was menacing, spawned from evil thoughts.

As Sam stared back with wide eyes, the beast opened its jaw to sound a blood-curdling roar. The sound pierced Sam's very thoughts and he tripped, falling onto the ground at the feet of the monstrosity. He couldn't move anymore. He didn't know if anyone could hear him over the roars, but he let loose a scream like no other. Something in him begged for it to be over and he didn't understand the feelings that drowned out his will to run. He could feel the hot breath on his face as the creature opened its mouth to strike.

He was waiting for the pain of the deadly jaws to close around him when, all of a sudden, he could feel two huge hands forcing him to stand up. He recognized them immediately. He then felt another set of smaller hands shaking his shoulders harshly. "Wake up Sam! Wake up!" Taren yelled.

Sam opened his eyes and, once again, he was screaming. The moment he recognized that the horrendous sound was actually coming from him, he stopped and blinked his eyes. He was standing in a clearing of the forest.

It was well past dusk now, and he could smell the faint odor of wood burning. Yetews was holding him up while Taren was kneeling in front of him with his hands still on Sam's shoulders. Keesa was staring at the scene from the side with worry in her trio of blue eyes. Her ears were twitching in every direction as if searching for something the others couldn't hear.

As he took in the scene, Sam noticed that he was also panting for air as though he had just been running a race and he was sticky with sweat that trickled down his face. Taren's eyes were serious and Yetews was biting his bottom lip as he continued to hold Sam into place. But more than anything, he felt confused. He wanted to know why he was screaming again and why everything he had dreamt seemed to be so real. As he stood there catching his breath, he couldn't seem to make himself speak the words he was so desperately thinking.

Taren was the first to break the edgy silence. "Are you alright?

What did you see?" His suddenly urgent words did nothing but confuse Sam further.

He still struggled to form the words and they came out slightly broken. "Yes...I'm...okay, I think. What happened?" Sam looked to each of his concerned party in turn, attempting to find clues to his puzzle.

Taren looked intently into Sam's eyes and then heaved a heavy sigh of relief, apparently relieved about something. He dropped his hands from their place on Sam's shoulders and glanced at Yetews briefly before he decided to answer the question. He stood up and backed away so as to give Sam more room as Yetews, too, let go his protective grip on him. Keesa had also calmed her disposition slightly and seemed just as intent as the others as to what Taren would say.

After brushing the back of his hand across his forehead, Taren spoke. "Yetews was carrying you and you fell asleep. We got to this clearing about an hour ago and decided to make camp so you could rest until morning. Yetews made you a place to lie, and things were fine until he laid you down. I had gotten a fire started when all of a sudden, you..." He stopped and looked concernedly at Yetews for a brief moment before continuing. Sam looked back eagerly. "Well, at first you just started to thrash around on the ground, like you were being attacked by something and I figured it might be a nightmare. But then without any warning you started screaming. We couldn't get you to wake up, so Yetews forced you to stand and we did everything we could to snap you out of it."

The floodgates of questions opened and drowned Sam's silent bewilderment of the situation. Once he opened his mouth, the questions were free flowing. "So that's when you woke me up? After I started screaming?" He didn't stop to wait for the answers. "Why was I screaming like that? Or how about this; *what* could make me scream like that? I've never felt anything like that before. I mean, wasn't it just a dream? What the heck just happened to me Taren?" He gasped for air after blurting out his desperate strain of questions.

Taren took two steps back and stared at Sam with a raised eyebrow. Something about what Sam had asked seemed absurd to him. He shook his head. Sam started to open his mouth to ask another question when Taren held up a hand to silence him. "You were having a nightmare."

Sam still didn't seem to grasp why he was screaming. "But if it wasn't real, then why did I feel like I was really there. I mean, I could hear and smell and see everything. I've had dreams before and I don't remember them feeling like…well anything like that."

"Not a dream, Sam. It was a *nightmare*. The more real it feels, the more convincing it is. The more convincing it is, the more scared you get. Everyone here has them and they can be quite terrifying." There was something more to his voice with the last remark.

It wasn't his tone that caught Sam off guard. A word that Taren had used caught him by surprise.

Scared.

He had never put the feelings together before this moment. A look of realization swept his face as he considered what he just heard. The knee-locking sensations, the feeling of helplessness, the need to cry out for someone; all the feelings began to make sense. But at the same time, it was incredibly confusing. He looked up at Taren and said, "Oh. So, you mean…that's why I was screaming? I was…*scared?*"

Yetews placed his huge hand on Sam's shoulder and squeezed gently to make his presence known. Taren looked at Sam as though he wasn't sure what he was seeing. But it was Keesa who was the first to comment on Sam's realization. "You say that as though you have never felt fear before. Were you not afraid when you were nearly swallowed by the deceptor? Did I not scare you when you first heard my angry calls from inside that trap?"

He had never considered the feelings that he was so perplexed by to be as simple as fear. He had never, in his whole life, remembered feeling scared of anything. His eyes unfocused and he placed himself back into the memories of his time since walking into the forest. It was so obvious now and he felt strange now that he understood. "I guess I never felt afraid before I came here. I remember feeling like I couldn't make my feet move. It was kinda like they were glued to the ground or something and my heart was going really fast even when I wasn't running."

Taren still had an eyebrow raised at Sam and replied to him, "Yes…that would be fear. You were afraid, and that was why you were screaming. That was why we woke you up."

"Oh."

"But I must admit that I've never had so much trouble waking someone up from a nightmare. I know they seem real because I've had some pretty nasty ones myself, but I'm curious..." His sentence drifted off as he considered something to himself.

"About what?"

Taren finished his thought. "What exactly was it that you saw?"

"Oh. Well...it was this...thing. Some kind of hairy creature that smelled really bad and was huge, like the size of a rhino. Have you ever seen something like that before?"

Taren laughed. "There are a lot of huge hairy things around here in case you hadn't noticed." After a fleeting glance at Yetews, he continued to listen as Sam struggled to explain what he saw.

"I can picture it in my head still. It was so real..." Sam faded off into the comfort of his mind. His eyes lost focus as they strayed into the dark woods beyond the fire and the mysterious shadows it cast. He closed his eyes and pictured the beast, clear as day, approaching him from the darkness of the trees. He could already picture those horrible eyes and the powerful jaws surrounded by the long matted hair. He could hear the twigs cracking and the bushes moving, just as he had in his nightmare.

All of a sudden, Taren shouted, "Yetews! Grab Sam!"

The sound of a bow being armed along with a long hiss and growl from Keesa forced Sam's eyes back into focus as he snapped them open, unsure what he had missed. Before he could absorb the situation, he was being lifted from his feet as Yetews placed him as high into a tree as he could reach. Yetews flipped back around and crouched into a defensive position under the branches that Sam desperately clung to. Keesa flanked him while Taren stood, armed and ready, for whatever was barreling through the trees towards them.

Sam's stomach twisted into a knot at the sudden turn of events. The sounds were getting closer by the second and he jerked when Taren aimed a warning shot into the dark. Taren's eyes must have been much more keen than Sam's because the arrow hadn't missed its mark. The dull thud was followed by a piercing howl and the forest moved with more anger as the very creature that Sam had dreamt of broke through the tree line into the glow of the fire. It was massive, standing now on its hindquarters with its fangs bared. It reached up with its claws and ripped the arrow out of its shoulder. It dropped down to all fours and growled as it looked at the three obvious threats. As it took another step closer, Taren shot another arrow. It flew, straight and true, striking the beast in the chest. It shrieked in agony.

Taren already had another arrow aimed and before the beast could react to the last blow, he shot again. This time, it struck the neck. Sam sat still as stone as he watched his friends in mortal danger below him. As Taren drew his bow back again, the creature ducked and lunged forward. This time his aim had failed.

Keesa sprung with stealthy precision. She darted around the creature and attacked it from behind. As fast as lightning, she was on its back, teeth sinking into the matted hair. The creature stopped in its tracks and roared in pain, shaking Keesa off its back. She was already backing into position with Yetews and Taren. Yetews refused to move further away than an arm's reach to Sam. The beast had stopped now, as if considering its next move. Taren shot three arrows, each hitting another part of the target.

The beast threw its head back and howled into the forest. It bared its fangs once more, before retreating back into the trees. No one moved from their positions. They could hear the creature's faint howling as it got further and further away. Taren was still aiming an arrow into the dark, as the last howl was nothing but a whisper of an echo.

"Well, *that's* a new one. Never seen one of those before." Taren broke the silence, making everyone jump in alarm.

Sam sat in the trees and gulped loudly as he looked at his protectors below. He knew now that what he was feeling was sheer fear for the events he had witnessed. This new feeling was going to take some getting used to. In a barely audible voice, he said, "I have. That was the thing from my nightmare."

The three looked up to him from below. "What did you say?" asked Taren.

Yetews reached up to retrieve Sam and placed him gently on the ground. Taren looked at Sam as though he was looking into the face of another one of those creatures.

Sam swallowed again and explained what he said. "That thing…it was the same creature I was telling you about right before it attacked us. It's the same from my nightmare."

Taren looked back into the forest for a long moment and then back to Sam. With what could only be described as fear, he looked into Sam's eyes and said, "You mean, you were picturing it in your head right before it attacked?"

"Yeah."

"Would you say you were imagining it?"

Sam thought. "Yeah. I guess so."

Taren shook his head, confused. "How did you do that?"

"Do what?" Sam was getting confused again.

Taren continued to stare at him nervously. "Sam," he said, "don't you know what you did? You just made that creature appear out of nothing...from your imagination."

Jessica Williams

Chapter Seven: The Guardian

Since Sam's arrival into this strange new world, he had heard and seen some fairly strange and outrageous things. Regardless of any of the happenings he had experienced thus far, the idea that he could actually bring to life something he had imagined would have normally been the least likely of things to shock him. Up until this very moment, he had been mostly convinced of the idea that the world he was so largely engrossed in, was in fact, entirely of his own making. It was simply his birthday wish coming to pass. Despite the fact that Sam had seen things that he never dreamt of in all his wild dreams, he had been convinced that nothing here existed before the fateful wish was made.

Now, with one sentence, Sam's perfect picture of this world was shattered. Taren's accusation of Sam's ability to create something so foul and dangerous shocked the very core of what he had come to believe. His claim was not what bothered Sam, but rather the fact that someone here was capable of connecting his imagination to this world. This meant that there was more to this strange place than Sam's mind could understand. For in Sam's world, no one knew of his imagination. Things were not as they seemed. Taren seemed as shocked by the creature's sudden appearance as the rest of them were but he was the only one that had drawn the sudden conclusion.

Sam had pictured the creature so vividly in his mind mere moments before its attack. The idea that he had imagined to life something that could hurt any one of his friends sickened him and the fact that Taren connected these dots was confusing. As these thoughts raced haphazardly through his brain, Sam wondered just where he was if it wasn't *his* world.

Everyone was still staring bewildered at Sam. Though only a

minute had passed since Taren's revelation, time felt as though it had stopped. Sam looked around at everyone. Keesa merely sat with her tail twitching patiently while Yetews simply watched him eagerly for his response. Taren, on the other hand, was still watching him as if waiting for a confession.

Sam had no way of knowing what he was to confess to. He knew that of all the creatures he would choose to bring to life, this dangerous one was not even an option. He'd never imagined something so frightening or menacing as the one that had just attacked them.

But there was no mistaking the coincidence of the situation. He had seen the beast so clearly and within seconds, the same image had appeared, real and monstrous, right in front of his eyes. If he truly was responsible for its creation, then it wasn't intentional, because the creature was spawned from a nightmare and not of his own creation. Sam was confused and the puzzle wasn't getting any closer to being solved with the silence.

In an attempt to start putting the puzzle together, he started with the first mildly coherent thought that crossed his mind. He looked at Taren and said, "Let me get this straight. You think that I brought that thing to life with my imagination?"

"Yes, I do."

"Why would you even think that?" Sam asked.

Taren was still absentmindedly shaking his head slowly. "I saw you when you were trying to explain what you dreamt. I saw the focus in your eyes as you tried to picture it. You tried to tell us what was in your nightmare and then that thing attacked us from out of nowhere." He stepped closer to Sam. "At first I couldn't understand how it was even possible that *you* brought that thing here, but then you said it was what you *imagined* right before the attack. That sort of sealed my suspicion. You imagined it and then it appeared."

Stunned, Sam asked, "You think that I *wanted* that thing to pop out of the forest and eat us all? Why would I want that?"

"No. It was more than likely unintentional. But one second it wasn't there, then the next second it was. How else can you explain it?"

"I have no idea, but I didn't bring it here. It's just impossible!" Sam was getting frustrated. The conversation was getting them nowhere.

"Do you have any other ideas then? Because I'd be glad to hear them." Taren folded his arms in patience.

Sam didn't know how he could possibly explain anything right now. It was only a moment before when this world made some sense. Taren may have wanted an explanation but Sam hadn't even yet explained how he'd gotten here. And now that it was obvious to him that this wasn't truly his world, he wasn't exactly sure if he even knew the answer to that anymore. The time had approached to come clean and Sam didn't quite know how to put his explanation into perspective. He looked guiltily at Yetews before turning to face Taren again. The idea that he would have to tell his best friend that he was merely a figment of an over-active imagination didn't settle well, but there was no getting around it now.

He mentally ran through his story, but in the end it sounded ridiculous and childish to take credit for the creation of an entire world. When he tried to start explaining things, the words failed him. "I don't know how any of this happened." Sam tried to go on, but the thoughts were all jumbled up.

He was becoming entirely too frustrated with everything now. Combined with the lack of sleep, Sam's mood was starting to waver severely. "Ugh! None of this is making any sense!" He stomped over to the fire and sat down with his back turned to everyone. He sat for a moment in silence and then mumbled to himself, "This is stupid. Why would I need to use my imagination if I'm already…" He cut off his thought, not knowing quite how to finish it. He must have spoken louder than he thought, because to his surprise, Taren finished his thought perfectly.

"You mean, why use imagination if you are already in an imaginary world?"

Sam's skin prickled with goose bumps. He sat there staring at the flames wondering how Taren knew?

Taren had already seemed so keen to this mysterious world. At first, Sam thought it to be mere coincidence. In his world, if he had imagined a person like Taren, he would probably be the know-it-all-rogue-warrior type. But it wasn't his world and Taren was not part of his vivid imagination. It solidified one fact. There was more to this place than Sam knew and this man he had befriended could help piece together the mystery.

The fire burned brightly, warming the clearing with its protective glow. He was still unsure what to say. He wanted to turn around to look back at the others but sat unmoving. He mindlessly played with a blade of grass and stared at the flames as they licked the night air. Taren knew more than Sam gave him credit for.

His perception of this world was changing by the second and he wasn't sure what would happen next. If he was really capable of unleashing a monster from his mind, then where did that leave his new friends? How could he jeopardize their safety? Especially Yetews. Now that he was no longer blind to what he was feeling, he didn't want to show anyone how scared he was at this moment. It was hard for him to admit this new sensation of fear in the first place.

As Sam sat and pondered what to say, Taren came to sit down next to him. They both stared into the fire. He sighed and looked over at Sam. When Sam refused to return the look, Taren placed a hand softly on his shoulder and said, "I know that you're confused and that this is hard to believe, but this world that you have entered is not yours. I know where you come from, Sam. I understand what you're thinking. I even know how you got here."

Sam finally looked over at him.

"And believe it or not," Taren assured him, "I even know why you came."

Those words sent Sam's goose bumps into high gear. His head was swirling now. As much as he felt the need to explain everything, he could tell by the tone of Taren's voice and the knowledge of his words that, somehow, no explanation was needed. "But, *how* do you know?" he whispered.

"I know more than you could possibly imagine."

* * * * * * * * *

Things weren't going at all how Sam had planned. From the very beginning of this adventure, he had been blind to many things. His lack of knowledge of what he had gotten himself into was right on the top of the list.

The mask of night was complete now, bringing with it a slight chill to the air. As a result, the four travelers were now huddled close to the warmth of the fire.

Sam was leaning up against Yetews. He had finally come to join Sam by the fireside after his initial hesitation. When he noticed how upset Sam was, he had an overwhelming feeling of helplessness for his friend and wasn't sure how to approach him. After Taren had talked to him, Sam had managed to regain his composure and asked Yetews to come over and join them.

Keesa also settled gratefully next to the fire. She seemed more eager than the rest for the unraveling of the evening's mysteries. She calmly, with front paws crossed gracefully in front of her, listened to every word spoken.

Not much had been said so far. Sam had been pushing Taren for a more thorough explanation of his most recent comment regarding his knowledge of things, but Taren was stubbornly avoiding the details.

Sam decided to push again. "Oh, come on! Why can't you just tell me more about this world? If you know so much, then it can't be that hard to just give me a few little details."

Taren rolled his eyes for the ninth time since this started. "It's not my place to explain, kid."

"Why not?" Sam whined.

"Well for one, I don't think your brain is going to take much more if you don't at least attempt to get some more sleep."

Sam threw his arms up suddenly, startling Yetews. He growled his annoyance. Sam ignored him and said, "Oh yeah! Sleep. Now *that's* a great idea!" His sudden rant was lined with sarcasm. "Uh…remember what happened the last two times I slept?"

Yetews grumbled a question to Taren.

Taren looked from Yetews to Sam. "Seeing as how you have an exceedingly vast knowledge of his undecipherable language, would you mind translating…again?" Then under his breath he added, "Which, by the way, is getting incredibly annoying."

Sam heard the snide remark and snapped back, "Don't get mad at him just because you can't understand what he says! And he asked you if you thought I might have another nightmare if I sleep. I wanna know what you think about that too."

"Well, first up, grunting and growling isn't exactly a language."

Yetews frowned and Sam patted him on the shoulder. "You are avoiding the question again. Am I going to have a nightmare every

The Gateway to Imagia: The Tale of Sam Little

time I close my eyes?"

Taren heaved a defeated sigh. "I can honestly say that I don't know. I'd venture to say the chances are pretty good, but everyone is different."

Keesa finally decided to speak at this, "You know, you really are quite cryptic. Or perhaps that is your objective. Do you, or don't you have any plans on explaining anything? I'd be more than amused to hear your take on this turn of events."

"Frankly," he answered, "I don't think I am the right one to explain anything to you." The feeling of annoyance flooded the atmosphere around him as he spoke. "Trust me. In the morning, you will get all the answers you want. We aren't that far away now. We'll be there shortly after the sun rises if we leave before dawn."

Sam was convinced that sleeping could only end with more screaming. The thought of waking up to hear his own blood-curdling cries again sent a chill up his spine. He shook off the sensation. "Can't we just leave now? I don't really feel like sleeping," he admitted.

"I told you already that we can't go gallivanting around the forest in the pitch black of night. Well, unless you have aspirations to become something's meal tonight. And in that case, you can go alone. I'm perfectly happy in my living form."

Sam swallowed hard. He could hear Yetews doing the same. Keesa was probably higher up on the food chain, so didn't seem phased by the idea of night travel. She had quite a few more advantages than the rest of them.

Sam gave in. "Fine. But I'm not sleeping so you might as well tell me something to pass the time." He took a page from Taren and tried to threaten with fear and added, "Unless you want me to accidentally imagine up another monster from my next nightmare."

Yetews snorted a laugh as Sam smiled a mischievous grin.

They both expected that they had Taren backed into a corner because it would be ludicrous to want to fight another creature if it was like the last one.

"Eh," Taren shrugged, "I've got plenty of arrows and I could use the target practice anyhow." He was smirking.

Both their jaws dropped slightly at the finality of Taren's retort.

No one spoke much after this. Yetews yawned loudly and laid his heavy head down on the ground. Sam teased him a little to keep him awake, but Yetews' exhaustion from the trek won out.

Keesa curled up into a ball, reminding Sam of Cooper again. Despite the fact that she was so intelligent, she looked more like a cat now than ever. Yetews was snoring softly as he slept on his stomach. Taren was standing with his back to them as a sentinel watching the darkness.

Sam fought the heaviness of his eyes for as long as he could, but succumbed, regardless. He slept again, this time more restlessly. When his mind would start to fade into dreams, the images would frighten him and he would wake up suddenly, nearly jumping off the ground each time.

When the early morning sun started to melt the black of night away, Sam found himself waking to his own screams again. The screams were nothing like the ones of the previous day, but they were enough to rattle his nerves.

Taren was first to speak as the three roused from their sleep. "Let's get going. If you carry Sam," he said to Yetews, "then we will probably make it there in two hours."

Yetews nodded and placed a yawning Sam onto his shoulders.

At first, Sam tried to argue the point so he could walk, but as he sunk down into his familiar perch, he realized how comfortable he really was and decided to go with it. There'd be plenty of walking to do later.

Keesa had already been up and hunted. The only sign of her doomed prey was the blue feather that now lingered on the tuft of hair by her mouth. She had been calmly licking herself clean when they departed the clearing.

The thought of her eating a raw bird wasn't exactly a pleasant thought, but Sam's stomach growled anyways. He hadn't eaten anything since his birthday cake. And by now there was no longer any way of knowing just how long ago that was.

Taren had doused what was left of the fire and started to lead them through the trees ahead. Sam looked behind them for a moment and thought about what his mom might be making for breakfast. His stomach growled again as he thought of her special chocolate-chip pancakes. But the thought left sooner than it came, and they all began trudging through the forest.

The Gateway to Imagia: The Tale of Sam Little

As Sam sat there, he absorbed every aspect of the morning gray forest in hopes of distracting his mind from the want to eat. Even louder than before, his stomach growled again. This time, Yetews cocked his head to look up at Sam. He grumbled a question.

"I know. But I can't help it. My stomach won't stop growling. I've never been this hungry before." His voice was longing as he thought again of food. "I hope there's food where we're going."

Taren overheard Sam. "Hungry, huh? There'll be food where we're going. I'm sure of it. But until then..." he stopped in mid sentence and then starting looking around the ground for something Sam couldn't see. He found a baseball sized rock and took aim somewhere into the tree above them. It was a direct hit to his target. The air was suddenly filled with small seeds that twirled down like miniature helicopters.

Sam watched them fall, amused at the scene. He reached his hand up and caught three in his open palm. He looked down at Taren from his perch and said, "Hey! We have a tree like this in our backyard at home. My mom calls it a whirly bird tree. Only our whirly birds are brown instead of purple."

Taren nodded. "And I bet you can't eat the ones from your tree either." He grabbed at a single seed and caught it effortlessly, amazing Sam at his natural stealth. He then put the bulbous end in his mouth and bit down. He dropped the feathery stem and, through his chewing, said, "They're pretty good for a snack if you can get to them before the wildlife does." He smiled. Then he added, "Eat up."

Taren threw another rock and released another round of the peculiar fruit. Yetews was already gathering them up with his hands while Sam reached in the air to catch them as they fell.

For a moment, Sam was hesitant. It was the first time he'd eaten since his dinner the night before and as strange as it felt to eat something new and unusual, his stomach growled again in protest. He placed the first one in his mouth and bit down.

The taste was sweeter than any fruit he'd ever eaten. They had enough for the journey and started walking again. Once Sam started eating them, he couldn't stop and by the time they ran out of seeds, he was temporarily satisfied.

Just as Taren had expected, it didn't take very long to reach their destination. Ahead of them, was another clearing in the trees, only this time the clearing was significantly larger. In the middle, there was what appeared to be a large grassy roof simply lying on the ground.

The closer they got, it was more obvious that the roof was actually a covering to a large hole that slanted downward. At the bottom of the slope, there was a rough, wooden door with no handle and one very dingy, circular window.

Next to the hole by the roof was a good-sized lump of rock that was covered in a mossy green growth. Taren held up a hand to stop them from going further. "Hold on," he ordered.

"Why? Isn't this where you wanted us to go?" asked Sam.

Taren just smiled crookedly. He seemed to be waiting for something.

While they stood there, Sam started to focus more on the strange place. His eyes wandered slowly over the picture and came to rest on the mossy lump that sat at the hole's entrance. It wasn't very big, but there was something oddly suspicious about it.

Sam saw that Taren was watching the rock intently. He wasn't sure what could be so interesting about it so he tried to look closer as well. The longer he stared, the more he couldn't deny that the mossy lump was actually moving. It was methodically rising up and down. The strange mound of earth was *breathing*.

It started to stir.

Sam gasped slightly as Yetews retreated a few steps. He'd noticed the breathing stone too.

Sam shot a look towards Taren, expecting to see his bow armed and aimed. It wasn't. Taren merely continued to smile and stare.

The earthy lump opened an eye. There would have been no knowing where to expect an eye and a chilling thought of the deceptor crossed his thoughts. The eye blinked. Four scaled legs suddenly emerged at its sides and the mossy lump was unexpectedly barreling for them.

Keesa hissed and Taren held up a hand for her to ease back. He reached into a pouch he carried on his belt and threw something onto the ground that looked like moldy mushrooms.

The creature skidded to a halt and gobbled them up. Taren bent down on one knee and started to talk to the weird creature, "Always hungry, aren't you? Doesn't he ever feed you?" He grinned back at Sam as he patted the creature's scaly head. If it weren't for the stubby snout and oversized eyes, it would have easily passed for a pint-sized alligator.

Sam slid down from Yetews. He slowly approached the strange creature, and asked Taren, "What the heck is that thing? Is it dangerous?"

"This harmless lump of a creature?" He scratched behind a hole in its head that served as its ear. "Nah. This is Warg."

Sam looked questioningly down at the creature. "Is this who you wanted to bring me to see?" It didn't even seem possible that something so unspectacular could be able to answer his many questions. But he knew better than to judge something for its size.

Taren laughed at Sam's speculation. "No. This is just his…well…for lack of a better word, his guard dog." He stood up and Warg rubbed up affectionately against Taren's legs. He was panting with his tongue lolling lopsided out of his mouth. It made him look almost cute. Almost.

As he watched the funny creature, he thought of what it would be like to have Titus here with him. He'd probably be enjoying himself. Though he felt greedy to think it, he wanted to have his faithful dog here with him too. It wasn't that he was unthankful for his granted wish and having Yetews by his side. It was simply that he truly missed his four-legged friend.

"A dog? Wow, my dog doesn't look anything like him. He doesn't even have hair. Cool!" Sam reached down to let him sniff his hand. He figured if it was like a dog, best be safe and let him get a good whiff before actually petting him.

Warg sniffed Sam's hand and then transferred from Taren's legs to his legs and started to settle by his feet for another round of attention.

Sam smiled at the funny little creature. Behind him, Yetews lumbered closer to him with a twinge of jealousy.

Yetews bent down to sniff Warg and received an unexpected lick on the nose. Yetews snorted and wiped off the slobber as he grumbled something low.

Sam laughed and said, "Actually, I think that means he likes you, Yetews!"

Yetews rolled his eyes and shook his head with a bit of disgust still lingering on his face from Warg's attempted affection.

"So if this is just the guard dog," asked Sam, "then who is his owner?"

There was a soft click of an opening door followed by an aged creaking of un-oiled hinges. Everyone looked down towards the hidden abode.

"Well, that would be him now," he answered while gesturing towards the hole.

Out of the morning shadows, stepped a large being. He was far from human and stood at least a foot taller than Taren. His head was a tad oversized for his body with a large jowl that jiggled as he made his way up the slope. His skin was smooth and mottled brown, resembling an overgrown salamander that walked upright. He had a large belly and long, thick tail that dragged behind him as he ambled his way closer. Two very beady, yet kind, eyes were sunken deep into his smooth, glossy skin. His clothes were simple and tattered from extended wear. A simple vest and short, roughly hewn pants were all he wore. His legs were bulky and he walked with a bit of a limp. As he approached, Sam was in awe at the aura of aged wisdom around him.

He reached one bony arm out and shook Taren's hand. Whoever he was, it was obvious that they knew each other. They exchanged pleasantries.

Taren looked over to Sam, who had stopped petting the still eager Warg. Sam was staring, bewildered, at them both. "Sam?"

Sam focused on Taren, but said nothing.

"Sam, this is Orga. The first Guardian of Imagia."

Chapter Eight: History Lesson

The morning was passing rather quickly. Sam felt that whatever world he may be in now, time didn't seem to move the same. Yesterday felt as though two days had been combined into one. Regardless that he hadn't been able to figure out what time it was, his stomach knew that it was well past time for a good meal.

So when the creature, Orga, invited them into his underground home for food, Sam could not have been more grateful. Truth be told, he was considerably nervous about what he might be eating. It was yet another surprise when the plate of food in front of him smelled so appetizing. He didn't have a name for any of the food, but he knew that it looked and smelled good enough to eat.

Orga had filled three plates of food and placed one down in front of Sam on the oblong, weathered table. Taren took his plate and sat it next to Sam. He even placed a plate of large purple fruit in front of Yetews.

On any other given day, he'd be a bit more hesitant on eating food he'd never tried before. But his stomach disagreed with this approach. He picked up something that resembled a lopsided muffin and closed his eyes. He bit into it with low expectations. As soon as it hit his tongue, he was ready for another bite. After he finished that morsel, he ate some berries and then moved on to a blue cooked egg and then something that looked like meat and tasted like chicken. He was thankful that he didn't know what it was. He settled for the fact that it was good and his stomach no longer grumbled.

Sam, much more content with a full belly, leaned forward and crossed his arms on the table. He listened while Taren explained the events of the past day to Orga. When he got to the part about Sam's imagining of the beast that had attacked them, Orga turned his focus to Sam.

He cocked his head in interest at him, as though he were an odd exhibit at a zoo and murmured, "Fascinating." Orga hadn't spoken much since their arrival. He had inserted the appropriate 'hmm's' and 'ah's' as Taren recounted their story. But the mentioning of Sam's imagination sparked his conversation skills.

Taren, too, was now watching Sam. "Yes. Fascinating indeed. I found it hard to believe that he is capable of imagining something into existence, but I thought it best to bring him back here to test the theory safely."

Both of them turned away from Sam to continue their conversation.

"Was he aware of his ability to imagine?" asked Orga.

Taren shook his head. "No. I don't think so. He's pretty confused, but that's to be expected I think."

"Yes. It's hard enough to understand this world for the best of us, let alone a small boy."

"I know." Taren turned suddenly solemn. "Should we be concerned?"

Orga shrugged. "It's hard to know for sure. It's good that you brought him here. We need to put his imagination to the test if it truly is how you explained."

Taren got wide-eyed. "But is that really safe? I mean, I didn't think it was possible that someone else could have the same abilities as..."

Suddenly, Sam cleared his throat a little louder than he meant to. He didn't like being talked about as though he wasn't in the room. Nothing they were saying made any sense and the questions were starting to form a line in his mind.

Everyone in the room changed their focus directly to him.

Now that he'd drawn their attention, he wasn't entirely sure what he should say. He cleared his throat once more and he said the first thing that came to mind. "I'm sorry, but what's wrong with my imagination?"

Orga smiled at him. "Nothing is *wrong* with your imagination Sam. It's just all very enlightening."

Confusion muddled Sam's thoughts now and it must have showed on his face, because Yetews had stopped gorging himself on the fruit and was patting Sam on the shoulder in reassurance. He was just as baffled, but was letting Sam know that he was there by his side to share the moment.

Orga, too, must have sensed Sam's puzzlement because he decided to continue without another question to go from. "The best place to start answering your questions is going to be with you, Sam."

"What do you mean?" he asked.

Orga made his way to the table and settled across from Sam. "For starters, where exactly do you believe you are at this moment? I would wager to guess that you don't believe you are at home, snug in your bed." He smiled slyly.

Sam assumed Orga was testing him and wondering if he believed he was dreaming. Sam knew better than to think something this real could be a dream. "Well, I think it's the world from my imagination. It doesn't have a name though. It's...my world...but different somehow." He wasn't sure how exactly to describe it.

Orga was nodding. "Yes. And no. That is what you are meant to think. Everyone who comes into this world is brought here by an important figment of his or her imagination. It's what leads you to believe that this world is solely yours. But I'm sure that you have noticed that many things here are not of your creating."

Sam nodded.

"Take me, for example. I am quite certain that you don't remember me from your made up world."

Sam thought for a moment and began to realize what Orga was trying to tell him. He was at a loss for words and merely stared back intently.

Something about Sam's response, or lack of, amused Taren and Orga, because they were both exchanging smirks. "Well, let me clear up the main source of your confusion right away. This world is not what you think it is. It is a place where the imagined things of your home world come into existence. Though it may have some familiarities, it is not *your* world. And it does have a name. It is called Imagia."

"Imagia," Sam echoed. This was already more information than Sam expected to get. He didn't know what exactly he was involved in, but it was nowhere near what he had expected when he entered the forest such a short time ago. It was so much more. He was eager, but at the same time worried, to hear everything that Orga had to say.

Orga wrapped his long fingers over Sam's shoulder. He looked into the kid's eyes and asked him, "You are about to embark on an incredibly detailed history lesson of this world. Are you sure you are ready to hear it?"

Sam thought for a moment. He looked to Keesa first who nodded her approval and sat patiently in the corner. Then he looked around to Yetews who was shrugging his shoulders and mumbled something while pointing to Orga. Sam nodded in agreement. "I guess we *all* want to hear what you have to say."

He removed his hand from Sam and took a cleansing breath through flared nostrils. "Very well then. Let's start at the beginning. Or I should say, we will start at *my* beginning. It is the only beginning I know."

Sam leaned back onto Yetews. He wasn't certain how long this would take, but he had an inkling that he should make himself comfortable.

Taren sat down next to Orga and started to pat Warg, who had come to join them after eating a large breakfast of moldy mushrooms.

Orga directed his focus to Sam as he began the story of his world. "I, as Taren already mentioned, am the first Guardian of Imagia. An extremely long time ago, I remember opening my eyes for the first time to this very world you have entered. I did not know how I came to be, but when I awoke, I knew that I had a purpose. Something called to me and I went to the source. I could feel the source of this calling connecting to my very soul. It was a powerful feeling that consumed my thoughts and I was curious what it was. When I reached the source, I was surprised to see that it was merely a small boy and that he was speaking my name.

"Before this, I didn't even know I had a name. But when I heard him call out, I knew that I was the one he was calling for. He saw me coming to him and he knew me at first glance. I, too, immediately knew him. His name was Cody. Somehow, I understood that my purpose was to bring Cody into this world for a time, protect him, and then safely return him to his home. I was his Guardian. I was the first of my kind and have existed in Imagia since."

Sam interrupted, "Who named it Imagia?"

Orga grinned. "No one really knows. It is simply what we called it when we came to exist. We are part of this world and, as far as I can guess, are born with the knowledge we need to carry out our duty. The things you see around you are from the minds of children all over your world. The more powerful the image is in a child's mind, the longer it exists in Imagia. Fleeting images are seen like an echo is heard. It will fade from Imagia nearly as quickly as it is born. Guardians are the products of very powerful imagination. That is why we continue to exist for so long. Do you understand?"

"I think so. So you're immortal, right?" Sam answered.

"Not always. Some Guardians will fade as the mind that imagined it dies in the outside world. Others, like myself, continue to be. As I said, the more powerful the image, the longer we exist. But then again, it's difficult to call us immortal. Even I could fade from existence at any given moment. There is no way to know for sure. I imagine that Cody's image of me was quite impressive."

"Where is Cody now?" Sam asked.

"I took him back home. When a child comes into this world, they only have a limited time here. The purpose of Imagia is to let a child live and experience the deepest desires of their imagination before they become too old to truly appreciate the power of their mind's eye.

"You see, I was the most important figment of Cody's imagination. That is why I was created in this specific image. No one knows why or how it happens. But as time went on, I witnessed the birthing of more Guardians. With the birth of each Guardian, a gateway would open to allow a child to enter this world. We all knew our purpose and as time passed, there became order. The laws were simple and each Guardian was created to uphold the structure of Imagia.

"It exists because of children. There is a period in a child's life that their imagination is strongest. When they reach their eleventh year, something in a child's mind begins to change and their imagination begins to weaken. Eventually they lose the ability completely."

Orga paused when Sam suddenly gasped. The idea of losing his imagination was a devastating thought and it shook his very core. "Lose imagination? But...but...how can that even be possible?" he stuttered.

Orga continued. "It is the way your mind was meant to work, Sam. But take comfort in knowing that you are one of a dwindling number of children who get to experience Imagia. Not every child will see the splendors of this world. There are a limited number of ways to open a gateway. The most common way is by wishing that your imagination were real. The second and most difficult way is to, beyond a shadow of a doubt, believe that your imagination is fact and not fictitious. It is a rare thing to enter that way. I've only seen it happen twice in my time and those children were...well...unique. The last way is to experience a tragedy that sparks your mind to retreat to its deepest imagination. This is the most dangerous way to enter. Those children have the hardest time leaving their Guardians behind."

Sam's mind began to piece the puzzle together. He realized that he must have opened a gateway into Imagia with his wish. His eyes brightened and he sat up straight. "I made a wish like that yesterday! That's how I got here then! Isn't it?"

Orga smiled and nodded.

"But then," Sam looked over to Taren who had saved him twice since entering Imagia, "that means that I have a Guardian too."

The room was quiet with silent anticipation as the thoughts caught up to him. Sam gasped again as he whipped around to Yetews who was looking guilty of an unspoken accusation. Then he turned quickly back to Orga and waited for the inevitable response.

He smiled warmly then said, "Yes Sam. Yetews is your Guardian."

Sam turned back to face Yetews. He looked up into his friend's familiar gentle eyes. He saw him in a new light now. Before, Yetews was simply his goofy sidekick with a tendency to shy away from the dangerous situations. Now, as he stared in awe at his best friend, he saw something new and majestic.

Yetews' smile changed as Sam looked up at him. He bent his head down to Sam's level and placed one massive hand upon his tiny shoulder. The goofy grin was gone and replaced with a look that comforted and reassured him. He nodded his shaggy head to affirm Sam's thoughts. He grumbled something to Sam and ruffled his hair adoringly.

Orga offered more information as Sam gazed at his Guardian. "It is a rare occurrence that a child seeks answers about Imagia. When they finally grow suspicious of this world, it is too late for them to get the answers they want. I understand that you sought answers very quickly from the time you have entered." He looked suspiciously at Sam. "Most children never discover the true purpose of their Guardian. They get no more than ten days in this world. That is the limit of their time. The Gateway will not stay open any longer and once it closes, it cannot be reopened again. Like the Guardians before him, Yetews brought you here."

Sam thought back to the night of his arrival. The rustling of the bush out his window, the animal he saw jumping into the forest. It wasn't a cat, or a dog, or a deer. "It was you outside my window that night...and your tail I saw jumping into the trees," he said to Yetews. "You were leading me to the gateway."

Yetews nodded and grunted his affirmation.

Orga continued. "Yetews' job as your Guardian is to watch over you and protect you at all costs while you are here. By the end of the tenth day, or earlier if you want, he is to do everything in his power to return you safely to your gateway. To return you home."

A sinking feeling began to form in the pit of Sam's stomach. Realization hit him as Orga explained the workings of Imagia. He was going to have to say goodbye to Yetews in nine days. He could feel embarrassing moisture forming in the corner of his eyes as he continued to look at Yetews. A single tear escaped but he caught it before anyone noticed.

Yetews leaned in closer to his precious boy and purred something softly to him with his goofy grin.

"But, I don't want to say goodbye to you. You're my best friend," whispered Sam. "You're my *only* friend," he added solemnly.

Yetews tenderly purred an apology to him and pointed to Sam's heart.

Sam jumped forward and threw his small arms around Yetews' neck and hugged him with all the might he could muster. Yetews wrapped his massive arms around the small boy and hugged him back, completely lifting him off of the ground. "I'll always be in your heart too," he whispered back as he muffled a sniff in Yetews' fur.

Though he never wanted to let go of this moment, he loosened his hold when Orga softly interrupted. "Sam, there is more to this history lesson that you must hear."

Yetews gently pried Sam's arms away and placed him back on the chair. Sam's feeling of joy for his granted wish had changed to one of sadness. He looked around the room through his glistening eyes and could see his sorrow mirrored in everyone's faces. Taren looked sullen and full of pity for him. Keesa's perfect blue eyes were shimmering with unshed tears. "What else could there be?" asked Sam.

"I've told you the purpose of Imagia and the Guardians. Now you need to know what went wrong." Orga's expression became grave.

"Wrong? What do you mean?" Sam placed this moment in the back of his mind for the time and listened intently.

"For ages, the order of Imagia was flawless. Not a single child ever missed the gateway home. You must understand that this world existed in perfect harmony with your world. When a child disappeared to come here, the gateway would hold that moment in time open so that the child could return to their home and their family would be none the wiser of their journey. Once the gateway closes, time resumes. They return and their adventure here eventually, as they grow, becomes nothing but a dim memory. If the child misses the gateway then they are lost here forever.

"It worked perfectly. Until..." he took a deep breath, "...until a single event changed the course of everything we knew and understood. It happened nearly three hundred years ago. I was there in the shadows on that fateful day – watching. If I'd known about the course of the events, I could have stopped it. But I was too late to react."

Taren finally spoke up at Orga's self blame. "You couldn't have known. It was impossible to predict." Orga turned to look at him. "If you'd have tried to intervene, you know the fate you would have suffered. You can't blame yourself forever, old friend."

Orga only sighed and bowed his head.

He turned back to Sam and explained. "Ten days before that fateful day, a young boy arrived in Imagia. He was, like you, in his tenth year and just as curious about the way this world worked. Two days into his arrival, his Guardian brought him to me. As you now understand, the love a child feels for their Guardian is real and can cause an immensely powerful connection. A Guardian shares that love for their child as well. But I don't believe I have ever seen a child so dependent upon their Guardian as this boy was.

"His Guardian had discovered that his boy could do something quite exceptional. He was capable of bringing small things into existence in this world using his imagination. The first time it happened, his Guardian believed it to be a fluke. But after repeated events, he was brought to me. It was spectacular to witness. It reshaped everything I knew about this world. It fascinated me." Orga bowed his head in shame.

"I chose to explain to him the workings of this world in hopes that I might also unravel some of his hidden mysteries. He did not want to accept the rules of this world. He broke down and begged his Guardian to let him stay in Imagia forever. He told his story to us. He explained that his parents had died and he had no one to return home to. Though, try as he might, he could not convince his Guardian to let the gateway close. After all his avenues were nothing more than lost causes, he accepted his fate and enjoyed the boundaries of Imagia for his remaining eight days. Never once again, did he murmur his desires to remain here.

"But regardless of this, I remained in the shadows of his journeys. I observed from a distance. I watched him create many things. As amazing as it seemed, there was never any sign of impending danger from his ability.

"On his final day here, I watched in the shadows as his Guardian led him back to his gateway. He was peaceful the entire time. As they approached the gateway, he turned to his Guardian and whispered one word. 'Please.' The Guardian embraced the boy for a last moment and explained that the law must be upheld and that he would never forget him. The boy said nothing in return and began to back away.

"Many things happened very quickly from that moment. I saw the boy smile and close his eyes. I knew he was trying to imagine something but I could never have guessed it would be something bad.

"A terrifying creature went barreling towards them. Of course, I can only speculate from here what I believe he meant to happen. But I am quite certain I am right. I believe he wanted to chase away his Guardian so that the gateway would close and he could remain here forever. The boy watched and waited for it to frighten away his Guardian. That's when things went horribly wrong. He had no control of the beast he imagined and it turned course, heading directly towards him. I saw the fear in his eyes as the beast made to destroy the very thing that created it. The Guardian jumped in front of his boy to protect him and was brutally killed."

Sam could feel Yetews' hands gripping his shoulders. He was silently assuring him that he would gladly do the same for Sam.

Sam could only sit and listen in shock.

"I was so stunned by the events that I couldn't find the ability to react," Orga said. "The events of that day are permanently engraved in my mind. I cannot describe the horror that this boy witnessed or the loss he experienced. It was devastating. The creature dragged the body of his Guardian into the forest and was not seen again. The boy was in agony. His own imagination had betrayed him and it, in turn, is what ultimately destroyed him. With his Guardian gone, he no longer wanted to stay. He frantically searched for his gateway but without his Guardian to guide him through, it was in vain. I think that the loss still drives him mad. He was forever doomed to roam Imagia's ever changing depths without the companionship of his Guardian."

Sam could almost feel the pain that the boy experienced. The sheer idea of losing Yetews, in any way, was nearly unbearable. But to watch him be dragged away from him in such a horrible ending was more than he could take. He felt his hands start to shake. He asked the only question he could. "What happened to him?"

"He is still here. Do you remember what I told you about the three ways to open a gateway?

Sam nodded silently.

"When a child experiences a tragedy, the place they seek refuge is in their imaginary world. He was already in that imaginary world when tragedy happened. His mind had nowhere to go. His reason for imagination had been killed so he slipped into a depth of imagination that no one had ever thought possible. He wandered the forests as his grief completely consumed his entire being. There was a time he completely disappeared. During that time, I believe he was honing his abilities.

The Gateway to Imagia: The Tale of Sam Little

"The more time he spent here alone, the more he grew to resent the Guardians. He blames them for trapping him here. It's obvious now that he believes if he cannot have his Gaurdian, then no one should. He is imprisoned here and wants every child doomed to share his same terrible fate. He brings horrifying creatures and beasts into existence using the power of his imagination. The control he has gained over these monsters in the last three hundred years is impressive. He unleashes them into Imagia with a purpose – to spread fear and to destroy Guardians."

Sam suddenly jumped up and yelled, "No!"

"Yes. I'm afraid that to be a Guardian is a very dangerous thing these days. Most of them, if they are lucky enough to succeed, vanish into hiding after returning their child to their gateway."

"No! If that's true then Yetews could be killed if I leave. I won't leave him to die here!" Sam was on his feet now and shouting.

Taren said, "Calm down, Sam. He will be hunted, regardless if you stay or go."

This didn't reassure him and he looked to Orga for some sign of hope.

"I'm afraid Taren is right. He was being hunted from the moment he was born. Not all Guardians are destroyed though. Look at me. I am still here after such a long time. That should give you some hope."

Sam took a cleansing breath and sat back down. "So, what now? I just leave and pretend that I don't care what happens?" he asked.

Yetews squeezed Sam's shoulders again. Sam turned to look at him, hoping for a better option. Yetews tried to explain something to him to ease his mind.

"No. I don't care how prepared you are to deal when I'm gone. It's not fair! There's gotta be something I can do to help." He faced Taren in desperation. No one reassured him and he stubbornly crossed his arms and said, "I'm not leaving."

Taren tried to convince him of the danger that he was in by staying here. "You have a family to return home to and this world is no longer safe for a ten year old boy."

Sam wasn't convinced. "No. You said that I imagined that monster to life last night. Right?"

"Yes. I believe so."

"And no one else can do that but me and this other guy?"

"So it seems."

Sam was nearly shouting as he tried to get them to understand his desperation for the situation. "If I can do that, then there has to be some way that I can help. If I can really do what you say I can do, then maybe I can fix things. You know…make it right somehow. There's just gotta be a way!" He dropped back into his chair and slumped forward onto the table, his head buried in his arms. He wasn't even sure he was convincing himself on the matter and felt flustered. Too many things were happening in a too short amount of time. In a muffled whisper, he said, "I won't do it Yetews. I can't leave you here to be hunted."

Yetews could do nothing to help ease his friend's worry. He sat next to him and patted him on the back gently. He watched the boy with a worried face as Taren came to kneel down beside him.

"Sam?" He spoke gently. "Sam, you don't want to stay here. Being here for even a short time is no longer safe. Regardless of how much he cares for you, Yetews' first duty is to keep you safe and return you home at all costs. If something were to happen to him…" he trailed off and changed what he tried to explain. "Without a Guardian to return a child back to their gateway, there is no way for them to return home. This madman wants to doom you to this world like he has doomed so many before you. You must understand that with his power, he has turned Imagia into a prison. We cannot ask you to stay here. Whatever wish you made, it was not for that fate."

Sam lifted his head up and looked at Taren. He furrowed his brow with agitation and asked him, "So is there any way to stop him?"

Taren glanced at Orga and they exchanged unspoken concern. He looked back to Sam. "There has never been anyone else who has shown even a small portion of his powers. His power of imagination has never been comparable to anyone. No one until…" he paused.

Sam felt all the eyes in the room on him now. He finished Taren's thought. "Until me."

Sam let his eyes wander to everyone in the room. There was silence now. He had always known he had a strong imagination. Now he wasn't sure he wanted that ability. Some small part of him wanted to return home where he could be safe. But the biggest part of him told him that if he really had some amazing ability to create things from his mind, then he could somehow try to fix this broken world.

He focused his attention on Yetews. His warm face and peaceful presence was all it took to convince the remaining part of his mind that feared the unknown. He thought for a moment about what he was getting himself into. He could hear the words of his mother nagging in the back of his mind. She always told him that his imagination would get him into trouble some day.

Perhaps that day had come. He asked himself if he was actually as brave as he always thought he was. Could he take the chance that he may not make it back to his gateway in time if he chose to stay? He battled the debate in his mind silently for a time until, finally, he shrugged and decided to be as brave as he always thought he had been. He took a deep breath and said, "So if I'm gonna stay here, I'm gonna need to know who the bad guy is."

Taren and Orga exchanged a hopeful glance and Orga said, "He is known in this world as Nadaroth."

Chapter Nine: Decisions

It had been a long morning. Quite a lot of information had been handed to Sam in the last hour. Though the history was now explained, there were still so many things that had been left unanswered. The history lesson itself had spawned a new batch of questions. Not only had he just learned who was responsible for the ultimate downfall of Imagia, but was also being forced to make a crucial decision about his journey here.

Sam, of course, was once again battling another round of confusion. His choice to stay seemed concrete at first, but now that he had actually come to think about his chosen words, he wasn't entirely sure he had made the smartest decision. His fascination with the world here was the driving force. Imagination had always been the biggest part of who he was. It defined him. In his heart, he knew that he wanted to help return normalcy to Imagia; that is, if one could call an imaginary world normal. But there was another part of his heart that was calling to him as well.

Home.

There was a home waiting for him outside of this unbelievable world. Though he had no friends that would miss him, he did have a mom and dad who would be heartbroken for the loss. He could picture all the things of his life outside that would welcome him home. He saw his parents, his dog, his cat, his bed, warm meals, and the safety of his home. These were all things that he would surely miss if he let close his awaiting gateway. Sam's heart was splitting in two ways.

Only minutes had passed since Sam's sudden decision, but the silence was almost deafening. Orga was the first to break the barrier. "You are so quick to leave your life behind you for a world that is not yours. Perhaps you should take more time and consider the severity of your actions."

Sam couldn't deny that he was grateful for this second chance to reevaluate his priorities. He had eight more days to discover the many wonders of this place. However, the idea of remaining here had its holes of doubt. He had nearly been killed more than once in the short time he had already roamed the wild. Up until now, he hadn't considered these moments as overly dangerous. As any child his age might, the idea that he could possibly be in mortal peril at any given moment was all but lost on him.

Between Orga's words of forewarning and his own sense of self-preservation, Sam's faith in this world began to waver. The choice in front of him seemed simple enough, but the decision was giving him a headache. "I don't know what I'm supposed to do," he finally sighed. "Um…what are my choices?"

"There are really only two options," answered Orga, "and I believe you already know them. You can head for your gateway and go home…"

Taren interrupted him, "Which you should do regardless of anything else."

Orga sighed and closed his eyes while he slowly shook his head. "Or you can stay and take the chance of missing your gateway; remaining trapped here for the duration of your life."

Orga was right. Sam already knew his options. Though they were spelled out, clear as day, in front of him, he still looked for another choice. As he thought about it, he could see another option faintly hovering in the back of his mind. "Can't I stay here for the rest of my eight days and help? After that, Yetews can take me back to my gateway and I can go home."

"No." Taren barked. "It's too dangerous. You need to go home, Sam. The longer you stay here, the greater chance that Yetews will be hunted down. If something happens to him, then you lose any hope of leaving."

"I d-don't care," he stuttered. "If I have the same power as this Nadaroth guy, then I might be able to help fix things."

"We haven't even tested that theory," Taren waved off that point. "This isn't some grand adventure you are on. It's real. It's dangerous. And you are just a boy."

Taren's anger started to show the more he spoke. He was very defensive of the situation. Even Sam, though just a mere boy, could feel the defensive tone and felt like a parent had just reprimanded him. His cheeks turned a shade pinker and he stared towards his feet again.

Yetews had joined Sam at his side and was listening intently. If it involved Sam, it involved him as well. Orga shuffled over and sat across from Sam once more. He watched Sam for a moment before speaking. "Taren is right. You *should* go to your gateway. It's safer and the right thing to do. We can guide you to your decision, but ultimately, we can not make that choice for you."

Sam looked into the creature's wise, beady eyes. "But...what about Yetews?"

Yetews nudged him and then grumbled reassuringly. Sam looked to him and said, "What if you're wrong? What if you can't take care of yourself?"

Orga answered him. "The longer you remain here, the harder it will be for him to hide. His first priority is *your* safety right now. Not his own."

Yetews nobly agreed and nodded his shaggy head.

"Oh," whispered Sam. It was embarrassing to realize how much danger he was causing his friend.

More silence followed, this time lingering more on the awkward side. Everyone awaited Sam's next words. When he continued to stare down at his feet, Keesa opted to break the silence.

"This morning has been very enlightening. I assume that a creature like me would not normally be privileged with such vast amounts of knowledge. I am ever grateful for your kind help, Sam. For your sake, I do hope that you return to the safety of your home. If

The Gateway to Imagia: The Tale of Sam Little

you cannot continue with me, I will understand."

Sam jolted upright. He'd almost forgotten what started this entire journey. "That's right! I almost forgot! What about Keesa's cubs?" he nearly shouted. Realizing that he didn't mean to forget about her, he quickly apologized, "Sorry Keesa. It's just that it's been a really weird morning and all."

Keesa smiled somberly at him. "It's quite alright Sam. There seems to me to be much greater things of concern here."

Orga was slightly thrown by the sudden turn of conversation. Taren remembered his promise to the cat, "Oh yes. I forgot as well." He spoke to Orga now. "I told her that you could explain the disappearance of her cubs. I believe that they have become marked beasts."

"Beasts?" Keesa growled in anger at Taren's accusation. "Is that what you think I am?"

Sam was about to speak in her defense when Orga calmly explained. "Taren means no harm by his words. That is simply the term that is used when Nadaroth captures them. You too will become a marked beast if you try to save them. If he truly has captured them, then it is a hopeless cause. He uses certain creatures of this world to strike fear into the hearts of those that remain and to hunt Guardians. I have seen it happen. He captures them young so he can train them and mold them into very dangerous pawns. He doesn't have the same power over creatures of Imagia as he has over humans. But he can imagine things that will drive them mad. In the end, they learn to do his bidding."

Sam couldn't believe what he was hearing. It was such a sad thing to hear and he felt pity for Keesa and her babies. Part of it didn't make sense to him though. "But can't he just imagine up creatures instead of training other ones?"

Taren scoffed. "Yes. He can. And he does. But if he can use creatures that have been more powerfully created through another child's mind, then they will exist longer."

Orga was nodding. "Precisely. He may be able to imagine powerful images, but because he has no emotional bond with what he is creating, they fade from existence much more easily. Kupa cats have been around for a very long time. Long enough that they have become capable of increasing in number. There are quite a few creatures here like that." He focused on Keesa, whose eyes were filled with tears of disbelief. "If Nadaroth has captured them, then your cubs are lost. To be a marked beast is a cruel fate. I am truly sorry."

Yetews and Sam watched her with pity. Sam had no words to comfort her. He could think of only one thing to say, "It's not fair."

She silently turned her back to them and moved to a remote corner in the room.

Things seemed grim in this world that Sam had so dearly wished to be a part of. And now it seemed that time was apparently of the essence.

It was difficult to make sense of everything he had learned. Still so much of it seemed like a good dream gone wrong. If he hadn't had nightmares while he was here, he would have convinced himself that none of it was really happening. Either way, he knew that he needed to decide what to do next.

The situation for Keesa seemed lost now. There were many things he was risking. The longer he stayed, the harder things would get for everyone. Though Imagia was beautiful and brimming full of life and possible adventures, he was coming to understand that things were not what they seemed. The idea of staying was thrilling, but to never return home again was frightening. He *was* only a boy and not a very intimidating one at that. He took a long, slow breath and looked to his Guardian. After all the bravery that Sam had once claimed to have, he knew that the choice he was about to make could change everything he had come to trust.

Sam couldn't look at Yetews when he spoke. He feared that looking into his eyes would make it impossible to say what he needed to say. It was fear itself that brought Sam to his decision. He started to say something but choked silently on the unspoken words. He looked at his feet and closed his eyes. He swallowed hard. In barely more than a whisper, he said "Take me home, Yetews." As the words formed through his lips, he felt as though someone else were speaking them.

He could once again feel four sets of eyes upon him. As he felt their stares boring into him, he was overwhelmed by shame for running away with his tail between his legs. For the first time in Sam's life, he felt as small as he was and completely insignificant. He

The Gateway to Imagia: The Tale of Sam Little

felt like a coward.

He didn't like it very much.

* * * * * * * * * *

Making the decision to go home was difficult. In fact, Sam wasn't entirely convinced that it was the best thing he had done. Taren and Orga spent the best part of the day debating whether or not to test Sam's power of imagination before taking him home. Taren seemed torn by the idea.

Sam was getting bored from all the talking. They weren't including him in their conversation. He spent the time pacing, tapping his fingers impatiently, and trying to get Yetews to entertain him.

Orga was eager to put Sam's mind to the test and in the end, they decided that the situation was much different than Nadaroth's, due mainly to the fact that Sam actually wanted to return home.

They weren't sure what the safest approach would be, but they ultimately decided to let Sam use his own creativity in the situation. After the details were worked out, they chose to move outside into the forest clearing for more room. Orga wasn't willing to have the inside of his home jeopardized by whatever might be imagined.

Sam was just grateful for something to do.

Once they were outside, Taren said, "Alright Sam. Try to keep it simple. You know…nothing that I'd have to shoot later, okay?" He readied his bow and nodded at Sam with a crooked smile. "Just in case." He winked.

Sam was back in the spotlight, so to speak. It was as if a teacher had just called on him for an answer he didn't know. "Er…so…something like a flower?"

Orga chuckled, "Well, that would definitely be safer than last night I'd venture to guess."

"Okay." Sam honestly had little idea how to even start. He couldn't remember what he had done on the previous night. He was barely convinced that he was capable of anything at all. But in spite of his doubt, he closed his eyes and tried to picture a flower. Then he opened his eyes, expecting to see everyone staring in awe at the same image.

Nothing.

"Did you imagine something?" Asked Taren.

Feeling a tad embarrassed, he meekly nodded.

"Keep trying."

He closed his eyes and concentrated again on what he wanted to imagine. After a number of failed attempts, he couldn't help but wonder if Taren had been wrong. He threw his arms up in frustration. "Geez! Nothing is happening! I don't think it's working. What if you were wrong?" he asked Taren heatedly.

"Hmm..." Orga interjected. He thought a moment. "Why don't you try again, but this time try to imagine like you would if no one else were around. Try not to think about it. Just...imagine."

Those were the words that he needed to hear. If he were back home, his imagination would still be second nature to him. He never had to think about what he was imagining. It always came to him so easily. To think that one day he would forget how to use his imagination seemed absurd.

He was so close to the age when this might happen that he was afraid he might actually be losing the ability already. It angered him and he forced himself to believe that it was impossible. He would force himself to break that mold.

Now, more determined than ever, Sam closed his eyes and tried to picture the same flower. This time he could see the flower in perfect detail. He could smell its sweet perfume dancing in the air around him. He could almost feel the soft, delicate petals as he imagined them, clear as day.

Someone gasped.

Sam opened his eyes. There, growing a few steps away from him, was a beautiful sapphire flower. Its petals were wide as it bloomed, perfectly planted in the ground as if it had always grown there.

"Fascinating!" exclaimed Orga.

"I don't believe it," Taren mused. "It just...appeared out of thin air."

Yetews went to Sam, smiling widely. He grumbled his pride of Sam's accomplishment.

He had done it. It wasn't hard or complicated in the slightest and he, the smallest person he knew, had done something quite extraordinary. He stood in amazement and stared at the flower.

Though he could hear the others talking amongst themselves,

Sam couldn't make out their words through his own thoughts. He hadn't believed Taren when he suggested that he was actually capable of some strange and impossible power. Now that the proof was growing just a few feet in front of him, he was having a difficult time understanding what it all meant.

His mind began to wander as he thought of all the amazing things that he could imagine while he was here. Images of his past adventures flickered through his mind in fast forward. There were so many times he wished he could bring those images to life and now he might actually be capable of it. Some images were more vivid than others, but each one was neatly tucked away in his memories so he could later pull them out for use any time he would need of them. He was remembering many creatures and scenes from his adventures back home.

In the middle of his mental slideshow, he felt Yetews shake him back into reality as someone shouted to get his attention.

"SAM!"

He blinked and refocused. When Sam looked around, he saw the familiar images from his sudden flashback. Creatures of various shapes and sizes were flittering madly around them. The sounds of twittering, cooing, and bellowing filled the air. Chaos was weaving its way between the group of Sam's unsuspecting and bewildered friends.

Then, just as quickly as the chaotic scene seemed to have appeared, the images began fading into nothingness.

All went suddenly quiet.

Everyone was standing in shock at what had just taken place. Taren had his bow still aimed at the ready, having never found a crucial target. Orga and Yetews stood with their mouths gaping slightly, while Keesa, who had finally joined them outside, was standing with her hackles raised and ears at attention. No one seemed to know quite what to say.

Sam watched them. Whatever had just happened was both strange and amazing. He wasn't sure what anyone else thought, but it certainly wasn't anything like what he expected. If no one else was going to say something, he was. "What the heck was all that?"

"Well…" started Orga as he half-glanced at a very wide-eyed Taren, "we were sort of hoping you could shed some light on it."

"What did you just do?" Taren asked, still flabbergasted.

Sam looked pleadingly to Yetews for an answer or some form of support, but his friend was still too shocked to move. "I didn't *do* anything. I was just thinking about...ya know...stuff. Things that I imagined in the past. Before I came here. But I wasn't trying like I was with the flower." Remembering the flower, he looked over to see that it was still there. It hadn't disappeared like the many images they had just witnessed.

Orga walked up over to the giant flower and caressed its petals as he thought.

Taren became impatient at Orga's silent reverie. "Is that how it happened with Nadaroth?" The concern in his voice was thick.

Orga blinked and looked from Taren's face to Sam's, concentrating on both. "I've never seen that happen before. For him to bring an image into existence with a mere glance of a thought is...impressive." He focused his gaze on Taren more intently and added, "Dangerously impressive."

Taren merely nodded once. He turned to Yetews. "You are Sam's Guardian. You alone can find his gateway. We've tested our theory and given him all the information he needs to understand this world. He made his decision to go home. The time has come for you to carry out your duty. This is a dangerous time for your kind. Do you understand what is at risk here?"

Yetews cocked an eyebrow. Though he was a Guardian, he was also the product of Sam's imagination and still retained the characteristics of his imagined form. He didn't exist before this, so was unknowing to the dangers that he was now in. He looked at Taren and then to his boy. Sam was looking at him so innocently. His Guardian instinct kicked in and he suddenly understood what he had to do. He grunted his affirmation and nodded determinedly.

"Good. If you're going to get there safely, then you stand a better chance with a Protector."

Sam asked him, "What's a Protector?"

"Protectors are those that have vowed to protect and defend the Guardians. They were children who were lost here when their Guardians were destroyed before they could return to their own gateways. I suppose you could call them self-appointed guardians of the Guardians." Taren smiled.

The Gateway to Imagia: The Tale of Sam Little

"Oh. So how do we find one of those then?" Though it didn't seem possible, things were getting more complicated by the minute.

Taren chuckled to himself. "You're lookin' at one, kid."

At first Sam couldn't think of what to say, but then he remembered that Taren had already saved them twice from hairy situations. It made perfect sense.

But then he thought about what Taren had just said and realized that he had lost his own Guardian. Losing a Guardian was a devastating thing. He couldn't imagine how difficult that must have been for him. It brought to light a new set of questions that he wanted to ask. "You don't look that old. How long have you been here? And what happened to..."

Orga stopped Sam in mid-question. "Taren's story can wait for the moment. There is still planning that needs to be done. How far away is his gateway, Yetews?"

Yetews looked around the forest behind him and silently calculated the journey in his head. He squinted his eyes in concentration. His expression was very serious and oddly different from the Yetews that Sam had come to know and love. For the moment that he stood there, he no longer looked like a goofy sidekick, but rather like a noble and wizened creature.

Then he turned to them and grumbled. He animatedly pointed in certain directions as he explained where to go.

Taren covered his face with both palms in frustration. "That is *really* getting annoying." He sighed and looked to Sam. "Translation?"

He had never considered how irritating it would be to others to not be able to understand Yetews. But before Imagia, he had never taken into consideration that one day he would actually need to worry about such a thing. As much as it annoyed Taren, he still couldn't help but feel even more connected to Yetews because of it. To him, Yetews sounded perfectly understandable and the situation made him smile.

"He said that if we start now then we could make it back in a day if we don't run into any problems."

Yetews grumbled something else and smiled slyly.

Sam smiled back and added, "And he also said that he thinks he knows a better way around that really annoying bit of forest we trucked through yesterday…if that's okay with you."

Taren raised an eyebrow and then rolled his eyes. "He's the Guardian." He shrugged. "I'm just here to make sure he doesn't lead you all back into the mouth of another deceptor." He smirked. Yetews snorted in irritation.

Orga suggested that they at least wait until the following morning so that they could have all eaten and rested. There were no objections. It had already been an eventful day. Sam was eager to prolong his stay in Imagia for as long as he could, so he was least likely to argue the point.

Orga disappeared into his underground home briefly. When he came back out, he handed Sam a small pile of tattered rags and told him it might be safer if he blended better into the background. It wasn't until then that Sam became aware of his appearance. He was still wearing his bright red and blue monster pajamas. Though they were sodden with dirt and grime, he still stood out like a sore thumb. It would be difficult to keep a low profile dressed as he was.

He looked over the pile of cloth in his hands and understood that they weren't rags, but rather roughly made clothes. He held the dull brown shirt up to his chest. It wasn't a perfect fit, but would make more sense to wear than his pajamas.

"It's hard to believe I used to be that small," said Taren.

Sam dropped the shirt to his side. He hadn't expected this. "You mean that these were *your* clothes?"

Taren nodded. "Orga made them for me after I missed my gateway. Let's hope that you won't need them for as long as I did. Why don't you go try them on?"

Sam looked over the pile of tattered clothes. He suddenly wasn't sure if it was appropriate to ask Taren how he got lost here. His ten-year-old sense of curiosity trumped his manners and he decided to ask anyways. "So if we're sticking around here for the night, then could you tell me what happened to you?"

"I think maybe we should concentrate on planning how to get you out safely. Besides, you're going to need some sleep tonight. It's going to be a long walk back tomorrow."

The idea of having more nightmares didn't appeal to Sam. He knew that he would have to try and sleep in the end, but at least he could try to keep his mind busy with more information. He shook his head. "I'm not really tired right now anyways and it's not even dark yet."

"Well," Taren started, "I think you ought to try. I promise to tell you about it tomorrow. Okay?"

Sam was slightly annoyed that he had to wait, but at the same time excited for the next day. Taren was such an interesting person so he was eager to hear more of how he became that way. "Okay, but you have to start at the beginning. I want to know everything." He couldn't seem to hide the eagerness from his voice.

Taren raised an eyebrow at Sam. He breathed deep. "Alright. But we best move back inside now. It's safer there."

Chapter Ten: The Gateway

Though they had only spent one day and night there, it was strange to be leaving Orga's home. Sam had felt oddly safe there. Before meeting Orga, he was blind to what this world was. He had planned to stay for a while and then return home of his own accord. All of his plans were jumbled up now.

Each creature or person that Sam had met so far, he had befriended. And each one found a place and a purpose in the group. Among the few things he was certain of was that Orga would be joining them on their journey back to his gateway. His knowledge of Imagia would prove to be useful and the stories he could tell were sure to be fascinating. So when Orga stayed behind, Sam was incredibly disappointed. He still had so many questions to ask.

He had spent the night fighting sleep. Every time he would feel himself slipping into his dreams, he would force himself awake with a jolt. Many a time, he was unsuccessful and had to be woken by the nearest individual if he started to scream.

But the night didn't last forever. Daylight had come to the forest at last and Sam and his friends were once again traveling through their expanses. Now that he had left, Sam wished he'd spent his night more productively. Orga wasn't there to whet his desire for knowledge and now the only one left to answer his questions was Taren, who was far from wordy when it came to explaining things.

The Gateway to Imagia: The Tale of Sam Little

He hadn't the same vast knowledge that Orga had. He admitted to this upfront when they started the long trek back. He explained to Sam that he would do his best to answer any questions he had, but couldn't promise his efficiency in doing so.

Sam had yet to ask Taren about his sad tale. He had a feeling that Taren might not be as willing to divulge that information now that they were on their way.

For a good while after setting out, the conversation was sparse. Sam didn't really know quite where to start and was still struggling with his decision to leave Imagia behind him. More importantly, he was fighting with the idea of leaving Yetews to an unknown fate.

Yetews saw the burden of worry and doubt that Sam carried now. He was completely aware that Sam felt remorse for his choice. He also knew that Sam didn't want anyone to know just how much it bothered him. He tried to break the awkwardness by being as playful and upbeat as he could. His attempt was at least partially successful because Sam agreed to ride in his usual place atop Yetews' shoulders.

As for Keesa, she had become much more sullen. Before they set off for the return journey, she asked to go with them. She offered herself as another form of protection for Sam. Though mourning for her lost cubs, when Sam accepted her offer, she seemed to benefit from her new purpose. There was renewed light in her eyes.

As they trudged along in silence, Sam's mind began to wander. He dwelled on the most recent thought of his last moments with Orga–

"Aren't you coming too?" asked Sam when he noticed that Orga wasn't making any preparations to leave his home.

Orga smiled widely and once more placed his elongated fingers over Sam's shoulders. Sam would never forget how warm they felt through his borrowed clothes. "I have no purpose in this part of your journey. I believe that you will make it back to your gateway safely. I would trust Taren with my own life." He chuckled and Sam watched as his large jowl jiggled. "In fact...I have trusted him with it many times. He's the best Protector I've ever met. You'll be plenty safe with him."

Everyone seemed to be more worried about his safety than he was. That was what kept driving him back to his gateway. His decision wasn't based nearly as much on his fear for being left behind and never going home, but rather based on the concern that he couldn't see. There was a nagging sensation that frightened Sam when the others would mention how dangerous a position he was now in.

Soon enough, he'd be securely tucked away in his boring bed with no more real adventures to ever put his small life in jeopardy again. Imagia definitely had more appeal to him than his normal life. But he couldn't stay. The fear he felt, though masked at the moment, was always looming.

Sam was staring at the flower that he had imagined into existence.

"I know what you are thinking Sam," Orga said. "You do have an extraordinary power. But you are also very young and quite vulnerable to the ways of this world. I will admit to you that I will always wonder if another child like you will come along one day and be able to return Imagia to its true purpose. But it is not your world to save. You do not need to feel guilt for leaving. It is the way it is supposed to be. You are meant to return home."

"I know. It's just that…well…what if I could help? If one kid could come here and make things go so bad, then can't one kid come here that could make things go good again? What if I'm that kid?"

Orga shrugged. "There's no way to know. But don't dwell on what could be. You are too young to worry so much. For now, just remember your time here as your grandest adventure. Yetews will always remember you. As will those you have met along the way. After a few days home, you will begin to think of this world as a beautiful dream. The dream will grow dim with time and then eventually, you will forget."

"But I don't want to forget," said Sam.

"It is simply the way of this world. No child ever wants to forget, but they always do. You will too."

"How do you know?"

"Because I'm a Guardian. I'm supposed to know," Orga answered matter-of-factly.

Orga handed him a roughly woven sack filled with food and water. He pat him on the shoulder one last time and said, "Sometimes it is a good thing to be able to forget. I don't believe I will ever forget *you* though." With a final smile, he said, "Be safe Sam Little."

The Gateway to Imagia: The Tale of Sam Little

As Sam remembered Orga's last words, he knew that he meant them to be comforting. But as hard as he tried to let it ease his mind, it simply wasn't working. He never wanted to forget anyone he had met or the awesomeness of Imagia. Forgetting was too painful.

He thought about what it would be like to walk back through his gateway. Seeing Yetews standing there and waving goodbye to him would be harder than anything he had ever done. He wondered if Titus would be waiting there for him just as he was the night he'd left. Getting here seemed so easy. Could leaving be just as easy if it is the way that Imagia works? And how could Orga be so certain that Sam would forget? How do you merely forget something as incredible as an imaginary world brought to life? Forgetting didn't seem even close to the realm of possibilities.

Yetews yawned and grumbled a question to Sam.

He popped out of his dazed state. "I was gonna ask him soon. But he might not want to talk about losing his Guardian."

Yetews nodded and sighed.

"You think I should still ask him then?"

He turned to look up at Sam and gestured with one of his hands towards Taren.

"Okay. So what should I say?" he whispered back.

Yetews made his suggestion clear with a long grunt.

Sam rolled his eyes. "Yeah, I guess that's a good idea. But what if he doesn't want to start at the beginning?"

Yetews shrugged and lifted Sam off of his shoulders. He nudged him gently forward so that he would be walking next to Taren.

Taren looked down at Sam and smiled knowingly. "You're going to ask me about my story, aren't you?"

Sam blushed slightly, realizing that his conversation with Yetews was not as private as he thought it had been. "Well...yeah. If that's okay still." He looked up hoping not to see any sign of sadness in Taren's face.

"I told you I would share it with you on your journey home. I won't go back on my word. But you should know that I'm not a very good story teller."

Sam nodded eagerly. He couldn't seem to hide the smile that was itching under the surface.

"Well, let me see...I guess you probably want to know how I got here."

"Yeah."

"As ridiculous as it sounds to say it out loud, I wished on a shooting star. I was eight years old. Much like you, I wished my imagination was real and the next day…I was here."

Sam got overly excited and interrupted Taren with a flood of questions. "What did you see? Who was your Guardian and what was he like? Did you go in through a forest too?" He looked up at Taren and saw him looking back with a raised eyebrow.

"Do you want to hear my story or would you rather keep asking questions?" he smirked.

"Sorry. Go ahead." Sam was mildly embarrassed.

Taren smiled again and resumed his tale. "First of all, I suppose you should know that I had a twin sister. Her name was Tessa. We both used to go together on imaginary adventures when we were growing up. We talked about how amazing it would be if it were real. One evening, we were sitting outside stargazing and agreed that the next shooting star we saw, we'd both wish that our imaginary adventures would become real. The next evening, we saw our Guardians standing at the edge of the woods not far from where we lived. Of course, we didn't know what they truly were, but we went to them nonetheless."

"What did they look like?"

He smiled solemnly as he remembered. "They were tigers, actually. Mine was white and his name was Tiberius. He was incredibly beautiful. And unlike Yetews, he was perfectly understandable," he joked. He paused long enough to watch Yetews roll his eyes. "Tessa's tiger was orange and her name was Atlantis. Of course, one gateway can only bring one child so our Guardians led us to separate places in the trees and then suddenly we were both here. It's not common for two to come together like that, but it does happen from time to time.

"So here we were, two naïve eight year olds riding on our tigers. We had no idea we had entered a world in the midst of dangerous times. We had only been here for two days when things took a turn for the worse…" Taren drifted off and got a far away look in his eyes. He shook his head as if shaking off a bad thought and continued.

"Out of nowhere, we were attacked. It happened so fast that there was nothing we could have done. The only warning we had was a massive shadow that covered us in darkness before it landed. It was a dragon. Our Guardians fought it the best they could, but it was a hopeless battle. Tessa and I stood helpless in the shadows of the trees and watched as the dragon killed Atlantis. Tiberius kept fighting. He was...so...so brave."

Sam watched Taren closely. He could tell that it was hard for him to relive that day. He felt guilty for asking to hear his story. He thought about asking him to stop, but so badly wanted to hear more.

"Tiberius got in a few good hits, but it didn't matter in the end. He died too. The dragon flew away, leaving us behind. Of course, we had no idea what any of this meant and that we would be trapped here forever. We sat by our fallen Guardians, scared and alone. We were there for hours before anyone found us. Tessa was inconsolable. She wouldn't stop crying and all I could do was hold her and try to tell her that it would be okay. Just when I had decided that we'd better find our way home is when I met Orga for the first time." Taren smiled warmly. "He happened upon us by chance and felt pity. We told him our story and he told us about Imagia. When Tessa found out that we were never going home again, she went into shock. Orga took us to his home and did what he could for us. He sort of took us under his wing. He truly is an amazing being.

"So, the years went by and Tessa never got better. She slept a lot and that's when the nightmares started. I, on the other hand, chose to go out and start to explore the world. Orga watched over us for a long time, but eventually I felt it was time to leave. In my travels, I came across a village full of people who had suffered the same fate we had."

"A village of kids?" Sam squeaked in surprise. "How many kids are stuck here?"

Taren shook his head slowly. "They aren't all kids, Sam. Many of them are grown now. Time ages us differently here, but we do still grow. When a child is left behind, they usually end up in the place I found. They call it the Village of Exile." He caught the flicker of confusion on Sam's face and explained. "Exile means to be sent away from some place and not allowed to return."

"Oh," answered Sam. He understood and it made him sad.

He noticed Sam's sad expression. "The name is fitting, really.

And it is sad. But a lot of us adjusted fairly well. We learned to cope with the nightmares and restless sleep. It's a tragic fate for any child to become lost here. They enter this world in joy only to be thrown into a nightmare. It pains me to see it happen so many times. That's what ultimately drove me to become a Protector.

"From the first moment I saw a Protector defend a Guardian as she returned her child safely home, I knew it's what I wanted to become. I learned from other Protectors and started going out and finding Guardians as they brought their children into the world. I would do my best to explain to them that they had to take their children back to their gateways as soon as they could. I watched over them and kept them both safe. After their child is safely returned, I teach them how to hide and what to avoid.

"Unfortunately, there aren't enough Protectors to help everyone. But we do what we can. If we're too late and we find a lost child, we take them to the Village of Exile. There, they are well cared for by the others. It's a place where compassion for the lost ones is not lacking."

Sam didn't look at Taren as he thought about what he'd heard. It was making his decision to go home seem simpler.

Taren watched the concern in Sam's face. He continued. "Anyhow, as far as my story goes, I'm afraid there isn't much else to tell. It's not a pleasant story for me to remember, but it happened a very long time ago. Time heals all wounds, so they say."

Sam looked at him curiously. Taren looked so young but sounded so wise to him. He wondered how long ago Taren had gotten trapped in Imagia. "How long have you been here? I mean…you don't look very old."

Taren laughed in response to Sam's observation skills. "Well, as I said before. Time is different here. I don't think that there is anyone here who could unravel the mysteries of Imagia. Not even Nadaroth. But you have to remember that children were not meant to exist here permanently. All I know is that after a certain time, I simply stopped changing. I have looked like this for a very long time."

"So how old are you?"

"Well, I've been in Imagia for 164 years. That would make me 172 years old."

"Woah…no way! You are super old! That's older than my grandpa! But you don't look like him at all. You're not wrinkly or anything!" Yetews snorted behind them and they all started laughing at Sam's candid comment.

Taren nodded. "But I bet your Grandpa didn't grow up in a strange world built by the power of imagination. So he has a good excuse for not looking like a twenty-five year old. I bet your grandpa never battled with a deceptor or a dragon either." He winked.

They were all amazed by this new revelation. Another piece of Imagia had been revealed. With Taren's tale finally told, and the mood of the group slightly uplifted, the outlook for the remainder of the journey had become significantly improved. And even though he was so close to leaving this world behind, there was a little extra bounce to his walk for the moment.

* * * * * * * * *

Yetews had been right about the length of time it would take to get to the gateway. He had just explained to Sam that they were very close and should be there fairly soon.

After translating to Taren and Keesa, Sam began to feel the imminent goodbye tugging at his heartstrings. It was unfair to leave so soon. And knowing now that he rightfully had ten days to be here with his best friend made the pain of it worse.

Sam had gotten tired of walking once again and had resumed his place atop Yetews. He wanted to treasure the last moments and remember exactly how everything felt. Taren knew this was a hard moment for him and did his best to comfort him by encouraging him it was the right decision. He promised that he would do everything in his power to protect Yetews and that he was in good hands. He even got a smile from Sam when he joked that the language barrier might prove to be a bit annoying, but they'd just have to use some form of sign language to get by.

The journey had gone smooth. They hadn't run into anything dangerous the entire time and spirits were high for it.

It was nearing evening of Sam's third day in Imagia, when finally, Yetews slowed to a stop. He looked up at Sam solemnly. He also felt the finality of the situation and the sadness couldn't be shrouded easily from either of their faces.

Yetews helped Sam down from his shoulders and watched him

carefully. Sam looked away from Yetews' stare to observe where they were. He recognized the large flowery bush he had mock ambushed and the clearing where he and Yetews had lounged in the broken rays of sun. The path that had led them to Keesa was near as well. He didn't know if he could get any words out through the lump swelling in his throat. So he sounded slightly muffled when he said, "So we're here then?"

Yetews nodded and pointed over to the shadows of a tree. There, still hanging just as he had left it, was his red super-hero cape. Under it, sat his green frog flashlight. Now that he saw them, he understood that the time he had dreaded the entire day had come. He didn't feel finished with this amazing world, but also knew that it might be his only chance to leave.

Yetews sheepishly grinned at his boy. He had brought him safely back and now it was time to say the words that neither of them wanted to say. It was time to say goodbye.

Taren made the first move. He moved to Sam's side as they stared towards the dark trees. He put a hand on Sam's small shoulder. "I know this is hard for you. But try to remember that it is much safer for both of you this way." When he didn't say anything back, Taren continued in a reassuring voice, "He'll be okay. And so will you." He finished with a smile.

Sam looked up and Taren saw the conflict in his eyes.

Keesa joined Sam at his other side and sat down on her haunches. "I am very sorry that my journey with you ends, Sam. I've grown quite fond of you in the small time I've been allowed to know you."

Sam looked into her crystal gaze. It would hurt to say goodbye to her too. She was such a kind and wonderfully interesting creature to have befriended. "I'm sorry about your cubs, Keesa. I wish I could have helped you. Are you gonna be alright?"

"Hmm. As the Protector said, time heals. But don't be sorry. It was never your burden to bear." Her smiled beamed through her saber teeth. "Good luck Sam Little." She turned and allowed room for Yetews. Taren followed suit.

Yetews had stepped in front of Sam and bowed his head so that he could look into his eyes. Sam had taken to staring back down at his feet again. One silent tear fell and wet the ground below him. Yetews put a finger under Sam's chin and lovingly lifted his face. Tears were

The Gateway to Imagia: The Tale of Sam Little

welling up and Yetews smiled his goofy smile in encouragement. Sam took one look into the big green eyes and jumped into Yetews' arms. He buried his face in the familiar fur as two large arms pulled him into a warm hug.

Sam couldn't help but let out a large muffled sniff as he fought back the tears. He wanted so badly to never let go and wished there were some way that Yetews could go with him.

As the Guardian held his child lovingly, there was a magical sound like the gentle tinkling of chimes in the wind as the gateway began to open mere feet away from them. Sam loosened his embrace on Yetews and gazed through the trees. It was as if he were looking through an open archway that led to his home world. He could see the lights of his house warmly glowing far across a long stretch of grass. The friendly glow beckoned to him as he watched from afar. It was still night in his world. Still the same night he left mere days ago.

All eyes were on Sam now. As they stood there in the evening light, more of the same magical sounds interrupted the scene. With Sam's gateway already opened, they all looked around, confused by the source.

A few yards from Sam's, another gateway had opened. A dazzling white unicorn was walking to the opening. It disappeared through the gateway for only a moment before it returned. It stood at the gateway and watched quietly, waiting. It lowered its gorgeous head serenely in expectation of something unseen to the small group of bystanders. A small girl came running through the gateway and threw her arms around the neck of the newly born Guardian.

The four travelers stood and watched as the girl's gateway dissolved back into the dark tree line. As the girl unwrapped her arms from the unicorn, Sam instantly recognized her. It was a girl from his school. Though they weren't in the same class, he knew her name. He whispered to Taren, "I know her. Her name's Elizabeth."

Taren looked down at Sam with a mix of confusion mingled with surprise. He had apparently never seen two children who recognized each other from the outside world. He turned to watch the scene unfold with concern in his eyes for the newcomers.

Keesa muttered, "Truly amazing."

Taren, obviously concerned for the situation, motioned for Sam to get to his gateway. "You'd better go, kid."

Taren barely got the words out when suddenly the trees behind them bent and thrashed violently. It was only a brief warning of what was coming.

Too brief.

The same strange and menacing beast from Sam's nightmare broke through the foliage and stopped only long enough to bare its fanged jaws and roar its deafening sound. It found its target all too easily and barreled towards the girl and her Guardian, destroying the peaceful scene.

Taren drew his bow instantly and took aim. He shouted over his shoulder to Yetews, "GET SAM OUT OF HERE! NOW!"

The creature heard Taren and its eyes flicked briefly to them. It wasn't enough to distract him from his goal and he dived for the unicorn. The Guardian pushed the girl out of the way with its flank and reared on its hind legs. It shook its head and neighed, then aimed its shining golden horn for the heart of the beast.

Sam saw the fear in the girl's face and ran to take her hand and pull her out of the way. Yetews had grabbed for Sam to hold him back but only managed to catch air.

Taren shot at the beast. It was a direct hit and it roared in rage as it stumbled forward towards the unicorn with its sharp teeth aimed at its primary target. The unicorn fell under the weight of the beast as a rain of arrows pierced the attacker from behind. The Protector's aim left the beast instantly dead.

Yetews had reached Sam and Elizabeth. They all watched in stunned terror as the fallen Guardian whinnied feebly and breathed its last breath. Yetews was trembling in fear for watching one of his own kind struck down so brutally.

The girl was sobbing into her free hand and shaking from head to toe. Sam felt pain and pity for her as he watched her and held her hand. He looked at his gateway and then to her. No one would ever believe him if he tried to explain her disappearance.

Taren turned, out of breath. He looked at Yetews. "The gateway is still open. He needs to go now before another attack. We have to get you out of here! Sam, you have to go now! Before it's too late. If a Guardian dies, the gateway seals itself instantly."

Elizabeth looked up at Sam through tear-filled eyes. Recognition washed over her as she saw his face. "Sam?" Fear shook her voice as she asked him, "What's happening? I'm so scared."

Sam looked into her scared eyes and felt her fear. This could so easily be him; Left to wander a strange world, unknowing and frightened. Time seemed to stand still as he realized what he had to do. He looked into his gateway at his home in the distance. His heart was pounding so hard that he could feel his shirt moving with every beat.

Taren was shouting orders in the background but they were muddled over his own thoughts. He looked to Yetews, whose eyes were so innocent and filled with panic. He had to do this before he could change his mind. He felt the girl's hand trembling in his as he started running towards his gateway, pulling her behind.

He got to the gateway and heard Taren yell to him, "Sam, you have to let go of her! She can't go with you! The gateway won't allow two to go through!"

Sam stopped dead in his tracks mere inches from the opening as he heard Taren's words of warning. He looked back at his three friends' faces and said, "I know." He focused on Yetews' familiar green eyes and whispered, "I'm sorry."

He turned to the bewildered girl and begged, "Please...tell my mom and dad that I'm okay."

Taren abruptly grasped what was happening and screamed, "NO SAM!" He sprinted towards him.

Elizabeth's face was confused and she had no time to react as Sam shoved her through his gateway. A sudden, unnatural gust of air ruffled Sam's hair as he watched the image of his home melt away, replaced by the dark shadows of the forest.

He turned in time to see three stunned faces staring back at him.

Taren had stopped in mid run. He looked into the small boy's eyes and whispered, "Sam...what have you done?"

He looked to Yetews and saw the fear of the unknown washing over his features.

Sam didn't know if he understood why he did it or what the consequences would be for his actions. But he did know that things were about to become serious.

"I...I...don't know," he stuttered.

Before his mind could catch up with his actions, the bushes where his gateway once stood began to shudder.

Four sets of eyes watched the shadows ahead as Taren drew his bow again, waiting for what was coming.

Chapter Eleven: Theories

The leaves where Sam's gateway had just been were rustling ominously. Something was fighting its way through the thick undergrowth of the forest. The dusky light of evening made it difficult to make out what kind of creature was about attack.

Taren was already prepared. His bow was aimed stealthily at the shadows. Yetews was already standing faithfully in his protective spot in front of Sam, blocking him from danger. And Keesa stood at Taren's side, preparing herself for the imminent attack.

Too many times, they had already experienced the quaking shadows of the forest. Sam could feel shock and fear welling up in his system and he could feel it on the brink of overwhelming him. Too much was happening too soon and he felt like he was just pulled from the mouth of another deceptor. He wasn't entirely certain what was happening, but he was sure that passing out again would not be ideal at this moment. He fought against it.

The events that had taken shape in the last minutes didn't seem real and it was far from being over. He was already beginning to understand that the snap decision he had just made was more dangerous than he could have ever imagined.

Though the recent attack was still fresh in his mind, Sam couldn't help but wish that this new threat would make its move. As crazy as it felt, he just wanted to get it over with. Yetews' body was blocking Sam from harm, but he risked a peek from underneath a protective arm out of sheer curiosity. The atmosphere was tense as the seconds ticked by.

The rustling of the leaves drew closer. Whatever this creature was, its size was apparently nothing compared to the monstrosity that Taren had just struck down. There was no wake of destruction like the fallen beast had left in its path.

Time felt as though it was happening in slow motion. Sam could hardly take the suspense any longer. He risked a question. "What is it?"

With his eyes not straying from the potential target, Taren whispered back. "I'm not sure, but whatever it is, it's hesitating. It can't be the same kind of creature as the last one."

In the quiet, Sam strained his ears. At first, all he could hear was the typical sounds of the forest mixed with the strange moving of the bushes. Then, for a moment, he caught a faint familiar sound. He couldn't quite place it, but the sound reminded him of something buried in the back of his memories.

Sam peeked further under Yetews' arm to take a closer look. The sound was clearer now. Despite the fear gluing his legs to the ground, part of him longed to get an even better look. He inched his way under Yetews' protective stance with wide and wary eyes.

Taren could see Sam's subtle movement out of the corner of his eye. "Don't move any closer Sam," he hissed.

Sam looked over to Taren. "But, I think I hear something. Listen. Can't you hear it?"

As soon as Sam spoke, the movement in the trees froze. Everyone refocused on the now silent spot. The only sounds they could hear now were the sounds of their own breathing. Sam wondered if anyone else could hear the beating of his heart as well as he could.

Taren took a hesitant step closer. Instantly, the quiet was interrupted by a low growl. Even this sound struck a familiar cord in Sam's memory, and against his own better judgment, he took another step forward making himself a more vulnerable target.

The Gateway to Imagia: The Tale of Sam Little

Something whined in the shadows.

Taren's bowstring creaked with tension and he glanced at Yetews to give an order, "Hold Sam back. Don't let him take another step."

It was then, that Yetews realized just how far Sam had inched his way out from behind his shielding stance. He grabbed the boy's shoulder and gently pulled him back out of harm's way.

In that instant, something significantly smaller than the last attacker leapt from the bushes, growling angrily.

Surprise washed over the face of the Protector as he saw what it was and he hesitated just long enough to hear Sam scream out as he fought Yetews' protective hold. "NO! DON'T SHOOT!"

The sudden surprise of Sam's outburst caused Yetews to tighten his hold on the boy and Taren to loosen his aim ever so slightly.

Sam struggled to get free with no sign of progress.

Taren was confused and looked to Sam for an explanation.

Sam wasn't paying attention to Taren's subtlety. He was consumed with his attempt to break Yetews' hold. This only confused Taren further and he pulled his bowstring back again out of fear for the situation.

Sam caught *that* slight movement and protested even louder. "NO! DON'T HURT HIM!"

This time, Taren didn't keep quiet. "Sam, it's not what it seems. It may look like a dog, but it's just another tool of Nadaroth. I have to shoot it before…"

"NO!" Sam interrupted him. "That's not just a dog! It's *my* dog! It's Titus!"

Everyone was stunned by Sam's recognition, but Taren was the one to ask the question that everyone else was thinking. "What do you mean Sam? He can't be your dog. That's…impossible."

Yetews was now protectively holding Sam with both of his arms snugly around his waist.

The dog watched Yetews and growled again, this time baring its white teeth at the Guardian.

Seeing that the only way they would let him go to his dog was by explaining things, Sam calmed down and stopped trying to kick his way free. "It *is* Titus. Just look at him! It looks just like him! I'd know him anywhere. Just let me go to him. Please!"

Taren didn't let his aim fully slide, but relaxed his position for the moment. He looked from Sam to the dog, unsure of the threat. His eyes came to rest on the growling dog and he shook his head. "Sam...this is a trick. Think about it. How could your dog get here? Gateways don't work like that. They are meant for kids. Not dogs."

Though the logic made sense to Sam, he shook his head too, refusing to believe he was wrong. "You don't know that! Gateways were only meant for the person that came here from it and I sent Elizabeth back through mine, so...so..." he hesitated while he desperately looked for a reasonable explanation. He wanted to run to Titus and throw welcoming arms around his shaggy neck.

Taren saw the look of desperation on Sam's face and pitied him. He was just about to lower his bow, when he saw the dog's eyes begin to glow red.

Sam gasped and backed against Yetews' chest.

Taren was right. It was a trick.

The glowing red eyes suddenly reminded Sam of his first nightmare here. It sickened him. It was such a perfect replica of his old friend. But he'd been wrong.

Sam had just enough time to feel the stab of pain in his heart as he realized that this imposter was the last image of Titus he would ever see.

"Run, Yetews!" Taren yelled.

After a split second's hesitation, Yetews turned his back to run from the attacking imposter and Sam was lost in a blinding blur of black hair.

There was commotion all around them.

Something in the trees behind Sam and Yetews was moving again and Sam's mind raced with the thoughts of what was about to happen. He silently hoped that the fake Titus was running away back through the forest. Even if it wasn't really him, he couldn't bear the thought of fighting against it.

He could hear the dog snarling and he thought he could make out the sound of Keesa growling back. There was more commotion and he couldn't place what was happening as Yetews took him further from the danger.

Taren was yelling something that Sam couldn't make out but then, very clearly, he shouted, "KEESA MOVE!"

Then Sam heard three things. The familiar warm sound of Titus' bark, the sickening dull thud of an arrow hitting its target, and a final yelp of pain echoing in the dark.

Yetews came to a sharp stop and quickly pivoted to see what happened. From a distance, all Sam had time to see was the image of his old comrade lying dead with an arrow pierced through him. Though he knew deep down that it wasn't really his dog, he couldn't separate the differences in his mind. The scene was too much for him.

He couldn't fight the feelings of fear and grief any longer as this image finally overwhelmed his mind. He could hear Taren's voice faintly calling to him as he gave up the fight and succumbed once again to the blinding darkness.

* * * * * * * * * *

Something was wet and warm on Sam's cheek.

It was a strange sensation, yet slightly comforting in an odd way.

He couldn't seem to open his eyes just yet. For some reason, they were strangely heavy. He could make out a couple of voices whispering in the background, but they weren't the ones that he had expected to hear.

Secretly, they weren't the ones he *wanted* to hear.

Part of the reason that he couldn't make himself open his eyes, was because he was desperately clinging to the idea that he had dreamt the events he had just experienced. He wanted to believe that when he opened his eyes, he would be home in his bed and waking up to the safety it promised him.

But he knew better than to trust this line of thinking. He knew that what had happened was no dream.

As he had started to think about it, he remembered everything perfectly. He thought back to his sudden choice to send Elizabeth back through his gateway. He ran through the events up until the point of seeing his dog lying broken on the ground.

He didn't want to see that again. The thought of envisioning this was all it took to force open his eyes.

When he had passed out...again...he expected he would have seen more nightmares. So he was pleasantly surprised to not dream at all. It was actually the first good sleep he had gotten since coming to this world.

He slowly fought through the fuzzy haze that held his mind near the brink of consciousness. The voices were clearer now and he was suddenly more aware of the wet sensation on his face.

He started to stir and someone said, "He's finally coming around." It sounded like Taren. "Sam? Can you hear me?"

Sam groaned and realized that the wetness he felt was a slobbery tongue. He feebly pushed whoever it was away. "*Blech*! Stop that!"

He blinked his eyes and looked around. It didn't take very long to understand where he was.

Orga's home.

"Feeling better?" It was Orga. He was standing next to Sam's side.

Sam started to sit up and Taren reached a hand over from his other side to help him. "Ugh...how did we get back here?" asked Sam.

Taren smiled slyly. "Interesting story. We'll share the details with you when you're feeling better. But for now, you might want to say hi to someone before he decides to bite my hand off. And don't be scared...he's not what you'll think he is."

The look on Taren's face was one of amusement and it baffled Sam. He was just about to ask what the heck he was talking about when he was cut short by a loud bark.

At first, a jolt of fear passed through him for the image of the imposter he had recently seen. But after a fleeting look at Taren, the smile on his face told him that there was nothing to dread. That same jolt of panic morphed into a wave of excitement.

"Titus?"

The dog wagged his tail and barked again in reply.

"Titus!" Sam jumped up and threw his arms around the shaggy dog's neck. "No way! But...I don't understand? I thought it was a trick. And what about..."

Taren cut him off with a chuckle as he held his hand up to silence Sam. "I'd say that we could get to the details later, but I suppose there's no convincing you of that." He chuckled again. "First thing's first. You need to eat. Orga has some food for you. You must be starving."

He hadn't really had time to consider his appetite. He still clung to Titus. He was trapped in a strange world, but now he had a small

The Gateway to Imagia: The Tale of Sam Little

piece of his lost home to keep here with him. It didn't seem possible that he should be so lucky to have Titus and Yetews at the same time.

As he thought the name, he remembered his Guardian and best friend. He looked around the room and saw that he was standing a few feet away by the nearest wall. He had a mixture of emotions on his face. There was joy, relief, worry, and something that looked a bit like annoyance. He sat with his arms folded across his chest. "Yetews! Can you believe it? This is who I used to go on my adventures with before you. I mean I always *pretended* that he was you, but now you are both here! And this is just so...so...cool!"

Having Titus with him was enough to dull the ache he felt for his losses.

But he knew that this joy couldn't last forever. It was merely temporary.

His Guardian walked over to him and sighed. He grumbled something too low for even Sam to catch and slightly rolled his eyes. He reached over to tousle his boy's hair like usual.

Taren cleared his throat. "Um, would that be a yes to the food?" He was waving a plate in front of him.

Sam blinked and stood to walk to the table. His stomach growled impatiently. "Yeah. I'm starving! How long have I been sleeping?"

Everyone in the room exchanged concerned looks. "Well, it's been a while. It's afternoon right now," said Taren.

Sam didn't understand why they looked so concerned. It was the longest he'd slept here and to the best of his recollection, it was nightmare-free. He started to dig into the plate of food and said, "So I guess I must have been tired or something if I slept all night. But hey! At least I didn't have any nightmares, right?"

Taren exchanged another worried look with Orga. "Actually, it's been two nights. After you passed out, we thought you would come around rather quickly like last time. But it was a lot for your mind to take in. Of course, Orga has a theory for everything."

This was not what he expected to hear. Two nights of sleeping without waking even once didn't make any sense to him. As far as he knew, he'd never slept that long in his whole life. He was beginning to understand why everyone looked so concerned.

It was actually very heartwarming for him to think that everyone seemed so fretful. However, he put this thought to the back of his mind so that he could concentrate on what he really wanted to know.

With Titus at one side and Yetews at his other, he felt secure and safe. He saw Taren eyeing him cautiously. "Why is everyone looking at me like I'm about to explode?"

Taren's eyes widened in response to that as if the answer was so easy to see. He tapped his chin with one finger and in a slightly amused voice he said, "Hmm...let me think. You've been asleep for almost two whole days, Sam. You just experienced massively shocking events. You have the same power as the person who is solely responsible for the downfall of Imagia and you *know* what traumatic events did to him. You just witnessed a Guardian dying, your dog being killed, were attacked by multiple monsters, and then trapped in a world where you can never go home again. You can't exactly blame us for expecting the worst right now."

"Oh." Sam hadn't even realized that the situation was so similar to Nadaroth's until now. He hadn't lost his Guardian, but he had seen the image of something he loved being killed so it was very close in its similarity. Things were still just too new to him in this world. It would take some time to understand everything. And now that he was truly trapped here, time wouldn't be a problem.

He was a lost one now.

The euphoria he had felt seconds ago already waned. The thought started to sadden him and he didn't want to cry in front of everyone. It would only make them more worried. He couldn't think of a better time to be brave. So he asked, "What happened after I..." He hesitated. He didn't like admitting that he had passed out but there was no other way to say it, so he finished, "...after I passed out? I still don't understand how Titus is here. I thought it was a trick. What happened?"

"Well," Taren started, "it *was* a trick. As Yetews was getting you to a safe point, a lot happened in that short amount of time. The imposter went after you and he started to change – to grow. When he did, Keesa went to stop it. But before she could reach it, something else came at us from the trees. It growled and jumped into the clearing, which was enough to stop that imposter dog in his tracks. When it hesitated, we saw that the creature that growled was another dog just like the first one."

"Titus," guessed Sam.

"Yes, but we assumed it was another trick. I drew my bow to shoot him while Keesa went after the original one. But before I could shoot the new dog, he attacked the first one. Right then, I knew something was off. The imposter kept trying to get free to run after you, but every time it did, the new dog, Titus, kept trying to distract him. It was like he was trying to protect you. So I made a snap decision to trust my instincts. I had Keesa pull Titus off the imposter and when she had him clear, I took my shot. Yetews turned precisely at the wrong moment. If he had turned a few seconds later, you would have seen the real Titus rather than the imposter one." He paused for a moment so that Sam could take it all in. "In the end, Orga believes that you would have still lost consciousness. Your mind had nowhere else to go to deal with all you'd been through."

Sam was still trying to take in what he had heard, but he couldn't understand something. "But why was there even a creature that looked like my dog?"

"I told you that Orga had a theory." He grinned.

Orga smiled back at him. "Yes. I do have a theory. When I saw Nadaroth go through something so similarly tragic, he remained awake. He never gave his mind a moment to heal itself. Your mind recognized that it was being overrun with overwhelming amounts of information and feelings. You are so young to see and deal with such horrific things. The reason you passed out was so that your mind could protect itself from further tragedy. Which is also why I believe you slept for so long. I'm curious. Did you dream at all?"

It took a moment for Sam to think about his answer. He thought back to his dreamless sleep. If he dreamt, then he had no memory of it. He shook his head. "I don't remember anything. I just remember waking up to something licking my face." He smiled. He'd just made the connection that Titus was the one doing the licking.

Orga continued to explain his theory. "There is a place between awake and asleep. It's the place where you are still aware that you are awake, but also aware that you are about to go to sleep. Do you understand what I mean?"

Sam nodded. He knew because every time he fell asleep here, it was the time he was most afraid. "Uh-huh. That's when I feel the nightmares starting."

Orga was nodding too. "Yes. That is the place where Nadaroth can connect with your thoughts and fears and imagine them into reality. I believe that he doesn't sleep. Or at the very least, he tries not to. His mind goes to that place in-between sleep where he can connect to other minds. He uses that connection to create nightmares in people and then uses his imagination to bring those images to life.

"You must have thought about Titus before you fell sleep sometime since your arrival here. Nadaroth imagined his own, much darker version, of Titus. He turned something you loved into one of your worst nightmares. I've seen that happen a lot."

Sam sighed. Imagia was getting more complex the longer he was here. He was wondering if there was any way that he would ever know or understand all of the strange secrets about this world.

He looked down at his faithful dog, not willing to accept that he could possibly be another fake, and scratched behind his ears.

From Sam's other side, Yetews frowned. He leaned into Sam's shoulder to get his attention. Sam reached over to scratch behind one of his long twisted horns.

Now there was only the unanswered question about Titus. "But how is Titus here? I don't remember imagining him. Is it really him?" His voiced started to trail off at the end of his question for fear of what might be said.

Titus looked up at Sam and wagged his bushy tail. It made a dull thumping sound on the aged wooden floor. If Sam didn't know any better, he would guess that Titus was actually enjoying the discussion and wanted nothing more than to join in.

Orga and Taren seemed to be having another silent conversational moment as if asking who would be the next to explain. Taren conceded and raised an eyebrow as he spoke. "Oh, it's him alright." He looked like he wanted to roll his eyes about something.

"How do you know?" Sam asked.

Taren sighed and looked at Titus. He gestured with his hand towards the dog and said, "Why don't you ask him yourself."

That threw Sam for a loop. He wasn't entirely sure if Taren was joking or if he was actually trying to say that Titus was able to speak. The idea seemed even more unbelievable than Titus being here. But then again, he was starting to think that this world held more mysteries than one person could possibly witness.

He waited for a patient moment for some sign that Taren was

kidding. There was no sign of joking in the atmosphere. He asked, "Do you mean that my dog can actually talk? So why hasn't he said anything yet?"

Taren didn't say anything, but instead gestured once more to Titus.

Orga saw the uncertainty in Sam's face. "I think he hasn't spoken out of concern for you. We explained much to him while you slept and he, like Yetews, is worried about you."

Sam didn't know what exactly to say. He'd always talked to Titus at home, but he had never dreamed that one day he would actually be able to talk back.

He chewed on his lip for a moment while he thought of how to start a conversation with his dog without feeling ridiculous. He stopped chewing on his lip and looked into Titus' glossy brown eyes. They looked wiser than he remembered them.

Titus cocked his head and one of his ears twitched forward in anticipation for Sam's unasked question.

Yetews nudged Sam on the back. He whispered reassuring words in his ear.

Sam swallowed loudly. He felt a bit silly about the whole thing. He opened his mouth, but all he could manage to get out was, "Um, hi."

Titus looked over to Yetews in concern.

Yetews grumbled something low.

Titus sighed, which in itself was unnatural for a dog. When he opened his mouth he spoke quite clearly in a deep soothing voice, "Hello Sam."

Sam jumped in surprise, nearly falling off of his seat. "Holy cow! You *can* talk!" He was momentarily shocked and slapped a hand to his forehead. "But how is all of this possible? I mean, when did you get here and why can you talk?" His voice got squeakier the more he asked. "How did you get through the gateway?"

Titus gently answered his friend. "Well, I honestly have very few ideas how this happened. I just know that after you told me to stay, I saw you disappear into the trees. The next second, I saw you standing there in a strange light. You looked like you were waiting for something and I thought it was me. So I ran to you and the next thing I know, I was jumping through the bushes into a clearing. I had heard your voice but barely caught a glimpse of you before I saw that evil creature attacking you. And…well…here we are."

When he finished, Sam sat with his mouth gaping in wonderment. It was as if he had always been capable of talking, but simply chose not to until this moment. He stuttered and then asked, "How come you can talk now?"

Titus shook his head. "I'm not entirely sure, but he has a theory about that as well." He looked to Orga expectantly.

Orga was nodding again. "Once again, yes. I do. I suspect that Titus is the first nonhuman to come here. When he came through, I believe that the gateway gave him the ability to talk. Why? I can only guess. Perhaps, in entering the gateway, Imagia bestowed him with the ability so that he could cope with the world. But these are only theories due to the fact that this is such a unique situation."

Talking to Titus would take some getting used to. Until then, Sam found it slightly easier to talk to Orga. "But I thought only one person can go through a gateway and I sent Elizabeth through."

Orga held up one finger. "Ah, yes…precisely. One *person*. Titus, as you well know, is not a person. I don't think that the Gateway registered his presence, just as it does not register the Guardians coming or going to retrieve their child."

"Oh." Sam looked down at Titus again. This new revelation made him think back to the night he'd arrived in Imagia. He could have easily taken Titus with him but left him behind. The guilt he felt was even more significant now that Titus was here and physically able to understand everything he said. He apologized to Titus.

"I'm sorry I told you to stay."

Titus grinned in a way that showed his sharp white teeth. It was slightly intimidating. "No harm done. To me it was only mere seconds that you were gone. But I am here now." He placed a paw atop one of Sam's knees.

Yetews leaned into Sam's shoulder once more making his presence known to his boy and Sam looked up at him. They smiled at each other and Sam thought he saw that same odd look of annoyance.

Though he was happy to have both Yetews and Titus here to share his life sentence in Imagia, it was also a forever reminder of what he left behind.

His heart began to ache as the joy wore thinner. Afraid that his friends would see the masked sorrow, he opted for his comfort zone and stared down at his dirty shoes.

Before he could think of any more questions for his dog, Orga said, "Speaking of 'no harm done.' I think it's time we have a little talk about what you *have* done, Sam. "

Though he knew that Orga was not one of his parents, he felt that a reprimanding was imminent. He sheepishly grinned up at the aged Guardian and waited for what would come next.

Chapter Twelve: Lost

The majesty that Imagia held was still a form of wonderment in itself for Sam. He believed that no one would ever experience all of the wonders it could possibly offer. Especially when so many of those wonders were still being created by the imaginations of children in the outside world. But this thought alone was no longer enough to bring him the joy he felt upon his arrival.

Another day was already nearly over. No one was completely convinced that Sam's spur of the moment decision to send Elizabeth through his gateway was the best course of action on his part. They replayed the events of that fateful evening over and over again, much to Sam's dismay.

They were very impressed by his selfless act of courage but also very disappointed by his apparent lack of respect for the danger he had put himself in.

Everyone had voiced an opinion on the matter to Sam. Keesa was genuinely worried for him. Yet she was content to still enjoy his presence and she had chosen to remain at his side until no longer needed. After realizing her cubs were lost, she developed a strange attachment to the small boy. She was showing an extraordinary desire to protect him as one of her own.

Taren remained adamant that Sam was unaware of the seriousness of the situation. Though even in his reprimanding, there was a hint of something more underneath. There was a spark of hope fighting to be free.

Orga had been less direct than the others. He seemed to weigh the negative and positive of the situation as he made his points. He always came back to the issue of Sam's power. If controlled, it could be just as powerful as Nadaroth's. But he was also quite concerned about the events that Sam had set in motion and was unsure what consequences may take place from sending someone through the wrong gateway.

Titus remained quiet, for the most part, only intervening when attention was drawn to him. He was still so new to this world that the only thing he was sure of was his loyalty to Sam. Everything else about this world was unsettling and would take getting used to.

But Yetews, especially, showed his true feelings for the matter. He had one job. And, by Sam's own hand, had failed. He expressed his feelings clearly. He was in the middle of another round of self-criticism as a Guardian when Sam finally shouted, "Stop it! That's enough!"

Everyone looked at him. He wanted to yell at them. The constant debating about a choice that he could never change was wearing thin on his already fragile ten-year old emotions. He had a million things to say, but if he tried to say them, he knew they would come out jumbled and confused.

A part of him wanted to stomp off to be alone and gather his thoughts. The reasonable part told him that no one would let him be alone right now so it would be pointless to try. Instead, he took a deep breath and calmed himself before trying to gather his thoughts before they could start debating again. He concentrated on breathing as the desire to throw a tantrum faded.

He got his best defense ready and looked around at everyone. "Sorry. I didn't mean to yell like that. But no one has let me say anything about this. You have no idea how I feel right now. I didn't even know what I was doing. I just did what I felt was right and now it's done. I'm really sorry, but I can't change what I did." He paused and bit his lip to fight back his true emotions.

They had no idea just how sorry he was. Sorry he would never go home. Sorry he would never see his family again. Sorry that he would never have his mom there to hug him when he was sad, or his dad to watch a movie with. Sorry that he'd put Yetews in constant danger. And sorry he'd never be able to tell anyone he loved that he was okay. He hung his head. "It's done."

"Sam," Orga said, "we are the ones who should be sorry. We shouldn't scold you for such a selfless act." He reached a hand over to comfort him. "The reason we are so upset is because we do care about you; some of us more than others. And you are right. What is done is done. I think by now you are fully aware of the seriousness of this situation. We will *all* try to be more understanding of your actions." He threw a very meaningful glance towards Taren and added, "And your loss."

Yetews had a guilty grin on his face. He grumbled something apologetically.

Sam grinned back. "Nah. I'm not mad. Are you mad at me?"

Yetews pat him a little too hard on his back and chuckled while shaking his head.

The tension was fading from the room. There was hope in this otherwise bleak moment. There were plans to be made and matters to discuss.

What now felt like weeks ago, they had all witnessed his ability to imagine. Sam had a remarkable power. There were both spoken and unspoken hopes that he could be the way to bring an end to the destruction that Nadaroth had brought to Imagia. It was time to think about the next steps he would take to do everything in his power to make everyone safe again.

It was a lot to think about. A week ago, the worst thing he had to worry about was where to hide his vegetables at dinner. Now he was being marked as the future hero of another world. He'd always imagined things like this, but never thought in all of his days that he would ever see such a time come to pass. There were dangerous outside forces working against him. It was no longer about controlling his imagination. Now it was as if his imagination were controlling him.

It was a frightening idea. But if ever there were a time to be as brave as he always believed he was, then it had come. He made a

The Gateway to Imagia: The Tale of Sam Little

conscious decision to hide his fear as best as he could.

It wasn't going to be easy.

Orga interrupted Sam's thoughts. "The question we need to ask you, Sam, is going to determine what will happen from now on. What do you want to do now? You have limited options. You could go to the Village of Exile and live with the lost ones of your world." Orga paused as if waiting for Sam to discover another option on his own.

Sam knew what his next option was. "Or I can try to fight Nadaroth. Right?"

"Yes," Taren answered. "And no. You can't just walk up to him and start fighting. It will take time and training to learn how your power works and learn to control it. And that won't be easy because none of us know exactly why or how you can do it."

Sam was nodding as Taren spoke. "Let's start now!" He didn't try to hide his eagerness. More than anything he was keen to do something to keep his mind busy. "I mean, we can go outside right now and I'll start trying to imagine things."

Yetews was voicing his disapproval of leaving the safety of Orga's home. Sam translated for everyone.

"We'll be fine here. Nothing dangerous has entered this area of the forest for a very long time thanks to Taren." Orga smiled at the Protector.

Taren looked like he could have blushed, but didn't. He merely half-grinned. The hope that he had buried before was starting to inch its way closer to the surface. "I suppose there is no better time than the present. Besides, Warg is still outside and would probably enjoy the company. He really has taken kindly to Titus."

Sam thought of Orga's strange crocodile-like pet and couldn't imagine a stranger pair when matched with his quite normal looking dog. He was excited to do something now. "Great! What should I imagine first?" asked Sam.

Orga got up slowly and motioned towards the door. "Not inside please. I'm quite fond of my home and I prefer it in one piece," he joked.

Everyone else followed Orga's lead and headed for the door. Sam was protectively placed in the middle of the group with Taren leading the way and Keesa guarding the tail.

As Sam walked outside, he could feel a change in his friends' demeanors. Their hope was starting to shine through and it warmed him. It was a nice change from the daunting fear.

* * * * * * * * *

"Good job Sam!" Taren's spirit lifted higher with every successful creation that Sam imagined. At first, his skepticism in Sam's abilities was not easy to miss. He didn't try to hide his feelings that this entire plan was nothing more than false hope in a small boy. After Orga reminded him that Nadaroth was younger when he came here and that his power was nothing to scoff at, Taren seemed to lose his negative edge.

At first, they tried to get Sam to imagine things that they would describe in their best details. Another flower to begin with, then a trio of trees, moving on to more complex things like birds and small creatures. Eventually they gave him more freedom to choose what he imagined. Sam enjoyed creating creatures more than the inanimate objects, so they just asked him to keep the creations to a low level of danger.

So far, Taren had only had to pull his bow out once purely out of precaution. It turned out that the strange horse sized hairy creature was totally harmless and it ambled away into the trees unscathed.

Orga was extremely impressed with how quick Sam was learning. His latest creation was a pale white butterfly that glittered and glowed brilliantly as it fluttered off into the dimming woods. It was one of Sam's own personal creations. As the glow of the butterfly moved deeper into the trees, Orga mindlessly scratched Warg and Titus' heads. He was deep in thought.

Sam watched him and wondered what he was thinking. "Did I do something wrong that time?" he asked quietly.

Though the question was not directed towards her, Keesa answered, "Not at all! That was, again, quite remarkable." With her new attachment to Sam, she had also grown very supportive of all he did. Though at times it bordered on annoying, Sam was okay with it. It reminded him of his mom, so was actually a bit comforting. He returned her smile.

After Keesa's encouragement, Orga answered as well. "On the contrary, you did that quite well. I was merely considering something.

The Gateway to Imagia: The Tale of Sam Little

It seems that even the images that are not solely of your creation are just as powerful. None of the images you have managed to create have faded away yet. The more strongly you are connected with the image you create, the longer they remain in existence."

Taren nodded in agreement. "But we already know that's how it works."

"Yes," Orga continued, "but, technically, the less important things, like the flowers, should have faded by now. When Nadaroth displayed his abilities so long ago, every image that I asked him to make faded nearly as quickly as it was created. Only the images he concocted remained solid."

Taren didn't respond. Instead, he beamed at Sam and his once masked hope poured freely from his soul.

Sam, of course, couldn't possibly imagine why everyone's hope seemed to grow so quickly. The idea of seeking out the monster that could do such evil things to this world was not something he enjoyed thinking about. So far only one quarter of the images that he'd tried to imagine actually appeared. He knew that it would take years of training to become capable of defeating such a dangerous foe.

He kept thinking of himself as being more like Taren. He hadn't told anyone, but he knew that he wanted to become a Protector too. He didn't know how fast he would grow up – or at the very least, grow bigger – but he was certain that it would take a while before he was big enough to learn the vast skills of his friend.

All the thinking and imagining was starting to take its toll on Sam. After all, he was still a ten-year old kid, and no matter how much sleep he had in his system, it still wasn't enough to keep his young eyes open indefinitely. Though he was far from sleep, he yawned hugely.

Orga noticed and left his silent thoughts behind him as he sighed. "I think perhaps it may be time to end our experimenting for now. Evening is upon us and so is dinner-time."

Yetews' stomach rumbled as if in answer to the suggestion. He rubbed his belly and growled in agreement.

They headed for the slanting entrance to Orga's home. Sam was playfully punching at Yetews in a mock fight as they walked slowly back. The idea of food gave him a new burst of energy.

Keesa was again patiently bringing in the rear of the group, when she suddenly stiffened and sniffed the air. She bared her fanged jaws and whipped around, ears laid back. Because she was behind everyone, no one noticed her sudden shift until she started growling.

Sam was too busy in his mock battling to understand why everyone was suddenly looking behind them. His heart sank when he noticed the looks on their faces. Then he heard a sound that he was all too familiar with. The bushes and trees were moving far too angrily and the sharp sounds of cracking branches were almost painful to his ears. His heart felt like it was fighting to break through his chest as he silently cursed the forest. He quickly thought of how comforting wide-open spaces would be, where trees couldn't hide your advancing enemies.

The scene was nearly the same as the night of that vivid nightmare. The only difference being that their party had increased by three. Titus had moved in front of Sam with his hackles raised. He growled in perfect sync with Keesa.

The creature that tore through the trees would have been a perfect replica of the one he had imagined before. It even had the same foul scent. But this one was significantly larger. The clearing that they stood in was wider than the one before, so they used that to their advantage.

Taren, Keesa, Titus, and Yetews were spread in an arc as Orga was pulling a very stunned Sam backwards.

The creature paused and sniffed the air to find its target. It growled low when it picked up the scent it was seeking. Sam looked over at his Guardian, certain the creature was about to strike him and yelled, "NO! YETEWS!"

The beast ignored the four obvious threats to its goal and charged for Sam through Taren's rain of arrows. Taren must have expected its target to be Yetews too because shock swept over him when he realized the monstrosity was aiming for Sam.

As Sam was being herded away, he lost his footing and fell hard. There was a sharp pain as something jagged tore through his pants and cut through the skin of his knee. He was aware that the wound was bleeding but didn't have time to react to the pain. He could feel the ground trembling as the creature closed in. He threw his arms over his head in anticipation of the attack.

The attack never happened. The beast howled in pain a few yards away. Sam risked a look and saw that Keesa was on its back, tearing through its thick hair with her saber teeth then clamping down hard on the neck. It flailed its arms furiously to pull her off, but failed. Titus had dodged through its legs to clamp down on a massive ankle. Seeing his dog react so viciously was unnerving to him.

There were arrows protruding from all angles of the monster's body. Yetews was behind it, standing on his hind legs, pulling the creature backwards to the ground.

Through the madness, Sam couldn't help but notice how impressively huge and strong Yetews was. He didn't have much time to think about this, for when the creature hit the ground, everyone scattered just in time for Taren to shoot a trio of arrows with fatal aim that inevitably removed the creature as a threat.

It shuddered once and then, after a feeble, gargling groan, was still.

Sam was already in Yetews' arms before Taren could speak. "Everyone inside," he ordered. Out of breath and hearts still pumping hard, they moved inside without the slightest bit of hesitation.

After composing themselves, they attempted to make sense of the sudden attack. There was something disbelieving in the stare that Taren held on Sam.

Sam was bewildered by the sudden attack. But more so, he was now overly aware of the throbbing pain in his knee and had thoughts for nothing else.

As Yetews put him down, Sam winced. Yetews immediately noticed what the source of his pain was. He scooped him back into his arms and placed him on the table, grumbling his worries all the while.

It became suddenly obvious to the others that not everyone came away unscathed from the attack. Orga was already fumbling around to find something to stop the bleeding and bandage the wound.

Sam tried to ease their minds with a brave façade. Though his words were for everyone, he directed them mostly to his Guardian. "I'm okay. Really. It's not that bad." He winced again when he moved his leg, revealing his true pain. He grabbed at his knee and gasped from the sudden movement. He tried to straighten his leg but it only made the pain worse.

Yetews rolled his eyes and gently tore the bottom half of his ruined pants away. He moved to Sam's side to give Orga room to work.

Orga had Taren make a tourniquet to stop the bleeding and began to wash away the blood. After the wound was cleansed, Sam could see just how bad it looked. The gash was wide and deep, straight through to the bone. The cut from his big bike crash last summer looked like nothing compared to this, and he had even gotten four stitches out of that. He didn't want to think about how they would fix this.

"What now?" Sam asked.

Orga, concentrating on the injury, said, "I'll worry about this, you just try not to watch. Focus on something else."

Yetews noticed the subtle glance from Orga. He knew that the look was meant to get him to distract Sam. He tried to converse with his boy and even tried to get him to look away, but to no avail.

Sam continued to watch as Orga's long, brown fingers elegantly worked on his injury. He was adamant to watch the whole thing until Orga squeezed a strange pod that oozed purple goo over the gaping wound. There was a hissing sound as the goo started to bubble. Suddenly, his knee felt as though it had burst into flames. "OW!" he hissed through gritted teeth. He clenched his hands tightly around the edge of the table and then closed his eyes.

"Give it a moment to work," Taren said to him. "The burning will stop soon." He was obviously speaking from experience.

Taren was right. The burning was disappearing, replaced by numbness. He decided that he didn't want to see what else Orga would do, so opened his eyes and focused on everything else in the room. He noticed that Taren was still staring bewildered at him. He hoped that conversation would take his mind off of the unnerving tugging sensation he now felt on his knee, so he risked a question. "Why are you looking at me like that?"

He frowned back and said, "What is it with you? First a dormant deceptor leaves its hole to try and eat you. Then the creature from your nightmare tries to kill us. Then there was the gateway attack followed directly by the imposter Titus. And now a larger version of the same creature that tried to kill us a few nights ago makes a cameo appearance specifically aimed at attacking – not your Guardian – but you."

Sam didn't know how to respond, so he just shrugged. "So? I

The Gateway to Imagia: The Tale of Sam Little

thought that was normal for this place now."

Orga, still working on the cut, replied to Sam's comment. "Taren is right. The multiple attacks are…unusual. Though there are many dangers in Imagia, never have I heard of so many directed towards a single target. Normally, they aim for Guardians, and even that is a random and unpredictable event. But all these attacks seem to center around your presence. They haven't even recognized Yetews as a viable target. That is highly unusual behavior."

Sam mumbled something about the gateway attack and how it only went after the unicorn Guardian, but was interrupted when Taren ignored his quiet reasoning. He looked at Orga and said, "It can't wait."

"What can't wait?" asked Sam.

Orga fidgeted as he worked. "I feared that your actions could have drastic repercussions. Apparently I wasn't mistaken. It looks like Nadaroth may be aware of your specific presence here. Whether he knows who you are or what you are capable of, I don't know. But he must be able to recognize your mind and link to it when you are falling asleep. It's the only way to explain why you have been targeted so often. Usually his connections to sleeping minds are random at best. Occasionally he finds specific or vulnerable minds that he can reconnect to twice in a night, but it's rare." His shoulders fell slightly as he continued. "The best way we know how to stop these attacks from happening is to avoid sleep for the night to break the bond. But I've never seen it go on like this. And seeing as how you can't stay awake forever, your only other choice is to stop the source or risk that one of his attacks is more successful. You have to stop Nadaroth. Soon."

Sam's heart skipped a beat when Orga spoke those last words. He couldn't understand how this was all happening so fast. He looked around, hoping that there could be some other way. It was too soon for him and he wasn't ready. He thought he had years to prepare for this.

When the faces in the room mirrored Orga's, he knew that he only had two options now. Wait here and hope that he could successfully hide and survive with Yetews in a constant state of fear, or be strong and fight against the very thing that was trying to destroy him.

It was hard to think that something so terrifying was capable of such a strong hate for him when they didn't even know each other. And he asked himself if he was even capable of any of this. He was, after all, only a boy.

As if Orga could read every emotion on Sam's face, he said, "I know this can't be what you hoped for, but if you want to survive in Imagia with Yetews, then time is no longer on your side. The only way either of you can be safe again is to stop Nadaroth."

When Orga finished with his leg, Sam swung it off of the table and pretended to examine it. It was stiff and felt swollen.

He was considering the situation he was in. When he could no longer pretend to be examining his leg, he looked over and met Yetews' watchful gaze.

As he looked into those gentle, green eyes, he knew that all the choices were gone, save one. He knew that, like so many before him, he was now one of the lost ones. This mess was mostly his fault. His actions had set into motion a very real and exceedingly dangerous adventure. He would make the best of his time here. He nodded and sucked in a deep breath. "Okay. So what do we do now?"

Taren walked over and grinned reassuringly down at Sam. He clapped a hand on his small shoulder and answered, "We train."

The Gateway to Imagia: The Tale of Sam Little

Chapter Thirteen: Tricks

Nearly three weeks had passed since the last attack on Sam. His knee was almost healed. It only ached when he was trying to sleep. Orga had done a fairly good job of patching him up considering his resources. There was a jagged, paling scar, but Sam didn't mind that so much. He had quite a few scars and he thought of them as battle wounds. The difference between this scar and the rest of them was that this scar was actually from a battle.

So far, Orga had proved to be a very gracious host. He had taken it upon himself to take care of the greater needs of everyone. There was always food and a friendly fire to keep them warm on the chillier nights.

Sam was also impressed to find that Orga's home was larger than he had originally noticed. The first time he had visited the inside of the home, they had never ventured further than the one over-sized room that they spent so much time in. Sam had never even noticed the hallway or the three small rooms that branched off from it.

He later found out that over time and with the help of friends, Orga had added a few rooms to his home to accommodate the occasional guests and lost ones that Taren would find. The rooms weren't especially cozy, but after a week of training, Sam used some of his sleepless nights to practice imagining inanimate objects. He started with a bed and by the end of his second week the room he was staying in very closely resembled his bedroom from back home.

The major difference was the massive, fluffy pillow that he had imagined for Yetews to sleep on. Yetews had insisted on sleeping on the floor, so they came to a compromise. Instead of a large bed, they settled for a floor pillow that looked something like a dog bed big enough for a buffalo.

Since Sam was still waking frequently to his own screams, he felt more comforted having Yetews sleeping close to him. Taren had decided to stay in the room across from them as a precaution. As there were no doors, it was easy for him to watch over Sam on the particularly bad nights when the nightmares were especially frightening. It was difficult for everyone to hear the screams and not feel compelled to rush to his bedside.

Titus was pleased to sleep on the foot of Sam's bed, much to Yetews' annoyance. Sam was becoming more aware of the jealously that had sparked in him since Titus' arrival. He was just happy to have them both with him, so he pretended not to notice.

Keesa had the most difficulty sleeping inside at night. Her preferred hunting time was night. But she'd changed that pattern most nights to stay close to Sam in his most difficult moments. She spent a lot of time hunting in the forest during the day, but when night came, she mostly just paced the hallway out of boredom. After tiring, she would inevitably settle in the hall outside of Sam's room.

All in all, the training was going well. By the end of the third week, Sam had imagined so many different things into existence that he was running out of ideas. Very few of the objects had faded and he had learned how to control himself much better.

There were, however, some challenges that Taren and Orga had asked of him, which he couldn't manage to wrap his mind around. For the last few days, Sam had been trying to manipulate the objects that he had already imagined. It was something that Nadaroth had mastered. He was capable of changing the things he had previously created as well as altering his own image. Sam was growing frustrated the more times he failed.

On this particular evening, it was actually raining outside. It was

The Gateway to Imagia: The Tale of Sam Little

the first time that the weather had changed so drastically since his arrival in Imagia. The amount of time they spent outside of the home was limited for fear of being attacked. Even on clear days, they were edgy and extra cautious of the forest around them. Rain, mixed with the sunless sky, made it more difficult to hear or see any unwanted guests. So once the rain started, they moved inside into the main room.

Sam had imagined a flower, much like the first one he created. It grew through the slats in the floorboards as if it had been growing there for years. He was focusing very hard on the oddly placed plant. His eyes were pinched in the middle, wrinkling his nose in concentration. He'd been trying to change the color of the flower from blue to red to no avail.

Finally, after another long minute of concentration, he exhaled quickly and relaxed his fists. His shoulders fell. "I just can't do it. It's impossible!"

It had been the tenth time today that Sam had made the same assumption, but Orga remained patient. "It was years before I saw Nadaroth's imagination capable of morphing. We are asking a great deal from you in a very short time frame. These things will take time. Your skills improve everyday. It's only a matter of practice."

It had been a long three weeks and Sam's irritation with the situation combined with the unfailing optimism that everyone was showing towards his abilities, was starting to annoy him. His brow furrowed when he looked up at Orga. He could feel himself about to lose his temper, but when he saw the sparkle in those beady eyes and the warmth of his gesture, he sighed and decided to not fight the matter. Instead, he voiced his concern for the situation. "I know you want me to do this, but I just don't think I can. I mean…if Nadaroth and me are the only ones who have ever been able to imagine like this, then how do you know that we are the same? I mean, maybe this is something I *can't* do. No one even knows how he does it. So, how am I supposed to learn it?"

Orga's face fell ever so slightly at this thought. He considered his answer very briefly. "That's a compelling question. Indeed. How can you learn something that no one knows how to teach? In reality, we are all learning. We can only offer suggestions. Make theories. We can only hope that we find the key to unlock the mystery of these powers you hold." He watched Sam's face fall. "I know that this feels hopeless to you Sam, but you are doing extraordinarily well. And we aren't going to push you out the door to send you to your doom. You've been free of attacks for nearly three weeks. I think we are safe to keep training for the time being." He smiled, hoping to raise Sam's spirits.

But Sam knew that Orga was merely trying to build his confidence and he appreciated the gesture. He answered with a half genuine smile so as not to disappoint the old Guardian's effort.

Taren, who had been leaning quietly against the wall, walked over to Orga and put a hand on his shoulder. "I think that it's time for a break." Sam thought he noticed a strange look in Taren's eyes, but it was gone before he could figure out what it was. "Perhaps we should take a break from training for the day. We can start again in the morning. Dinner might be the best thing for us all right now."

Orga, not seeming to see the strange look that Sam had noticed, simply nodded and said, "Yes. Let's eat, shall we?" Both Orga and Taren disappeared into another room and Sam, exhausted from the constant concentration, slumped down in front of Yetews. He rubbed his eyes and yawned loudly. It was easy to notice the faint shadows underneath his eyes that he had developed from his restless nights. He leaned back against one of Yetews' massive arms.

He felt the exhaustion settling in and in fear of falling asleep too soon, talked to Yetews. "I'm starving. Do you think we are having those really good cakes that he makes?"

Yetews groaned hopefully.

"Yeah. I hope he has more too. But they aren't as good as my mom's cookies. She makes the best cookies in the world. I wish you could try them. I bet you'd eat a hundred of them! There's no way she could make enough." He laughed and so did Yetews.

But after the laughter stopped, Sam started to feel the pain of never seeing his mom again. When his face noticeably shifted moods, Yetews instantly knew that he needed to change the subject to spare his boy the heartache.

He grumbled a question.

Sam shrugged. "Nope. I don't think I can change the stupid thing's color no matter *how* hard I try." He looked over at the flower and then up at Yetews. There was a familiar hint of optimism in his innocent eyes. "You think I can do it too, don't you?"

Yetews shrugged his hairy shoulders and then nodded sheepishly.

Sam looked around the room and noticed that even Titus and Keesa had some form of confidence in their faces. Though he knew that they didn't mean to annoy him, the atmosphere of the large room started to irritate him. When he made his wish to make his imagination real, this isn't exactly how he planned things would turn out. He never asked for this.

Keesa grinned from the darkened corner of the room. "You'll find a way to master this ability. I've seen you do many things already. You must be a powerful young cub to do what you do."

Titus trotted over to him and dropped his head into Sam's hands. With a caring nudge, he said, "It really is amazing, this power you have. Nothing like you had back home."

Titus agreeing with everyone else was the last straw. His dog was the last shred of home and normalcy that he had in this place.

He suddenly wanted everyone to stop being so hopeful and realize that they were putting too much faith in him. It was silly and absurd. His mind started reeling with ways he could leave the room so he didn't have to deal with it any longer. He didn't understand how they couldn't see the hopelessness of the situation. "You guys don't understand. This just feels impossible!"

As if on cue, Taren and Orga came back into the room. "You're right, Sam," said Orga. "There may be a good reason why Nadaroth can do this and you cannot."

Taren added, "We were just having a discussion about your age. When Nadaroth came here, he was younger than you. Maybe you are too old. Perhaps your imagination was already in the process of slipping away when you arrived and that's why you keep failing. We really should just be thankful that you have any power at all and accept that your imagination has reached its limits. We simply need to work with what you *can* do and stop pushing you to do what you can't. We can only hope that you won't lose your imagination completely over time."

Orga added, "Don't worry Sam. We will just keep concentrating on imagining things. It's okay that you can't morph objects."

Sam couldn't believe what he was hearing. They were so sure of him minutes before. Now they seemed to have given up so easily. He had wanted them to understand how hopeless things seemed, but to believe that his imagination was on the verge of disappearing was too much. It was about to send him over the edge. He'd already lost so much since coming here and he wasn't about to lose his imagination as well.

Everyone was watching him carefully as if he was a ticking time bomb and about to explode. But Sam didn't want to react irrationally.

He wanted to prove them wrong.

He stood up and looked over at the flower growing in the middle of the room. He was furious with the situation now. He was determined to let everyone know that he would never lose the ability to imagine no matter what they said. It meant too much to him. He looked at Taren and realized that he couldn't – wouldn't – accept his assumption.

Sam closed his eyes and bowed his head. Unlike the many attempts before, he felt completely relaxed. Despite his anger, his hands didn't clench into tight fists and his face was no longer pinched in concentration. He could see the flower, clear as day in his mind and slowly began to shift the color from Blue to Red. He watched through closed eyes as brilliant shades of red bled into the deep blue hue of the petals until the flower was a scarlet masterpiece.

When it was exactly how he wanted it, he slowly looked up to see all eyes on the flower. It had worked. Sam smiled defiantly.

Taren had a sly smirk on his face and glanced over to Sam then shifted his eyes back to Orga who looked ecstatic.

"Apparently all it takes is the proper form of motivation," Taren stated.

Now Sam was confused. "Huh?"

A devilish smile kicked the corner of his mouth up. "It's simple, really. I convinced Orga that your previous signs of attachment to your imagination could work in our favor if we planned it just right. Though he didn't exactly agree that threatening another loss of something you hold so dear was a particularly kind act, he agreed that it was worth a try."

Still confused, Sam said, "I don't understand."

Taren tried to explain. "My theory was that if you were properly motivated, that you would be able to morph the flower. I know that you don't like the idea of losing the ability to imagine so I simply

The Gateway to Imagia: The Tale of Sam Little

pushed you into believing that it was happening already. Did it make you angry?"

Sam nodded as he began to understand.

"Then my plan worked. You wanted to prove us wrong and...well...you did."

"Oh," was all Sam could say. He knew that he should be mad, but he felt more pleased than anything. Even if it was a sneaky trick, at least he knew he was capable of morphing.

Taren looked smug about the whole thing. Orga chimed in with an apology. "I hope you can forgive us. I know that you are still dealing with so much for such a young age. We meant no true harm." The excitement he showed for the recent success was now muddied with regret.

Sam looked over his shoulder at a beaming Yetews then back to Orga. He didn't want to ruin this moment of joy for them so he said, " S'okay." And now, longing for a subject change, he suggested what his exhausted body wanted most. "Can we eat now? I'm starving."

Accepting this as a sign of forgiveness, Orga nodded and scrounged up the dinner. Including, to Sam's delight, the tasty cakes.

Keesa eagerly left for an evening hunt in the forest. On the odd occasion she left the confines of Orga's home at night, she would rarely be back to sleep with them inside. They would always wake up to find her outside basking in the early morning sun.

The rain was hammering on the roof and showed no signs of letting up. Sam kept peeking outside expecting Keesa to return to the dry indoors. He figured that she was soaked to the bone by now.

Taren reassured Sam, "She's fine, Sam. She's used to sleeping in the forest. Remember? She'll find shelter."

Sam glanced once more out the dingy window and then walked back over to Yetews. "Yeah. I guess I keep forgetting where we found her. She just seems so...I dunno."

"Human?" Taren completed his thought.

Sam nodded. "It's just still a little weird."

Taren was silently agreeing with him. "You get used to the strangeness over time. Trust me."

Another day was coming to an end and the unusual gloom of the day pushed everyone into an early sleep.

Sam, mentally exhausted from the trials of the day, slumped into his bed without a further thought. The rain had slacked off and the soft plinking of it outside was relaxing. Even Yetews yawned wider than usual.

It didn't take long for most everyone to drift into sleep. Sam feared another night of disturbing dreams and nightmares. But the exhaustion of the day seemed worse than usual. He felt like he'd worked twice as hard today than the days before and he'd only imagined half as much. His concern for this was fleeting though. He barely even tossed and turned until he found a comfortable position. He felt himself slipping into the familiar place between sleep and awake.

Of his entire night, this was his favorite part. He never saw anything bad here. It was mostly just pleasant images of his past or present. It was like a mental diary that he kept right before going to sleep.

Images and thoughts began to flutter through his mind haphazardly. One image stood out among them. It was a beautiful glowing creature that bore a likeness to the one he saw in his first dream. The one difference between them was that this creatures face reminded him of his mom. It was warm and lovely. He could hear her whispering his name in the dark of his mind.

As he listened to her, he realized that she was calling to him. It sounded a bit like his mom too. As he heard the soft voice, it hurt. He felt his eyes fill with tears. He couldn't tell if the tears were a part of this dream or if they were real.

It was hard to hear her voice and see her face and know that it could never really be true. He also knew that it wasn't really his mom. This creature had inhuman features and glowed like an angel. Yet he wanted nothing more than to run to this creature and feel the warmth of its embrace. The longer he watched her, the more like his mother she appeared to become. His heart ached harder.

A loud crash of thunder suddenly shook Sam awake. His cheeks were wet from the tears that spilled over from his dream. He wiped them away with the back of his hand and as the thunder rolled away, something caught his ear.

A whisper.

It was the same voice from his dream.

"*Sam...*" the voice whispered.

The Gateway to Imagia: The Tale of Sam Little

Sam's heart raced. He looked around the room at his sleeping companions. Either they hadn't heard it yet, or he was still dreaming.

"*Sam...I'm here,*" it whispered again.

He looked around the darkened room and decided to sneak past his friends to find the source of the voice. He tiptoed past Taren's room, down the hall, and towards the door to the outside. The voice hadn't called to him again, so he climbed up and peeked though the dingy window of the door to see if anything was outside.

At first all he could see or hear was the rain as it came down steadily. There was a flash of lightning followed by another clap of thunder.

Something touched his hand and he jumped, nearly falling from his stoop atop the box he'd moved to stand on. It was Warg. He was happily looking up at Sam, waiting for affection.

"Shhh...do you want to wake everyone?" He reached down and pat the scaly head and Warg waddled away to his corner to go back to sleep.

As the light from the lightning faded, a soft glow took its place. Sam saw it from the corner of his eye and looked back out the window.

He blinked and tried to place its source. But he couldn't manage to see where it was coming from. It was a pale, white glow from somewhere outside.

He started to feel a twinge of fear and thought perhaps he should wake Taren. Then the voice called to him again.

"*I'm here, Sam.*"

Sam's heart raced. He had an overwhelming urge to go to the voice. He looked around hesitantly, but convinced himself to get a closer look. He opened the door as quietly as he could. He was sure that the rusty hinges would give him away, but there was no sign that it had woken anyone.

He inched up the slanting entrance of Orga's home. He plodded through the rain. As the water dripped down into his eyes he saw that the glow became brighter. As he stepped into the clearing, he saw the woman-like creature from his dream. She was smiling warmly at him.

She opened her arms, beckoning to him.

Sam froze, unsure what to do. He took a half step back.

Then she smiled at him again and said, "I'm here Sam. Come to me."

She sounded and looked so much like his mom. He tried to convince himself that if Titus had found his way here, that maybe his mom had found a way too. And if the gateway could change Titus, then it could have changed his mom as well.

She spoke his name again and spread her arms wider. "Sam."

The temptation to leap into her arms was building. He hesitated before he spoke, but then said, "Mom?"

She smiled wider.

He watched her and as much as he wanted to believe that it was true, he knew that it was impossible. The only feasible explanation for her likeness to his mom was that he was still dreaming. And if he was dreaming he might as well enjoy the moment.

One foot slowly broke free of its frozen state and the next foot closely followed. His bare feet squished in the mud and he became oddly aware that he wasn't wearing shoes.

He inched closer to her. There were only a few yards between them now. He was about to start running to her when he was faintly aware of the door behind him opening again.

It was Taren. "Sam? What are you doing out here? Are you...?" He stopped mid question when he noticed what Sam was about to do. "SAM!"

Sam turned away from the glowing creature to look back at Taren. When he saw Taren's eyes wide with fear, he didn't understand. He didn't want Taren to frighten the creature away. He looked back around to tell her to not be afraid.

But when he turned to face her, she was no longer beautiful. Her eyes glowed red and her hair turned to fire. It was a terrifying image. She called to Sam again, but this time her voice was rough and raised the hairs on Sam's neck. He stumbled back two steps through the mud and slipped, falling on his backside.

Taren was in front of him before he could make sense of the situation. He was without his bow, but reached down into his boot and pulled out something that gleamed silver in the falling rain. With a tactful flick of his wrist, the dagger shot though the air and caught the creature in the chest.

It shrieked in pain but the dagger only managed to anger it more. The flames that encircled its head now consumed it. The creature shrieked like a banshee and fell forward onto her hands. It shuddered and morphed into a blazing wolf-like beast. It took a step forward and the puddles of water hissed and sizzled as the fire touched it. It flicked its tail like a bullwhip and snarled low. The image of Taren desperately shielding Sam reflected in its eyes as it watched them.

It pulled back, preparing to lunge. Taren yelled, "NO! RUN, SAM!"

Sam couldn't run. He was frozen in shock.

The creature lunged at them. In mid jump, something from the left made hard contact with it and there were now two bodies entangled as they fell to the ground. Taren and Sam looked over and saw a mess of wet tawny hair circling the stupefied creature. It was Keesa. She roared at the beast and suddenly the two were entangled again. The creature was stunned by the sudden attack and retreated into the dark of the forest, Keesa in pursuit. The eerie glow of the creature faded along with the silhouette of Keesa.

Taren pulled Sam up and forced him harshly down the ramp, back into the safety of the home. Out of breath from the ordeal, he shook Sam's shoulders roughly and gasped out between breaths, "What...were you...thinking? You can't just wander outside like that! Are you trying to get yourself *killed*?" He was livid.

Sam had never seen him like this and didn't know how to respond. He felt ashamed for being so easily tricked. It was like the deceptor all over again.

By this time, everyone had woken and come to see what the ruckus was all about. Taren was suddenly aware that he was still gripping Sam a little too firmly and eased his hold on him. He seemed to be trying to make some sense of the confused stares.

Orga squeezed by Yetews, who appeared horrified. "Taren, what happened?"

Taren sighed and pinched the bridge of his nose. "Apparently Sam thought it was a nice night to take stroll in the rain," he said sarcastically.

Yetews growled his frustration with his boy and himself for not realizing he was gone.

Sam still couldn't find the words he needed. He was still much too embarrassed and in shock to try and explain himself.

Taren tried to clarify to everyone what he had witnessed, but left open gaps for Sam to fill. "Warg woke me up. I figured while I was up I would check on Sam. Only, when I went to his room I found him missing. That's when I thought I heard him outside. He didn't sound like he was in trouble, but I had no idea what he could be doing out there. The door was cracked open so I knew he had gone outside. When I went to check on him, I saw him walking directly towards some mysterious, glowing creature. As soon as it caught a glimpse of me, it morphed. I hit it with a dagger, but it barely fazed it. If it weren't for Keesa's timely intervention, we'd probably all be dead." He looked down angrily at Sam.

"Was it alone?" Orga asked. He spoke quickly with concern riddled through his unsteady voice.

"I think so, but I can't be sure. I'm going outside to search the perimeter." As he opened the door to leave, Keesa was standing there, panting.

She was soaked, as Sam predicted, but also had slight scorches on her wet fur from the fight she'd just had. Sam expected her to run in and yell at him for his foolishness. Instead, she ran to his side and said, "Thank goodness you're alright. What was that thing?"

Taren answered her. "We don't know exactly."

"Well, whatever it was, it didn't make it much further before it faded away."

Taren raised an eyebrow. "It's gone then?"

"I believe so," Keesa said.

"Well, I was just about to go check for any other signs of danger. Keesa, would you be willing to make a wider scan? You can cover more ground quicker than me."

"Certainly." She was out the door again before Sam could even thank her for saving his life.

Sam looked up to see Taren begin another frustrated glance at him. But when Taren saw Sam's sadness, he quickly softened then turned to address Yetews. "Try to get him to talk. I think he's in shock."

Yetews nodded and sat on his haunches next to the soaking wet boy. Orga came over to drape a rough, brown blanket over Sam's shaking shoulders.

The warmth of the blanket made Sam realize how wet and cold he was. It brought him back to the present. He'd been rethinking the events of the night over and over in his mind. Looking up into his Guardian's pleading eyes, he knew that he had to explain what happened.

Yetews grumbled a question. Sam looked away for a moment to gather his thoughts. "I...I...don't know what I was thinking. I was starting to fall asleep and..." he trailed off and stared at his muddy feet.

On the other side of the room, Orga had started a fire and Sam felt his shivers start to quiet. Titus leaned into his other side. He gently whispered, "Take your time. Just tell us exactly what happened."

Yetews was grumbling his agreement with Titus.

Sam continued to concentrate on his feet as he started to talk. "It was in that place between awake and asleep. That's where I saw her." He looked up enough to see a couple of questioning stares. He tried to elaborate. "The creature that Taren saw me going to...I saw her in my...well...not my dreams. But, I saw her before I was all the way asleep."

Orga tried to help Sam find the word he was looking for. "That place you are talking about. The one between awake and sleep? We call it the in-between."

"Oh," Sam thought aloud. It was yet another part of Imagia unfolding in front of him. "Well, then I saw her in the in-between. Then the thunder woke me up and I heard someone calling to me. It was the same voice I had heard from her before. She sounded just like..." Sam didn't want to admit that she reminded him of his mom, but there was no better way to explain, "...my mom. And I couldn't help it. I mean...I knew she couldn't really be here, so that's when I figured that I must've been dreaming. But I was wrong. Again. And...I'm sorry." The last two words were barely a whisper and, though he tried not to, he shed a single tear and hung his head in hopes no one would notice.

Yetews gave him a reassuring pat on the back while Titus put a paw on his knee. Orga tried to ease Sam's guilt a fraction by saying, "It's not your fault. You had no way of knowing what you saw was of your creating or someone else's. Now you should go sit by the fire to dry off. You're absolutely drenched."

As Sam was warming himself, Taren and Keesa returned.

"It's all clear. We didn't see any sign of anything else out there. But if I could wager a guess, I'd say that it won't be the last attack. There's a good chance others know Sam's here. We have no way of knowing for certain that the creature disappeared. It could have morphed again before Keesa noticed. And if it saw Sam, it can vouch for our whereabouts." There was regret in his voice and Sam knew that he was blaming himself for letting the creature get away.

He felt he needed to apologize to Taren too. He'd caused a lot of trouble so far. "I'm really sorry Taren."

"Don't worry about it, kid." The anger was dissipating in Taren's voice. Sam's hidden tear was not so easy to hide from Taren's keen eyes. "The bad news is, we have to leave as soon as possible. It's no longer safe here for you." Then he addressed Orga. "If we don't leave soon, you won't be safe here any more either, Orga."

Orga nodded in understanding.

The fact that he had put more than just himself in danger made Sam feel even worse. Ever since coming to Imagia, he'd never felt so helpless. Despite this strange power he had, he was only just beginning to learn how to master it. Even though his heart told him the answer to his next question, he asked anyways. "When do we have to leave?"

Orga answered him, "I'm afraid I was wrong to tell you that we wouldn't push you out the door too soon. The sooner you leave, the better. I'm afraid tonight will be your last night here Sam. I'm sorry, but you will be safer the more you move. It is obvious now, that you can't remain with me any longer. But Taren will continue to help you train. Once you master the morphing as you have the imagining, you will be fine." He smiled ruefully. "I will spread the word from my end to all the Protectors. They will help you when they can."

Sam felt like he had swallowed a brick. He knew the time would come to leave again, but he'd hoped it would be years rather than weeks. He didn't feel ready to fight a battle...or perhaps it would be more like a duel. Either way, he could feel swarms of angry butterflies fluttering around the brick in his stomach. He was nervous and scared and totally unsure what was going to happen next. "W-where will we go then?" It was all he could think to ask and it came out very shaky.

Yetews was still patting Sam reassuringly when Orga said, "No one knows exactly how to find Nadaroth. We only know that he is far from here, past the Impossible Way. To get there, you will have to go through the Village of Exile. There, you can talk to some of the people who have tried to find Nadaroth. They may be able to help you."

Sam considered the word 'impossible'. "But if it's an impossible way, then how can we get past it?"

Smiling again, Orga simply said, " Ah, yes. It would of course be impossible to anyone else. But they don't have your power of imagination, do they?" He winked one of his beady eyes. Then he added to Taren, "This won't be easy. Gather all the information you can."

"Yes," Taren said. "Tonight we sleep. Tomorrow, we begin our journey."

Chapter Fourteen: Preparation

Sam awoke to the sound of Taren's voice. It was muffled slightly so he figured that everyone was in the big room, making plans. He hadn't gotten much sleep over night, so his muscles seemed to contradict every move he made. When he finally got into a sitting position, he couldn't bring himself to leave the room.

Yetews, Titus and Keesa weren't in the room to greet him this morning. They had apparently awoken early. He didn't know if anyone knew he was awake, but he preferred it that way. He simply wanted to sit and think.

He knew that he was about to leave behind the closest thing to a home that he would probably ever have again. And to make matters worse, he had no idea where he was going or what was going to happen to him. He was certain that three weeks of constant training of his imagination wasn't enough to prepare him to do what everyone expected of him.

As he sat on the bed, contemplating whether or not he should go join the group, he thought back to a conversation he had with Taren a week into his training.

While they were resting under the shade of a nearby tree, Sam had obviously had a concerned look on his face and it caught Taren's attention. "What's eating at you, kid?"

The Gateway to Imagia: The Tale of Sam Little

"I dunno. I guess I was just thinking that I don't understand why this happened to me. I mean, why can I make my imagination come to life? What's so different about me?" Sam paused, then added, "Why me...and why *him*." He spoke the last word with a twinge of disgust.

Taren sighed deeply and let his gaze wander to the sky. "Hmm...well, no one can ever really know why. Sometimes, things just happen. That goes for the good *and* the bad. Orga would tell you that it's all about the choices we make. But he and I haven't always seen eye to eye on that little point."

Sam was curious what that meant. He couldn't see Taren arguing with Orga about anything. "What do you mean?"

His gaze didn't stray from the sky when he continued. "As you already know, I didn't exactly choose to stay here. Neither did my sister. We were forced to stay here as a consequence for the choices of someone else." He glanced down to see Sam's puzzlement. He tried to elaborate. "If Nadaroth wouldn't have come here before me and chose to destroy this world, then I would have had my ten days here and gone home. It's the same for many others. The suffering that he has done to so many..." he stopped and Sam saw him clench his hands into tight fists before relaxing them a moment later. Through clenched teeth, he said, "Why a creature so vile...so evil, would be bestowed a power that could cause so much pain, makes no sense to me. Is there a reason for all of this? Who knows? But if there is a reason, then I haven't found it yet. But I can tell you that if given the choice to stay or leave Imagia, I'd be hard pressed to find someone who would have chosen to stay."

Before Sam could respond to anything, Taren started talking again. "I've seen Nadaroth do a lot of strange and terrible things. I've always believed, since coming here, that nothing good can come from that power he has. And then *you* came along." He smiled down at Sam.

"But I haven't done anything on purpose to hurt anyone. I'm not like him! I swear I'm not!" Sam returned defensively.

Taren put his palms up in mock surrender and laughed. "Hey, now! Simmer down, kid. I didn't say you were just like him. I'm just saying that if Orga is right, and things happen because of choices made, then there must be a reason that you are here. You have had to make some of the same choices that Nadaroth did. And you are choosing differently. You are both so alike and yet completely different at the same time." He paused for a moment and stared at Sam's face as if looking for something hidden and then quickly shook it off and said, "Look, I know that all the hope you feel from us annoys you."

Sam opened his mouth to protest, even though it was true. But Taren stopped him.

With a knowing look, he said, "Yes. It does annoy you. You try to hide it, but I can see it from time to time. But you have to understand that the hope comes from years of seeing your same power in its destructive form. You're becoming the opposite of what Nadaroth has become. I know that you don't think you are capable of doing so much, but you are. You're stronger than you think you are, Sam. You'll see."

Sam felt it was strange that Taren would know him so well after such a short time. It was a bit comforting. "Er...thanks, I guess."

Taren nodded once to acknowledge the thanks. He went back to sky gazing as he said, "I don't know. I suppose that everything that Nadaroth does stems from a single choice he made. He could have used his power to do good things for Imagia. But then there would be no need for Protectors. And I wouldn't be here." There was a sense of longing in his voice.

Sam felt sadness for Taren. He understood the sorrow in his voice. He wished there was something good he could find in all the bad. He didn't know if there was a reason for everything that was happening, but then he had a thought. "Well, if none of this had ever happened, then we would never have met. And I'm really glad I got to meet you."

Taren barked a quick laugh and tousled Sam's hair, much like Yetews liked to do. "If nothing else, then you've sure got optimism, kid." He laughed again. "Not that I don't still think it was a mistake for either of us to come to Imagia. But still, I'm glad we met too."

Taren seemed to be touched by his observation. Sam was glad to see him happy. But he shrugged at the idea of coming here being a mistake. He'd met too many friends here and that was something he had never really had. Even though he had lost things, it was nice to know what friendship felt like. So he said, "My mom always told me that we learn from our mistakes."

The Gateway to Imagia: The Tale of Sam Little

Taren merely smiled at his genuine words, roughed up Sam's hair again, and then went back to gazing at the passing clouds. Sam smiled too and joined Taren's gaze towards the sky. For the moment, he felt like he was sitting next to the older brother he never had and never even knew he wanted.

As Sam sat on the bed, remembering that moment he had spent with Taren, it helped him to understand the choice he had to make right now. He could choose to hide away and hope for the best while others tried to fight this battle for him, or he could get up and join the planning happening in the other room.

It was an easier decision than he thought it would be. He knew that he needed to get up and face the world. One day at a time.

As though Yetews had somehow heard his thoughts, he popped his head around the doorway and grinned goofily. He grumbled something questioningly.

"Yeah, I'm hungry," answered Sam. "I'm coming. I just got up."

Yetews must have noticed the far away look of worry in Sam. To try and brighten his mood, as Sam started to walk down the hallway, Yetews scooped him up and placed him on his shoulders. He had to crouch to manage it, because of the ceiling.

"Whoa! Yetews," Sam laughed as he said his name, "you don't have to carry me. It's not that far to walk."

Yetews shrugged and glanced back just enough to see the grin on Sam's face. He grinned as well.

Though Sam knew it was silly to be riding on Yetews' shoulders inside, it was still really nice to be in his familiar place again. Since their return from his gateway, the opportunities to ride on Yetews were practically nonexistent. In spite of the absurdity of it, it felt good. For the moment, things felt simple again. He dug his hands into the thick fur and enjoyed it while it lasted.

It didn't take very long for them to reach the others in the big room. Sam was right. They were busy making plans. Though the rest of the night was free from any other attacks, Taren had made it a point to keep watch all night. Sam was the only one who hadn't had a turn on watch. Even Titus and Warg took a turn. Oddly enough, Titus and Warg seemed to enjoy each other's company.

Yetews didn't take Sam off of his shoulders and neither of them seemed to mind. They settled across the aged table from Taren and Orga, who were so engrossed in their talk, that they barely noticed Sam.

After a few minutes of Taren explaining how far he thought they could travel safely, Orga looked up and saw Sam. "Are you hungry Sam?"

Sam nodded and, with a bit more enthusiasm than he intended, said, "Yup! Starving!" He bit his lip when he heard how forced it sounded.

Not everyone noticed his misplaced exuberance, but Taren and Yetews both raised an eyebrow as Orga went to get Sam's breakfast. Everyone knew that Sam was dealing with a lot at the moment so Taren didn't say anything. Rather, he turned and grabbed a knapsack from beside his feet and pulled a tattered piece of folded parchment from it.

Sam thought of all the pirate movies he had seen and it reminded him of a buried treasure map. He wasn't far off. When Taren unfolded it on the table, it had markings and sketches from edge to edge.

Noticing how Sam eyed it, Taren said, "There's no X to mark the spot, if that's what you're looking for. But it *is* a map. Or better yet, a rough guide. Parts of Imagia change from time to time and there are places no one has gone since before Nadaroth."

Sam stared at the aged map and noticed a small drawing that resembled Orga's home. He was surprised how intricate it looked. It was slightly faded and not labeled. He slid down from Yetews' shoulders and walked over to the table. He reached a hand hesitantly over to the map, afraid that he might smudge it if he touched it, and pointed at the familiar looking sketch. "Is that Orga's home?"

"You noticed that, did you? Yes, that's where we are now."

He saw names for all the other drawings on the map and didn't understand why Orga's home had no label. "Why isn't it labeled?"

In a matter-of-fact voice, he explained. "Protectors make maps of where they have been. It helps us when we are searching for Guardians. But there's no guarantee that our maps won't fall into the wrong hands. There are quite a few who wouldn't mind finding Orga. He's...well known."

"Oh."

"Yeah. We try not to label everything in case it falls into the wrong hands. You'd be surprised who or what is hunting Guardians. And not just for killing. Nadaroth would love to find Orga or the other original few Guardians left here. The more he knows about Imagia, the better. Mine is a bit more detailed than the others, but we try to keep it fairly simple." His face seemed to swell with pride when he added. "We've never lost a map to date."

Sam couldn't stop looking at the map. It was fantastic. He saw small sketches of creatures and even saw a familiar sketch of what he thought could only be a deceptor. He couldn't believe how big Imagia looked on the piece of paper. As he looked, Taren studied it carefully. "It's really cool. Did you draw all of this?"

For the first time, Taren's cheeks actually looked as though they changed a shade pinker. He cleared his throat then said, "Yeah. Well, I don't remember much about school, but I remember art time was my favorite. I suppose I would have been an artist in your world."

Sam thought it was strange that Taren would call it 'his' world when he used to belong there too. But then he remembered that it wasn't really his world anymore either. Imagia would forever be his world now.

Taren cleared his throat again and then pointed at a spot northeast of where they were. He said, "We are headed here. The Village of Exile."

Sam remembered the name from the history he'd learned of Imagia. It was where he would probably end up living someday, but he didn't want to dwell on that thought so he asked, "When are we leaving and how long does it take to get there?" When the question left his mouth, he realized that he didn't really want to think about that either.

Taren gave Yetews a fleeting look of concern. Yetews put a hand in comfort on Sam's back before bending down and gently answering the question in his ear.

Sam's face instantly betrayed him. He was trying so hard to be strong about everything but Yetews' words were harder to hear than he expected they would be. As he looked at the ground, he said, "But…I'm not ready."

"Yetews knows we have to leave for both your safety. That's why we have to leave this morning. The more time we travel during the day, the better it will be all around. I don't have Keesa's perfect night vision to help and we can't expect her to never sleep."

Keesa chimed in. "I can survive on very little sleep if need be." She joined them at the table. "I will do my part to protect us."

"Yes. You are an asset that we are lucky to have." Taren stated. "But even the best of us work better with a little sleep under our belts."

"Agreed." She bowed her head slightly as she said the word. "But please don't worry about me. I won't disappoint you. Especially where your protection is concerned. Kupa cats are quite resilient. I can hold my own." Her lips curled up in the same feline smile Sam so often found amusing. He didn't think he'd ever get used to seeing a cat smile. With her saber teeth, it could be truly menacing to someone who didn't know her.

Taren merely said, "So I've seen."

Keesa looked adoringly at Sam and said, "I will do everything I can to protect you Sam. You are the closest thing I have to a cub, now."

Sam found himself, once again, wanting to reach over to her and stroke her head or scratch behind her ears out of appreciation for her kindness and friendship to him. But he still wasn't sure if she would welcome the gesture, so he just said, "Thanks Keesa," and smiled back at her. She really did remind him of his mom and it warmed him for the moment. He felt like he had a second wind that would help push him out the door.

"So after I eat then we have to leave?" asked Sam. As he looked around, there were several answering nods.

Orga had returned with food and Sam ate as slowly as he knew he could get away with. He felt that every bite he swallowed was like another step closer to the door.

His old self would have seen this as an adventure, but now that he was wiser to how real adventures worked, it was difficult to find the enjoyment.

Then he remembered riding on Yetews down the hallway. The brief feeling of joy it gave him nearly drowned out his fear of the unknown and he remembered what it was like to pretend. If only for a moment he could convince himself that this was just another grand adventure, perhaps it wouldn't be as frightening.

He was only moderately aware of the bustle of everyone behind him. He could hear the chatter as they prepared to leave. Orga and Taren were discussing the finer details of where they would head after they reached The Village of Exile, but they could have been talking about the weather for all Sam could tell. He was too selfishly lost in his own thoughts to pay full attention.

Keesa was joining in the conversation every so often to ask what distance she needed to scout for them in the woods. Yetews was helping pack the odds and ends that they would need, such as water and food. Though he wasn't technically a beast of burden, he was the closest any of them came to it. He was also easily the strongest. So Yetews would be carrying a bulk of their supplies in a pack made to fit around him. Titus nervously paced and panted behind Sam. He was just as anxious about this trip as Sam was.

Sam chewed the last bite of fruit until it all but disintegrated in his mouth. He hesitantly swallowed then stood up and walked to his room. He'd spent so much effort in creating it just how he wanted it. He sat on his bed and put his shoes on. He rubbed his still healing scar on his knee and looked around the room.

He'd imagined everything so close in detail to his room from back home. It was starting to feel like home in a way. And now he would have to leave it behind again. His heart ached from the familiarity of it all.

He was deep in thought remembering a photo he had of him and his parents that hung on one of his walls. It was one of the details of his room that he had left out intentionally because it was too hard to think about. But he sat on the bed, eyes closed in thought; he saw the picture in his mind. It had been taken on a summer day when they went camping about a year ago. It was one of the best days he remembered and had asked his dad to hang the picture in his room.

He imagined the photo in his mind and then in his fingertips he felt something that could only be the glossiness of a photo. He opened his eyes to find that he was holding the photo. One salty tear dropped onto it, staining the corner.

Yetews walked into the room and saw what Sam was looking at. He grumbled reassuring words. He was genuinely worried about the boy. But, without warning, Sam's emotions spiraled downward suddenly and he ran to his Guardian. He buried his head in Yetews' hairy chest.

Yetews did all he could do to comfort Sam. He hugged him and purred soothingly while Sam cried.

Sam had been as strong as possible these past weeks, but it had been harder than he thought it would at times. He sobbed once more and then he felt the deep humming purr in Yetews' chest. It eased his mind. He knew that he would always be grateful for Yetews. The thought that something out there wanted to remove him from his life ignited a spark in his mind.

He couldn't let anyone take away his Guardian. His friend. He wouldn't let them and it was time to do what he needed to do to prevent it from coming to pass. He silently promised himself that he would be as strong as Taren thought he could be. He slowly backed out of his Guardian's loving hold.

Yetews extended a large pale thumb and wiped away the remaining tears on Sam's cheek.

Sam sniffed and wiped his nose on the back of his sleeve. He folded the photo in half. After he carefully put it in his pocket, he looked up at Yetews and said, "Okay. I'm ready. Let's go."

* * * * * * * * *

It was as if he was leaving for his gateway all over again. Sam had said his goodbyes to Orga and Warg. It was harder this time around. Before, he had merely enjoyed the company and stories that Orga offered. Now he would genuinely miss their presence and the comforts they brought to him.

Though Titus was more than capable of speaking, he still managed to whine when he left. Titus' fondness of Warg's company made it even harder for Sam to leave. He hated the fact that his friend had to suffer a loss as well. He hadn't dreamed that Titus would befriend something as strange as Warg. It turned out that their common background of being someone's pet is what fueled their attachment to one another. Titus even had some strange ability to understand some of Warg's gurgling noises and managed to translate what he could from time to time.

It was a milder version of Sam's understanding of Yetews. The oddest part was that Titus seemed to understand a fair amount of what Yetews said as well. It was another mystery that Orga only had rough theories about.

They had everything packed and were out the door before Sam had time to digest the idea that they might not be coming back again. Before they set out, Yetews spied him peeking again at the picture he imagined. He was ready to find a way to distract Sam of his thoughts. So they didn't make it far out the door before Yetews had Sam on his shoulders.

Orga hadn't said much this time around. He was genuinely worried for them. Taren's last words to him were, "There are two Protectors scanning the perimeter of the clearing. Once the enemy knows that Sam's no longer here, you'll be safe again. I'll send word once we reach Exile. Good luck, old friend."

Orga merely replied, "And luck for you as well. Watch Sam close. Nights will be the hardest for you all." They shared a firm handshake that seemed to mean more than Sam had ever seen a handshake mean. Orga smiled at Sam and said, "Good luck Sam. I hope we meet again soon." Sam feebly turned one corner of his mouth into a smile and debated whether it was okay to hug the wise Guardian. He decided that it didn't matter what the formalities might be and reached up on his toes to hug Orga.

The gesture took Orga by surprise, but he warmly hugged the boy back in response.

Titus whined again, nudged Warg's shoulder with his cold nose and then bolted off to the head of the group. With no more words left between them, they set off into the depths of Imagia.

Sam turned back once, but couldn't see the welcoming morning glow of Orga's clearing through the thick of the trees. They were barely a stone's throw away, and he already yearned to go back. He knew it would only get harder from here on.

Sam looked suspiciously around the trees. Although it was most likely not meant for his ears, Sam had overheard the last words shared between Taren and Orga. He was finding it difficult to make sense of it. He didn't know how it was possible that two other Protectors were already here when the attack had just happened last night. He was desperate to find out how they knew to be here so quickly and was waiting for the perfect moment to ask Taren. As he looked around, he wondered where the other Protectors were and if they could see him.

The morning seemed to inch by at a snail's pace. The forest was thick and every odd noise seemed to cause nervous twitches through the group of travelers. Though Sam was glad to be atop his friend's shoulders once more, it hardly felt like one of his old adventures. There was a heavy weight hovering above them, ready to drop at a moment's notice.

The five had spoken very few words since their departure from Orga's home. Sam couldn't tell if the silence was for safety reasons or if it was simply because there was nothing to say. Nevertheless, it made for a very long and boring hike. At one point, Sam felt quite close to nodding off and decided the best way to keep awake was to busy his mouth and his mind.

He shifted slightly on Yetews' shoulders and asked, "So how far away are we from the village?"

"Actually, we just passed the halfway point a few yards back," Taren answered. "It's taking a little longer than usual, but we have to be extra careful." As they set out, he explained to Sam that this wouldn't be the longest stretch of their journey in the slightest but that it would likely be the easiest.

Between Taren's warning, Keesa's constant state of alert, and everyone else's concerned glances, it didn't make for a very pleasant trek. Sam was determined to find a way to change the heavy atmosphere. He wasn't sure what he could safely ask or say, but he figured there was no better time to ask about the question ruling his thoughts. "Can I ask you something Taren?"

"Sure, just try to keep your voice down."

He realized as soon as Taren said it, that his voice was entirely too loud in the still of the forest. "Sorry," he said as he bit his cheek. "Well, I was sorta wondering about those Protectors you told Orga about."

"Hmm," Taren seemed to mull over his thoughts for a moment. He gave Sam a knowing look. "You weren't meant to hear about that, but I suppose you already know *that* too, don't you?"

Sam nodded and shrugged at the same time and then felt Yetews shaking with silent laughter.

"Well, I suppose it doesn't really matter in the end, but what is it you want to know about them?"

Nearly everyone else seemed just as eager to be informed as Sam was. Keesa was the only one who didn't change her pace. "Why are

The Gateway to Imagia: The Tale of Sam Little

they even there? It doesn't make sense. How did they know they needed to be there? Did you send a message or something?"

Taren looked over to Keesa before answering. She nodded slightly and shot off into the forest ahead of them. Taren noticed another question in Sam's eyes. "Before you can ask about *that*," he jerked his head towards the direction Keesa ran, "she already knows what I'm about to tell you and is going ahead of us to scout for danger." When he saw Sam's face lose its questioning look, he continued. "Alright. It's fairly simple. The Protectors knew to be there because I asked them to be there. After your merry little jaunt into the arms of the enemy," he paused for Yetews' annoyed reaction to the obvious sarcasm, "I had Keesa and Titus stand guard while I sent word that Protectors would be needed for Orga.

"I was hesitant to leave, but I couldn't leave Orga unprotected. I thought it would take me longer to return, but luck was with me. I ran into Garrett halfway. He's another Protector. I gave him the message to send two back to Orga's by morning. And judging from your disappointed expression, I'm assuming that you were expecting something more interesting, like mind-reading or something similar?" He smirked as he asked his question.

Sam shook his head. He didn't want to admit that Taren wasn't far off from the wild answers he had considered before asking about it. "So why wasn't I supposed to know about them then?"

"That part's a bit more complicated. Orga would have me hiding a lot from you. But as I've said, we don't always agree about everything. Personally, I doubt you'll stop wondering about it so I'll just tell you so you can ease your busy mind. They arrived before you woke up. I explained the basics of everything to them that they weren't told by Garrett. The reason Orga was hoping to keep it from you was in an attempt to guard you from feeling the pressure of expectation."

"I...don't understand," Sam said.

Taren hesitated briefly. He looked as though he had made his mind up about some unspoken internal argument. "The hope is already spreading Sam. Hope in *you*."

"Oh." His cheeks reddened slightly.

Taren continued. "We know the pressure you are feeling can't be small. A great weight has been laid on your shoulders. Whether you

168

feel it now or not, you will inevitably feel it as word spreads of your abilities. Orga simply wanted to keep the pressure from you for as long as possible so as not to affect your imaginative growth. I'm not sure how far word will have spread, but I wouldn't be surprised if every person in the village is lining up to see you. Waiting to see if you are real.

"Orga never wanted to say anything to you, but there are some who have wondered if another one with Nadaroth's powers would come to Imagia one day and help set it free from the darkness. After so many years of waiting for such a person, the hope of its possibility was all but lost. Many of those that originally believed in such a possibility are gone. By the time I arrived in Imagia, the hope had become barely a whisper in the dark."

Titus trotted up to Taren, closing the gap between them. Since his coming, he had become highly curious about the ways and workings of Imagia. Sam occasionally felt out of place listening to the conversations Titus would have with the others. He was still trying to cope with the idea of his dog being so intelligent and verbal. "Why wouldn't Orga want to tell Sam about this? Doesn't he have a right to know?"

Taren looked down at Titus and looked as though he was wondering the same thing. "Honestly, I think he had Sam's best interest at heart. He didn't want to give him more burdens to bear." He lowered his voice to barely a whisper and said something only to Titus. The only part that Sam could make out as he strained to hear was, "…already needlessly suffered so much."

The two looked back to Sam. It made him feel uncomfortable when the others talked about him like this. It seemed to happen more frequently the longer he was here.

As if they hadn't had the hushed conversation, Taren continued. "Sam, don't be upset with Orga for keeping this from you. No one knows how Nadaroth came into his powers. The chances that another could have the same abilities, was almost impossible. But, as word spreads of you, the hope will return. I can already hear the whispers growing louder."

Through a low growl, Titus said, "All the more reason to tell him everything. I still think he has a right to know what you expect of him."

The Gateway to Imagia: The Tale of Sam Little

"Placing the fate of an entire world on the shoulders of a young boy with such a powerful gift is a dangerous thing to do."

"Sam is strong." Titus said proudly.

Taren raised an eyebrow. "Yes. He is strong. But a child's mind can be a fragile thing. You've seen what great power can do in the wrong hands, Titus."

"Yes. I have seen it. But Sam is not like that monstrosity you speak of." Titus looked back to Sam, nearly growling again. Sam smiled back at him, glad that his friend was defending him. He didn't enjoy being compared to something so terrible.

Taren looked down once more at Titus and said, "You're right. Sam *is* different. And that, my friend, is why the hope will spread."

Sam didn't say much after this revelation. He spent the remainder of the journey trying to figure out how he could avoid becoming the center of attention once they reached their initial destination. He didn't want to be attacked, but he did hope for some form of distraction from his anxious thoughts. He contemplated whether he should practice using his imagination for something to keep his mind busy.

Every once in a while, Sam would imagine a plant or flower, or even a few bird-like creatures or strange harmless critters. They'd pop up in odd places and cause Taren to jump back in surprise from time to time. He would say something along the lines of, "Sam! Warn me first!"

At which Sam would say, "Oops! Sorry." Then he and Yetews would share an amused look and a quiet laugh.

Yetews even grumbled a few suggestions to Sam to aid in the passing of time. Before long, the dusk of evening was beginning to shroud the never thinning trees. The sun had nearly set when they finally broke through a particularly thick part of the forest. It was the first time that Sam had seen anything in Imagia that wasn't completely surrounded by trees.

He stood in awe at the roughly trodden path that led into a village. It was bigger than he thought it would be. He could see multiple hut-like homes that spread too far for his eyes to take in. People moved amongst the buildings, not noticing the odd group of travelers standing within their borders.

They stopped at the edge of the town.

Titus said, "Do your eyes see this, Sam? It's amazing."

Sam couldn't respond. He just continued to take it all in as Yetews grumbled in agreement with Titus.

Keesa hesitated going further and said, "Fascinating. I've never been out of the forest before. I had no idea there were so many humans."

Noticing Sam's sudden tied tongue and taking advantage of the moment, Taren said, "Welcome to the Village of Exile."

Chapter Fifteen: Exile

Taren had asked Keesa to remain at the border of the forest before they went in. He told her, "Many of the people here will see you as something brought here to terrify them. As I told you before, Nadaroth uses Kupa cats as weapons. It's best to wait in the safety of the trees until I can explain you to the others."

Keesa was fidgety. Sam had never seen her so nervous. She was uncomfortable being in the open. Her home had always been in the safety of the forest and she was more than willing to remain there until they sent for her. "I can keep watch from here for approaching danger." She nodded and darted back into the tree line. Sam squinted his eyes to see her but she was already hidden in the shadows.

"What about Yetews?" Sam asked Taren. "Is he safe to go in? Will they be afraid of him too?"

Taren unexpectedly laughed and then seeing that Yetews was not amused, he quickly apologized. He cleared his throat. "Um, sorry. But I can't expect that anyone would find him frightening, especially with a small boy on his shoulders. They will expect him to be a Guardian. Most of them have lost theirs, but they are not blind to the bonds of others."

Though Yetews didn't seem entirely thrilled with Taren's response, Sam was convinced but was confused about a small part. "What do you mean by 'most of them' lost their Guardians? I thought that...well...you know."

"You wonder why they are still here if their Guardians lived."

"Yeah."

"Sometimes the Guardians don't die in the attack. All that has to be done is to stop the Guardian from keeping the Gateway open for their child. If one is rendered unconscious or time runs out, then the child would still be lost. But there aren't very many instances like this."

Sam was intrigued by the idea of meeting other Guardians. He'd only met two, but they were both amazing. He pushed this thought to the back of his mind and looked into the village. "Okay. So what now?"

Taren waved them forward. "Come on. We need to see what we can do about gathering as many Protectors as we can. We need to find out as much information as we can about the paths we are going to take. I've spent the majority of my time in the western areas of Imagia. Others will have more information. From what I've heard, Nadaroth resides somewhere in the far North. I've never been there."

"And others have been?"

Sam could tell from the way Taren avoided his eyes, that he was hiding something else. "Perhaps. But those who might have reached those lands never returned unless Nadaroth brought them there. Parts of this world never existed before him. You have to remember that the imaginings of other children can change Imagia."

Now everyone, minus Keesa, walked into Exile. Taren would occasionally nod at some of the people and they would curiously glare at Sam and his Guardian. It made for an awkward part of the journey.

As they headed through town, a deep, rough voice spoke from behind them. "So this is the child with the great imagination."

Taren pivoted and smiled at the man. "Zane." He reached his hand over Sam's head and they firmly shook hands. "You're just the man I was hoping to find."

"Indeed," Zane replied. As he spoke, he shifted his eyes nervously towards Sam. The look made Sam feel uncomfortable and he averted his eyes, pretending to be looking around the village. "Word has traveled that you were bringing a boy back with you. Are the rumors true then? Can he imagine?"

Taren proudly defended the rumors. "Yes. The rumors are true.

The Gateway to Imagia: The Tale of Sam Little

But before I explain further, we need to gather every Protector we can find. I'll explain everything then. There is much to be done and much to be shown."

Zane seemed hesitant to leave. Sam could feel his eyes boring into him even when he tried to avoid his stare. Yetews must have felt the boy's anxiety for the situation and caught Sam's eye. He winked and started to lumber off towards the shadow of the nearest building egging Sam to follow.

As they moved, a few others took notice. Taren gave directions to Zane. "You know where I'll be. I'll prepare them," he gestured to Sam, Yetews and Titus, "for the gathering. Spread the word. And tell them that we have also befriended a kupa cat."

"*A kupa cat?*" Zane nearly spit the words. "Taren, are you *mad?* They're vicious creatures! You can't possibly..."

Taren held up a hand to silence him. "The boy found her and saved her. She is not a marked beast, but a free one. Don't fire on her. I'll escort her in tonight after dark so as not to create panic."

"But...a...kupa cat?"

"Yes. She has become strangely attached to Sam." Taren looked over to Sam as he spoke. "You will see. Tomorrow. Gather all you can." He clapped Zane on the shoulder. "There may be hope on the horizon yet, my friend."

Zane scowled over at Sam before disappearing slightly unwillingly into the village.

Taren led them to a shabby looking place in a more remote area of the village. Unlike the other homes, it was dark on the inside. The evening light was quickly fading and this place was the coldest looking. The other homes had warm glows of firelight coming from inside.

The buildings were earthy. They appeared sturdy though obviously hand built. As Sam looked around, he realized that it truly felt like he was stepping into another time. The homes matched the clothes that he was given by Orga. No bright colors or manufactured details, each building was built by the hands of men. No two looked exactly alike. But the dwelling that they were walking directly towards looked strangest of them all. It looked as though it had never been lived in. It was rough and unwelcoming.

As Sam walked past the lighted windows of the earthen homes,

174

he longed to be back with Orga. Deep in the forest, where he was most comfortable for his time here.

They entered the shabby excuse for a home and Taren said, "It's not much, but I don't stay here often." His words indicated to Sam that this was his home. But there was remorse in his tone that didn't go unnoticed.

Though he knew before the words were out of his mouth that he shouldn't ask now, he couldn't stop himself. "Why don't you stay here?"

Taren walked to a dusty table in the middle of the room and lit what looked like a rusty old oil-based lamp using a torch that he had acquired on their walk here. Sam wondered momentarily how things like that even existed in this world as he waited for Taren to answer his question.

But Taren didn't answer. He went around the room and lit three more lamps. The light was brighter than expected and it brought out the details of the large open room.

It was covered in dust and there were odds and ends scattered all over. Other than a few worn chairs and the weathered table, there wasn't much to see. The only sign of previous life was an overturned, cracked pitcher in the middle of the table. It had dried stems spilling out that looked like old flowers. Sam could tell that someone lived here once, but it had been a long time since it was a place anyone called home. He still waited for some kind of response and tried once more to prompt an answer. "Taren? Why don't you stay here? Isn't it your home?"

Taren sighed quietly, his back to Sam. And even more quietly, he said, "Yes. It *was* my home. Along time ago..." He trailed off in thought and Sam knew from the heaviness of his voice that he should leave well enough be for the time.

Yetews and Titus both seemed comfortable enough. They didn't require the same comforts that Sam was used to. They both settled on the floor. Yetews' hair had a fine sheen of dirt around the edges from where he sat and Titus plopped down near him, raising a small cloud of dirt into the air. Sam pulled up a chair to the table and fiddled with a loose string on his tattered shirt.

Once the sun had set and night's cover was hiding the paths to their refuge, Taren went out to retrieve Keesa from the forest. It didn't take long for them to return. Without the rest in tow, Taren and Keesa were a stealthy duo.

Nerves were on high alert for the time. Anticipation for the events of the next day could be felt by nearly everyone.

Though none of them felt like sleeping, Taren managed to scrounge up a pile of uncomfortable looking blankets. He led Sam to one of the two other rooms in the house. "This was my room. The bed isn't exactly what you're used to, but it's better than the floor." He smiled faintly and handed Sam an extra brown blanket.

Sam was grateful for the bed, even if it wasn't soft. But he also knew that he could easily create another bed if he wanted to. As Taren turned to walk out, Sam asked, "Can I make a new bed? Or would that not be...er...okay right now?"

Taren seemed to mull over the idea, but said, "Let's hold off on that for now. If you're bored enough and there's no attack on you tonight, you can redecorate tomorrow." He chuckled dully and then waved goodnight. Before he left the room he said, "I'll be close if you need me." He hung one of the rusty oil lamps on a peg by the door before he left.

Yetews, who had barely been able to squeeze in through the small opening to the room, settled beside the bed. He annoyingly watched Titus jump up onto the foot of the bed then asked Sam a question in his rumbling tongue.

Sam shrugged. "I guess we'll just have to wait and see until tomorrow. I don't know what kind of gathering he means, but I would guess maybe a few Protectors want to know what is going on." Sam frowned as he considered the possibilities. He wondered if he could skip the gathering or if, perhaps, he wasn't invited at all. He had a bad feeling that the focus would be solely directed upon him and he hoped that if they wanted him to imagine something, he would be able to perform under that kind of pressure. Which reminded him of Taren's words. "I guess they were right."

Yetews grumbled questioningly back at him.

"About the pressure that Taren warned me of. What if they want me to imagine something in front of everyone? I don't know if I'll be able to do that."

Yetews growled reassuringly and Titus responded to him, "Of course he'll do fine." He drew his focus to Sam. "You will be perfect.

We will be there for you."

Yetews nodded in agreement and patted the bed. He was implying that Sam should lie back and relax.

There wasn't a pillow to lie on and he didn't feel like he would sleep well if he was too uncomfortable. He thought that it wouldn't be too obvious if at the very least, he imagined a nice soft pillow to sleep on. So he closed his eyes and pictured a soft feather pillow. As he imagined it, he made sure to make it match the dingy colors of the bed so that it didn't look too perfect. He didn't want to anger Taren.

When he opened his eyes, the pillow was there and perfectly soft. Yetews cocked his head to the side in mock disapproval and clucked his tongue. He turned to look for intruding eyes at the door. When he looked back at Sam, they were both grinning. Sam put one finger to his lips and said, "Don't tell Taren, ok?

Yetews ran his large fingers across his mouth and pretended to lock his mouth and throw away the key. The three of them laughed silently and Sam laid his head down on the pillow.

Sam didn't know if he wanted to sleep, but he knew after the long day that he was likely exhausted from the journey. He only had time to think about how much he missed the smell of his freshly washed pajamas. It was only as he remembered how his mom would wash them and put them, perfectly folded, on his bed, that he realized how tired he was. He took advantage of the moment and fell asleep almost instantly.

There was no in-between sleep for him and for that, he was subconsciously grateful. He dreamed briefly through the night. Only flashes of memories, good and bad, flickered through his mind from time to time. Yetews woke him up the next morning and Sam was relieved that there was no sign of distress from his night. Too often, he would wake up sore or with a destroyed bed from his constant thrashing.

His stomach growled as he followed Yetews. Sam sat at the table, noticing that Taren was nowhere to be seen. He was just about to get up and look out the window, when the door swung open and Taren stepped inside with the man they had met the previous evening.

They were muttering to each other about something Sam didn't understand. However, when they noticed that they weren't alone, they stopped immediately.

The Gateway to Imagia: The Tale of Sam Little

"Sam, you remember Zane?" Taren asked.

Suddenly, Sam felt himself swallow hard. He felt as though someone had stolen his tongue and he couldn't get words out properly. He settled for awkward nodding. Zane's frigid attitude from the previous night, seemed melted away this morning.

He was beaming down at Sam and then stuck his hand out to shake Sam's hand. Sam shakily took Zane's hand and they shook briefly. "It's a thrill to meet you Sam! Taren speaks so highly of you. You must have extraordinary abilities. I am most excited to see what you can do."

The feeling was starting to come back to his tongue, but Sam still couldn't quite get the words out. He numbly thought that this was what Orga predicted would happen if he was dropped into the spotlight.

Zane, feeling the awkward silence, realized that the boy might have noticed his harshness when they'd met previously. His smile only faltered briefly before he apologized. "I'm really sorry I was so cranky when we first met. It had been a long day for me. I had lost a Guardian earlier. I was...well...unpleasant company." He smiled wide and waited for Sam to respond.

Taren took notice of Sam's uncharacteristic silence. He stepped forward to try and bring the shaken boy back into his comfort zone. "Zane is a Protector, Sam. He is the one who taught me a lot of what I know." He smiled warmly and Sam suddenly found his tongue.

He looked at Zane in silent awe and then said, "Wow. That's great!" Sam knew that if this man was anywhere near as fascinating as Taren, then he wanted to know more about him. "Glad to meet you too."

Seeing that Sam was getting more comfortable, Taren knelt down to his level. In a voice meant only for Sam's ears, he whispered, "There are more Protectors coming soon. They should be here within the hour. You'll be fine. Just try not to worry, kid." He winked and handed Sam a piece of fruit and some bread that smelled delicious.

As he devoured his breakfast, there was a knock on the door. It was a man with longer blonde hair that was pulled back much like Taren's was when they'd first met. He was tall and slender and had the same muscular kind of build that apparently all Protectors seemed to have. His long face was friendly, but there was something more the closer he got. Sam noticed a jagged silvery scar that went from his eyebrow down to his chin. He shook hands with both Zane and Taren and was quickly brought to Sam.

Taren introduced them. "This is Garrett. He's one of the newest Protectors. He's only been Protecting for around twenty years."

"Twenty-two, actually," Garrett proudly corrected him.

This time, Sam seemed in better control of himself. "I'm Sam. Sam Little." He couldn't stop staring at the scar.

Garrett noticed and eagerly said, "It's a nice scar, isn't it?" He beamed. "Dragon. I'll tell you all about it while we wait for the others."

Sam could tell that he would like Garrett. He was, by far, the happiest individual he had met since his arrival in Imagia. His disposition seemed almost contagious. Sam couldn't stop smiling as Garrett entertained them with the tale of his scar. Sam was impressed to find that his first act as a Protector was battling a dragon to save a boy and his Guardian.

Sam had never seen a dragon and hoped that one day he might be lucky enough to catch a glimpse of one. When he mentioned this, Garrett said, "Amazing creatures! Terrifying, but amazing nonetheless. Of course, they are fairly plentiful here. I'm sure nearly every child has imagined a dragon at least once. But you'd best steer clear of them if you can." He ran a finger lightly over his scar. "Scars from dragons never stop burning."

Sam touched his own cheek and thought about feeling a constant fire on his skin. He quietly admired Garrett for his strength. He wondered if that was another common trait of Protectors and if he could ever be strong enough to be one.

Within an hour, the room became packed with a large number of people. Sam counted thirty-seven, including Taren. There were even three female Protectors. When they first walked in, it caught Sam off guard. He had only met men Protectors up until then, and it was strange to see a lady. They were just as strong and impressive as the rest and Sam hoped he would get to meet at least one of them before the day was done.

One Protector was actually standing next to a strange looking creature with tentacles on his chin and the top of his head. After Garret noticed Sam staring, he nudged him with his elbow and

The Gateway to Imagia: The Tale of Sam Little

pointed to the duo. He whispered, "That's David and the strange looking fellow he's with is his Guardian, Lugo. Now those two…you don't want to mess with them if you're a bad guy. I'll introduce you later." He winked with his scarred eye.

Apparently the gathering was complete because Taren cleared his throat loudly and held up a hand for silence.

Sam was comfortable sitting next to Garrett. But when everyone was quiet, he immediately felt a swarm of butterflies reeking havoc on his stomach. He wanted to run behind Yetews' body for cover but knew that he'd never make it unnoticed.

Taren started the meeting. "You all know why you are here. Word has spread that a boy has come to Imagia that has the same power as Nadaroth – the power to imagine."

Someone that Sam couldn't see said, "So it's true then? You've seen him use his power?"

"I have. I've witnessed him do amazing things."

Taren proceeded in telling Sam's story in its most basic form. He left out the finer details, but made sure to explain the key points.

No one interrupted Taren as he explained Sam's discovery of his ability and Orga's various theories on the circumstances. The more he spoke, the more passionate his voice became. Sam was sure he could feel the stares of everyone. In fear of seeing thirty-seven sets of eyes looking back at him, he picked at the dirt under his fingernails and pretended not to notice.

When Sam's nails were cleaner than they had ever been, he heard Taren finish with, "So as you can see, it's become obvious that Nadaroth has discovered that Sam is here and that he could be a danger to him. The threats on Sam's life have become increasingly worse. Nadaroth knows he is a hazard to his reign of power on this once good world. There is no other choice but for Sam to find him. And when he does, we need all the information that anyone can offer to aid us on our quest. Sam is the only one who has ever come here and stood a chance against that nightmare of a creature. If we do not act now, then I fear for the fate of Sam and his Guardian."

There was a brief moment of silence followed by a wave of murmurs throughout the crowd. The same faceless voice from before spoke again. "What's to say that he isn't going to be just like Nadaroth? How can we trust him?"

Every eye in the place turned on Sam and his butterflies turned into stinging bees. Many others in the room affirmed the legitimacy of the man's question. The harsh mood change in the atmosphere prompted a protective reaction from Yetews. He placed himself between Sam and the crowd of Protectors. He growled as he stood there, towering over even the tallest man.

Titus followed suit and was growling in sync with Yetews one step in front of him. Sam felt his face grow hot. He looked up at his Guardian in all his magnificence and remembered why he was here. He had to be brave, so fought back his instinct to hide. He touched Yetews gently on the arm and peered around his massive body.

Yetews pricked an ear backwards in Sam's direction, not taking his eyes off of the crowd. Sam whispered, "It's okay Yetews."

Yetews turned to look at him and, still frowning, saw the gentle look of trust in Sam's eyes. He quickly softened his posture. Titus stopped growling as well when Sam touched his back and whispered, "It's alright."

Sam looked out into the sea of unsure faces, feeling smaller than he'd felt in a long time. He hesitated for a moment until he saw Taren's reassuring look through the crowd. Garrett winked again with his smile still bright as ever. So Sam opened his mouth, afraid that the words might not come, and said, "I'm not like him. I don't want this world destroyed. Now it's my home too." His voice nearly broke at the end but he stood as tall as he could when he said it.

Taren smiled and nodded once. "He's right." Everyone turned the focus back on him. "He isn't like Nadaroth. I was there the night he became a lost one. I watched as he sacrificed his gateway to a young girl that would have suffered the same fate as us. And I ask you all, could you have made the sacrifice he chose willingly to make? We all know the sting of his loss. I am a first hand witness to the pain and nightmares he has already endured. If you doubt him, then you doubt Orga and you doubt me."

Another wave of murmuring filled the air. Taren waited patiently until the last whisper faded. Garrett was the first to speak. "I've talked with Sam. I look at his face and see nothing evil there. I trust Orga and Taren…I trust Sam."

Others turned to look at Sam. A new voice spoke. It was one of the female Protectors. "How can one so young handle such a heavy burden?"

The crowd agreed with her and Taren held up his hand again for silence. "He won't be alone. I'm going with him. He also has Titus and Yetews. But we are lucky enough to also have another aiding our journey. He nodded to Zane who was standing in the back by the door.

Zane nodded back and held his hand on the door waiting for something.

Taren spoke with caution. "Please do not be alarmed by our fifth party. Do not draw your weapons on her when she comes in. She is a friend." He pointed at Zane who opened the door.

Keesa walked in, blinking her crystalline eyes at the wary crowd. She made her way to Sam's side through a sea of whispers.

Garrett whispered in awe. "Amazing! Good for you, Sam. She's perfect!"

Sam couldn't help but smile back at his exuberance.

The rest of them were much more hesitant to accept her as she walked through the crowd. Everyone eyed her suspiciously and kept their distance from her.

As she finally settled next to Sam, she rolled her three eyes and muttered, "Hmph! Humans...paranoid group of creatures." With that, the tension lifted almost instantly. Nearly everyone laughed at her observation.

Soon the uncertainty began to turn to trust. The faceless Protector that had voiced his concerns in the beginning made his way through the crowd towards Sam. He squinted his eyes as he looked into Sam's face. The rest of them watched.

As difficult as it was, Sam stood his ground and stared back. The Protector relaxed his face and said to the boy, "I guess the hope of Imagia is on you now." All skepticism gone from his voice, he placed a hand on Sam's shoulder and said, "May our hope not be wasted. My name is Brock. And if you truly are set on facing our enemy, then you will need to know what I have to say. For I have seen the way to his lands and it will be nothing short of a miracle to find passage there again."

* * * * * * * * *

The Protector, Brock, was deep in conversation with Taren and a few of the others. After Sam had turned three shades whiter than he was, Taren had suggested that Yetews take him back to the smaller room to regain his senses.

Sam was sitting on the grungy bed with both hands covering his face. Yetews stood over him, worry deep in his eyes. He stroked Sam's back to attempt to relax him. Titus was in the room as well, but after seeing that Sam was in well enough hands, he suggested he might be better used to listen to the happenings at the gathering.

As he trotted out the door, Sam sighed heavily. Yetews, still worried, grumbled to him.

Sam mumbled through his hands. "How? How is this okay? I don't know what I'm doing here. You heard the Protector, Brock. He told us how impossible this is going to be. And they think that I'm the one who can find a way to get there. *Me*!"

Yetews responded hesitantly.

Sam dropped his hands from his face suddenly and briefly laughed hysterically. "Oh Yeah," he said sarcastically, "Sure, Yetews. It's going to be just great! But even if we do somehow make it to Nadaroth's land, I'm supposed to find some way to stop him. How the heck am I supposed to do that?"

Yetews opened his mouth to respond just as Taren walked into the room. "We will be there to help you, Sam."

Sam jumped. He didn't expect Taren. He preferred not to seem so helpless, but he wasn't sure what other options he had. "Taren, I don't even know what I have to do, so how am I supposed to do anything at all?"

Taren walked over and sat down next to Sam on the bed. "We have a lot of information from the gathering of Protectors. I won't lie to you. It's going to be a challenge. But I believe you will be capable of more than you know. It's at least a five-day journey to the Impossible Way. We have some time to plan and practice."

Sam's face fell even further. "Five days? But...how are we getting there?"

"Well, unless Yetews can sprout wings, then we'll be walking. We'll go through parts of Imagia I'm unfamiliar with. We have to be careful. Especially when you sleep."

After Taren mentioned wings, Sam had a thought. He got excited as he sputtered the words out. "Wings! I can imagine something for us to fly on...like...like...big birds or something!"

Taren, though slightly amused at the thought, shook his head. "That would be a good idea if times weren't so dangerous. Nadaroth has dragons scouting the lands for him. The skies are likely more dangerous than the forest." Seeing the sudden disappointment in Sam's face, he added, "But it was a great idea. That's the way you need to be thinking, going up against Nadaroth."

It raised Sam's spirits to know he was doing something right. His jitteriness started to dissipate. "Okay then. So where to from here and when do we leave?"

Taren stood up. He took a deep breath. "Once we have all the supplies and information we need, we should be good to go. It'll be a long journey to the Impossible Way. I haven't been there, but I know of the way. We'll get a good night sleep tonight and then leave at first light." He started for the door.

Sam didn't want Taren to think that he was weak from the hopelessness he expressed earlier so he said, "Sorry I freaked out Taren. I think I'm okay now."

Taren turned and didn't say anything. He just smiled quickly and then left.

The gathering lasted into the evening. Towards the end, Taren brought Sam into the middle of the room. The others were eager to see Sam's powers first hand. He was asked to imagine something for everyone so that they could witness with their own eyes the power that he held.

Sam could feel his hands shaking slightly. He was terrified that he might freeze in the midst of all the eager stares. He could feel the pressure of expectation weighing heavily on his shoulders. For a split moment, when all eyes were on him, he thought he might have forgotten how to imagine at all. Time felt like it was standing still and he was sure that everyone in the room was getting impatient.

He asked Taren, "What should I imagine." There was a trace of shakiness to his voice as he spoke.

"Anything you'd like. Preferably something that doesn't tear the roof off from over our heads." He winked so that only Sam could see.

As he thought about what would be best, he remembered the flower growing so perfectly in Orga's home. He didn't have to think of its beautiful petals and large green leaves for long. He had barely closed his eyes for a second when the room filled with sounds of awe. A few jumped and even cursed when the flower grew instantly through the floorboards.

Many requested that he show them more, even after Sam had imagined two more flowers, a beaver-sized scaly creature, a chair, and five twittering birds. He decided to get more creative the more confident he became. He decided to imagine something more entertaining. He opted for a group of ten fuzzy creatures that resembled tennis ball-sized black cotton balls with eyes, two tiny arms and oversized feet. They chased each other around the room taunting as they went. They ran amok up the legs of the Protectors. Some of them jumped and pretty soon, the room was light with laughter.

After awhile, Taren quieted the crowd. They rounded up the creatures that Sam called fuzzy footed migglewumps, and released them into the forest. Before long, they went back to planning.

By the time the sun was set, the last of the Protectors were departing. Garrett was the last to leave. He had spent a good portion of his time entertaining Sam who found him fascinating. Just being around him was a relief. He was the most upbeat person Sam had ever met. Even Yetews enjoyed being around him. Garrett wasn't bothered by the communication gap between them. Either Taren's life as a Protector wasn't as exciting or Garrett simply enjoyed divulging his tales to anyone who would listen.

Sam secretly hoped that Garrett would join them on their journey. But he knew that it would never happen because he was one of the three who were to keep guard over Orga.

Finally, when the drab house was no longer buzzing with life, Sam dragged his feet to bed. Now that his power was exposed, he figured that it couldn't hurt to change a few things to the room. Taren had followed him to his room and he could see that Sam was thinking about something. Taren already knew what Sam was going to ask. But he waited patiently, nonetheless, for Sam to speak.

"So would it be okay if I imagined a new bed now? You could use it the next time you come home or I could make one for you tonight too." Sam was nervous to ask. He felt like an intruder in Taren's home.

The Gateway to Imagia: The Tale of Sam Little

Taren didn't deny him the request, but instead, said, "I tell you what, kid," he started, "if you can *morph* the bed that's already here, you can go right ahead and make me a cozy bed of my own." Seeing that Sam wasn't exactly thrilled with the idea he added, "It's good practice."

Sam groaned. He didn't relish the idea of sleeping in that musty old bed another night, but he was still so unsure of his ability to morph existing objects. He'd only done it once before and it required a stern form of motivation. Regardless of his lack of confidence, he said, "Fine. I'll try."

"Just try to remember how you did it last time."

Sam closed his eyes. Just as he started to clench his fists he remembered that the key to his last success was in relaxation. He pictured the bed in his mind. He remembered morphing the flower. He felt the surge of confidence as he realized that he knew he could do this.

He slowly began to change the ragged old bed. The dingy mattress and old blankets brightened and fluffed as the splintered boards holding it together smoothed and straightened. It wasn't the same as his beds before because he had to change what he saw instead of start anew. The dull brown of the pillow he'd imagined the night before washed away into a perfect shade of tan. It looked just right in his mind and he grinned to himself.

He opened his eyes and saw Taren shaking his head in disbelief. "Amazing," he whispered.

The bed had been successfully morphed and it was just as Sam imagined it. "You still want me to make you a bed then?" he smugly asked Taren.

"Nah. I have a lot of planning to do tonight. Maybe I'll let you make me one when we come back." He tousled Sam's hair briefly and turned around to leave. "Try to sleep soundly, kid. We have a long journey ahead of us. We leave at dawn."

Sam was having trouble falling asleep. Even with a more comfortable bed, he couldn't manage to find the peace he needed to sleep. And he knew, from experience, that these sorts of nights weren't likely to go without incident. He was geared from the day, anxious for the night, and weary for the journey he was about to make. He didn't know how he was ever going to fall asleep.

But he did.

He felt the familiarity of the dream he was in. He'd walked this part of the forest before. As he treaded softly across the cool green grass, he started to remember what he saw the last time. There used to be a boy with his beautiful angel-like creature standing close by. He walked the same path, hoping to find the boy and his creature, but they were nowhere to be found. This time, there was nothing but the shadow of the trees.

Still, something drew him further into the darkness. He didn't want to go, but something forced his feet on. As the light from the sun waned, he realized he was lost. All familiarity was gone and he felt his heart begin to race inside his chest. The darkness closed in around him and he tried to feel his way back to the safety of the sun.

When all hope of finding his way was lost, a red glow broke the darkness behind him. Sam's knees locked and he could feel the panic rising. He wanted to stand as still as stone, hoping whatever demon gave off such a light would fail to see him, but his hands betrayed him when they started to shake.

He wanted to run or at least face the enemy that lured him here, but couldn't find his legs. Then, when the fear didn't feel as though it could worsen, a raspy, chilling voice spoke from behind him. "Sam," it hissed slowly, "Turn and face your doom, child."

Sam couldn't help himself as he turned to face the creature that beckoned him. When he turned he buckled to the ground in fear. The demon was shrouded in shredded black garments that were wisps of smoke in the air. Where a face would have been were only two glowing red demon eyes that penetrated everything good and warm in Sam. It was as if every nightmare ever dreamt was combined in the form of this horror.

Spiders, snakes, and terrifying creatures of all shapes were crowding in from all sides as the darkness closed in.

He felt the scream building in his tightening chest. He wanted to scream for Taren or Yetews or anyone who could bring him back from the gloom.

In a snap of a motion, it cocked its head in morbid curiosity as it watched Sam quake. It finally spoke again. "Imagia is mine, boy."

"No..." whispered Sam. He wanted to say more, to fight back, but couldn't find his courage. The sweat dripped into his eyes and his breathing became ragged.

The creature, more vile than any of those he'd seen before, hissed three last words before Sam yelled out. "You…will…*die*…"

"TAREN!" Sam screamed. He knew he was having a nightmare but he couldn't wake. The creature vanished plunging him back into the blackness. He hoped that someone would hear his screams and lead him back.

"YETEWS!" Sam screamed again, fighting his way back through the darkness. And just as if someone yanked him out of ice-cold water into the warmth of day, Yetews was shaking him awake.

Sam was gasping for air and yelled again, "Taren! TAREN!"

Though Taren was already by his bed, Sam didn't see him until he caught Sam's shoulders and forced him to turn. "I'm here, Sam! What happened?"

Nearly out of breath, Sam said, "I saw him! It was…him! He said I'm going…to die!"

"Who Sam? Who did you see?"

"It was *him*. I saw Nadaroth."

Chapter Sixteen: Southern Shores

It was only an hour before sunrise when Sam finally became brave enough to close his weary eyes again. No one left his side the rest of the night. Every time that he was close to sleep, his eyes would pop open and he'd shift restlessly.

Though he felt as though he'd only just fallen asleep, Yetews was already nudging him awake. As Sam's tired eyes fluttered in the early light, Yetews grumbled his concern for Sam's exhaustion.

Sam yawned and rubbed his eyes. The dark circles always looked worse after nights like this. He tried to put his Guardian's worries to rest for the moment. "No. I'm all right…really. I just need to eat some breakfast and I'll be better." He smiled and yawned at the same time.

Yetews cocked one very unconvinced eye. But Sam told him to go on ahead of him and get something to eat. When he was alone, Sam pulled out his family photo, already frayed at the edges. He knew that today was only the next step of a journey that he was terrified to take. He sighed heavily, folded the photo again and put it back in his pocket for safekeeping.

He knew that he had to get up and take the first step. But the longer he sat there thinking about it, the more he thought about how incredibly fast things were happening. He breathed deep and closed

The Gateway to Imagia: The Tale of Sam Little

his eyes. As he stood up and walked to the door, he wished that everything around him would slow down enough that his mind could catch up.

Everyone was gathered around the table looking at Taren's map. They turned worried eyes on Sam when he walked into the room. It was the same looks he had been getting since his nightmare last night. He didn't exactly enjoy the feeling it gave him so he tried to draw attention elsewhere. "Are we leaving soon?" he asked grumpily.

Taren exchanged a look with Keesa that was so fast that Sam might have missed it if he weren't paying such close attention. She nodded infinitesimally and loped gracefully out the already open door. "We'll be leaving as soon as you are ready."

Sam glanced towards the door but was too tired to really care why Keesa left. He just said, "I just want to eat first then I guess I'll be ready. Or I guess as ready as I'll ever be." He felt like he should laugh, but it was too true. He sat down heavily to eat. He didn't remember ever feeling so drained in his life. Even chewing his soft bread took extra effort. He wanted so badly to go back to sleep, but after seeing Nadaroth, he was dreading slumber more than any one thing he had to do at the moment. Nightmare laden sleep was far worse than no sleep at all.

It didn't take long for the five to set out once more. As they came to the northern border of the Village of Exile, Garrett met them with two other Protectors that Sam only vaguely recognized. Keesa was standing with them. Sam realized that she must have gone to alert them of their departure.

Sam could feel the doubt on his face. He knew that he wasn't hiding it well enough, so he wasn't surprised when Garrett said, "I know you carry the weight of our world on your shoulders Sam. Try not to think about it. Just remember to avoid dragons and you should be okay." He tapped his scar lightly and winked.

Sam gazed at his scar one last time. He couldn't help but to grin. "Alright. Thanks Garrett." Of all the people he'd met during his short stay in Exile, he'd miss Garrett the most. His enthusiasm for Protecting and the genuine sparkle of joy he carried was contagious. He wished once more that Garrett would join them, but by the looks of his pack and the sense of purpose he exuded, it was obvious that this hope was fleeting.

Taren explained to the three Protectors, each in charge of separate things, "After last night's nightmare encounter with Nadaroth, you will have to be very cautious for awhile. We still don't know what he saw in Sam's mind during our stay here. He may send others here to look for Sam. Anywhere that Sam's been is sure to be a target. There's no doubt now that Nadaroth knows about Sam. Anyone he has met could essentially be a target now." He looked very meaningfully at Garrett. "Garrett, *please* be careful. You've left an impression on Sam in our short stay. It could be especially dangerous for you."

Garrett nodded. "Don't worry about me. I'll be fine."

Though Taren didn't look entirely convinced, he nodded back and turned to look at Sam. "Okay Sam. It's time."

They said goodbye to the three Protectors and headed back into the forest.

Leaving Exile behind didn't impact anyone nearly as much as leaving Orga's home. The silent weight from before was absent and the five travelers were freer in conversation. Titus was always finding something to talk to Taren about. Sam could see the changes that Imagia was bringing out in him. Though he was still his dog and friend, Titus had become like a soldier at war that was on the verge of outranking his comrades. He was always on alert and attempting to form some plan of action. Sam admired his desire to conquer the fear that this world could bring.

For the first time, Sam was actually the quietest of the bunch and eventually, Taren started to take notice of his lack of interaction. They had been traveling nearly the entire day without conflict. No attacks or set backs had tampered with their journey's beginning but Sam's demeanor was not mirroring the day. Taren finally decided to slow his pace to match Yetews'. In an attempt to bring Sam back to life, he said, "Did I ever tell you about my sister?"

Sam perked up at the sudden willingness to share part of his story. "Um, only that you are twins and that she wasn't happy to be trapped here."

"Hmm," Taren continued, "yes, she never really adjusted to life in Imagia. Even after we made a home in Exile." He looked down waiting for Sam to show enough interest to continue.

The familiar curious light beamed from Sam's eyes. "So that

The Gateway to Imagia: The Tale of Sam Little

house was where you both lived?"

"Yes."

"So…where is she now? Was she one of the lady Protectors?" Sam asked.

"I'll get there. But first you should know a little about her." He smiled. Sam was himself again and his plan was working. "Tessa was always more sensitive to things than I was. She was also more connected to her imagination than me. That made the death of Atlantis very hard for her. I was deeply saddened for my loss of Tiberius, but it was nowhere near the sadness that Tessa felt.

"As we grew, Tessa didn't get better. She slept constantly and as you have found for yourself, sleep in Imagia is not always good. She was constantly plagued with nightmares. Some of them were of Nadaroth's creations, but others were of her own. She ultimately began to fear sleep."

Sam sympathized and felt sadness for Taren's sister.

Taren continued. "Over the years, she began to only sleep briefly and it was a stretch calling it sleep at all. She began to mutter to herself. I would come home, only to find her curled in a corner, rambling nonsense. Every once in a while, I could understand a sentence or two. But none of it made any sense. Eventually, the only thing she would say was 'Find the end.' I assumed it was nothing and I was too late in finding that it had meaning."

Sam could hear the regret thick in his voice. "What happened?" he asked.

"Well, I'd been away for two weeks. It'd been a busy time. Many Guardians were born that needed protecting, and by the time I got home…she was gone. No one knew where she went because she left in the night. But word traveled and someone spotted her heading north. In the very direction we are headed now, to be precise."

Sam realized what Taren was saying and he gasped suddenly. "You mean she…she…" He couldn't manage to finish his thought.

Taren was shaking his head from side to side in disgust. "She went to find Nadaroth. There were tales of people who had tried to cross this place we so eagerly are trying to reach. The moment I found her missing, I started to search. She was foolish to go and I had never traveled this far north. By the time I reached the end of my search, I knew she was gone."

Taren's face was filled with regret and Sam knew that it wasn't easy for him to tell this story. "What happened to her?" he asked hesitantly. He wasn't entirely sure he wanted the answer because the same thing could easily happen to him.

"She tried to cross the Impossible Way two days before I reached it. And like those before her, she failed. She was gone."

"I'm sorry," said Sam. He had thought Taren's sister was still around and that he would meet her someday.

"It's okay," Taren shrugged. "It was a long time ago."

"Oh." Sam didn't understand how Taren could simply shrug off the loss of his sister so easily. Even though his parents were still alive, he'd felt as though he'd lost them. He felt incredibly sad that he'd never see them again. He would imagine that losing someone in such a permanent way would be more devastating.

Taren could tell that Sam was upset by something and he must have realized what it was, because he said, "I don't *seem* bothered by her loss now, but I am. You have to understand, Sam. It was nearly one hundred years ago. Over time, the pain of losing someone you love starts to lessen. It never goes away, but it does get easier."

Sam didn't say anything. He hadn't thought much about how old Taren really was. In fact, up until now, he'd almost completely forgotten because he looked so young. As he considered what Taren had told him, he asked another question. "So what did Tessa mean by 'find the end'?"

"Well, one of the only other things I could understand from her was that she wanted the nightmares to end. She figured that finding Nadaroth would end her suffering. I don't believe she wanted to find him to fight him. She wanted to find him to end the pain."

Sam didn't know what to think about this and the uncertainty was thick in his expression.

In hopes of interjecting a subject change, Yetews growled a question and Taren looked to Sam for the translation.

"He wants to know what makes the way so impossible."

"It's a very wide body of water," he raised a finger to stop Sam. He could see the question brewing before it was asked. "And no, a boat won't work. And before you ask, swimming won't work either. There are strange and terrible things that stop you from entering the water."

The Gateway to Imagia: The Tale of Sam Little

Sam jumped in, "You mean like the deceptor?"

Taren laughed from Sam's connection. "No. Not quite. Actually, I'm not entirely sure because I've never tried to cross. I've only heard stories, but no one who has tried to cross has ever come back so I imagine the stories are only speculation."

Titus, who was also engrossed in Taren's story, asked, "But why is it even there? I say we should try to simply go around it. Bypass the water entirely. Surely it has an end."

Taren looked down to Titus. "No. Think of Imagia as a globe. In the middle, there is a river that splits the globe into north and south. Some parts of Imagia are never changing and this is one of those parts. There is no beginning and no end. But what I do know is that before the nightmares took hold of this good world, the passage could be crossed by anyone. I was never able to go, but the older Guardians tell us that it leads to an amazing place that is home to the largest creatures of Imagia. They call it the Land of the Behemoths."

Sam was alight with excitement. His mind raced with the things he might see in such a place. It was the first time in a while that he actually felt excited. "I wonder what we'll see when we get there."

Taren was pleased to see Sam in such high spirits. "I don't know, but I've heard tales of giant beasts of burden with long gray hair that shimmers silver in the sun. And there were many dragons there, though rumor has it that Nadaroth has imprisoned and all but exterminated them from those lands."

Sam was almost glowing with anticipation. He didn't say anything more as they walked on.

There was new life in Sam's face that nearly erased the dark circles from his tired eyes. Yetews looked gratefully to Taren. He grumbled something low to him.

There was no translation needed because they were both thinking the same thing. He quietly replied, "You're welcome."

Yetews slowed his pace to become more in stride with Sam. He noticed the boy losing ground as he became further engrossed in this thoughts. He scooped him up and placed him on his shoulders without missing a beat.

Sam barely noticed.

* * * * * * * * *

When Sam opened his eyes, it was nearly dark and they had stopped moving. He couldn't even remember falling asleep. But he was thankful that he had. He felt more rested, but his eyes still felt heavy. He wasn't sure where they were or how long he'd slept.

It was obvious that they were still in the forest because trees surrounded them. Unlike the other times he had stayed overnight on the forest floor, there wasn't much of a clearing to speak of, just a thinning of the trees. Sam began to wonder if the entire world was covered in a forest.

Keesa was resting on a large tree limb above Sam when she noticed that he was awake. The tip of her long tail twitched methodically. "Good evening, Sam. I hope you rested well."

Sam was slightly startled by her voice. "Um, yeah, kind of. I didn't even know I fell asleep. Where are we?"

"Not far from the border of the forest," she whispered. "Taren and I agree that it might be safer to not make camp in open clearings if we can avoid it. There is more safety in the cover of the trees. You still look exhausted. Why don't you try to go back to sleep. I will watch over you until morning."

Sam yawned and the others noticed. Taren was building a small fire from the timber that Yetews was busy gathering. He had also just noticed that Titus was lying protectively near his head.

No one else said anything to Sam. He yawned again and felt the heaviness take over his eyes. The last thing he saw was Yetews' lopsided grin as he slipped back into slumber.

* * * * * * * * *

Sam jerked upright from his sleep, startled by the sound of rustling underbrush. Taren was there to calm him with a hand on his chest.

"Calm down. It's nothing to worry about."

"What is it?" Sam almost yelled. He'd become all too familiar with the sounds of lurking danger in the trees.

"It's just a Guardian and her child. They're heading to their gateway."

Sam could see the Guardian through the trees as she passed them. She was a tall human-like creature, only her skin was smooth as satin and the most stunning shades of blue. She was shrouded in flowing robes of indigo and scarlet. She was strange and beautiful and as she passed, she peacefully peered down at Sam. She was holding her girls hand and guiding her through the dark. The girl, younger than Sam, took no notice of the strangers in the dark. She knew she was safe with her Guardian.

Taren quietly said, "You can go back to sleep. You're safe."

Seeing another Guardian with a child for the first time started his mind to thinking. "I don't know if I can." Sam looked around and saw that Yetews was snoring about a foot away and Titus was following in suit. They had made a protective barrier around him with their bodies.

"You should take the chance to sleep while you can. The last time you slept well was nearly eight days ago when we left Exile."

Sam couldn't believe they'd been traveling for over a week. They'd seen so many strange creatures and places that it felt like there could be nowhere left to journey to.

In the back of his mind, he remembered a time when he'd dreamed of setting off on weeklong adventures. But those were simpler times when his adventures weren't plagued by fear and exhaustion. He longed for those times. He missed so much of his old life. But he knew that his past life was in the exact same state as he was – lost.

He splayed his fingers out and examined how filthy they were. He thought of his mom and how she would practically have to drag him, kicking and screaming, to bathe every night. As he wiped his hands on his pants, he found himself suddenly missing something as simple as a bath.

And as far as simple things went, he missed peaceful sleep. It seemed that every time he closed his eyes lately, there was something awful waiting for him in his nightmares. Or worse. There was something waiting for him in his vulnerable in-between. He'd spent the times when they rested practicing imagining. He found it too difficult to force himself to sleep, so he'd use the time to hone his skills. The good thing was that he'd become increasingly good at morphing. The bad thing was that he was completely drained by evening.

Everyone seemed to notice the toll it was taking on Sam. They helped as often as they could, but no one could take the pressure fully away from him. They had good times, when Sam would be genuinely happy, but after the fifth day, things took a turn for the worse.

Now, on day eight, Sam was losing his focus. He was having trouble imagining things as clearly. Taren was convinced it was due to his lack of sleep. But Sam knew better. He was sure it was his loss of hope for the situation. He trusted Taren to know where they were going, but he'd expected to be to their first destination nearly three days ago. He was afraid to mention it, but in a desperate attempt to avoid falling back asleep, he asked, "Taren, why is it taking so long to get there? I thought you said it would only take five days."

Taren was nodding before Sam finished the question. "Yes. I know. But the last time I took this journey, I was alone. I didn't take into account that there would be five of us. And one of us who would be running on very little sleep." He flashed Sam a slightly accusing look.

"Oh. So, let's say I got some sleep. How much longer would it take then?"

"Hmm…" Taren stroked his chin in mock thoughtfulness, "I'd say we'd be there tomorrow. Midmorning." He smiled then added, "But that would be without you sleeping as well. I was going to tell you earlier but you looked like you were close to sleep in Yetews' arms so I didn't want to disturb you."

"Tell me what, exactly?" asked Sam.

"That we are nearly there. We will reach the Impossible Way shortly after we leave in the morning."

Sam was shocked. He couldn't understand why they didn't simply keep going and reach it tonight if they were so near. He was almost angry at the thought of prolonging the journey further when he barely slept anyways. What would it hurt to miss another night of restless sleep? He could feel his eyebrows pinching in the center, giving away his frustration.

Once more, Taren's uncanny intuition for Sam's thoughts came through. "Now don't go looking at me like that, kid. We aren't prolonging the trip to annoy you. I want everyone to be as keen as they can tomorrow. I don't know exactly what this place is going to throw at us. That's why everyone is sleeping in shifts tonight."

Sam was slightly embarrassed for getting frustrated and all he could manage to squeak out was, "Sorry."

The Gateway to Imagia: The Tale of Sam Little

"Don't sweat it. Just *please* try to sleep. You're going to need to be as alert as you can tomorrow. I know the harder you push yourself the more exhausted it makes you. I need you running on full steam, okay? We can get you there safely," Taren said as he gestured to the other three sleeping soundly around them, "but if Orga was right, once we get there, it's all going to be on you and your imagination. You're gonna need all the rest you can get."

Sam took Taren's words to heart. Knowing that they were so close to something so important put things back into perspective and, strangely, it helped him sleep. He knew that their fate may very well rest on his shoulders tomorrow and he found the will to fight the fear and drifted back to sleep.

Whether it was pure exhaustion taking hold of him or the uncommon lack of dreams, Sam finally slept soundly. He didn't know how they moved him and walked so long without waking him up, but when he opened his eyes, he was once again being cradled in Yetews' massive arms.

Yetews noticed Sam stirring and grumbled to him in greeting. He growled something else and, slightly startled, Sam said, "We're almost there? But how?"

Keesa answered him. She was in her alert mode, but still managed to sound sweet. "You were sleeping so peacefully that we didn't have the heart to wake you."

Titus snorted. "Not that we didn't try though. You would simply roll back over and say 'five more minutes' like you did when you had to wake to go to school. It was pretty entertaining." He smiled doggishly.

Sam laughed lightly. His mom was always telling him he was a lazy morning person and that waking him was like waking the dead.

They'd been traveling in and out of hilly grasslands and even thicker forests for two days. Now the forest was once again behind them. There were still trees, but the grass stretched far around them. They were battling a rather steep hill at the moment. The blades of grass in these lands were so high that Sam's head barely reached the top at times. It'd proved to be perfect camouflage for Keesa and Titus while Yetews seemed quite at ease for his part.

Sam never thought much about what Yetews liked to eat, but he was perfectly happy to munch on thick mouthfuls of grass every so often to compliment the berries he'd managed to forage.

Sam, now walking beside his Guardian, noticed how appetizing the crunch of the grass sounded and thought that he might try a bite. He plucked a few blades and placed them in his mouth. He then promptly spit them out in disgust. Yetews snorted and laughed. He grumbled to Sam.

After wiping his mouth on the back of his hand he said, "But it looked good when you were eating it. Yuck. That was gross."

Yetews started laughing again only to be stopped short by the sound of Taren's reprimanding voice.

"Yetews," Taren said in all seriousness, "I need you to keep Sam close." He turned to address Keesa next. "Stay on my left flank and keep Sam in your sight." Lastly, he looked to Titus. "Right flank. And let me know if you smell any sign of danger." He paused, slowed his pace, and then said, "We're here."

They came up over the hill and at the bottom was water so wide that the other side didn't registered in view.

The five made their way to the water cautiously. Keesa was poised for attack and Taren's knuckles were white as he grasped his bow. Sam's heart was pounding so hard that he could hear it beating in his ears.

There was no sign of danger in any direction. Even the water looked without peril. Sam had tried to picture the water from Taren's vague description. He'd expected black water and torrential waves that thrashed across the surface. But it was nothing like that. The water moved, but only from the warm wind that weaved its way through the tall grass. It wasn't clear water, but it wasn't menacing either. It held the same mystery that a common lake might hold.

As tense as the situation felt, the shoreline seemed clear from both east and west. For all the danger they had experienced so far, this seemed almost harmless. Sam looked around, like everyone else, only to see nothing in any direction. There wasn't so much as a bird in the sky.

They were only a few yards from the water's edge now. "I don't get it," Sam finally said. "What's so impossible about this? It looks easy."

Yetews quietly agreed with him.

Taren didn't respond to Sam's observation. He just stood silently as if waiting for the inevitable to happen. He looked over towards Titus who was sniffing the air repetitively. "What is it?" he asked him.

Titus shook his head and sniffed a moment longer. "I don't know. Something isn't right about this place."

"I smell it too," Keesa agreed. "It's almost as if..." She cut short and her ears laid back flat against her head. She bared her teeth and let out a low menacing growl the same time as Titus did.

Titus' hackles were stiffened straight up and he backed up to stand directly in front of Sam.

The change in their behavior was so sudden that Sam felt the hairs stand up on his arm.

A strong stone's throw away, the water began to quake and stir. Something massive was moving under the surface and it was heading straight for them.

As Sam watched the wake of the water quickly approaching, he realized that whatever he had said before about this being easy was spoken too soon. The ground began to tremble and he suddenly wished he had never said anything at all.

Chapter Seventeen: The Impossible Way

Taren readied his bow and took steady aim, still hesitant to fire. He only glanced back once to make sure that Sam was well enough protected between Yetews' arms.

Whatever was lurking beneath the water began to rise. The water swirled and something smooth and glossy began to break the surface. It was muddied shades of greens and browns and looked as sleek as the skin of a dolphin. As it rose, a colossal, frayed dorsal fin appeared followed shortly by an equally worn tailfin that could only belong to that of water-bound creatures. The last thing to break through the water was its gargantuan head. Its eyes were relatively small compared to the size of its body, but still easily the size of a soccer ball. And floating snakelike on the water just above its mouth were tentacle-like whiskers.

Taren pulled his bowstring taut, but still hesitated to strike.

Sam was in awe. He knew exactly what he was looking at but never dreamed that one could ever be the size of a small whale. He didn't know what compelled him to do it, but he couldn't stop himself. He looked at the creature and spoke directly to it. "Holy cow! You're a catfish!"

The beast shifted in the water and focused one glassy eye on Sam. There was a slight milky haze deep inside the black pupil. The kind that only appeared in the eyes of the old. Yet, the eyes held vast wisdom.

Taren was shocked by Sam's sudden outburst and looked back to the creature as if waiting for some form of response.

The water-bound beast took a raspy breath and then, to everyone's surprise, it spoke directly back to Sam.

"Come here, boy," It spoke in a deep, booming voice that gurgled slightly from the water in his mouth.

Sam, strangely without fear, got one foot forward before Yetews had the instinct to hold him back. Taren quickly interjected to the creature's demand. "The boy isn't going anywhere," he said as he steadied his aim.

The creature's eyes swiveled to face Taren before it returned its stare back to Sam. "Hmph! Then tell me, boy. You spoke like you knew I'd respond. Why?"

Sam saw everyone turn eyes to him, waiting for his response, and he swallowed hard before he answered. "I...don't know. I just always liked catfish. My dad let me throw them back when we went fishing and...well...he told me that we let them go because they were the wisest of the lake. He said the biggest ones were the wise old granddaddies." He stopped to look closer at the giant fish. "And you must be the oldest catfish ever because you're *huge!* So you gotta be the wisest!"

The air was filled with a booming laughter and the fish's mouth turned up slightly at the corner. Then without warning, it disappeared back beneath the water.

"What happened? Where did he go?" Sam asked.

Everyone was too shocked to know what to say. Then, nearly a minute later, he resurfaced. Taren was the first to jump back into position, standing steadfast at the front.

Like so many he'd met in Imagia, there was personality in the catfish's face. Sam wasn't sure he'd ever get used to that.

He tugged lightly on Yetews' arms in hopes of him letting go. He wanted to approach the amazing creature. He had an odd feeling that it wasn't the danger that they needed to concern themselves with. But when Yetews refused to give him any slack, Sam decided that he had no choice but to ask from where he stood. "Excuse me. But where did you just go?" He decided he should speak loudly because he wasn't entirely sure where the ears were at on a catfish.

One of the catfish's eyes was still focused directly on Sam. He took another gurgling breath and said, "Ah...sorry 'bout that. Large gills, you know." He rolled in the water enough to flap his gills for Sam to see. "Takes me a bit to take a good, deep breath." He swiveled his great eye on Taren briefly then said, "You can tell the Protector to relax. I'm just a sentry to these waters. I'm not here to harm you."

Taren jumped in before Sam could say anything. "A sentry? If that's true, then what is your purpose if not to guard us against crossing?"

The catfish asked Sam in a lighthearted tone, "Is he always this much fun or is it just because a giant fish is talking to him?"

Though he knew that Taren meant well, Sam couldn't help himself but to smile. "I think he's just being safe. We've been attacked by a lot of stuff since I got here."

Taren looked over to Sam in silent warning. "Sentry or not. I'll let my guard down when I can guarantee the boy's safety."

The catfish looked surprised. He looked at each individual before he focused back on Sam. "Hmm." He considered for a moment. "A Protector's duty is to defend Guardians, not children. Interesting. What's so special about you, boy?" When the catfish saw Taren's warning hand towards Sam, he dipped back down for another breath. When he resurfaced, he said, "Alright, Protector. Keep your secrets then. But know that I am here as a forewarning. Listen and heed my words well.

'To pass these waters, you must be
Much more clever than even me.
Dangers in the deep await.
Tempt to swim and you tempt fate.
Disturb the water and there's no doubt,
What goes in, shall never go out.
For the strength you have is the wrong kind.
The power you need is from your mind.
Think twice about the choice you make,
It could truly be your last mistake.
If you dare not this dangerous game.
Go back the way, from which you came,
Because in these waters you will rot,
For pass I can, but you cannot."

The catfish was eerily silent after his warning. Taren, obviously convinced that the sentry was not a danger, lowered his bow and turned to Sam. "Let him go, Yetews."

Yetews fought against his instinct to protect Sam and looked down at him with concern. The catfish had already gone below for air. By the time he resurfaced, Sam had already gotten as close to the

The Gateway to Imagia: The Tale of Sam Little

water as Taren would allow.

The catfish watched the boy closely as he stood there with curiosity thick on his face. Sam finally spoke when he knew what he wanted to say. "I'm Sam. Do you have a name?" He could hear a sigh from Taren. When he turned around to see what the problem was, Taren was rubbing both of his hands over his temples. It made Sam wonder why saying his name was really so bad.

The catfish considered for a long moment. At first Sam thought that he wasn't allowed to speak anymore and he started to feel slightly uncomfortable. But finally, the catfish answered. "Ah! I remember now! My name is Dolimus." He looked very pleased with himself and repeated his epiphany. "Yes. Dolimus is what I was called."

"You forgot your name?" asked Sam.

"Well, it's been a long time since someone's actually asked me."

"Oh. Well, I've never met a catfish before. Nice to meet you, Dolimus."

The others were standing behind Sam, confused for the moment. They kept glancing nervously at one another while Sam continued to converse with the giant fish. But of all of them, Taren was most impressed with Sam. As the conversation went on, he realized that Sam was more than likely doing something that no one else who had tried to pass the Impossible Way had ever attempted to do before.

It was as though Sam was fraternizing with the enemy.

Sam was still busy talking to Dolimus. "So if you aren't the one we have to worry about, then what is?"

Dolimus seemed torn by an internal struggle. "I don't know exactly what I can tell you. This way is not meant for passage any longer. I can only warn you of the dangers that are waiting for you should you try to pass. And there are a whole lot of dangers, boy."

Taren stepped forward next to Sam and interjected before Sam could get his next words out. "These dangers you warn us of. If I understand you correctly, they are only meant to attack if we try to cross. So that is why it is impossible then."

Dolimus opened his mouth to respond, but as he did Sam corrected Taren. "No. He said that if we touch the water then we would be attacked. 'What goes in shall never go out.' That means if we touch the water then whatever is in the water will take us and we will never go out. Right?" He looked to Dolimus for affirmation.

Dolimus chuckled. "Intelligent little human you have there, Protector. But I am not permitted to reveal the dangers to you or the answers to the riddle. However, if I were you, I would not try to cross. Go back the way you came, Sam. I like you, boy. I don't want to see you lost to these confounded waters like so many before you." There was an element of disgust in his voice.

Yetews, who had stepped next to Sam, grumbled a question. Sam translated for them. "He wants to know why you can cross and if that means you are an enemy?"

Dolimus made a clucking sound and sighed deeply. "I don't wish you – or anyone else for that matter – harm. But no, I am not your enemy. I am neither friend nor foe. If there was more time I would gladly tell you my story, but I think it best if you simply leave. It is impossible to cross. I shouldn't speak of this, but…"

They watched as Dolimus was making a decision about his internal struggle. Sam prompted him to finish. "But what?"

He'd made his decision and offered them his information. "The only one who has ever crossed these waters is the very same that made them dangerous. He made it this way. It is impossible for anyone but him."

In unison, nearly all of them said, "Nadaroth."

The catfish's silence affirmed it.

"But you said," Sam paused as he tried to remember the catfish's exact words, "you said that the power we need is the power of the mind."

"Yes. That is the warning I gave you. And now I must wait here for your decision. Will you choose the impossible? Or will you remain in the safety of the south?"

Taren looked around to everyone and answered for all, "We have no choice. We must find passage. We must cross the Impossible Way."

Dolimus sighed regretfully. "Very well. Then my final warning to you is this:

> *'The only safe passage this way can bestow,*
> *Must come from something in the waters below.*
> *You were given a choice; the decision is made.*
> *You have but an hour, to find your way."*

Taren was shocked. The color slightly drained from his face. He

The Gateway to Imagia: The Tale of Sam Little

looked from Sam to the old catfish. "An hour? We have a time limit? What will happen at the hour's end?"

Dolimus took a final look at the curious group and let his eye rest once more on Sam. He didn't answer Taren's concerned questions. He only said, "I'm sorry. I can say no more. Good luck, Sam. Of all the ones who have tried, I hope *you* will find a way."

Without another word, Dolimus disappeared. At first Sam thought that he was merely taking a long breath. But after several minutes, they all knew that he would not resurface again.

He was gone.

Taren turned to Sam. He knelt down on his level and held his gaze. "Sam. I don't know what will happen in an hour. But there is a reason that no one has returned from this place. It is in your hands now. We must find safe passage to the northern shores."

At first, Sam was in a mild state of disbelief. He wasn't sure what he was supposed to do and his mind was clouded with the events of the past weeks. But Taren shook him lightly on the shoulders and gently said, "Sam?"

When Sam began to focus, he shook off his haze and nodded. He knew what he needed to do. He cleared his mind and sat down on the ground. He mumbled parts of Dolimus' warning to himself as he thought about what he had to do.

Taren knew what Sam was doing. But it didn't seem to help him gain patience for the situation. One hour was going to pass too quickly and he was already edgy. During their talks with Orga about Sam's abilities, he knew that in order to do the impossible, Sam would have to use his imagination in ways that would have to stretch his power to new levels. He folded his arms and waited, keeping alert to their surroundings.

While Sam deliberated, the others cast wary looks to one another while they nervously looked around, waiting for something to attack them. Keesa, being completely out of her element, found herself pacing like a caged creature. She consistently checked over her shoulders with every turn she made. Her ears swiveled in fluid motions as she moved.

Yetews sat, ever vigilant, next to Sam in an attempt of moral support. Titus joined Taren and together they attempted to mask their own impatience and hushed words of concern.

After a quarter of their time was spent, Sam stood up. He looked over to Taren and said, "Do you think we only have one chance to try? Because I'm going to try something and I don't know what will happen."

Taren could hear the uncertainty in his voice and tried his best to reassure him. Out of the corner of his eye, he saw Keesa and Titus go on alert while Yetews stood protectively by Sam's side. He said, "I don't think it works that way. I think we have one hour to cross."

Sam took another shaky breath as he silently wished that he still had his watch. He closed his eyes and pictured the most obvious way he knew to cross water. As he pinched his face in concentration, he knew that his imagination was successful when he heard the others whispering.

He'd imagined a boat. Small, yet perfect for the five travelers to fit in comfortably. He smiled to himself when he saw it. But the instant he took one step forward towards it, the water around the boat shook fiercely. From under the boat, the water turned black as night. The shadow of some rising beast dwarfed the small vessel.

Everyone backed away from the water, nearly falling over each other in their desperate attempt to flee from the shore. Sam expected to see a fierce creature rip the boat in half before their eyes. Instead, it happened slowly.

It was an eerie sight. Thousands of thread-like white tentacles felt their way up the wooden sides of the boat. The tentacles weaved in through the tiniest imperfections. While they watched, the wood began to shred and splinter away, piece by piece, into the water. The tentacles slowly pulled the boat under into the darkening abyss. The only thing left was the rippling of the water where the ship had once been.

Taren spared no moment for shock. "Try again Sam. We are running out of time."

Sam didn't reply. His fingers began to shake as he considered what to try next. He looked at the water and then gazed into the sky. Deep down, he knew that what he was about to do wouldn't work but he tried it anyways – even if it was mostly for sheer curiosity.

The lack of birds flying in the sky wasn't as noticeable until the sound of one lone bird broke the silence. Everyone looked into the sky at Sam's newest creation. They watched as the bird left the safety

The Gateway to Imagia: The Tale of Sam Little

of the southern shores and began to cross the skies above the water.

Just when Sam had the tiniest spark of hope that he'd found a way across, the water thundered. The same tentacles from before shot through the air and grabbed the unsuspecting bird from the air. The speed at which it moved was significantly different this time. But, it crept back into the watery depths with the same ghostly movements, devouring the poor bird with its descent. Whatever this creature was, it gave no warning to its attack.

The attack had happened so fast that Sam didn't even realize he'd fallen back to the ground in shock. His fingers shook harder as he stood back up.

Taren was even a bit unsteady when he said, "I guess *flying* over is out then."

Titus considered for a moment and then said, "The warning from the fish said the only way we can cross must come from the water itself."

"Yes," said Keesa. "But how is that possible?"

Taren angrily replied, "It's not meant to *be* possible. That's the problem."

As they argued between themselves about what they should do, Sam watched them and thought frantically about Dolimus' words of warning. The words jumped through his thoughts until he could no longer hear the panic from the others. He slipped into the comfort of his mind and suddenly the great catfish's words made perfect sense.

He didn't know if the others were aware of what he was doing, but he didn't care. He turned to the water and focused his mind deep below the surface of the water. He knew what he had to do.

He couldn't hear anyone or anything. Things simply began to take shape in his mind. He felt as though he purposely stepped into a self-made dream. He concentrated harder. Finally, the spot where he was focusing began to swirl. Three dark shapes were heading straight for the shore.

Taren was the first to notice and he immediately looked to Sam. Though afraid to break his concentration, he asked cautiously, "Is this your doing?"

Sam was nearly whispering when he spoke. "It had to come from below." He turned to look at Taren whose face was tight with concern. He spoke a little louder now. "They'll take us across."

Just as Taren was about to ask what Sam was talking about, three boulder-sized heads emerged from the water. The heads were nothing compared to the massive humps that trailed behind. They stopped mere feet from the shoreline.

Everyone stood in awe at the sight. Their eyes were those of gentle beasts and they patiently looked to Sam as they dipped their heads to listen. Sam looked back, smiling, at the shocked faces of his friends. "Sea turtles. They come from below, they won't leave the water, and we can ride them across." He turned back to the three whale sized turtles and asked, "Will you take us to the other side?"

The middle turtle nodded once. In a voice that mirrored the gentleness in her eyes, she said, "We will."

Though he tried to hide his sense of amazement, Taren still felt compelled to ask, "I still don't know how you did this, but how do we get on them without touching the water?"

Sam simply blinked twice, grinned slyly, and glanced around Taren.

Taren turned back around when he heard Titus say, "Remarkable, Sam."

A large set of wooden steps had appeared that jutted out just before the shore's edge, careful not to touch the water or pass the shoreline. It created a sort of dock-like structure.

The five hurried up the steps and made their way onto their turtles. Sam and Yetews were on the lead female. Keesa and Titus followed on a slightly smaller male and Taren rode alone on the smallest male.

They were all slightly nervous initially, hoping that the eerie tentacles wouldn't return for the turtles as well. When nothing happened after a few minutes, they settled nicely on their mossy shells, concentrating on not falling into the murky water.

Sam was elated to be riding something amazing that he had actually created. He was nearly lost in his busy mind again when something familiar surfaced beside his turtle.

It was Dolimus. "Amazing, boy! How did you do this?"

Sam startled and Yetews grabbed him before he slipped. Seeing the big catfish got his heart pumping for a moment. Dolimus was nearly the same size as the turtles. He watched the giant fish glide effortlessly next to his turtle and couldn't help but feel a little excited for the sense of adventure. "I have the power to make my imagination real. Just like Nadaroth. Only I'm not bad."

"I believe you aren't." Sam could see his gills working as he swam. "I now understand why the Protector is so jumpy. I've always hoped that another child would come to remove Nadaroth from his self appointed throne."

Sam was confused. "But I thought you worked for him."

"No. I do what he orders me to do because I am the last of this once great river's Sentries."

"I don't understand," Sam replied.

The two other turtles were close enough that the others were listening to what Dolimus was saying. Taren, who sat alone with his bow in hand, said, "I've heard the tales before by the oldest Guardians. But, I thought you were all wiped out when Nadaroth took hold of the northern shores. Do you still live because you are a traitor to the good of Imagia? Are you Nadaroth's pet now?"

Taren's harshness offended Sam. He didn't understand why Taren would be so rude to Dolimus when he had never done anything wrong to them. Sam was about to say something but Dolimus spoke first.

"Don't be angry with your Protector, Sam. He is half right." When Dolimus saw the confusion and disbelief over Sam's face, he spoke again. "Before this world was in essence destroyed, I was a Sentry to this river. Children enter through their gateways on the southern half of Imagia and many of them, led by their Guardians, would travel to the river to cross to the north. There were many things to see and Sentries would aid them in their passage.

"When Nadaroth took over the lands, he staked claim over the northern side of Imagia. Against his will, we continued to ferry children and their Guardians back and forth when we could and he warned us to cease. It was our duty to aid children and so he littered the waters with evil. He made it so no one could cross and began to hunt us down, one by one, until I was the last of my kind. He used his followers and dark creatures to capture me. I was trapped in a net, unable to move. They held me until Nadaroth came. He was horribly frightening; like nothing I've ever seen before. I was chilled to my very core at his presence. I could barely look at him." Dolimus shivered in the water, sending extra waves of ripples out across their path.

Taren, anger still on his face, sat quietly and listened openly to the fish. The others followed in suit and Sam prompted Dolimus to continue. "What did he do?"

"They tortured me." He paused and Sam could tell he was hiding the details. "I will not relive this moment, so please do not ask me to. But in the end, he gave me a choice. He said that he would allow me to survive, grant me protection, if I would stay and deliver his message to those who dare cross. Or I could be tortured into doing as he asked and forever live a life of pain. I chose to do his will. Not because I was a traitor, but because I wanted to save whom I could from the horrors that he created in this water. But I was alone. And many children and Guardians found out too late that they could not cross."

The sadness Sam felt for Dolimus and the many who were lost was great. He wanted to say something to help, but he couldn't manage to find the right words. He hoped that when they crossed, that the turtles would serve as friends for him. He'd put a great deal of effort into creating them to be kind and gentle creatures.

Even Taren had warmed his misplaced icy expression.

It had been at least a twenty-minute ride before they could see the shore growing closer as the turtles brought them to their destination. Their hour mark was dangerously close. There was thick forest along the entire shoreline, hiding what might be waiting behind its dark wall. Dolimus finished his tale more quickly. "You seem to hold the power that Nadaroth would fear if he knew you existed."

Taren jumped in at that. "We think he already knows. It's the only way to explain the numerous attacks. Will you tell him we crossed?"

Dolimus thought for a moment and the eye closest to Sam swiveled to watch him. "I will do what I can to keep it hidden from him." They could tell that this may cost him greatly.

"Thank you," Taren said. Yetews grumbled his thanks as well.

"You can thank me by doing everything in your power to protect the boy." His eyes swiveled once more to Sam and then back to Taren. "Perhaps the world will be a good place again."

Yetews grumbled something and Sam went to translate for Dolimus. "Yetews says that…"

The Gateway to Imagia: The Tale of Sam Little

Dolimus interrupted him. "I understood him. No translation necessary." Everyone was shocked and waited in silence for an explanation. "I understand all Guardians. It's part of being a Sentry." He smiled again as best as a fish could smile.

Yetews raised an eyebrow and waited for the response to his question.

Dolimus answered. "In response to his question, the answer is yes. Though I have never seen anyone cross successfully before today, I imagine that you will be safe once you leave the water. But you must hurry. You still have to find a way to get off of these amazing creations without touching the water and your hour is nearly up. I can feel the evil in the water waiting to strike."

They were very close to the other side. Every so often, they could see shadows swimming menacingly beneath them. A warning that one slip of the foot could end their journey all too quickly. It took the turtles nearly half an hour to cross, leaving them with barely a few minutes for Sam to imagine another cleverly designed set of steps to help them off their gracious hosts.

Dolimus swam to the shore, waiting and watching in awe at Sam's ability. Nearly everyone was safely off the turtles' backs. Keesa was the last to make the small jump to the steps. But when she jumped from the turtle's back, she slipped on the mossy shell and barely caught the edge of the wooden steps. Her muscles rippled beneath her tawny fur as she heaved herself back up. Taren was already running back up the steps to help. She was on all four feet before he got there, but slightly shaken from the brief ordeal.

The five, slightly disorientated from the journey, returned safely to the shore. Everyone but Keesa walked to the waters edge to speak once more to the wise catfish. Keesa was the worst for the wear of the crossing. She willingly disclosed her strong dislike for water, making Sam smile. She was more like a cat than he took her for.

Sam was closest to Dolimus. "Um…thanks for crossing with us. I hope the turtles help you to be less lonely." He wasn't sure that it would help at all but he hoped silently that maybe the turtles could become Sentries one day as well.

Taren was next. "It looks like we made it safely. Thank you for keeping our secret." He looked over to the wooden steps and realized that their passing couldn't be kept secret for long no matter how little the Sentry disclosed.

Dolimus saw what Taren was looking at and said, "Yes. It won't take much to figure out that someone has crossed. But I will not reveal your names, Protector."

Taren nodded once in thanks.

"Thank you, Sentry," Titus said.

The others uttered their appreciation as well and Sam understood suddenly what they were referring to. "The steps!" He clapped a hand on his forehead and said, "Oh shoot! I didn't even think about that. I was just trying to find a way across and..."

"And you did beautifully, Sam," Taren interrupted. "There isn't a fix to every little problem in that amazing little brain of yours." He tousled Sam's hair. "You did good, kid. Now let's get going. We still have a long journey ahead of us."

Sam turned back to Dolimus again to say goodbye. "I hope to see you again. I can't wait to see what kinds of creatures there might be over here. But after seeing you, they might not be as cool." He smiled, hoping that Dolimus would understand his gesture of friendship.

He smiled his fishy grin. "You are an amazing child, Sam. I wish you all the luck you need. But don't make the mistake that every creature you meet is friendly. Children have not visited these lands in many years. These waters were but a first taste of the now strange and wild ways you are about to embark on. Be careful. Some things are not as they appear."

Dolimus said goodbye and then was gone. The turtles were already silhouettes in the water. As everyone hesitated by the water's edge, the dark shapes that loomed below began to grow. Their hour was up and the evil in the wild water began to rise.

To Taren's surprise, he watched Sam take a step closer to the water and his toes were but a few inches away. As he peered curiously at the stirring shadows, Taren barked, "Yetews, pull him back!"

The water became more violent and Sam felt Yetews pull him back hard at the same time as he realized how much danger they were about to be in. The ground began to tremble around them as they breeched the edge of the wild forest, unknowing as to what they were about to find on its other side.

The Gateway to Imagia: The Tale of Sam Little

Chapter Eighteen: Wild Ways

The difficulties that the southern forests of Imagia held paled in comparison to the northern woods that the travelers were now risking passage through. Everyone, including the forest born kupa cat, were worse for the wear since their departure from the river's shoreline.

Yetews was in the lead. His brute strength was proving useful once more. Twigs and leaves seemed to stick out of the majority of his hair and he had a bandage on his hand. He'd cut it while trying to move a rather large fallen tree from the only path they could manage to find. Sam had imagined the white cloth that now covered the wound.

Keesa's once sleek tawny fur was matted from the muddy ground that never seemed to be dry for more than a few yards. Her mood was noticeably worse than her generally gentler nature. Sam heard her grumble, more than once, that she 'loathed being filthy.'

Titus was seemingly the only one whose spirit hadn't been dampened by the gloom of the woods. Though he was walking with a slight limp on his front right paw, he was ever vigilant. He continued to verbalize his newest strategies to a very patient Taren who had a long gash on his right forearm where a thorny branch flipped back and hit him. The wound had ceased bleeding, but the bloody stains soaking through the bandage on his arm couldn't mask the damage underneath.

Sam, on the other hand, was by far the worst worn. They'd been traveling in the murky woods, only to find themselves seemingly no closer to an end than when they'd first entered a few days ago. As they pushed their way through the thick underbrush, he was constantly tripping over exposed tree roots and was getting stuck in goopy mud puddles. He'd gotten so many more scrapes and bruises than he'd ever had and he wondered what his mom might say should she see him like this. He'd bumped his scarred knee a few times so it was sore. He wondered if it would ever heal completely.

Sam was also exhausted. He couldn't sleep very well since they'd left the northern shores of Imagia. He was afraid that the closer he got to Nadaroth, the easier it might be for him to step into his dreams and take control. Yetews had helped him when he could, but Sam refused in fear of getting too comfortable and falling asleep.

His first few nights in the woods were not peaceful ones. There were strange creatures lurking in the trees. It had been a long time since an actual attack had been made on Sam and Taren's theory was that it was probably due to their constant movement.

Yet another evening was approaching, dulling the colors of the wild woods even more than they were. And to make matters worse, a light rain was sprinkling, stirring up the already muddy forest floor.

Titus had trotted back to Sam and informed him that up ahead was a more sheltered place to rest for the night. He'd noticed the dark circles under his friend's eyes and lingered for a moment. "Are you okay, Sam? You look so tired. Perhaps we should stop here." Everyone mirrored the concern as he spoke.

Sam shook his head and quietly said, "No. I'm fine." But even as he said it, he realized how unconvincing the words sounded to even him.

The spot that Titus spoke of was nearer than Sam expected and they reached it within moments. Sam wondered how bad he must look if Titus didn't think he could make it another five minutes. Regardless, he was beyond ready for a rest.

They found a good place to make a small fire. As Sam was finding a place to settle, he stumbled into a deep patch of thick mud at the base of a mossy, hollowed out tree stump. His shoe was stuck and

The Gateway to Imagia: The Tale of Sam Little

he decided to sit down and take it off rather than fight his way out. He sat down heavily and started working on getting his foot free. Before he could attempt to fish the shoe out of the mess, he suddenly jerked around with a gasp. He thought he felt something moving behind him. He squinted his eyes, searching for the source and he felt the hair on the back of his neck stand up.

Concerned for his sudden wariness, Keesa joined him and asked, "What is it? What do you see?"

"I thought I felt something moving right behind me." Both of their eyes scanned the area and found nothing. So Sam shrugged, rubbed the back of his neck and said, "I guess it was nothing."

"Would you like me to search the trees?"

"No. I think I'm just tired. It was probably just the wind or something."

Keesa smiled at him. She turned to join Taren and her tail gently brushed Sam's cheek. Sam felt a brief moment of comfort from the soft touch and wondered if she'd meant to do it.

Sam took another look behind him and noticed the tree stump. It wasn't all that unusual of a sight in the woods, but it gave him a chill, nonetheless. Trying not to look too frantic over something so silly, he quickly tugged out his trapped shoe.

As he hastily tied the laces, he felt a brush of moist hot air touch the bare nape of his neck. He knew instantly that it was too warm to be the rain. Before he had time to react, two bone thin arms with unnaturally long fingers folded around his shoulders and locked him in place.

A cold sweat flooded his vision as he struggled violently to break the hold of the sickly green creature. In his fear, he'd nearly forgotten how to scream. But once he realized his silence, his frantic yelling didn't go unnoticed. Sam looked up and saw the creature open its multi-hinged jaw wide enough to swallow a full-grown pig. There were multiple layers or razor sharp teeth that dripped with pungent strings of saliva.

Taren was taking aim, but didn't shoot in fear of hitting Sam as he flailed madly in the creature's grasp. As he anxiously tried to find a safe place to shoot, Keesa looped around the tree stump from which the creature was still inside. She leapt, full force, onto the thing's back, locking her sharp claws into the vulnerable flesh.

216

She clamped down on the long exposed throat, digging her saber teeth into its leathery jugular. Its jaw snapped and cracked noisily back into place as it gagged on the air it was barely sucking in. It still held onto Sam, despite the attack. But the distraction gave Yetews and Taren time to pull Sam free from its weakened hold on him.

Keesa locked her deadly jaw around the creature's throat, but it wasn't as fleshy and unprotected as the rest of its body. Her claws were digging into the sickly green flesh and the creature shrieked in agony with every new wound. She shook her head, trying to increase the damage she was inflicting, but the creature was fighting back just as hard.

It tried to reach its eerily long, clawed fingers back to remove the burden to no avail. At best, it was only causing minor discomfort to Keesa and she clung tighter to the attacker.

Once Sam was at a safe distance in the protection of Yetews' care, Taren yelled to Keesa, "Get back, Keesa! I can't get a clear shot!"

Keesa pulled away, releasing the deadly hold on the beast. But unexpectedly, it turned on her as she retreated. It snapped its fierce jaws and she took a hard hit on her right side. The blow knocked her to the ground, throwing mud in every direction.

Sam watched her fall in disbelief and saw the red tinge of the mud below her body. "KEESA!" He fought desperately against Yetews' hold to go to her. Yetews grumbled orders to Sam with fear in his eyes for the inevitable fate of their fallen comrade.

Taren didn't hesitate in taking the shot. The wounded beast was still a threat for a moment long enough to reach for Keesa's limp body with its unhinged jaws. It had settled for dragging Keesa back into its dank pit as its captured prey. Sam screamed again and Yetews drew him closer to hide his eyes from what he knew was sure to come.

But the creature didn't have enough time to pull Keesa into the tree stump with it. Its bloodstained body went suddenly limp as it slumped lifeless over the dead tree.

Yetews let go of Sam when he was sure the monstrosity was no longer a threat. An arrow had pierced its skull directly and next to the body, Keesa lay motionless, remaining partially in the jaws of their attacker.

There was nothing holding Sam back now and he ran full force to

The Gateway to Imagia: The Tale of Sam Little

her side. Taren was right on his heels and worked to remove her from the jaws of the fallen creature.

When she was free, they both knelt down next to her. Sam saw the blood dripping from a deep bite on her ribs. Her three beautiful eyes were closed and he started to panic. "Keesa? Keesa, please get up," he begged.

She didn't respond and Sam didn't know what to think. She'd attacked that creature and risked her life for him. But when she didn't respond, he knew that this was one of those moments that held no hope. He stroked her face and whispered, "Please...please don't die."

Taren knelt beside her with Titus next to him. Yetews started to pull Sam back from her body. But just as Sam was about to protest, Titus said, "Wait. She's still alive!"

Taren put his hand on her chest and felt his hand barely rise with her weak breathing. "You're right, Titus. How could you tell so easily? Her breathing is so shallow."

"I heard her heart beating." He spoke so matter-of-factly. "It started to beat harder when Sam spoke to her. I think she might be able to hear us." They looked over to Sam and waited for him to say something else.

Sam felt his own heart skip. He stroked her again and said, "Keesa? C-c-can you hear me?"

Unbelievably, she stirred under his hand and her eyes fluttered open. The crystal blue of her eyes seemed duller somehow. She weakly raised her head enough to meet Sam's gaze. Breathing raggedly, she said, "Sam...are you...alright?"

She was lying there dying and all she could think about was him. Sam could only find the ability to nod silently.

She let her head slump back to the ground and whispered, "Good."

Taren looked down at her and warned her of what he was about to do. "I'm going to check your wounds and see what the damage is."

She could barely find the strength to nod back.

After examining the damage, Taren looked up uncertainly to Yetews and shook his head while Sam wasn't watching. Yetews, understanding his meaning, looked to the boy, who was still trying to comfort Keesa. He wasn't sure if Sam could handle the death of a friend after all he'd lost already.

Taren discovered that the attack left her with broken ribs and deep cuts from the bite in which the bleeding was showing no signs of stopping. There were several minor cuts inflicted by the creature's claws as well, matting her fur with blood in several places. Her breathing was steady but weak. As she rested, Sam could do nothing but sit idly by and watch.

He looked over to Taren. "Can't you help her?" he begged.

"She's losing a lot of blood. It looks like there is some kind of anticoagulant from the creature's saliva that is causing the wound to continue bleeding."

"But can't you stop it? Sew it up like Orga did for my knee?"

Taren started to say something but then simply shook his head and said, "I'm sorry. There's nothing I can do."

Sam could feel a sob hanging in the back of his throat as he looked back down at Keesa. He had finally lost his uncertainty for showing affection to her and continued to comfort her by stroking her head. She didn't seem to mind in the slightest. As the rain dripped from Sam's hair onto his face, masking the escaped tears, he closed his eyes and wanted so badly to help her more. He wondered what good having his powers were if he couldn't even help his friends.

Just as he thought this, he contemplated if there might be some way to help her. He knew how to imagine and morph objects, but to change the state of a living creature that he had no hand in imagining was something completely different. He didn't know if he could help her but after all of the amazing things he had seen and done in his short time here, he was certain that it would be ridiculous to not try.

Sam couldn't stand seeing her lying there so weak and helpless. He'd felt the pain of loss too much already. First his family, then his home, and now was he meant to lose his friends as well? It was too much. He knew that he had to find some way to save Keesa. She saved him and now it was his turn to repay the favor.

His body was suddenly filled with a sense of euphoric hope for the situation. He reached down to the wound and ran his fingers over the bump where the ribs were fighting to protrude. As his shaking hands traced the wound through her blood soaked fur he started by trying to mend her injury in his mind.

In his mind, the bleeding slowed as the wound knitted back together. He wasn't sure by this time whether the mending was all purely in his mind or if it was really happening. But Taren was standing there and Sam heard him say, shocked, "I don't believe it."

The others gathered around as the last puncture of the lingering bite mark sealed closed. Sam felt her breathing get stronger under his palm and could feel the protruding ribs, still broken under the skin. He didn't know if he knew what he was doing, but felt deep into her fur and tried to make a whole picture of what her undamaged ribs would look like. He pictured the broken ribs transforming back to whole again and snapping back into place.

Keesa suddenly jerked and yowled in one moment of blinding pain. There was a sickly cracking sound as the ribs set and were mended. She panted for a moment, beyond weak from the loss of blood, and slowly rolled off of her side, staring in bewilderment at Sam.

Everyone was watching him in silence now, unable to believe what they had just witnessed.

The loss of blood was still too much for her body so Keesa slumped back to the ground and closed her eyes with a sigh. She'd need rest to recuperate from the attack.

Sam hadn't realized it, but he, too, was nearly out of breath from his effort. He watched as the others stared back at him in their silent disbelief. Whatever he'd done must have worked, but he was having trouble focusing. He heard one last thing as he felt Yetews' warm, supporting arms take hold of him. The world began to spin around him as Taren and Titus said, "It's impossible."

It was all too much and he was far too exhausted to fight his tired eyes any longer. He smiled tiredly at Keesa as Yetews held him and he succumbed to the sleep.

* * * * * * * * *

The forest was thinning and the feeble light of day was beginning to show its warmth once more. They'd already spent too many nights in the dreaded gloom of those woods and it was quite enough as far as any of the five were concerned.

Though Keesa's worst wounds were mended, she was still far from perfect. She was moving slower than even Sam was. And though Sam had set her bones back in place, his lack of anatomy knowledge made her healing slower. The ribs were still causing her somewhat significant discomfort and the bruising was still there. She tried hard to hide her winces when she moved too quickly. Either way, she couldn't stop showing her gratitude towards Sam since the night it happened.

Sam had slept till morning the day after the incident in the woods. It was a restless sleep filled with visions of being attacked by dozens of his would be killer if it weren't for Keesa's selfless act. They might have gotten further if she wouldn't have had her injuries to cope with. But nevertheless, there was finally hope on the horizon.

They left behind the thickness of the trees and set foot on wildly overgrown lands that stretched far and wide. The exit of the forest was at the bottom of a steep incline. It was as if they had passed from the forest into another world. There were trees here as well, but more scattered and blended into a land of distant mountains and grasslands that together made an all too amazing sight. The trees themselves, reminded Sam of the Redwood Forest he'd seen in books back home.

But more amazing than the landscape was the herd of creatures that were now standing directly in front of them. Sam looked out with the others at the behemoths that lazily grazed on the wild land. There were over two dozen of them and some stood nearly a hundred feet tall. Their bodies were covered in long silvery-gray hair from neck to tail. Each one had a long tail that balanced out the lengthy neck. Their heads were smaller, each one having unique sets of horns that elegantly curved from their skulls. They had four cloven hooves like so many beasts of burden often do.

Sam was the first to speak. "Awesome." Though he was still tired and weary, he managed to smile from ear to ear.

Yetews grumbled his agreement to Sam's eloquently stated observation and they grinned at one another.

"Unbelievable. Simply unbelievable," exclaimed Titus.

Taren, having seen so many things in his life, expected that he would be unfazed by anything they might happen upon in their travels. But this was more than even he expected out of Imagia. The creatures were beautiful and graceful in their movements despite their mammoth size. And even Taren found himself staring in awe at them.

Keesa said, "These must be the beasts of burden you spoke of, Taren. Absolutely fascinating. Do you think it's safe to cross?"

The Gateway to Imagia: The Tale of Sam Little

Taren shrugged, "Only one way to find out. It would take at least a day to go around them. When Orga told me about these behemoths, he said that they were gentle creatures that were a favorite of children. But Dolimus warned us that the ways are wild now. We need to be careful. We are nothing more than specks of dust to them."

Sam didn't believe that he could be so much more impressed by Imagia. He was certain that by now he'd seen it all. So as they walked through the legs of the creatures and gazed up at their inquisitive faces, he couldn't help but feel happy again. He hadn't felt this happy since his first days here.

They were cautious in their choice of direction, afraid that one wrong move might frighten or anger the behemoths. Sam wanted so badly to touch one but Yetews grabbed his hand when he tried and shook his head, discouraging the attempt.

Sam was soaking up every moment, never wanting to forget this. He stopped when the nearest creature caught sight of him. It was easily the largest of the herd and had the biggest, most intricate horns. Taren noticed and held a hand up to stop everyone. "Nobody move."

Just as Taren whispered his warning, the giant made a soothing trumpeting sound to the others. It reminded Sam of whale songs. Before anyone could react, every creature in the herd was suddenly looking directly at them.

The five looked around at one another. Sam asked, "What do we do now, Taren?"

"I'm not sure. Just…just don't make any sudden movements."

The entire herd was cooing and trumpeting softly to one another. The big one must have been their herd leader because they all seemed to be responding to its calls. Taren and the others formed a protective circle around Sam. The giant slowly shifted and as he moved, the ground trembled. It lowered its head towards the ground in a fluid motion that only creatures of this size could manage.

Taren was spreading his arms wide as a protective barrier, unsure how to react to this situation. His eyes darted in every direction as he tried to formulate some plan of action.

The creature's head was massive but velvety smooth. To their surprise, once it was on their level, it began to make a sound that could only be described as purring. The sound was deep and thrumming and it resonated around them. It seemed to have singled

Sam out of the group and was leaning more towards him than anyone else.

Everyone looked as though they were certain to be trampled to death. Everyone, that is, but Sam. Sam was positively alight with amazement. The sound coming from the behemoth was soothing and he wanted nothing more than to pet the creature's velvety face. And he was almost entirely sure that the creature wanted the exact same thing.

So without warning to the group, he reached over Titus and stroked its muzzle. When Taren held an arm up to protest, Yetews unexpectedly grumbled something and grabbed his wrist to stop him.

Taren asked Sam, "What did he say?"

Sam smiled wider. "He understands them."

"You're joking."

"Nope."

Taren rolled his eyes and sighed. "Naturally," he said sarcastically.

The creature trumpeted again and Yetews smiled. He relayed the message to Sam for translation.

Sam continued to stroke the creature's soft muzzle when he looked to Taren. "He says that they're happy to see a child again." He paused for more translation and then said, "They think this means the world is changing…that children are finally returning to Imagia."

As Sam translated the words, he was struck by their innocence. Though he wanted to stay here in the presence of these remarkable creatures, he also wanted nothing else so badly as he wanted to give them their desire. They wanted children to return to the world of Imagia.

As the creature gently nudged Sam, eagerly wanting more attention, he realized how important it was to find Nadaroth and do everything in his power to free Imagia. He still wasn't convinced he was the one who could do this, but he also knew that he wanted it more than anyone else. But he also knew that not even Taren had a solid idea where they were supposed to look. They were simply going on blind faith that they would find Nadaroth in the farthest north.

Sam thought for a moment and then asked Yetews, "Can *they* understand *us*?"

Yetews grunted his uncertainty. So Sam figured it couldn't hurt to try. He stopped petting the gentle giant. He didn't know exactly how to talk to him. But he realized that he had his attention and cleared his throat. "Uh, hi. I'm Sam." He paused to give room for response.

The creature merely cocked his head curiously so Sam continued. "Well...I was wondering if you know who Nadaroth is?"

The creature snorted angrily, disturbing the ground around them. It stepped back and then trumpeted angrily. The others responded with similar sounds. The leader leaned in closer to Sam and shook his great head, his silvery hair flowing fluidly as his neck turned. Even in anger, they were beautiful.

Taren said, "I take it they understand."

Sam agreed. "Um...we're going to find a way to bring the children back. But we need to find the way to Nadaroth. Do you know how to find him?"

Sam waited while the giant bellowed and purred. He looked to Yetews for an answer. Taren was showing signs of impatience for having to wait through two translations instead of just the one. Sam thought the look on his face was entertaining but figured it best not to laugh at the hilarity of the situation.

"So?" asked Taren. "What did he say?"

"He says that there is a darker place in the farthest north...past these lands." They all looked towards the direction that Yetews was now pointing. "There's a mountain range that's at least a week or two away from here in that direction." He pointed too, but it wasn't visible from where they were.

Sam wanted to know if Taren had any idea where they were right now.

So Taren pulled his aged map from his pack and mulled over it for a bit. Meanwhile, the giant creature nudged Sam for more attention. Three other creatures joined him and Sam made the rounds and tried to give attention to each of them.

Finally, Taren said, "The best I can figure, we are right on the southern edge of the Valley of the Behemoths. That mountain range makes up the northern border. It's going to take some time to reach it. The map won't be of much use beyond that though. It's not been traveled by any Protectors I know of."

Titus said, "Then we best start moving. Sam, do you need to rest or are you okay to go on?"

In truth, Sam was beyond tired. What he truly wanted was to stay here for a while and enjoy the soothing company of these gentle giants. But he knew that this journey wasn't meant to be a vacation. They were on a mission. And after seeing what Nadaroth's presence had stripped Imagia of, Sam realized just how important this task was. No child should have to miss an opportunity to witness something like these fantastic creatures.

He looked to the creature and apologized. "I'm sorry, but we have to go. We have to find a way to stop Nadaroth." He looked over his shoulder towards the mountains. "And it's going to take us forever to get there." He sighed.

The largest creature lifted his head and looked to the north. He dipped his head back down once more and bellowed. As he did, two others lowered their heads, mimicking his moves.

"What's he saying?" Taren asked.

To everyone's surprise, Sam walked up to the creature, who was now kneeling on his front two knees so that his head was touching the ground. Without hesitation, he used the spiraling horn growing out of the side of the creature's head and its thick strands of hair to climb onto his neck.

Taren jumped forward, befuddled by Sam's action. "What are you doing? Are you *crazy*?"

Titus echoed his concern as well, "Sam, what's going on?"

Yetews was already hesitantly pulling himself up onto the giant to sit with Sam.

While Sam adjusted himself behind the head, just where the silvered hair began, he motioned with one hand to the others. He smiled at Taren who looked as though he might scream. "Come on. They're going to take us to the mountains."

"What? Are you sure about this, kid?"

"Yep. Can't you feel it?"

"Feel what?"

"The peace. I can feel it when they're purring."

Taren shook his head strongly. "Don't you remember the deceptor at all?"

"Yeah, but this is different. It just feels right. It feels like the night I came to Imagia. I think…" Sam stopped. He didn't know how to explain to Taren what he felt.

"You think what?"

"I think these creatures are a part of Imagia. I think they were meant to take us where we need to go."

Taren and Keesa looked at each other, doubt in their eyes. Keesa voiced her concern first. "These creatures are massive. They could kill us instantly if you are wrong about this."

Taren agreed. His eyes darted towards the other two creatures. They seemed to be waiting patiently for Keesa, Titus and Taren to mount them.

Sam couldn't understand why the others were so hesitant to trust the gentle giants. He could only think of one thing to say. "It's safe. Trust me."

They admitted defeat and climbed onto the other two creatures. Taren helped Titus up onto one and climbed up after him while Keesa leapt carefully onto the other one, trying not to use her claws for support. She winced when she landed, still not fully healed.

Once they were settled, the creatures stood to their full height and began moving towards the mountains. Though they felt as though they were moving slowly, the ground that the mammoth creatures covered was significant with every step. The entire herd traveled together.

Though the day and the valley were both dreary from the foggy mist that seemed to cover everything, Sam was enjoying himself immensely. Through Yetews, he talked with the creature and learned that most called them lorthaxes. This completely changed what any of them thought of the term used to describe Yetews before. Apparently not all lorthaxes were unintelligible. They were simply untranslatable to everyone. He spent the journey trying to learn as much as he could about the origin of their kind. Unfortunately, they didn't seem to know a great deal about Imagia.

Sam was right, however, about their purpose. They aided children in their journeys if it was asked of them. The others weren't as overjoyed as Sam was atop the mighty lorthax. The wind was warm, despite the weather and it felt refreshing as they made their way across the rugged landscape.

Keesa and Titus were having difficulty riding. Though their necks were wide, Keesa was concerned with her own stability without the use of her claws. Titus, on the other hand, despite his nervousness, was lucky enough to have Taren with him. He managed to keep a steady hold around Titus for extra support.

By day's end, they'd reached the halfway point. The herd was ready to rest by a massive lake. The riders dismounted their gracious hosts for a time to rest and recuperate by the peaceful water. Sam gazed up at the stars that poked through the still cloudy skies. It was hard for him to believe at this present moment that Imagia was capable of harboring evil. He listened to the purrs of the herd as they swayed in a standing sleep above them.

The next thing he knew, he was being prodded awake so that they could set out on their journey once more before dawn. The second day of travel moved even quicker than before and before they knew it, they were at the edge of the mountain range.

As they dismounted, Sam felt a pang of sadness for leaving them behind. There was something more to these mighty creatures. He couldn't quite place how he'd understood this, but they protected his dreams when he'd slept. Not only did he not have nightmares as he listened to their soothing purrs, but he had a beautiful dream that left him refreshed the next morning. It was hard to leave that kind of peace behind him.

He hoped that they might get to return this direction some day so that he might meet them again. He learned on the journey across that they were just one of many giants that occupied these lands. The mountains were still a part of the Land of the Behemoths and they were likely to meet more creatures on their way.

Sam stroked the leader on his velvet muzzle one last time before they trumpeted their farewell and turned to head back to the safety of their trees.

Keesa and Titus were thrilled to be using their own legs again. Even Yetews seemed to be relieved that they weren't a hundred feet in the air anymore.

But Taren, on the other hand, was actually smiling. He looked back at the departing herd with a sense of fondness. He caught Sam's curious eyes and nodded. "You were right."

"What do you mean?" asked Sam.

"About the peace. I felt it too. And I haven't felt that…in a long, long time." He smiled again as though he was remembering a far off memory.

While they stood, gathering their bearings, their peaceful moment was horribly interrupted by a menacing sound that shook the rocks around them.

The roar mixed with the sounds of clanking metal. The commotion they were hearing sounded close, just through the ravine ahead of them.

Both Keesa and Titus were growling and stood, hackles raised, in the front. Yetews already had Sam behind him and Taren was moving slowly towards the ravine. He stopped at the entrance and what looked like the only passage through the mountains.

All became still for a moment and there was an eerie silence in the air.

Sam watched Taren inch closer to the ravine and wondered what he was thinking. He couldn't take the silence any longer. "Taren?"

The stillness was broken by the sound of another roar that raised the hair on Sam's neck. Taren turned around with wide eyes and said, "I know that sound. That's a dragon."

Chapter Nineteen: False Impressions

Everyone stood at the base of the mountain near the entrance to its hidden paths. Whatever creatures made a home in the mountain were hidden well past the rocky entrance. The ravine was quite wide. It appeared as though each of them could walk shoulder to shoulder with no lack of comfort. But the steep sides were jagged and unwelcoming. They could only assume where this may lead them because the path veered directly left.

They stood at the entrance, ready for anything that might come barreling out, but when no threats emerged, Taren looked around the group while deciding their next move. Sam, on the other hand, was finding it difficult to think that he might be so close to a dragon and still not see it. But even as much as he desperately wanted to see an actual dragon, he found himself remembering Garrett's warning to steer clear of them.

Sam was picturing Garrett's scarred face. He wondered if after all he'd seen and survived, if he too might someday have a similar wound. Though his knee was scarred, he wasn't willing to count that because he wasn't a Protector yet. Either way, he was excited at the prospect of seeing a dragon – even if it was from a far off glance. He couldn't mask the excitement in his voice. "Is it really a *dragon*? I mean…are you sure?" Sam squeaked.

Taren nodded. "But of all the things to be excited about, a dragon shouldn't be one of them, kid. Dragons are marked beasts. There

The Gateway to Imagia: The Tale of Sam Little

hasn't been a friendly dragon in the skies since before I came to Imagia." He seemed slightly annoyed by Sam's misplaced enthusiasm.

The idea of marked beasts was still a disturbing one. The act of taking an innocent creature and torturing it to do evil bidding seemed horrible at best. Sam's mind strayed to thoughts of Keesa and her lost cubs. Though at first glance, he could see how one might assume her as a threat. Nothing with saber teeth like that could initially appear friendly. But after traveling with her and getting to know her so well, the idea of her intentionally bringing harm upon the innocent was far fetched.

After considering his thoughts for a moment, Sam decided to mention his point of view. "Just because a creature is a marked beast, doesn't mean that it is evil. I mean, look at Keesa. She's a marked beast, but she's not evil. Not even a little bit. Maybe this dragon is friendly." He was happy with his observation.

Keesa was pleased in part as well. She looked back at him and smiled warmly through her pearly teeth. "For what his heart tells him, he is right." Her eyes became suddenly wary. "Though...I do not doubt what the seeds of evil can grow in the innocent. I'm sorry Sam, but Taren is right in his concern. We must use extreme caution."

Sam could feel the rush of blood to his face. He felt like he had raised his hand to answer a question in class to which he had the wrong answer. He looked down at his feet while Yetews reassuringly patted him on his back. He grumbled apologetically.

"Sorry Sam," Taren said. "We can't take any chances. We'll have to turn back and find some other way if the dragon crosses our path. I can't take down a fully-grown dragon – even with help, it would be difficult."

Sam frowned. "Garrett took on a dragon all alone."

"Yes. Well, Garrett was extremely lucky that all he came away with was a scar."

Sam mumbled something too low for anyone to understand but his message that he was mad did not go unnoticed.

Taren rolled his eyes and shook his head at Sam's pouting. Knowing that his word was final, he said, "Now let's move. We'll be easy prey in that ravine. If something wanted to trap us, it wouldn't be too hard to achieve. We'd best move with haste."

When Taren was like this, he was hard to argue with. Sam knew by now the difference in his demeanors. At times, he was easygoing and very likeable. But then there were times like these that were harder for Sam to understand. Taren would switch and become almost callous in the things he said or did. Sam knew that years of fighting and being a Protector were to blame for his more military side. That fact alone was enough to justify Taren in his worst state. After all he'd probably seen and done, it couldn't be easy to be happy all of the time. Perhaps he was once more like Garrett – a free spirit full of pride and optimism. But the wisdom that time brings does not take kindly to foolish arrogance.

Sam decided to save any more arguing for later. There was still a chance that they might not cross paths with any dragon at all. He realized his arms were crossed stubbornly over his chest and then quickly dropped them to his sides and started walking.

They went cautiously forward. They were surprised to find that the ravine was a short one. The path led them right into the mountains. Unfortunately, directly ahead of them was a rock formation that jutted out from the ground and there was a great deal of commotion coming from behind it.

Taren motioned for everyone to fall back into the ravine and they quietly complied.

A menacing string of snarls escaped from behind the rocks and caused everyone to jump back a few steps. Yetews pulled Sam closer to him and Taren readied his aim for an attack. He began to back off slowly and indicated the others to follow his lead. He whispered to them, "We'll find another way."

What happened next was most unexpected. The snarl subsided and a hidden voice, deep and rumbling, spoke. "I can hear you, vermin. Show your faces so as I can snap them off after I break these chains!" The sound of constantly clanking iron followed the threat.

Taren watched Sam's frightened face carefully and moved his finger to his mouth for silence. Sam clapped his hands over his open mouth to stifle any noise that might happen to escape.

They started to sneak back towards the ravine, but just as they did, the voice spoke again. "I can hear you breathing. If you are so brave as to hunt me and capture me then step forward. Claim your prize, you cowards!" it hissed.

The Gateway to Imagia: The Tale of Sam Little

Taren watched Sam struggling to keep silent and thought it better if he were to speak first. "We are not your captors and we mean you no harm."

It became silent again with only the occasional tinkling sound of the chains as the hidden beast shifted its body.

Everyone looked to Taren as if waiting for his guidance, though not even he knew what the next move should be. It was apparent that the dragon, still hidden behind the rocks, must have been restrained in some fashion. But to move forward could be unwise.

The dragon growled in frustration and finally said, "If you truly mean me no harm, then come and release me of my bonds so that I may go free."

Taren shook his head. "We can't do that. We only want safe passage across these mountains. And you're a dragon, are you not?"

"Yes. But I too, mean you no harm. I only mean harm to the filthy rats that dared imprison me." The callousness was thick in his voice.

Sam's eyes were pleading. His emotions shifted quickly from fear to excitement as the dragon pleaded with them. His heart was fluttering madly and he started to struggle against Yetews' hold. He wanted so badly to go around the rocks and see the great beast in all his magnificence. He couldn't hold his tongue any longer. "If he's trapped then it can't hurt to keep going. And there didn't look like any other way into the mountains."

Taren was already sighing from Sam's decision to speak, revealing another number of their party. But all things considered, he knew that Sam was right. This was the best way to continue their journey.

Titus said, "He's right. We should use caution but we must go forward."

Taren hesitated for a moment and then nodded. "But Yetews, you better keep him close," he indicated to Sam. "He's got a history with these situations you know." There was a hint of teasing in the lines of his face.

Yetews nodded in agreement and gave a knowing glance to his boy.

They carefully made their way towards the rocky formation. When they breached the gap between themselves and the dragon, they all stopped in surprise at what they saw.

Indeed there was a dragon on the other side. It was trapped amongst the shadows with chains that bound it to the ground. A thickly woven net was tied around its midsection, binding its wings to its body. Dark green scales, almost the color of the forest, covered its body from head to tail. As he moved, the light that strived to break free from the cloudy sky touched his body, making his color even more brilliant. He had sharp claws that had damaged much of the ground from the struggle to escape and a crown of horns atop his head. But most shocking of all was its size.

It couldn't have been much larger than Keesa.

Sam was more surprised than the rest and like he so often did, spoke without thinking. "But...you're...so tiny! Aren't dragons supposed to be huge?"

The dragon made a sound, scoffing at Sam's innocent observation. "You shouldn't make judgments based solely on the perspective of size, child. Nevertheless, I implore you once more to reconsider. I beg of you. Free me from my chains, small one."

The dragon's choice to speak to Sam directly didn't go unnoticed and everyone immediately became nervous for what Sam might choose to do.

Sam began to walk closer only to be stopped by Taren's hand on his chest and Yetews' hand on his shoulder. "No Sam. We can't trust him. Big or small, he's still a dragon. Can't you see that?"

The dragon roared in frustration. It was an exceptionally impressive sound, coming from something so little. "*I* am not your enemy! I swear to you that no harm will become you." Suddenly, he jerked his head to the side and sniffed the air. He growled and added, "At least no harm from *me*."

Sam was about to ask what he meant when an unfamiliar voice from behind them said, "Hmm...you'd promise them anything to get free, wouldn't ya? Filthy dragon. Can't trust them for nothin'. Ain't that right?" he said.

A second voice answered the first, "You got that right. Look at what it's come to for him. Begging!" The two voices laughed.

Everyone whipped around and searched for the source of the voices. But they weren't searching low enough. It wasn't until they spoke again that Sam spotted them. The first voice said, "You don't want to be trustin' him, folks. He'd say just about anything to get free."

When Sam saw what he was looking at, he couldn't resist his urge to smile. The voices came from low to the ground. They were two ferrets. They stood on their hind legs and walked upright, just like miniature people. They were a little larger than normal ferrets, but only by a bit. One was sable with a black raccoon-like mask across his eyes and the other was chocolate brown with a white chest and feet.

Oddly enough, they were also dressed much like the people in Imagia were. If it weren't for their size and the fact that they were actually ferrets it might be hard not to mistake them for people.

The sable one was casually leaning up against a tree sapling and the darker one was standing with his arms crossed as if bored. The sable ferret spoke again. "You folks just best be movin' along. You know? For your own good and all." He smiled slyly.

The dragon snarled and yelled, "Filthy vermin! Release me!"

"Well, would you listen to that? He's callin' us vermin!" said the sable one. He was holding a paw over his chest in mock heartache.

"Yes. Very rude indeed. You'd best watch yourself dragon, or we might just leave you here to die."

The dragon simply fought his bonds in response.

Sam and the others were baffled by what was taking place. They stood between the ferrets and the dragon, clueless. They looked to one another for any signs of what to say and Sam was the first to speak.

He looked down at the ferrets and said, "Um, who are you?" Yetews echoed the question.

The ferrets, which were a few yards back, dropped down on all fours and scurried over to Sam. Once they were there, they stood back up and introduced themselves.

The sable one looked up to Sam and said with great pride, "I, good sir, am Ignatius Oswald Tavarius the 3rd. Pleased to meet you." He took a bow.

The dark brown one stepped forward next and said in the same fashion, "And I am Artemus Xavier Waldamere the 1st, at your service."

The sable ferret started to laugh, "Arty, you can't keep introducing yourself like that. There's no such thing as a 'first'. It makes you sound like an idiot." He looked over to Sam, who was stifling a giggle, and motioned with a thumb-like claw to his comrade. "He's always been jealous of my name. Made up all that rubbish just to sound important."

The brown ferret retaliated instantly, "Well that's not true at all!" He also looked at Sam. "He's just angry because my name sounds more superior. Besides, you can't be a 'third' when there was technically no first or second."

"Technicalities, my friend...technicalities. Now," he addressed the others, "You can call me Iggy."

"And you can call me Arty. And you would be?" he waved his hand around the group for introductions.

Sam opened his mouth to introduce himself. He liked these two. They were funny and interesting characters, to say the very least. But before he could get the words formed, Taren interrupted him.

"*We* are no one important. Why do you want to know?"

Iggy said, "Well aren't you the rudest person I ever met. But there's no reason. Just curious I suppose. It's not normal, ya know. Having a conversation with a dragon."

"That's right," agreed Arty. "You ever met anyone who wanted to talk to some thick-skulled dragon? They're not very bright creatures, ya know."

They both started laughing as Iggy added, "Yeah! And they reek like a bag of lorthax dung too!"

"Ha! Good one Arty!"

The dragon growled, "I'm not deaf, you wretched pests. And when I escape, rest assured, you'll be the appetizers to my meal."

"Do you hear something Arty? Because if I didn't know any better, I'd say that there pile of dung is tryin' to speak!"

"Yes, well perhaps we should move downwind before it tries to speak again."

"Wise idea Arty. Wise idea."

While the ferrets and the dragon bantered amongst themselves, everyone else was trying to make sense of what was going on. There was an air of awkwardness among the group. They had obviously stumbled into something that they wanted no part in.

Taren whispered to the others, "I don't think we are in any danger here. But let's go, before we get drug into this mess."

The Gateway to Imagia: The Tale of Sam Little

Yetews and Keesa nodded while Titus said, "I agree."

Everyone started to move away from the three while they were busy taking jabs at one another.

Everyone but Sam.

Yetews turned around when he sensed Sam's hesitation and grumbled a question to him.

Sam looked at Yetews. "It's just...well...I don't know." He looked back at the dragon, bound to the rocks. He felt pity for the poor creature, even if he *was* a dragon. He was a small dragon and he seemed sincere enough from Sam's perspective. He truly believed that he meant them no harm. He felt guilty for leaving him in that condition.

The others stopped. Taren saw the look on Sam's face and instantly knew what his intent was. "Oh no. Sam? Sam, we can't interfere with this. There's no telling what would happen if you tried to free that dragon. He may be small, but I'm sure he could do a fair bit of damage if backed against a wall. And at this present time, that's exactly where he is – backed against a wall!"

Sam shook his head. "But Taren, I just feel like it wouldn't be right to leave him there. What if he's a good dragon? He might even help us...tell us which way to go or something." He tried to look as serious as he could. He was willing to stand his ground as long as he could. "I want to help. It just...feels right."

"Sam," said Keesa, "it's not safe. You should listen to Taren."

Sam frowned. Of all of his friends, he expected Keesa to understand the most. "What if Taren would have been with me when I found you? Wouldn't you have wanted me to try and free you, even if he told me it was a bad idea? You're a marked beast too. I thought *you'd* understand."

Keesa bowed her head, slightly ashamed. She looked at Taren and said, "He's right."

Taren looked at Sam and remembered some of Orga's final words to him. He had pulled Taren aside and explained to him that Sam's compassion and pure heart were the things that made him different from Nadaroth and that he should be wise to remember that. He glanced from Sam to the captured dragon and knew that if Orga were here, he'd commend Sam for such a choice. He sighed then threw his arms up in surrender. "Fine. But, good luck in freeing him.

236

Those chains aren't exactly going to break."

Yetews grumbled something in an annoyed tone behind him. Sam smiled and said, "Yeah, I know Yetews. I remember. But wasn't I right about Keesa? So I know it'll be fine."

They walked back and realized that the bantering was silent for the moment. Iggy and Arty were watching Sam with wary eyes as he moved towards them. But Sam walked right past the ferrets and towards the dragon, with Taren by his side.

Iggy hollered to Sam, "Hey! Are you mad? Don't let his size fool you. That's still a dragon, ya know."

Sam replied, "Yeah, I know. I want to free him."

"Oh no you don't!" Arty said, suddenly irate. "That's *our* catch. We caught him, fair and square!"

Then Iggy said, "Yeah! Do you have any idea what the bounty on a live dragon is?"

Sam was shocked, he turned around and stared, open mouthed, at the two. He was starting to think that he might not like them as much as he did initially. "You mean you are trying to sell him? To who?"

"Well there's only one that's buying, isn't there?"

"Who?"

Iggy looked at his counterpart in confusion and then somewhat whispering, he said, "Nadaroth of course. He's always lookin' for more creatures to do his bidding and dragons are hard to catch. He's worth a fortune to us."

Sam was disgusted and he heard Keesa growl her disapproval. "Well, we'll definitely be freeing him then, so that he doesn't have to suffer by doing anyone's dirty work."

They moved towards the dragon, who was being uncharacteristically quiet, and Arty said more calmly, "Look, kid. I admire your guts. I really do. But Nadaroth's been here a long time. We don't like what he does, but we gotta survive somehow. He's just a dragon."

"Arty's right. We're ripe with guilt about it."

"Yup. Ripe."

"But you just can't change the way things work around here. Besides, we'll just have to stop you if you try anything funny."

"That's right. We don't want trouble with your lot. Just keep moving like you didn't see a thing," Arty suggested.

The Gateway to Imagia: The Tale of Sam Little

Sam looked at Taren who was now standing directly behind the ferrets. He had turned back and drawn his bow. He had two arrows pointing directly at the ferrets' heads. He raised his eyebrows and grinned. Iggy and Arty turned around and yelped.

"Hey! That's not a fair fight!" squeaked Iggy.

Taren smirked, "Who said anything about fair?"

Both the ferrets gulped and then Arty added, "Um, Yeah. Well, it's just that...we're uh...we're more of the 'hand-to-hand' combat type." Arty smiled sheepishly through his sharp teeth. But when they realized that they were without choice in the matter, they looked at each other slyly and crossed their arms.

They conceded, paws high in the air, and Iggy said, "Okay, fine. Have it your way. But good luck getting those locks undone. Those are one-of-a-kind locks. We made them ourselves." He pulled a small ring with a key on it off of his belt. He jingled it around. It was tiny until he twisted the top and it instantly popped open, much like a switchblade, into a much larger key. "It takes a real special key and I've got the only one. I'll swallow it before I surrender it to you."

Taren eyebrows pinched in the middle. He was getting annoyed with them. Bowstring still taught, he said, "Hand over the key. Now."

Iggy smiled again, and quick as lightning, retracted the key back to its smaller form and stuck it in his mouth. Now his words were muffled when he said, "Put the bow down or I'll swallow it."

Arty started laughing and pat him on the back hard.

Iggy started gagging and coughing. When he got his breath, he looked angrily up to Arty and said, "You idiot! Look what you did! I went and swallowed it! Now how are we supposed to unlock him?"

Arty started chuckling.

Angrily, Iggy asked, "What's so funny?"

"It's just...well..." He started laughing harder then said, "*That's* gonna hurt coming out later!"

"Aww, Arty! It's not funny!" He smacked his friend upside the head.

Still laughing, Arty said, "Sorry! I thought you were gonna swallow it anyways."

"I was only bluffin' you moron!"

The two continued their bickering, occasionally taking swings at each other with their small paws.

Taren stretched the string back further on the bow to intimidate his targets and said, "Well...they *are* pretty annoying. We could always just kill them and cut the key out."

Keesa said, "Excellent idea. Would you like any help with that?" She took one threatening step forward.

They stopped their squabble almost immediately and looked up at the pointed ends of the arrows, aimed so steadily towards them.

But Sam said, "No Taren. It's okay. I got it." He turned his back to the ferrets and began to concentrate. He tried to remember the exact shape and size of the key. He wasn't entirely sure he'd gotten a good enough look at it, but regardless, he closed his eyes and pictured the same key in his hand. It was a strange shape. Not straight like most keys. It curved in a claw-like shape with four, square parts attached to the tip. It had three intertwining circles for a handle and was the same silvery color as the chains. When he opened his eyes, there was what appeared to be, an exact replica of it sitting in the middle of his palm. He raised an eyebrow and showed the ferrets.

They stood in disbelief and kept staring at the key in Sam's hand. After they couldn't find the right question, they simply said in unison, "How'd you do that?"

Sam looked over the odd little key and just smiled.

Still baffled and rubbing his stomach in confusion, Iggy said, "But I know I swallowed it. What kind of trickery is this?"

For a moment, Sam considered telling them but decided not to. "I have no idea what you're talking about. You dropped it and I picked it up." He knew the lie was completely unbelievable, but pretended not to notice.

Arty, now slightly more suspicious, said, "You're lying. But still, pretty nifty trick for a kid. Come on. Tell us how you did it."

Before Sam could say much else, Taren jumped in. "Look, it's a long story and I'm not sure you get to find out anymore about it, so quiet down. Got it?" He thrust the arrows closer as a warning.

"Okay, okay!" Iggy said. "We're quiet now." Then under his breath, he mumbled, "It'll be a miracle if the key works anyways."

Arty smiled back at him.

Sam looked back at Taren for reassurance. Now that he was closer to the dragon, he wasn't sure if he was making the right decision. Even though the dragon was small, it was still very intimidating to be so close to him.

Taren simply said, "Go on Sam. Just be careful."

Yetews started to follow Sam and was quickly on his heels before they reached the dragon's bound head.

The dragon was oddly silent and no longer fighting his bonds. Sam could hear every breath that the dragon took and watched as the puffs of dirt moved on each exhale. They'd reached him and were unsure what to do first. So, following with his previous encounter of a trapped beast, he decided to start with small talk. "Er...hi. I'm Sam. Do you have a name?" He almost felt silly as he asked, but he remembered feeling similar when he first met Keesa, and that thought eased his mind.

The dragon, hesitant at first, looked up as best he could. Which, due to his chains, wasn't easy. He spoke. "I do, child. I am called Enoch."

"I want to set you free if I can."

"I would be forever grateful. Even if you fail, I will be grateful that you tried."

There was a true sincerity in his deep voice that Sam could not ignore. It was as if he was meeting Keesa all over again. He couldn't help but wonder if all marked beasts were like this. It made him all the more confident of his decision. "I believe you. So, you won't try to eat me if I unlock you?"

The dragon laughed. It was a booming sound that echoed through the ravine just past the rocks. "No. I won't harm you or anyone under your protection. Despite popular belief, dragons don't eat anything that just happens by them. Truth be told, I'm actually quite picky. Though," he paused and looked towards the now silent ferrets, "I do make exceptions for filthy rats that attempt to sell me for selfish gain."

Sam looked back at Iggy and Arty and saw that they were feigning innocence. He shook his head and said to Enoch, "I'm sorry that you are a marked beast. I hope that I can help you. I'll do everything I can."

"I believe you will. But how exactly are you going to do that with no key? Those fools ate the key and these aren't ordinary chains."

Sam realized that the dragon must not have noticed him imagining the key he spoke of. He opened his palm and showed

Enoch.

"But how? I thought I heard them say it was swallowed. Unless…" Enoch slowly turned his head sideways to look closer at Sam. The pupil of his eye became a small slit as he focused on Sam's face.

It was enough to spark Sam's self-consciousness. He forced himself to stare at the key in his hand instead of into the dragon's eye as he asked, "Unless what?"

Enoch's eye dilated back to a wide circle of black. "Nothing. It's not important right now. Perhaps we could try the key?"

"Okay." Sam looked closer at the chains and counted ten locks, each identical, in random places. He turned the key over in his hands and stepped bravely forward to the dragon's side. He inhaled deeply and caught Yetews' eye before he inserted the key into the first lock. When Yetews smiled back at him, he put the key in.

Instantly, the lock popped open with a harsh click. It startled him and he jumped. He didn't even have to turn the key. The second lock was the same and he continued with the other eight. Yetews helped Sam untangle the chains from Enoch, setting his body free from captivity.

Sam heard one of the ferrets behind him say, "Crap."

Then the other one said, "Yup. That about covers it."

"Well…we're dead."

"Definitely dead. Been nice knowin' ya Iggy."

"You too, Arty."

Taren poked them again with the point of the two arrows and said, "Shut it, you two."

Enoch, wings still bound by the thick net, stretched his legs and turned to Sam. "Thank you."

Sam smiled. "No problem." He was so ecstatic that he could hardly contain himself. He was actually talking with a real, live dragon and to top it all off, it was a nice one that wasn't two seconds away from eating him. But then, as a distant thought popped back into his mind in full force, he could only think of one thing he wanted to ask this remarkably small dragon before he flew away. "I'm sorry, but I was wondering, if we are in the Land of the Behemoths, then why are you so small? I mean, shouldn't dragons be…well…"

But Enoch finished his question for him, "Giant?"

The Gateway to Imagia: The Tale of Sam Little

Sam nodded sheepishly. "Well, yeah. Giant."

Enoch smiled, revealing a long row of razor sharp teeth. "Yes. As I stated before, you should never judge one by their size. Take you, for example. I've seen men more than twice your size cower in my presence for simple fear of what I am. You are small, but I do not doubt your courage for a moment. Free my wings, and I will show you why I belong in these lands."

Then Iggy suddenly burst out, "NO! Not his wings!"

Arty echoed him, "Not his wings! Keep them bound!"

Sam ignored the warning even though the others were showing sudden signs of nervousness. He looked over the net and saw that there were two more locks; one was on each side of Enoch's body, hidden just in the fold of his wings. He unlocked the first and then went around to the other side.

He held the key an inch away from the final lock and, for a mere fraction of a second, wondered if he were really doing the right thing. But before he could talk himself out of it, he shoved the key in and heard the crisp crack of the lock opening.

Enoch stepped back from Sam and Yetews. "Please stand back, young one." He reached one of his powerful arms around to his back. He grabbed the net and pulled it free. Two perfect wings were folded to his sides and without warning, he sprung forward into the air, wings spread wide. The instant his wings were full spread, he burst into a full-sized dragon. He was so massive that Sam couldn't imagine something more impressive.

Enoch flew up and circled once then dived down to land not more than a few yards from where Sam stood.

Sam didn't move until he felt Yetews pulling him backwards, away from the leviathan.

Enoch stood, wings spread wide, in front of them. He lowered his head to Sam's level and said, "I am a shrinking dragon, Sam. I show my true size when I spread my wings. When I fold them…" he folded his wings in demonstration. As if growing backwards, he shrunk almost instantly into the small dragon that Sam had freed. Once he was small, he finished his explanation. "When I fold them, I return to this."

Sam was flabbergasted. "That's awesome! I can't believe just how…how…*awesome* that is!"

Enoch was flattered. "Unfortunately, my ability to do this makes my kind very valuable."

"Valuable?" asked Sam, wanting to know more.

"I'm the perfect hunter. I can stalk my prey when I am small and quiet but when I attack, I am a lethal size. Perfect for watching from a distance then deadly when the time calls for it. I have seen many of my kind changed to do the bidding of evil."

Sam suddenly thought of Taren and his sister. He remembered that a dragon is what killed their Guardians and how terrifying that must have been. To think that Enoch would have been made to do the same thing to someone one day was a disturbing thought. He couldn't be more confident of his decision now.

Enoch looked past Sam and Yetews now. He was focusing on something behind them and Sam could tell that he looked much angrier than before. "Speaking of which, I can't believe I was outsmarted by two complete idiots."

It was then that Sam became aware as to what Enoch was looking at and of his earlier vow to eat his captors.

Enoch spread his wings and burst back into his full size in mid-flight. He flew up to circle around towards Iggy and Arty who were now in a full panic. Despite Taren's drawn bow, they started to run frantically about in an attempt to flee. They settled for hiding behind Taren's legs, which took him by complete surprise.

Even though Sam wasn't sure about the two bandits, he knew that he didn't want them to die. So he ran as fast as he could to stand between them and a vengeful dragon. He placed his arms up and yelled, "NO! STOP!" He jumped in front of them just in time, as Enoch was about to strike.

He landed and growled menacingly. "Out of my way Sam! My revenge is not with you!" He kept his wings fully spread to maintain his size.

Sam frantically searched for the right words, "No! No. You said that you wouldn't harm anyone under my protection."

Enoch practically spit as he said, "But they are vile creatures with no concern for others. They would just as soon betray you if it meant profit for themselves."

Iggy popped his head out from behind Taren's boot. "That's not true! He doesn't know what he's talking about!" He pleaded nervously with Sam.

Sam, noticing that his arms were still raised, lowered them. He turned to face Iggy and Arty. He was conflicted for what to say or if he should believe them. So he settled for the best he had at the moment. "I...I don't know what to do." He looked around at his friends' faces, hoping for help.

The two looked uneasily at each other. Arty finally said, "Truly. If we can do anything for you, just say the word."

"Yes," Iggy said. "Just spare us. *Please.*"

Whether it was the desperation in their pleas or simply his own general nature, Sam agreed. "Okay. But you've got some explaining to do."

"A lot of explaining." Taren added.

Enoch was confused by Sam's choice. "Why do you want to protect them? They've done nothing to earn it."

Sam looked down at Iggy and Arty. They were not evil. He knew this somehow in his heart, but he wasn't thrilled with what they were doing to Enoch. He thought for another moment. He swallowed hard. Sadness took over his face. "I don't want to watch them die." As he said the words, he knew they were true. He didn't know how much he could take before his bravery might start to slip away. He hoped that his sympathy for them would do some good somehow.

Enoch's face softened and he stepped back, slightly calmer. He was shocked by the compassion in such a small boy.

"Look. It wasn't personal, dragon. Just a job." Iggy grinned innocently.

Arty said, "Yeah. And we swear we won't try to catch you again."

Enoch growled again. "If not me, then some other creature. You deserve to be disposed of," he hissed.

"Look, " Iggy said, "We weren't always in this trade. We'd just as soon be rid of Nadaroth as much as you. But, you know what they say? If you can't beat him..."

Arty finished for him, "Pretend to join him."

"And hope that he doesn't grow a brain and figure it all out."

"Not to mention that you'd just as soon put a shrinking dragon down his pants than actually join him." Arty laughed as he finished.

Taren chuckled quietly at the thought.

Iggy laughed too and said, "Yeah. We aren't evil ya know. We're just tryin' to survive in a world gone mad."

Enoch snarled. "The only thing *mad* about this is the fact that two annoying pests such as yourselves can actually find a way to capture a dragon at all."

Arty, not able to resist the moment, replied, "Well, really you're more like a fifth of a dragon if we're all being honest with ourselves."

Enoch snarled.

Taren was suddenly curious for the situation. It hadn't dawned on him of the difficulty that the two small creatures must have encountered in capturing an actual dragon. He was also slightly annoyed that they were utilizing his feet as their protective barrier. He tried to shake Iggy off of his left foot and then asked them a question. "That's an interesting point the dragon makes. Just how did you capture him and what exactly were you planning on doing with him once you had him bound? It's not as if you have a direct line to Nadaroth and could just drag him there." He smirked at his own thoughts.

Arty shook his head and started to ease his way out from behind Taren's boot. "No. Not a direct line. But we have a connection to his collectors."

"Collectors?" asked Taren.

"Yeah, the ones that have joined him. They hunt down the marked beasts and look for potential new ones."

Iggy added, "And they give you things of value for capturing one. The more valuable the find, the better your pay is." Suspicion thick in his face, he asked, "And how, exactly, is it that you aren't aware of this information?"

Taren didn't answer, only adding to the suspicion.

Titus, curious as always, repeated one of Taren's points. "That still leaves you with a dragon chained to the ground and no way to move him without getting eaten."

Iggy grinned and crossed his arms. "We *were* about to go find the collector and bring him back here until your lot decided to…er…intervene."

Sam was listening intently to every word the ferrets were saying. He started to put together everything that he'd just heard and then all of a sudden, he had an idea. "That's it!" he said mostly to himself. He turned around and saw Taren, Titus and Keesa staring back, confused.

Sam looked back at Enoch and then to the ferrets. "I think I know how you can help us." He turned to Taren and said, "I have an idea."

Taren focused on the three and considered what Sam could possibly mean. But after a few moments it dawned on him just what Sam was thinking. He raised an eyebrow and turned one corner of his mouth up in a smile. He looked down at the cowering duo still clutching to his boots, and said, "Perfect."

Chapter Twenty: Trades and Traitors

It was raining – again.

Sam's hair was dripping water into his eyes and he had started shivering. Though the course of the day had offered plenty of amazing and unbelievable things, it still wasn't quite enough to erase the fact that he was wet and cold.

Yetews had wrapped his arms around Sam in a hope to keep him warmer, but his long hair was also soaked. Sam didn't have the heart to tell him that it only made the situation worse.

He'd asked yet again if he could create a shelter, but Taren and the others agreed that unless he could find a way to make it disappear when they left, that it would be too easy to connect it to them. If someone were trying to find them, it wouldn't be hard to miss such clues. After all, they weren't entirely sure just how far word had spread about Sam and his abilities. It was just safer keeping a low profile.

He knew that he hadn't developed his morphing skills enough to change objects regularly or confidently, so he silently sulked about their situation and longed to go back to southern Imagia. It seemed warmer there.

The Gateway to Imagia: The Tale of Sam Little

Luckily, though they had barely entered the mountains, there seemed to be many more options for protection than the previous forests had offered. Enoch had already proven himself to be quite the ally. He'd lived here long enough to have knowledge of various shelters that he'd inhabited over time.

Enoch led them to a small cave that was embedded into the rocky crags not too far from where he'd been chained. It was just big enough to fit them all inside. If Enoch weren't a shrinking dragon, then it might have proved to be difficult to fit so comfortably.

Sam went inside and decided to try and imagine a nice fire but his mind was so concentrated on his chattering teeth that he couldn't manage it. He realized at that time just how much he had to learn and it worried him about what they were going to do if they actually found Nadaroth. He hoped that his confidence would grow so that he might not have the fear he seemed never able to shake himself of.

Taren, not oblivious to Sam's sudden disappointment, looked over to him and smiled sympathetically. He knew that it couldn't be easy to be in his position or situation. He watched Sam's face fall as he lost his concentration once more. He looked at the disappointed child and walked towards the back of the cave where there was some dry grass and twigs – remnants from previous inhabitants. He squeezed Sam's shoulder as he passed him and said quietly, "Rest your mind, kid. I got this one." And then he smiled warmly.

Sam stopped staring at the stony ground and glanced up at Taren who was working on getting a fire going. He half smiled when he understood that Taren was trying to make him feel better so he wouldn't beat himself up.

It'd been a long day and everyone was tired and eager to dry themselves by the fire that was now warmly blazing in the protection of the cave. When they were all warmer and slightly dryer, the atmosphere in the cave started to relax significantly.

Things had changed drastically by the days end. Sam and his companions had set out across the wild northern lands of Imagia with no plan in mind in regards to their journey to seek out Nadaroth. Up until then they were relying solely on the hope that they were going in the right direction. To their great surprise and fortune, a plan had nearly fallen into their laps.

The northern lands were far more lost to the ways of Nadaroth and his intentional downfall of the world. He'd developed a control on the inhabitants and come to construct ways to have others do his dirty work for him.

Evening had already come and wherever they were, they all were hopeful of finding a more solid direction to point themselves in. And, though they were hesitant at first, it became obvious that the two bandits they'd met just happened to be the key to that potential success.

Everyone was quiet for the moment as they warmed themselves, which left Sam to his own thoughts. He became lost in the glow of Enoch's scales as the firelight reflected brilliantly off of him. He thought back to earlier in the day, remembering what had happened.

After Sam released Enoch of his iron bonds, they discovered that Iggy and Arty were quite knowledgeable of the way of these lands and the inhabitants there in.

Sam had thought through what he'd heard between Enoch and the ferrets. He realized that if the three of them would be willing to help them, then they might be able to find some way to not reach Nadaroth, but possibly the next best thing – one of his collectors.

The hardest part of explaining this newly formulated plan was getting the three key characters to agree to it. Sam proceeded to try and explain his idea to the others. "If we can find one of the collectors, then they might know how to find Nadaroth. And if they can find him, then we can find a way to force one of them to tell us the way."

Taren nodded. "It's a good idea, but we can't do this by force. We have to go about this in a smart way or we could have a lot more trouble on our hands than we bargained for."

Iggy was shocked by all this talk. "What's all this nonsense? No one wants to actually see Nadaroth face-to-face. It's been said that not even his collectors can look him in the eye without cowering in fear. And here you are, a bunch of rogue do-gooders who are rushing to find him. Why? Is there something wrong with your brains?"

Taren shook his head. "We can't give you the details unless you agree to help us."

Iggy raised his furry brow and came to an unspoken agreement with his friend. He finally replied, "So what exactly does a big strapping guy, such as yourself, need with two helpless little creatures like us?"

He tried to work out the details for everyone. "What we need is bait and someone who is familiar with dealing with the collectors. Which, of course, is where you three can help. Iggy and Arty, you can inform the collector about capturing a shrinking dragon. When he sees what you have, you two will need to convince him that you're the only ones who can deliver the dragon because of your locking system. Tell him that you have lost the key. Tell them you will need to describe the key to Nadaroth personally so that he can make a new one. After you have the best course, we'll meet back up with you. Then you can lead us straight to Nadaroth. You've survived this long, so you must know a bit about how to work the system. If you are as efficient at lying as you are at being annoying, then it shouldn't be a problem." He slyly looked down at Iggy and Arty who were standing with their mouths open. "It's perfect."

"Perfect?" Iggy suddenly said aghast. "You call this perfect? That's a wretched plan!" He looked at his counterpart who merely shrugged indifferently. They were both confused as to what might be going on in the heads of these near strangers. "You are aware, of course, that the collectors are all but savages that Nadaroth has complete control over and that they'd kill any living thing that deceives them or threatens them in any way. Right?"

Sam looked around at everyone who all seemed completely uncaring for the moment. He waited for Taren to answer Iggy.

He simply said, "I figured as much." He waited for the two to decide if they would help them. After neither of them seemed to choose, he began to grow impatient. "Well," he said, "you are obviously the key to success. So will you aid us in our plan?"

Iggy rubbed his paws on his head as if warding away a coming headache. "But we don't have a prisoner anymore. You went and set him free. Which, by the way, thank you very much for that. It's exactly what we were hoping for – having a hungry, vengeful dragon on the loose who has a personal vendetta with us. Thanks so much!" His sarcasm was thick.

Taren rolled his eyes at the mockery. "Well, that's where it would get tricky. Enoch," he turned to face the dragon, "how opposed would you be to being the bait if we could swear to protect you to the best of our abilities?"

Everyone watched the dragon's face intently, waiting for a response. After remaining quiet for a long moment, he looked down at Sam. He folded his wings, instantly shrinking down to his less threatening size. He walked up to Sam and said, "I have reason to believe that there is something truly remarkable about you, child. If I am right, then I would be willing to stand with you. Though I'm slightly disgusted by the idea of being led away in chains by the likes of those two, I will do what I can to help you, Sam. If it weren't for your uncommon compassion I might be in the same situation only with less promising ends."

Sam felt honored that Enoch was so willing to help after so little time in knowing them. It helped fuel the small spark of hope that was building in him. Yetews nudged him with his knuckles, proud of what Sam had done.

Enoch also said, "But will you be willing to share your story with me so that I may know what it is that you stand for?"

It wasn't what Sam, or anyone for that matter, expected to hear. Sam felt a surge of excitement go through him at the prospect of having a dragon on their side through all of this. He didn't know if it was what Taren wanted him to say, but he followed his own instincts and answered, "Yes. We'll tell you everything."

Arty's mouth fell back open with a barely audible pop and he shook his head. "So let me get this straight? You expect us to just willingly throw our hands up in the air and do whatever you want us to do simply because you're on some weird suicidal trek to find the most dangerous being in all of Imagia who will probably kill us at first chance. Is that 'bout right?"

Taren looked around the group briefly and smiled back at him. "Yeah. That pretty much covers it."

Arty and Iggy looked at each other for a few seconds, glanced around the group and then back to each other. They seemed to have some silent communication as they considered their options.

A sudden clap of thunder rolled from the dark clouds that were gathering above them. Everyone looked up at the warning storm clouds quickly forming.

Then, after taking deep, cleansing breaths, Iggy and Arty clapped their paws together and rubbed them eagerly. Together they both said, "Okay then! We'll do it!"

The Gateway to Imagia: The Tale of Sam Little

Iggy quickly added, "But we want to know the kid's story too. That trick with the key wasn't just a random event and if we're joining you on some hopeless trip to our ultimate demise, then we want details."

"Our time's up anyways," Arty added. "The dragon was our last chance and it was a long shot at best."

Sam furrowed his brow. There was something more to these two and he wanted to know what it was. "What do you mean 'your time's up'?"

"We'll explain later. But I think we'd best find some shelter from that storm. It's gonna be a nasty one."

As Sam finished recalling their last dry moment, he realized that he was finally getting dried out and no longer shaking. He looked around the cave and watched the strange shadows, cast by the firelight, dance on the stones.

Yetews was sitting next to him and no longer dripping. Now that everyone was warmer and less prone to chattering teeth, it was high time that someone began explanations.

Iggy and Arty were sitting inches away from Taren, having utilized him as a temporary shield. Enoch had been glaring at them every chance he got. They were whispering amongst themselves when Sam decided to grill them about their past. "So Artemus and Ignatius, I was sort of wondering what you meant earlier about your time being up."

"First of all," Arty answered, "you really can call us Arty and Iggy. Much easier to say, don't you think? But as far as *our* story goes, if we have plans on dying at some point in time for whatever crazy plan you have, then you get to go first."

Sam didn't know how to respond.

Iggy spoke his part as well. "Besides, it looks a bit like you need us more than we need you so why don't you go ahead and let us know what's going on?"

"Actually," Enoch pointed out, "If it weren't for their protection, little rats, I'd have already digested you. So perhaps it's *you* that needs them more." He seemed pleased with his observation and made a slight rumbling sound that wasn't quite a growl.

Taren decided he needed to mediate on the situation. "No, it's okay, Enoch. Thank you, but I think they have a point. They deserve to know. As do you." He turned to look at the ferrets while considering something. He knew that judging from their nature, they might be compelled to turn them in at some point in time for their own benefit. So he quickly formulated a backup plan. "But if they try and run, I give you full permission to go right ahead and dispose of them as you see fit." He smirked.

The ferrets gasped in not entirely true resentment. "We wouldn't dare!" It was hard to tell which one actually said it.

Everyone eventually settled as close as they could around the fire. Sam sat with Yetews on one side and Titus on his other.

Keesa winced quietly as she settled herself beside Titus. He noticed and whispered to her, hopefully out of Sam's earshot, "Is it still not healing?"

She replied, "Not really. But I suppose I'm getting accustomed to it."

"Do you think you will ever fully mend?"

She closed her blue eyes for a moment and said doubtfully, "Only time can heal. So I must wait and see." She noticed Sam attempting to listen and tried to hide the doubt in her heart. She quickly added, "But it's better than the alternative was." She hoped that he didn't hear their hushed conversation. She knew that Sam had healed her to the best of his ability and she couldn't have asked for more given the circumstances.

But Sam did hear them and he instantly felt a surge of guilt for the pain she was trying to hide. He wondered if saving her life was a fair trade for any damage he did to her. Every time he saw her wince, he told himself that he would never try something like that again with his powers.

"Sam?" It was Taren.

"Huh?" he snapped out of his thoughts.

"I think this might be easier if we just show them what this is all about. Do you mind?" He looked around the rather close quarters and then added, "Something small and preferably immobile." He smiled and winked.

Sam nodded. "Okay." Now that he was warmer and dryer, he was feeling better. He hadn't been imagining much lately for lack of the want or need to. After he imagined the giant sea turtles, it seemed like

The Gateway to Imagia: The Tale of Sam Little

it was harder to concentrate and he didn't really understand why. But that was days ago and his mind felt stronger now.

When he seemed to hesitate, Yetews grumbled words of encouragement to him. Sam closed his eyes and tried to think of something he could imagine that wouldn't put them in any danger.

As he was concentrating on what he wanted to imagine, the ferrets voiced their inevitable confusion. Iggy asked, "What's he doin'? What did you mean by 'small and preferably immobile'?"

No one answered Iggy's questions.

Sam tuned them out completely and escaped into his mind. He thought of Orga and Warg, safely sitting in the underground home he'd come to enjoy. He caught himself smiling when he thought of the beautiful flower he'd imagined that was probably still growing in the center of the big room. He decided that it would be the perfect thing to imagine now, in such a dreary moment.

He opened his eyes and began to picture it just how he remembered it, only in brilliant fiery shades of oranges and yellows. This time, instead of having it merely appear, he imagined it growing from the ground. Even as it broke through the hard earth with a muffled cracking sound, he could hear two distinct voices in shock.

Sam ignored the gasps and let his mind slip further into his memory. Soon after the flower appeared, an aged wooden table and benches appeared, followed by a change in the floor. The ground began to creak as the stone disappeared, replaced by aged wood and dusty makeshift rugs. The cave began to morph into what looked like the main room in Orga's home. As everything began to take form, Sam felt himself jerked out of his subconscious, back into the cold of the cave. Yetews was the one trying to force him to stop.

Sam saw that everyone was up and had backed against the cave walls, moving away from the heart of his imagined memory. The memory didn't have time to become strong enough for his entire image to remain permanent. The room began to fade almost immediately, leaving only the perfectly grown flower in the middle of them all.

Arty, obviously shaken, peeled himself quickly from the cave wall and yelled, "Impossible! It's true! It's him!"

Iggy backed away a few paces to fall in step with his friend. "Maybe he isn't a boy at all! Maybe this is just a trap! Arty, we've gotta get out of here."

Arty was torn between shock and amazement. "The rumors are true. Iggy, we stumbled into something truly amazing, my friend."

"No," Iggy protested. "If we get caught helping this kid we'll end up worse than dead! We might as well just let the dragon eat us now!"

Taren almost yelled over their sudden hysteria. "What in the name of Imagia are you two babbling about?"

Iggy, much more eager to leave than his friend, said, "The boy. Do you have any idea how much he's worth? We thought it was just a rumor, but it's all true!"

It suddenly dawned on Taren as to what they were saying. "You know about Sam." It wasn't a question, but a statement. "How far has word spread about what he can do?"

Iggy shook his head, still inching towards the cave entrance. "I don't know exactly, but there are rumors amongst the collectors of a boy who can imagine and that Nadaroth wants him. No one believed it could be true."

Titus was up and concerned about what was taking place. "What do you mean Nadaroth wants him? For what?"

Iggy shrugged. "We don't know. Rumor was that he would be traveling with a human that protects him, his Guardian and maybe two or three others. We had no names, but we should have realized with the key. It wasn't a trick." He paused for a moment and then said, "I'm sorry. We can't help you. Right, Arty?"

Arty's shock seemed to be changing more to awe. He stared at Sam, who was looking a bit shaken as well, and then looked to his friend. "I suppose you're right. We can't. We won't turn you in, but please let us go on our way."

Taren sounded close to panic as he tried to explain. "But you don't understand! Sam is the best chance Imagia has now. We can prove it if you'll just hear us out! If you don't believe us by the time we are done, then we'll happily let you go on your way. Dragon free."

Both ferrets nervously considered their options for a moment. They cautiously paced the ground, never taking their eyes from Sam. Finally, after considering the alternatives they had yet to share with the others, they nodded to one another and Iggy said, "Okay. We'll listen and then decide from there. But start from the beginning. From the very moment this boy set foot inside his gateway."

The Gateway to Imagia: The Tale of Sam Little

Yetews' ears suddenly perked up and he looked suspiciously at the two small creatures. They noticed him watching them, but made no effort to inquire why.

No one else seemed to take notice to Yetews' sudden shift in posture and demeanor.

Taren proceeded to explain everything he could to the newcomers. They all sat quietly in the cave and listened intently to every word that he spoke. Sam filled in a few blanks from when he first arrived to the point when he met Taren. Titus and Keesa added a few key points from their perspective.

Sam hadn't realized just how much had happened in the months he'd been in Imagia. When the story was told, he felt exhausted from reliving it in his mind.

As Arty gathered his senses, Iggy began to walk up to Sam, who looked down at him in return. What he said next was perhaps the most unexpected thing any one of them could have predicted. "Do you have any idea how long we've been waiting for this?"

Sam, slightly confused by the sudden mood shift, said, "Waiting for what?"

Arty finally came to his senses and let out one hard laugh. "Ha! *You* of course! Or someone like you, at the very least. Long ago, on the rise of Nadaroth's power, others said that it was possible that another one could learn to do what he does and stop the madness! When the rumors of you started, it was impossible to believe that another child had come with the same power as Nadaroth. You've learned to imagine! You are the one we've all been hoping for!"

"You're pretty short, mind you," Iggy observed, "but nevertheless, you're the one everyone hoped might come one day."

Enoch hadn't said much during Taren's explanation of things. He finally had something to say. "I had a feeling this child was something special. I knew it from the moment he turned back to free me with a key that shouldn't exist."

Sam could feel his ears burning. All the attention that was being directed towards him was a bit unnerving. Every time someone referred to him as special or when he was told he was the one whom Imagia's existence relied on, he found it difficult to concentrate through his embarrassment. He hoped that he could live up to the challenge that was being set before him, because at the moment, he

256

felt exactly like what he was – a very small boy in a very large world.

Yetews, still looking suspiciously at Iggy and Arty, grumbled a question to Sam to relay to them. Sam translated. "He wants to know if this means that you two will help us?"

There was a noticeable change in their mood. Neither Iggy nor Arty could seem to contain their newfound enthusiasm for the situation at hand. They were positively giddy as they chattered on and on about what they'd just heard and seen.

Iggy stepped forward next to his friend and said, "This moment has been the hope of every Guardian that walks the unsure paths of Imagia. Of course we will aid you."

"In every way we can," Arty added in all sincerity.

At Iggy's words, Taren unexpectedly stood up with a jolt, startling nearly everyone. The flames of the fire made him look fierce. He was angry that two creatures with a need to betray the life of another creature could compare themselves with beings so pure as Guardians. More than offended by such an idea, he asked the two bandits, "What could you two possibly know of the hopes and troubles of Guardians?"

They turned to face him, casting a knowing look to Yetews who looked as though he already had the answer to the question. Both the ferrets laughed smugly. They crossed their paws over their chests.

Iggy looked at Arty for a moment then said, "We know quite a bit actually." They were truly enjoying the emotions that they were bringing out in Taren.

Taren looked even more irate at their smugness. "You hunt marked beasts. Is torturing knowledge out of Guardians one of your other trades?"

"Not exactly," Iggy answered.

Taren scoffed. "Then exactly how is it that two small bandits such as yourselves can know anything of Guardians or those that protect them?

Arty raised his furry brow and his ears perked forward. "Because, as the kid's Guardian has probably already figured out, we just happen to be a couple of Guardians ourselves."

* * * * * * * * * *

The Gateway to Imagia: The Tale of Sam Little

Yetews was shaking his head in disgust. After finding out that Arty and Iggy were actually Guardians, Yetews explained that he suspected it the moment that they mentioned Sam's gateway. The way that they referred to his gateway revealed what they more than likely were.

Taren wasn't surprised of Yetews' insight into the two. He explained that Guardians tend to have a knack for sensing when other Guardians are around.

Regardless of anything, Sam wasn't the only one who was shocked by this revelation. Even Keesa found it difficult to accept. The fact that two creatures that could turn another creature in for a reward could be of like mind as someone like Yetews or Orga seemed a cruel comparison. She even threatened them. She hissed quietly between her sharp teeth, "I should personally deliver you to the dragon simply for your blatant betrayal to this world."

Her statement genuinely offended Iggy and Arty. Iggy, momentarily fearless, stormed up to Keesa and defended his honor the best he could. "Now look here, cat! We are *not* traitors!" Arty was vouching for him in the background.

She hissed back, "Though I am only beginning to understand the way Imagia works, I know that to turn your back on your child and become a personal servant to the enemy is nothing short of a betrayal to what you are."

Arty threw his paws up in the air in frustration. "You have no idea what you're talkin' about."

"Yes," said Iggy. "We gave you a chance to explain yourselves. We deserve the same courtesy." He flipped around to Sam, who was still trying to make sense of everything. Sam looked at him and Iggy asked, "Don't you think so, Sam?"

He couldn't seem to focus on the question. As he looked around at everyone's faces, he wondered what he should be saying. He processed the question as quickly as he could. For some reason, despite the fact that he was only a ten-year-old boy, so often, things managed to come down to what he thought. However, in all truth, his own hand was what was sparing the ferrets' lives and he had to make a choice in the matter.

Sam didn't want to give up hope on the two. If they were Guardians at one point in their lives, then they couldn't be all bad. He considered that perhaps there was more to their story below their tough façade. He found his tongue and said, "Yeah. They're right. We should let them explain." He looked to Taren for any sign that he might be wrong, but when all he saw was a subtle nod of his head he knew it was okay.

Everyone moved into more comfortable positions. The only one that couldn't seem to wind down was Taren. He continued to stand for the time being.

Sam asked the first question. "If you are really Guardians, then why would you be working for Nadaroth? He's the reason that Imagia is so bad now. I mean, doesn't he *kill* Guardians?"

The sincerity and sadness in the boy's blue eyes struck something in the two ferrets. There was no hint of a joke about them now when they answered him. Iggy began. "It's a lot more complicated than that."

Taren and Yetews snorted doubtfully at the same time and Iggy and Arty shot them an annoyed glance. Taren verbalized what he and Yetews were thinking. "Enlighten us. Please."

Iggy and Arty moved to place themselves closest to Sam. Their small, thin bodies were silhouetted by the brightness of the fire. Iggy, seeming to be more of the storyteller, began. "Well, as we said. We *are* Guardians. We came to exist right around the time when the Crossing Waters were still free to pass."

Sam quickly asked, "Crossing Waters?"

"Yes. I believe you would now know it better as the Impossible Way. Anyhow, we came into the forest on the south shores with our child. His name was David.

"His gateway was very close to the water and it was the first place we went. His first three days here were all spent on the northern shores. That was when things turned for the worse." He paused to look at Arty, who looked grim at the recollection.

Iggy went on. "Well, unfortunately we weren't exactly privy to Nadaroth and his growing control of Imagia. On David's third day, word was spreading of something foul in the Crossing Waters that would stop anyone from passing. Instinct took over us and we tried our best to find safe passage to David's gateway.

Others were crossin' the waters so we thought we'd be safe to do the same. We were wrong."

The Gateway to Imagia: The Tale of Sam Little

"Dead wrong," Arty added. "'Something foul' was the stinkin' understatement of the year. It was mass chaos! Everyone we saw on the water that day..." Arty couldn't get any more words out. His small ears laid back and sorrow filled his face. He turned away and gazed into the fire.

Sam watched him and didn't know what to feel or say, so he remained quiet and waited with the others for one of them to continue.

Iggy softly pat his friend on the back and then turned back around. There was a deep sadness in his eyes as well. "Everyone – Guardians and children alike – they all died that day. They were dragged into the water, screaming, by beasts that had no shape. There was no warning. Only white tentacles that, as it pulled, devoured everything that touched the water. Then everything went dark and *he* appeared. It was like he came out of nowhere. All we could see were the red flames of his eyes and hear a voice saying, 'None may pass. The way is closed.'

"There was nothin' we could do but watch. And when it was over, word spread pretty quick of Nadaroth. David was devastated. But we protected him as best we could."

Arty shivered suddenly. He put his paws over his eyes and then said, "I can still hear it. When I close my eyes, I can hear them in my mind. The *screams*." He shivered again then shook his head as if it would force the memories out.

Less harsh this time, but still skeptical about the two, Taren asked a couple of questions. "David must not have been able to return to his gateway. Where is he now? How did you survive this long? Because, if what you say is true, then you have been in Imagia far longer than any of us. That is a long time to survive; even in the south."

"Yeah," Iggy agreed. "Which was my next point, if you wouldn't have interrupted me."

"Sorry. Go on," Taren gestured with his open palm to continue.

"David grew up like all the other lost children do. Villages were built. More children became lost as the years went by. Gateways in the north opened, but there were so many creatures attacking Guardians that the newly born ones barely stood a chance. Most of them never made it to their gateways to bring their children in. But children that did arrive and lost their Guardians had barely a choice as they grew. Some agreed to join Nadaroth and do his bidding for the sake of promised survival. And some helped. They called themselves Defenders, much like you, if I could guess from your defensive nature." He indicated to Taren.

Taren replied, "We're called Protectors. We watch over Guardians and their children when we can."

Arty chimed in suddenly. "Different name, same game."

Iggy was silently agreeing with him. "Yes. Only the difference is that there aren't many Defenders left to do the defending. They are just as hunted as Guardians are."

Taren looked confused. "I thought that gateways only opened in southern Imagia. Have they always opened in the north as well?"

Iggy and Arty both nodded. Iggy said, "As far as we know, that's always been the case. At least since we came to be."

Sam couldn't hold back the question that he was dying to ask. He wanted desperately to know what happened to David. It was obvious that he wasn't here with them today, so he knew that there had to be more to his story. But just as much as he desired to hear the story, he also didn't want to know. Because he knew that there was little chance that it could be a happy ending. In a hesitant voice, he asked, "What happened to David?"

Their somber looks returned in full force. Iggy was shaking his head slowly. "David. He's the reason we are what we are today. If you want to speak of betrayal, then you really ought to talk to him. Arty can tell you this part better. He was the conscious one through this part of our story." He looked behind his shoulder at Arty who was still staring at the fire.

As he turned to face Sam, there was a new look burning in his small eyes. It was anger. "David started disappearing from time to time. We didn't know why at the time or where he was goin'. Best we can figure is that he was meetin' up with some of Nadaroth's scum and they talked him into joining them. That night...well...he turned on us. He tried to kill us both. He knocked Iggy out cold and then tried to do the same to me.

"When I asked him why he was doing it and begged him not to kill us, he said the reason he was doing what he did was because *we* were responsible for his entrapment in Imagia. He left us barely alive. We never saw him again after that night."

Sam felt the knots in his stomach twisting violently. He was

The Gateway to Imagia: The Tale of Sam Little

sickened by their story. He couldn't understand how anyone could betray their Guardian. He looked over at Yetews who must have been thinking the same thing. He looked down at Sam and they couldn't find anything to say to each other. Even Taren was speechless. Everyone was too astounded by the tale.

But the story wasn't over yet. The madness had to lead them to where they were today and so Iggy continued. "When we healed as best as we could, we had to adapt our ways just so we could survive. We found an in with Nadaroth's crowd. We learned of marked beasts and started finding ways to catch them."

He noticed the sudden agitation amongst the others and quickly defended his statement. "Look, I don't know how it is in the south. But here, it's either eat or be eaten. Besides, we only did what we did if we needed more time."

Taren was confused. He had been under the impression, as were the others, that they were paid something of value for their captures. "You said Enoch was valuable to you. What's so valuable to you that you would turn in another creature's freedom for?"

Iggy looked almost ashamed, but very sincere. "Our lives. We found a Collector named Ognotz. Pathetic creature. Specially imagined by Nadaroth as the captain of his hunting party. He was amused by our attempts to survive and gave us an option. He would give us a job to do and if we could do it, he'd give us a certain number of years of amnesty – freedom from being hunted.

"So we agreed. We wanted to survive. That's why we were hunting the shrinking dragon. Ognotz said that if we caught one then we'd have ten more years of amnesty."

"But our time's up now," Arty said.

"Which is fine by us 'cause now it looks like we have a reason to fight instead of flee. Sam, we never wanted to do damage, but we did what we did to live on. We aren't proud of it, but we wouldn't be here talkin' to you if we didn't do any of it."

By the way that they spoke, Sam could tell that they were trying to ask for forgiveness. Though it was in his nature to forgive them, he wasn't entirely sure that it was his forgiveness that they needed. Before he answered, he looked around the small cave. Once more, he found all eyes towards him. But the one he turned to was the only other Guardian there.

262

Yetews' blameless eyes looked deep into Sam's soul. Their connection was a deeper one than any two in the room and he knew what the boy was thinking simply by looking at him. He knew that Sam was worried that if he offered forgiveness to Iggy and Arty for their actions as Guardians, that it might disappoint everyone – that it might disappoint him. Yetews knew that Sam's heart was so pure that he couldn't refuse to give a second chance to such creatures. So he grumbled and growled his support for Sam and he tried to reassure him that it was okay – on every level.

Sam nodded his head and faced the small Guardians. After only a moment's hesitation, he said, "I…I don't know what all you've done. But…I guess I can understand. It must have been really hard to have David betray you like that. I can't imagine why any kid would do that. It's just so sad." He glanced back to Yetews and added. "I could never do that."

Yetews smiled as if he had no doubt about it.

Arty watched Sam share his connection with Yetews and sighed. "There's a lot that no one can understand about this world anymore."

Sam moved so that he was kneeling in front of Arty and Iggy. He looked at them with all the seriousness he could muster. "Then everything is forgiven. Does that mean that you will help us find Nadaroth?"

Iggy nodded. "Yep. We'll do everything we can. But as far as your plan goes, I'm afraid we agree that it's still…well…horrid."

"Yes. Awful plan. Wouldn't stand a chance." Arty chuckled.

Taren stood up, agitated. He circled the fire and asked them, "And what exactly is wrong with the plan?" It was obvious he was offended by their opinion.

Titus joined Taren at his side and stated his confidence. "Yes. There are some details that would have to be worked out, but it could definitely work."

"Well first of all, my furry friend," answered Arty, "Collectors might be ugly, but they aren't exactly dumb." He tapped his head with one of his claws. "They've got brains and anyone with half of one would know that they wouldn't just hand over the keys to the castle. If ya take my meaning."

Sam didn't want there to be a fight about what to do. He asked them, "Okay. So what should we do then?"

The Gateway to Imagia: The Tale of Sam Little

The two shared a devious look. Iggy raised his brow. "We've got a much better plan."

Sam watched Yetews who seemed worried about what these two might have in store for them. Taren was donning a similar look that was mixed with frustration. Sam wasn't entirely sure what to expect either. He looked around the cave and saw all of his friends, old and new ones alike. He finally had a flicker of hope. This morning they were walking blind into the darkness. Though they were still in the dark, at the very least, they now had a lamp to light the way.

Chapter Twenty-one: Hoodwinked

Settled deep in a valley in the heart the mountains was a village. What was once meant as a safe haven for children to stay in and explore in their short time in this world had become a sinister, unwelcoming place. The laughter of children that once rang through the air was replaced by whispers of dark dealings and the constant battles between lost souls. With Nadaroth's control, the village was now the perfect place that one might go to deal with the twisted transactions of Imagia. It was the kind of place that any child, sane beast or Guardian would avoid unless given no other option. And Iggy and Arty were now standing in the shadows of the trees on its borders, waiting for the perfect moment to enter.

They had left the rain behind them when they set off for the closest meeting place of the collectors. It had been two straight days of traveling through the muck and mire of the stormy mountain pass. They were headed for the best place they knew of that they could be guaranteed to find what they were looking for. Though those that frequented the place might call it a village of sorts, it was anything but. Those that lived there or stopped in for a time were not the kind of beings that were to be trusted.

And despite the nervousness that being there brought, it was exactly right where they wanted to be. The dusk of evening was setting in and both ferrets lingered for only a short while longer as they gathered their wits and worked out the details that were essential to their survival in this dangerous position.

Arty kept throwing uneasy glances over his shoulder into the trees behind him. Iggy noticed his edginess for the last time. "You're gonna get us killed if you keep twitching like that."

Arty, unaware of his obvious anxiety flipped his attention back to his friend. "I'm not twitching, I'm observing the situation from all angles."

Iggy smiled. "Yes. I'm sure *that* will be convincing." He smacked Arty in the back of his head and said, "Now stop twitching! For the love of pity, we've been here dozens of times and you've never acted like this before. Sheesh. Grow a spine, Arty."

At first, he was merely annoyed by the smack to his head, but he realized that it was what he needed. He was rubbing the place Iggy had hit him as he pulled himself together. "You're right, but this isn't exactly like the other times, is it? We got a lot more ridin' on this little jaunt into the pit of ravenous beasts."

Iggy looked into the village and sighed. "Yeah. But Ognotz can smell fear, so pull it together mate. He may reek like a rotten sack of meat – and look like one too – but he's not a complete idiot. Besides, he's not about to pass up what we have to offer this time."

Arty thought for a moment and slowly began to shake his head. "I don't know. What if this doesn't work?"

Iggy finished packing his rucksack and shrugged. "Well, I suppose we'll just wing it; like we've always done."

"I don't know, Iggy. Something about this just don't feel right. What if Sam–"

"Aww, come on! Now don't start with that again," Iggy interrupted him. "We've gotta do this…for our own good."

Arty breathed deep while nodding. "I suppose you're right." He patted his counterpart on the back. "Well then. Shall we?" He waved his open paw towards the torch-lit borders.

Iggy nodded and Arty glanced once more into the trees as they started to leave the safety of the forest.

As they entered the streets, they tried desperately to remain as discreet as possible. They weren't exactly easy to spot, being as small as they were, but they wouldn't be completely unnoticed. So they kept from view as often as they could, ducking behind barrels and boxes that littered the unkempt paths through the buildings.

It didn't take them long to find the building that they were looking for. It was the biggest one in the town. It was also the most occupied. The stench of stale, rotting food stung their nostrils with every breath. They dodged the feet of humans and creatures alike as they silently approached the busiest table in the huge room.

Before they could even approach, a deep, mocking laughter cut through the crowded noise like a rusty knife. Iggy and Arty stopped dead in their tracks along with half of the room. They both stood, arms confidently crossed at their chests.

From the center of the largest table, a booming voice mockingly said, "Well, well, well. Look who it is! Someone set out the traps. We've got a little pest problem on our hands tonight!"

Laughter echoed throughout the room. When it finally died down, Iggy calmly smiled and said, "So, Ognotz, does that mean you aren't going to invite us to join the party?"

Everyone laughed again, including Ognotz. "Ah. I see you still have a sense of humor. But apparently your sense of self-preservation is lacking, because…" he paused to sniff the air with his wide nostrils, "I don't smell a dragon. Just the lingering stench of a couple of worthless Guardians." He grinned widely, revealing a jagged row of misshapen, lethal teeth that lined his over-sized mouth. His harsh, yellowed eyes gazed around the room for a moment before stopping to focus on the two Guardians. He stood up from the table, kicking his chair back to the point of falling.

He placed his fat, gnarled hands on the table and leaned over the middle, revealing his putrid gray-green color in the light of the lamps. His skin was heavily wrinkled, despite the scaly texture. And his fat stomach fought to escape his dingy clothes as it pressed into the table. Though only the size of an average man, his wide stature and foul disposition was enough to bring alarm to even the bravest soul. He sneered at Iggy and Arty, making the skin on his large frog-like jowl stretch unnaturally. The evidence of previous fights littered the helmet that covered most of his head. There were trophies from kills dangling around his neck like charms. And hanging from the top of his helmet was a long tuft of black hair that looked like it came from a horses tail

The Gateway to Imagia: The Tale of Sam Little

– trophies from fallen Guardians

"Now, Ognotz, we mustn't forget our manners. Besides, do you really think we would be stupid enough to come here empty handed?" Iggy asked. "A little credit, please." Arty was being oddly quiet. Even though Iggy was normally the one to do the talking in these situations, Iggy could tell that there was something more to his silence. He silently hoped that he was the only one noticing.

"Hmmm…point well taken," Ognotz replied. He sat back down and gestured for the two to join him at the table with the others that were there. "Do humor me, one last time."

They joined the rabble of collectors and hunters at the table. Once they climbed to the top of the stool, and feeling quite small in the meantime, they waited for Ognotz to finish slopping down his pungent, brown drink before they spoke their part. "I believe we have a transaction to make tonight."

"Does this transaction involve a shrinking dragon?" Ognotz wiped the drippings of his drink from his chin.

"Naturally," Iggy replied. "Isn't that what you asked for?"

"Ha!" Ognotz laughed heartily. "So you actually did it then? Amazing. You two rats never cease to amaze me. Just when I think I'll get bored of your pathetic desperation for existence, you surprise me again!" A lanky man set another mug of the brown drink down on the table and Ognotz instantly began to chug it down.

Iggy inconspicuously nudged Arty in the ribs while Ognotz drank. He was hoping for a bit more involvement in their conversation. He was beginning to worry that Arty was going to ruin their only chance at success.

Luckily, their lifetime of friendship helped him realize what Iggy wanted and he spoke up. "Yes, well you have no idea what we went through to capture Eno…that dragon." He caught himself before he could say Enoch's name, but he quickly added another thought in hopes of hiding his slip. "Nearly bit the head clean off my shoulders! Nasty day, it was."

Iggy kept his cool even though he heard his friends slip, clear as day. Luckily, Ognotz wasn't quite as observant. Iggy took advantage of the moment and covered for Arty. "Yes, but what's done is done. Now, if you don't mind, we'd like to get on with our exchange. I haven't had my supper yet." From the corner of Iggy's eye, he caught

Arty in the middle of a nervous glance to the exit. He hoped desperately that Ognotz missed that as well.

But before there was a chance to hold on to that hope, Ognotz turned his focus entirely to Arty. His eyes squinted and he cocked his head every so slightly to the side. He asked Iggy, "What's he so nervous about?" He jabbed a calloused thumb in Arty's direction.

Lucky for Arty, Iggy was much smoother than him in tight spots like these. He always seemed to know exactly how to find the right thing to say and Arty knew that he could count on him to get them out of a hot spot when they needed to.

This was one of those moments.

"Ognotz," Iggy clucked his tongue. "You know as well as I do what we have ridin' on this little transaction. Out there in the woods, we have a very angry dragon ready to shred us to bits at a moment's notice. Now, you know our chains are iron clad."

Though not fully convinced, there was a definite shift in his suspicion. "Yes. I still can't figure out how exactly you manage those chains, being as puny as you are. I may throw on a couple of years if you share that little secret."

Iggy knew he was close to closing the deal now, and he smiled crookedly. "Tempting, but we'll have to decline for the moment. However, iron clad or not, no chains will hold if his buddy dragons are anywhere near and half as angry as he is. Hence, we might lose our catch. We lose our catch, and well…I think you know what that means, eh?"

Ognotz watched Arty, who had finally pulled himself together, for a moment longer. Finally he seemed to make up his mind. "Let's get this over with. Take me to the dragon."

Iggy nodded once. "We'll be waiting outside the front entrance when you're ready."

After the collector agreed, the two Guardians headed towards the door as quickly as they could without adding to any distrust they'd already achieved.

Once they were outside and well out of earshot, Iggy looked at his friend, shocked. "What's with you tonight? You *tryin'* to get us killed?"

Arty scratched behind his ear in frustration. They both knew what his problem was. "Iggy, I just don't know about this. There's going to

The Gateway to Imagia: The Tale of Sam Little

be a whole lot more than just an angry dragon to deal with if this doesn't go well. Something's bound to go wrong and you know it!"

"Yeah, but at least I'm not showin' it on my shoulder. Pull it together or we're gonna blow our only shot at this. Stick to the plan. It's gonna work. It has to. If we do this right then –" He cut off mid sentence when the door opened.

It was Ognotz and he had two other collectors at his flanks.

Iggy turned away and felt himself lose confidence for only a split second. They had hoped that Ognotz was going to retrieve the dragon alone. They both knew that this would interfere with their plan but Iggy quickly started to reformulate things in his mind just in case things went downhill.

He regained his composure and they both led the trio of collectors into the woods of the mountains.

It didn't take long to reach the trees. By the time they were pushing through the maze of trees, it was well into the night. The torches that the collectors carried kept the way brightly lit. Iggy had informed the three that they were getting very close to where they had the dragon restrained.

The collectors were trudging along, not attempting to be silent. They broke through a thick group of trees and there, chained between two large trees, was Enoch. His wings were restrained and he had his mouth tied closed. There was silent fury burning in his eyes.

"Just as we promised. Isn't he a beauty?" Iggy exclaimed.

Ognotz snorted. "Impressive. Never seen one so big with his wings bound. Can't wait to see him full size."

"He was almost impossible to catch." Iggy said. He knew this was the moment they had to make their move. He swallowed hard. "Which brings me to my next point. I'd say a dragon this size is worth a bit more. Don't you agree Arty?"

Arty wasn't expecting Iggy's question. His eyes widened slightly and he stuttered his response. "Y-yes. V-very valuable I think."

There was no hiding the uncertainty in his response and Iggy closed his eyes and cursed himself for pushing Arty's nerves too far. But it was too late and there was no way he could cover this one up.

Ognotz had been looking over the dragon when he heard Arty's hesitation. He whipped around, scowling at the Guardians. "You little weasels are hiding something from me," he hissed menacingly. He turned to the other two collectors and barked orders. "Apparently, I have some unfinished business with the rats. You two, take the dragon."

The chains were clanking and straining under the pressure as Enoch fought against them to no avail.

Arty looked at Enoch and lost all sense. He was already yelling before Iggy could stop him. "NO!" He jumped forward towards the chained dragon but it did no good. Ognotz had already closed the gap between them and reached down to grab Arty by the throat.

Things were happening like a whirlwind. Iggy put his paws up and ran to Ognotz. "NO! WAIT! You're right! We *are* hiding something! We have the boy!"

Ognotz loosened his grip on Arty's throat just enough so that he didn't restrict all airflow, but still enough that he had to gasp for breath. He looked down at Iggy; his curiosity sufficiently peaked. "What boy?"

"The one Nadaroth's looking for. The one who imagines." Iggy barely made eye contact with the collector. He kept watching his friend, hoping that he wasn't taking his last breath.

Ognotz hesitated and then shook his head. "You're lying."

Iggy snapped back, "No! He's hiding and waiting for us to return. He thinks we are trying to help him. The dragon was aiding him and his Guardian. We convinced the boy that we needed the dragon in order to find help. We came here to turn the dragon in and we were going to go back for the boy after that."

The collector closed his gnarled fingers tighter around the Guardians throat and Arty gasped hopelessly for air. Ognotz looked at the small creature and hissed through his teeth. "Is this true? Lie to me and I'll snap your neck."

Arty was barely able to speak. The words were short, but clear through the gasps. "Yes…all…true."

Ognotz ground his teeth together and let Arty go. He crumpled when he hit the ground and Iggy ran to his side to help him up.

"Why did you try to stop us from taking the dragon then?" Ognotz asked them, fury burning in his eyes.

Once Arty was standing and rubbing his throat through wheezy gasps, Iggy sighed and said, "Leverage."

"Leverage? What do you mean?"

"I mean leverage. There was always a chance that you'd suspect something was going on. That you'd find out we were hiding something. If that ended up being the case, then we would need the dragon for ourselves," Iggy said.

Ognotz was getting more agitated. They weren't explaining fast enough for him. "What do you mean for yourselves? What is this madness?"

Iggy watched Arty carefully. He looked hard at his friend waiting for something before he answered. Arty, still trying to catch his breath, looked over at Enoch and then back at Iggy with doubt lingering in his eyes. He nodded which was all Iggy needed.

He answered in all seriousness. "We want out. We want permanent amnesty. And we need the dragon for that."

Enoch strained harder against his bonds as Ognotz laughed heartily. "You're joking! And how do you expect to get complete amnesty with a dragon?"

"Well, we *were* going to use the boy, but I suppose that's not an option now that you know about him. So we'll use the dragon. We'll take him to Nadaroth ourselves."

Arty, finally regained his voice. With a raspy voice he said, "If we can take the dragon to him personally then we can see him. We'll plead our case, telling him about turning the boy over to you, and then give him the dragon."

"Ha!" Ognotz laughed again. "You really *are* crazy! He'll never give you what you want. He's not interested in being entertained by your fleeting need for survival like I am. You'll be dead before you get the words out."

Iggy's ears laid back and he scowled. "That's *our* concern."

Ognotz considered the situation. He crossed his large arms then asked, "So why don't I just kill you now and save you the trouble?"

Being nearly choked to death was enough to bring Arty to his senses. He answered before Iggy had a chance. "If you do that, you'll never find the boy. And the next time you sleep, your master will surely enter your mind. He won't be too happy finding out that you had a chance to get the boy but gave him a dragon in his place. Maybe then he'll find the need to create a new captain to do his bidding."

Iggy had to muffle a slight snicker that fought to escape. He was also surprised at Arty's sudden need to take charge of the situation.

The idea of displeasing his master was obviously not settling well with Ognotz. His eyes wandered from the dragon to the ferrets until he finally came to a decision. He turned to the other two collectors who had silently been waiting for orders. "You two. Leave." Once they disappeared into the trees he turned back to Iggy and Arty. "What do you propose?"

Arty replied, "A trade. You give us the directions to Nadaroth and leave the dragon here for us. We take you to the boy and his Guardian. Once you have what you want, we come back for the dragon and you remain Nadaroth's favorite pet."

Taking a few steps forward, Iggy knew it was time to seal the deal. "What do you say Ognotz? Do we have a deal?"

He mulled over his options. There was still some small hint of doubt lingering in his expression. "How do I know you're not lying about the boy just to save your own hides?"

Iggy already had a response for this because he knew how the collector's mind worked. It was a common trait to have constant distrust and suspicion. He noticed that Arty was starting to get that worried look again so before it could get worse, he said, "If we get there and there's no boy, you can kill us. Then you can come back and take the dragon for yourself. Either way, you profit."

The collector sneered, showing his yellowed teeth. He let out a short laugh before agreeing. "You two really do amaze me. Unfortunately Nadaroth isn't so easily impressed. But it's your death. Either way, this is the last deal we'll ever make." He crouched down as close to the ferrets as he could and grinned wickedly. "We have a deal."

He was so close to them that Iggy and Arty could smell his hot, fetid breath on their faces. They nodded, sealing their agreement with the collector.

"I'll give you the details to find Nadaroth on the way." Ognotz turned to look at Enoch once more before they left. "It's a shame really. He's a good catch. Nadaroth would have been pleased."

Though he couldn't move his arms from the way he was restrained, Enoch dug his front, clawed hands into the ground in rage. His chest was rising faster with every breath he took. But he couldn't manage to budge the chains that once again held him captive.

"Take me to the boy," Ognotz barked.

The Gateway to Imagia: The Tale of Sam Little

Iggy nodded and then turned to his friend. "Arty, go check the locks before we go." He looked at Enoch and smiled crookedly. "Make sure the knots on his mouth are good and tight too. We wouldn't want him to get any bright ideas about warning the boy. Now would we?"

Arty mirrored Iggy's crooked smile and agreed silently. "Be right back."

Ognotz was losing patience already. "Make it quick."

While Arty hurried over to Enoch, Iggy asked Ognotz about the directions. Arty finished his check as quickly as he could without causing the collector more impatience than he already had.

The three left Enoch behind in the dark of night. They could hear the strain of the chains growing more faint as they traveled back towards the cave where they'd left Sam and the others waiting, hopeful, for their return.

Chapter Twenty-two: Double Crossed

The two-day journey to the valley where Iggy and Arty found Ognotz was significantly shorter on the return. There was no rain for a change. So naturally, this eased their journey. It was early afternoon and the sun was shining on the mountainside through the dense trees.

It was a quiet journey for the most part. Neither Ognotz nor the ferrets were too interested in small talk when their purpose was solely business based. Iggy and Arty were having a difficult time trying to refrain from speaking to one another out of fear for Ognotz overhearing.

The silence between them made it easy to hear the subtle change in the quiet of the woods. There was a voice in the not too far distance and Iggy and Arty heard it first. When they stopped without any warning Ognotz nearly stepped on Arty.

"What are you doing?" Ognotz snapped angrily at them. His annoyance for the trek didn't help his conversation skills.

"Shh!" Iggy held a paw up to warn Ognotz from speaking.

The three of them listened carefully. When they located the direction the sound was coming from, they slowly crept through the high grass and bushes. When they reached the source of the voice, they silently watched at a safe distance, well hidden from prying eyes.

Ognotz, being significantly larger than the other two, had to crouch in a more uncomfortable position to stay out of view. He whispered harshly, a hand on the hilt of a large curved dagger on his belt. "Is that the child?"

Arty gave a wary glance to Iggy. They knew that chances were small of it being anyone else, as they were very close to the cave. They watched as the boy stood in the small clearing of the mountainside. He was standing in a relatively barren bit of ground. And without any warning, a small bush appeared in front of him from out of nowhere. Yetews came lumbering into view and it was obvious that it couldn't be anyone else but Sam.

Iggy closed his eyes for a brief moment and cursed under his breath. He looked back at Ognotz who was looking rather baffled by what he just saw. Iggy said, "Yes. That's him. But you have to let us go to him first. We'd better make sure he and his Guardian are alone. If you go rushing in there, he's going to get scared and imagine a creature that will most likely kill you."

Agitated by their lack of respect for his abilities, he pulled his dagger out and it made a sound like iron cutting through stone. The sound caused Sam to whip around suddenly. He was looking straight in their direction now, Yetews by his side. All three of them noticed and Ognotz closed his mouth before he had a chance to speak his mind.

Arty whispered, "He trusts us. Let us bring him to you."

Ognotz's eyes were barely slits as he considered just how far he could trust them. He sheathed his dagger and nodded once. He whispered back, "Make it quick. I don't like waiting."

The way he spoke was meant to be a threat and Iggy and Arty knew better than to take that idly. Before Sam could suspect anything more of the noise he'd heard, they walked quickly into the bright clearing.

Relief washed over Sam's face when he saw who it was. "Hey! You're back!" Yetews instantly mirrored his sense of relief. Sam started to ask them a question. "Did you guys –"

Iggy held up a paw to silence him while Arty threw a wary glance over his shoulder from the direction they'd come. "Sam, why are you out of the cave?"

"Well, we needed food and seeing as how imagining food doesn't seem to work right yet, we –"

Iggy raised his paw to silence him again and interrupted. His eyes darted nervously around for a moment before he said, "Are you two out here *alone*?" He seemed almost reprimanding as he asked.

Sam opened his mouth to answer right as Ognotz came into view from behind Iggy and Arty. His eyes were still suspicious. He was apparently unwilling to wait. The two ferrets looked unsurely at one another and turned around towards the collector.

Once Ognotz was close, Yetews pulled Sam back by the shoulders and kept him tucked close by his side. He backed them off a few steps. Neither one was comfortable with this stranger's presence.

"I think it's obvious that they are alone," Ognotz said. "And as for you two," he was indicating the two ferrets, "well done. I must admit, I didn't think you'd follow through. Now come here, boy."

Yetews growled and his ears lay back against his black hair, nearly hiding them from view. Sam looked down at Iggy, uncertainty running high. "Iggy, what's going on?"

Neither of the small Guardians answered immediately. They kept nervously searching the trees as if waiting for something to attack them. Iggy finally looked at Sam and regret filled his voice. "Sam, we're sorry. We didn't –"

"Enough!" Ognotz snapped. "Don't make me regret letting you both live. Our deal is complete. You're free to leave and retrieve the dragon. I can handle the child and his Guardian on my own."

Yetews snarled again and Sam couldn't understand what was happening. But the instant that the collector mentioned a dragon he couldn't stop himself from asking. "Dragon? Is Enoch okay? Where is he?" He could feel his heart speeding up as he watched Iggy and Arty shake their heads. He was starting to understand what was happening and he couldn't wrap his mind around it.

"Ahh…" Ognotz mockingly replied. "So the dragon had a name. Fascinating. But irrelevant." His face became even more threatening than Sam or any of them thought possible as he hissed his demands again. "Now…come with me willingly boy, or I will kill your Guardian slowly and painfully."

Yetews rose to his full height and stepped in front of Sam, using his body as a shield.

Ognotz let out a deadly laugh. "Guardians. So pathetically faithful. Even at their end." Without any further warning, he pulled a dagger out and pointed it directly at Yetews. "Last chance, Guardian. Move or the boy will watch you die now."

The Gateway to Imagia: The Tale of Sam Little

Arty suddenly yelled, "No! You can't kill the Guardian! Not yet! Nadaroth will want them both!"

Ognotz sneered down at him. "Better the boy than nothing at all. And the boy is what he'll get." He pulled his arm back to throw the dagger with lethal aim at Yetews' heart.

Sam screamed, "NO!"

Iggy and Arty gasped and looked away but there was no sickening sound of dagger meeting flesh to justify their reaction. There was only the dull sound of metal hitting wood. There, high enough to protect Yetews, was a wooden shield sticking out of the ground. Where Yetews' still beating heart would have been, was the dagger. It was deeply embedded in the imagined wood.

Ognotz roared in anger and reached around to his back to pull another, much larger dagger out. But before his hands could pull it free, something stopped him dead in his tracks.

"I wouldn't move if I were you." It was Taren. He had an arrow pressing into the back of Ognotz's unprotected neck; the point threatened to break through his thick skin. Ognotz slowly moved his hands out into the open as Taren asked the panic stricken ferret, "Iggy, who is this?"

Iggy replied nervously, "This isn't what it looks like. Forgive us."

Taren looked down at him, not sure what he was saying.

Ognotz suddenly laughed. "Groveling won't save you now! Your betrayal is complete."

"What is he talking about?" Taren asked.

Ognotz seemed to take pleasure in explaining for them. "These little rats traded with me. I let them keep the dragon and they led me to the boy. You meant nothing more to them than an easy means to bargaining for their pathetic existence."

Sam was dumbstruck by Ognotz's words. He couldn't seem to fathom the idea that his friends would betray him. He didn't want to believe what he was hearing.

From beside the targeted collector came Keesa's voice. She'd come out of the trees just moments before with Titus. She was livid. "You betrayed us to save your own lives?" Her teeth were fully bared as she spoke. "Taren, we have to destroy them to protect Sam. *All* of them."

Taren shifted his attention for a split second towards Iggy and Arty. He seemed just as shocked as Sam and Yetews were. He refocused almost immediately on the threat at hand. The arc of his bow creaked as he pulled it farther back. His voice was slightly shaken when he said, "Yetews, take Sam away. I don't want him to see this."

Iggy began to panic and began to back away. But Arty stood his ground and tried to explain. "No! You don't understand. It wasn't supposed to happen like this!"

Keesa said, "You are Guardians. We trusted you."

Titus growled, "And I suppose you're going to tell us that you didn't keep Enoch captive, because he's certainly not here. Traitors!" He barked loudly.

Iggy was pulling on his friend's arm, trying to get him to move before it was too late but Arty refused and continued to plead with them. "But that's just it! When Ognotz found out we were hiding something we had to change the plan. We told him we needed to check the locks. When I went to check them, I told Enoch to wait until we were out of sight and to fly back and warn you. I loosened the ropes on his mouth, unlocked one of his arms and dropped the key on the ground. He should have been here by now. S-something must have gone wrong. Maybe another collector – "His voice was filled with true panic and he trailed off at the end, not wanting to consider the possibility.

By the time Arty had explained this much, Ognotz was nearly shaking with rage. "You...you...YOU FILTHY TRAITOROUS SCUM! I'll rip you limb from limb!

Taren, undecided what to believe, quickly pushed the arrow deeper into Ognotz's neck. This time it punctured the surface and dark red blood trickled out. As he twitched under the pressure, Taren warned him. "Move again and you're dead."

Ognotz's face turned deadly as he said, "You're about to make a very grave mistake."

Taren responded in his most dangerous voice. "I'll take my chances."

Sam was no longer sure who was telling the truth. If Arty was lying and Enoch was gone, then he felt it was his fault. He wasn't sure who to believe and everyone in the clearing seemed to reciprocate the feelings of distrust. The atmosphere was growing tenser by the second as if the balance of life and death hung by a thread.

Iggy and Arty were speechless but now stood their ground in hopes of regaining trust. But there wasn't a chance for redemption. There was movement in the trees. Keesa and Titus turned to face what were now five other collectors, brandishing the same weapons that Ognotz had.

Iggy recognized them from the table where they'd spoken with Ognotz a couple of nights ago. There were three human men, a tall hooded creature with four arms, and another that looked similar to Ognotz, only much larger. "You had them follow us?" he asked, shocked.

Ognotz replied, "You look surprised. Trust is fleeting. You should know that by now." And while his captors were distracted by the appearance of five extra threats, he took his moment. The instant he felt the pressure of the arrow in his neck slacken slightly, his elbow made swift contact with Taren's jaw. The blow sent Taren flying onto his back.

Taren was on his feet nearly as quickly as he'd landed. When he saw that Ognotz was heading towards Sam, he yelled, "Sam, run!"

Everything happened so quickly. Sam was still focused on the new threats when he heard Taren's words. He didn't know where he was running, but he felt his feet moving and could hear Ognotz closing in on him. He ran down the mountain's sloping landscape, trying to leave the open clearing behind him. He tried to imagine boulders and trees growing behind him to slow his attacker down, but had no idea if his attempts were successful.

He couldn't keep up with the increasing downward slope and he slipped. His feet went out from under him and he fell onto his backside. He was sure he was as good as caught when he heard the ruthless threat of his enemy.

"You will watch as I rip every limb from your Guardian's body!"

Sam was breathing so hard that his lungs burned. He turned to look behind him. The collector was more than a few yards away, struggling to get past a random maze of rocky formations that weren't there before. Realizing that his imagination had worked under pressure gave him a new wind. He stood up and started to run again, the back of his mind nagging him to the whereabouts of Yetews. He was so close to the thicker woods ahead.

"I'll kill you myself, boy!" Ognotz shouted from behind him.

Suddenly, a shadow covered the ground around Sam and he stopped before he had a chance to run any further. He looked up into the sky and saw a massive shape landing between him and the furious collector.

It was Enoch.

Sam managed a weak smile when he realized that Iggy and Arty weren't lying. They had never really betrayed them. It fueled his hope for the moment.

When Enoch landed, Ognotz didn't move. Everyone in the mountainside clearing, good and bad, were staring at the magnificent beast as he stood between Sam and the enemy. "You will not touch the boy," Enoch growled. He turned his body around and whipped his tail at Ognotz who barely dodged the blow.

The clearing filled again with the sounds of fighting but Enoch wasn't about to leave Sam unprotected with the threat of Ognotz still looming. Just as he was about to strike the enemy with his deadly jaws, he heard Taren yelling at him.

"Enoch! We need him alive!"

Sam watched as Enoch took flight and swooped over Ognotz, pulling him high into the air. He realized that Enoch was trying to take the source of danger away from him. Before he could get too much height, Ognotz pulled a smaller knife from a belt around his ankle, reached up and sliced deep into the back of the dragon's leg. It was enough that Enoch roared in pain and dropped his captive onto the imagined rocks below. He landed with a sickening thud and made no attempt to get up.

Enoch couldn't move in the clearing with his wings at full span, so he had no choice but to land and return to his less helpful size. He limped on his injured foot to help Yetews, who was battling with the biggest of the five threats.

With no one standing guard over Sam, he decided he should go and help his friends who were doing everything to defend him. He'd never seen a battle before, but this was as close to one as he'd ever hoped to be.

He stood behind the largest of the boulders he'd imagined and watched. Each one of his friends was in the midst of fighting someone. Keesa and Titus were circling the tall, four-armed creature. Each arm held a deadly weapon that threatened anyone who came near. Taren was fighting with two of the humans. The third man was lying facedown on the ground with an arrow in his back. Yetews was hurling heavy stones at the largest creature from a distance.

Taren's quiver was empty of arrows and he had only one long dagger for defense. But despite his fighting, he noticed Sam from the corner of his eye. He turned his head, disapproving of Sam being in the middle of this. "Get out of here Sam! Hide!"

"I can help!" Sam yelled back. He was about to say something else when he saw one of the humans about to hit Taren in the head with a jagged sword. His eyes went wide and he gasped. "TAREN!"

Taren turned just in time to see the sword coming down from above his head. He placed an arm over his head in a last attempt to block the blow. No one was more surprised than Taren when he felt the sword strike a wooden shield that had been perfectly imagined onto his arm.

Though it was only for a moment, he beamed with pride at Sam. His pride empowered his desire to defeat his enemies. He seemed to be fighting with more passion than ever before.

Still, each friend was in the direct path of danger and now Sam knew he had to put the power of his mind to its first real test. First he imagined Taren's quiver full of arrows, but Taren was too distracted to notice. So Sam called out to him. "Taren! Your bow!"

Taren reached over his back. As soon as he felt the feathers touch his fingers he grinned defiantly and took aim. The collectors were so surprised about this, that his first shot was a direct hit to a shoulder that disarmed one of them.

Sam had no idea how to help Keesa and Titus who were dodging many strikes at them. But he then noticed that Iggy and Arty were on Yetews' hump, anticipating the largest of the collectors' moves and yelling snide remarks at him in-between to goad him on. Sam had a strange feeling that they were actually enjoying themselves. The best he could do for them was to imagine a protective stone barrier to protect them. Enoch was doing his best to attack the creature from all open angles.

Sam then pictured a heavy woven net dropping down on the four-armed collector still trying to defeat Keesa and Titus. It worked for only a moment until he cut himself free. Sam had never used his imagination in a situation so serious and he felt his limits being stretched.

He'd paid so much attention focusing on the others, that he'd left himself totally unprotected. He hadn't given a thought to where he was standing. A gnarled hand reached around his stomach and pulled him off of the ground. He let out a scream that was cut off by another hand over his mouth.

Sam bit down hard on the scaly flesh of Ognotz's hand. For a split second his mouth was free to yell again. Luckily, nearly everyone heard his scream and now all focus was directed at him.

It didn't take long for Yetews to rush to Sam's aid. But Ognotz now had a knife to Sam's throat, pulling his hair to keep his throat exposed. He snarled through his blood stained teeth. "Stop! Or I'll kill him!"

Still atop Yetews, Iggy called his bluff. "No you won't. Nadaroth would never let you live if you did."

By now, Taren had joined Yetews and had an arrow aimed steady, ready to release it to its target. Ognotz was struggling with what to do and when Yetews took another step, eyes wide in fear for his boy's safety, he moved the knife down to Sam's shoulder. "You're right. I won't kill him. But I will do this." He slid the knife across Sam's shoulder, slicing through his shirt. Blood instantly stained the fabric and Sam screamed. He'd never felt pain such as this.

Yetews quivered in fear to hear Sam hurting so badly. He reached a hand out and grumbled, pleading for Ognotz to stop. The blood was already soaking through the front of his shirt and he began to turn pale.

In a last effort to escape, he tried to focus once more as he started to feel even weaker. He imagined a large beast of burden coming from behind Ognotz. It barreled through the trees, smashing everything in its path. It did exactly what he wanted it to. It distracted his captor, causing him to turn and fight. He let go and Sam crumpled to the ground.

The creature resembled something like a buffalo, only it was the size of a bus and hairier. It plowed over the collector and loped off into the mountains. Sam held his aching shoulder and heard Taren run to his side as he managed to get up on his knees. "Are you okay?"

The Gateway to Imagia: The Tale of Sam Little

"It hurts." Sam began to shake all over.

"You're gonna be okay, kid," Taren said as he checked the wound.

Ognotz started to cough. He was lying on the ground, blood spraying the air as he mocked them with his laughter.

Taren was already standing over his broken body with an arrow aimed at his heart. "Iggy, Arty, did you get what we needed from this scum?"

Still perched on Yetews, Arty said, "Yes. We know how to find Nadaroth."

Laughing again as he choked on his own blood, Ognotz said, "It's too late. He...already knows...where you are."

"What do you mean?" Taren demanded.

Through gasping breaths, he answered, "Showed him...when...unconscious. He saw...everything. You'll...all die."

Taren turned to look at Sam who was turning another shade whiter. "Yetews, get Sam out of here. We'll find you. Keesa and Titus can track him. They know his smell." Yetews nodded and scooped Sam up in his arms. Then Taren turned back to Ognotz and added. "He's seen enough bloodshed today."

There were still faint sounds of the others in the clearing fighting the remnants of the collectors that hadn't run away. And Sam, through his hazy thoughts, had nothing but worry for his friends' safety. When they left the battle behind, he felt the throbbing in his shoulder with every step Yetews took. He wearily asked Yetews, "Can we rest for a minute? I just want to stop moving. Just for a little bit, okay?"

Though hesitant at first, and despite Iggy and Arty's protest to the idea, Yetews placed him gently on the ground so they could rest. He grumbled something to Sam.

Though exhausted from the ordeal, he still managed to grin. "Yeah. Some adventure. Never imagined stuff like this back home."

Yetews laughed his urmph-urmph laugh and tousled Sam's matted hair. He gently looked at his injured shoulder and sadness swept his eyes. He gently stroked the wound and looked at the blood on his hand. He grumbled again.

Sam looked up at him. He could tell that Yetews felt responsible for not protecting him. His blood loss caused him to shake harder, but he fought hard against the feelings. "You were great Yetews. Bravest

Guardian out there I bet." He then yawned loudly. "I'm so tired. But, I think I'm okay now. Let's get going."

Standing up slowly, Sam decided to try walking but Yetews protested. Even Arty said, "I don't think it's such a good idea, you walkin' and all. You look about as pale as they come."

Sam turned his head and shakily said, "I'm okay. Really." And when his head was turned, he didn't see the hidden hole in the ground directly in front of him.

The hole, no wider than he was tall, swallowed him up without any warning whatsoever. As he fell the short distance into the dark, he felt his head hit something on the way down. All he heard was someone asking if he was okay before he closed his eyes and focused on the spinning world around him. Before he could answer the calls of panic several feet up, he let himself find the sleep that would hopefully take away the many aches in his body.

And in the dark of Sam's mind, he was not alone.

Chapter Twenty-three: Connection

The scene was so familiar. Sam had often dreamt about it while sleeping in this world. He was walking the familiar paths of the forest he'd left behind him in south Imagia. He knew that there should be a boy with his angel-like Guardian frolicking in the warm sun. And he knew that through the shadows of the twisted, old trees waited the one thing he feared most – Nadaroth.

Sam had come to expect the fear that it induced when he connected with the mind of his foe. It was the very fear he thought of every time he closed his eyes to sleep. He'd avoided it for so long only to find that it was, once again, waiting for him.

The nightmares and dreaming were always the same anymore. But this time, something was different. For one, he could sense the conscious world calling to him. He'd never been able to do that before. But outside his mind, he could hear the voices of his friends begging him to awaken.

He could hear Yetews' worried grumbles and sifted through the voices until he heard one more clearly than the rest. It was Taren. "Sam? Sam, are you okay down there? We're coming to get you. Can you hear me? Sam?" There was a pause and then he heard Taren speaking to the others. "He must be hurt. Can you grab some heavy vines, Yetews? I'll climb down. When I tell you to, pull us up."

Sam wanted to call out to them and tell him that he was okay and that he could hear them. But then the other part of his mind longed to focus on the dream, because it was playing out differently than before. Though he could see the shadows of the trees that he'd walked into before, they weren't drawing him in this time.

He felt in total control of what he was doing for a change. It was as though he were looking into someone else's dreams instead of his own. It was definitely different.

So Sam tuned out the outside world as best as he could and focused on his dream. He turned away from the darkness and faced the sun-touched forest around him. He looked into the distance where he once saw the boy and his angelic Guardian. He didn't expect them to be there, so was surprised when he heard the boy's laughter from somewhere he couldn't see.

Sam rushed forward through the trees until he reached the source. It was a new place. A place in the forest he'd never visited. And standing there, in all her glory, was the angelic Guardian and her boy. By the time Sam had reached them, the joy was gone; replaced by the boy's tear-filled eyes.

The boy whispered something to her but Sam was too far away to know what he was saying. She responded by embracing him lovingly. He sobbed into her shoulder and nodded.

Something very familiar about this scene gave Sam's heart a jolt. He watched as a Gateway opened and the Guardian walked away from the boy, waiting for him to follow her. He turned to follow, but stopped suddenly when she offered her outstretched hand to him.

The boy stared at her open hand and suddenly backed up two steps. As Sam watched the boy smile and close his eyes, something familiar sparked his memory again but he couldn't quite place what it was. While he witnessed from afar, he could still hear the voices of his friends trying to reach his unconscious body.

He pushed the voices to the back of his mind and continued to watch the boy. The child opened his eyes to the sounds of the forest being trampled by a great monster storming through it. Suddenly, the monster began heading directly for the two. The Guardian's eyes were filled with terror. Only she wasn't frightened for herself, but rather all concern was directed towards her boy.

Sam watched as her fear turned to panic when the monster changed course. It was going for the boy, who instantly looked as though his world was turned upside down.

The beautiful Guardian leapt into the beast's path, taking the full force of the attack. The boy fell to the ground and watched as the

The Gateway to Imagia: The Tale of Sam Little

creature destroyed the life of his precious Guardian. There was one last look of anguish from the now broken Guardian as the beast dragged her away into the darkness.

Sam remembered seeing this moment unfold in his mind as Orga told him the story so long ago. But something was different. The boy didn't look around for his Gateway; he simply dropped to his knees in defeat and sobbed helplessly into his palms.

There was such a sadness there that Sam had never hoped to feel and he was filled with pity for the small boy. He couldn't help what he did next. He quietly approached the boy and placed a consoling hand on his back.

Whatever Sam's good intentions were, they were in vain. The boy jumped up and looked at this intruder in utter shock. He looked at Sam as though he'd committed the murder himself and he was no longer a grieving child, but a vengeful soul full of hatred.

His tear stained eyes began to burn red and his body was enveloped with a ghostly cloak that moved like smoke in the stillness. Everything around Sam went pitch black in an instant. When finally the shadows shrouded him, he started to feel the fear take over whatever pity he had for the boy. He no longer felt like a stranger in his dream. He was back in the recognizable nightmare and it quaked his very core. Even though he'd been here before, he couldn't stop his knees from locking or his heart from pounding.

And in an instant, his connection to his conscious mind was severed. The sounds of his friends trying desperately to help him were no longer there to comfort him in the dark.

By now, the frightening figure of his enemy had become a part of the darkness. Sam waited for his chilling voice to pierce the stillness, but none came. Instead, the red glow he'd seen before was a white mist that began to form an image. A section of the dark was light, as if looking at a dream within a dream. He was peering at an image of himself standing with Yetews. The light widened and he saw Taren appear, followed by Keesa and then Titus.

He had no way of knowing what was going to happen, so when an army of creatures of many shapes and sizes descended on them from behind, Sam was unable to control himself. He shouted out to his friends, but they couldn't hear him.

One by one, they were attacked and dragged away from him

while he stood helpless, a prisoner to his own fear. Yetews was the last to be taken and an exceptionally terrifying beast stole him away.

The image faded, leaving Sam alone again. Though he had no memory of doing so, he had fallen to his knees, tears spilling from his eyes. Suddenly, while still deep in the nightmare, he was able to hear Taren's faint voice. As he felt his body being pulled up the hole he'd fallen into, he knew that what he'd just seen could only be part of the nightmare; a vision of the future to heed as a warning.

Unlike the many nightmares before, he felt a sense of control of his actions. Sam stopped crying and pulled himself off of his knees. He spun. Blind in the darkness, he yelled out, "It's not real! You're making me see these things! It's not real!"

Evil laughter flooded the darkness. Sam could feel the icy chills running down his spine as he waited for Nadaroth to speak. When he did, the dark ahead turned a hazy red and the terrifying, smoky image of the enemy ghosted into view. "It *will* be. I know your mind. You are coming to me," he hissed in his deathly voice. His words were spoken slowly, as if it'd been a long time since he'd spoken to anyone.

Even though he was trembling and having increasing difficulty staying on his feet, Sam tried to threaten back. He looked down at his feet and whispered in his most hostile voice. "I warn you. Stay out of my mind," he whispered harshly while looking at his feet.

The image of Nadaroth was gone when he found the strength to look up again and the absence of his presence was infinitely more terrifying. Sam waited for an answer to his threat and in the deafening quiet of the dark he got his response. Silently standing behind Sam, Nadaroth hissed into his ear. "Stay out of *mine*."

The sound of his voice so close to Sam was all it took to bring him to his knees again. He fell to the ground, covering his ears. He tried to fight the fear but knew he was losing the battle as he heard himself screaming out.

At the same time he was screaming he could hear Taren's voice start to clear a path into his muddied mind. "I've gotcha kid. Yetews, pull us up!"

Sam could feel someone holding him tightly around the waist. But even though he could feel and hear the outside world, he couldn't seem to completely awaken from the place in his mind just yet.

The Gateway to Imagia: The Tale of Sam Little

Something seemed to be holding him back.

So he fought harder. He tried with all his might to stop screaming and uncover his face. When finding the courage to open his eyes in his nightmare, he found himself waking to the sight of Taren holding a grouping of vines with one hand. Someone at the top of the hole was pulling them both to safety.

The first thing he noticed was how badly his arm hurt in the position he was in. Then he looked at his shoulder and saw blood everywhere. It hurt and his stomach flipped when he saw his red, soaked shirt.

Taren glanced down briefly and saw that Sam was awake. He smiled briefly and Sam could see a trail of blood coming from his swollen bottom lip. He turned away too quickly to see the extent of the damage. Within a few short moments, they broke free of the dank hole and a very strong hairy arm lifted Sam the rest of the way out.

Yetews helped Sam onto the ground while his other hand was steadily holding the vines for Taren. When the Protector pulled himself out completely, everyone gathered around Sam to make sure he was okay.

Looking around the group was almost harder than witnessing the tense battle they'd all taken part in. Even though Taren was still catching his breath from the ordeal, Sam simply had to know. He asked, "Is it over? Is…is everyone okay?"

Though his eyes searched the faces around him hesitantly, he quickly replied, "Yes. It was a small battle and the odds were fairly even. But you did really well, Sam. Everyone's alright."

The look of uncertainty was enough to make Sam look around the group. At first he simply counted the faces. When everyone was accounted for, he began to notice the damage that had been done.

Titus moved closer to Sam, to sit by his side and reassure him. But as he walked, Sam saw him favoring his front, right paw. There was an unmistakable limp to his gait now.

Yetews, who had been fretting about the deep wound across Sam's shoulder, had a large gaping gash of his own that was camouflaged under the matted hair of his cheekbone. It looked like it was no longer bleeding, but his hand wasn't so lucky. Along the back of it, the skin was raw and still bleeding from the constant strain of his muscles.

Iggy and Arty, who were still perched atop Yetews' shoulders, seemed the least scathed. Arty had a knick out of his ear that left a small trail of dried blood onto his shirt while Iggy appeared perfectly fine.

Keesa was licking a wound on her front leg and her once pearly saber teeth were now stained by a faint reddish hue. She was sitting close to Enoch who was in his significantly smaller form. Though he seemed unharmed from the battle, Sam remembered seeing Ognotz slice through his scaly skin before being dropped into the rocks below.

Sam's eyes finally came to rest on Taren. Taren had moved to Sam's side and was assessing the damage that Ognotz had inflicted on his shoulder. He reached into his pack and pulled out a pod of the purple goo Orga had used to numb him on his knee. As he worked, Sam tried not to wince too often. The goo finally started working, but not nearly as quick as before.

Sam watched Taren work gently on his wound. When he'd hurt his knee, Orga had fixed him up really well and he'd remembered thinking it was a very bad wound. As he watched Taren's fingers, he realized the blood covering his fingers was his own and not from Taren. Suddenly, he felt dizzy. He snapped his eyes tightly closed and fought the queasy sensation by breathing deeply through his nose.

Taren noticed. "Sorry, kid. I'll work fast. It's pretty bad. I could sure use Orga right about now."

Sam nodded and the dizziness passed. He opened his eyes and made it a point to look anywhere but his shoulder. He couldn't help but notice that Taren was easily the one who suffered the most from the fight. Sam wasn't surprised. Taren seemed to have been fighting twice the battles of their comrades. It explained why he was such a skilled Protector. He was proud to have Taren on his side.

But still, seeing him so worn from the battle couldn't help but to make Sam feel completely responsible for his state. Taren's lip was no longer bleeding, but the cut hidden somewhere in his hair, was still flowing freely. He wiped the trail of blood away before it trickled into his eye. There was a faint purpling on one of his cheeks where a bruise was sure to develop later. A torn and bloodied shirtsleeve revealed a hidden lesion underneath. His hands had traces of blood, but there was no telling from who or what.

The Gateway to Imagia: The Tale of Sam Little

Seeing all of their faces, still filled with silent hope, made it even harder for Sam. He understood what each of them had risked and why they were doing it. But he also knew that he needed to tell them about everything he'd just experienced. He wasn't entirely sure where to begin.

Luckily, Taren took that worry out of the equation. Still breathing heavy from his trek into the pit, he spoke to Sam. "We know that you're worried about us just as we are worried about you. But something was happening to you down there. Even after all of the nightmares I've witnessed from you, that one was something more. What happened?"

Iggy, now perched comfortably from one of Yetews' spiraling horns, added his take on the situation. "I've seen a lot in my time. Heard a lot too. But I sure haven't heard anything quite like that. It's like you were havin' a conversation with someone that wasn't there and then all of a sudden, well…"

Arty finished his thought for him. "You were screaming like your skin was on fire."

Yetews grumbled questioningly to his boy while he tried to cover Sam's wound with a dirty rag. Everyone turned to Sam for a translation except Titus. He was becoming increasingly efficient at understanding the Guardian.

"Sam?" Taren asked. "What did he say?" His tolerance for the language barrier seemed to be getting better.

"He wants to know if it was Nadaroth again. You know. In my nightmare." Sam looked around at all of his friends – old and new. He could see that they were concerned and curious at the same time. But saying everything out loud would make it real. Nadaroth knew he was coming and the time was upon him too quickly. It was time to put his mind to the ultimate test.

The time to face Nadaroth had come and his friends needed to know. There, on the calm of the mountain, Sam explained everything to them.

"When I went to sleep, I thought I was having another dream. But I think I was connected to Nadaroth's mind. Only this time, I was in *his* dream."

"How do you know?" Titus asked.

"Because of the story that Orga told me. The one about Nadaroth and the day he missed his gateway – when he was still a boy like me. I think I've been in his dreams before. I watched his gateway open and then…then that creature killed his Guardian. It was so sad."

Taren was listening intently. "Fascinating. Then what happened? Why were you screaming?"

"I dunno. When I was seeing *his* nightmare, I could still hear all of you. It was weird. Kinda like I was awake and asleep at the same time."

Taren was nodding, excited by what Sam had just said. "That's the in-between. You've just done what Nadaroth has been doing all along. You connected to another mind in the in-between." He paused for a moment then smiled. "Amazing."

Sam wasn't entirely sure if this was something to be excited about. To him, it was just another mystery of his strange ability. Taren was looking at him as if he had accomplished an amazing feat and it made him feel self-conscious. He turned away and continued explaining his experience. "Well, whatever it was didn't last very long. Because, when the boy saw I was there, he got angry. *Really* angry. He turned into something really scary and then everything went black." Sam stopped and looked at the faces around him. He didn't want to tell them about his darker visions. Putting it into words would make it seem like a possibility. So he hid it from them.

Yetews smiled at Sam and urged him to go on as they all waited patiently for him to continue.

He skipped over the vision Nadaroth showed him and then said. "He told me that he knows we're trying to find him. But I don't know how."

Arty was nodding. "We do. Ognotz showed him. He told us how to find Nadaroth and after he found out that we…well, that we double-crossed him…he made sure to let his master in on that tidbit of information."

Iggy winked at Arty. "Well, he won't be sending anymore messages, now will he?"

Sam wasn't sure what had happened in the clearing after he'd left. But despite how evil the collector was, he was positive that he didn't want to hear the details. He tried to ignore the insinuations that Iggy and Arty were making.

Taren noticed Sam's sudden discomfort and shot a warning look

The Gateway to Imagia: The Tale of Sam Little

at the two. They continued no further.

Both Keesa and Titus' ears were swiveling nervously as they listened to the wilderness around them. Taren noticed and looked around uneasily as well. He said, "We shouldn't be sitting here so idly. If Nadaroth knows where you are then he's liable to send out others to retrieve you."

Sam frowned. "But he already knows we are going to him. Won't he just wait for us now?"

Taren scoffed at the idea in sync with the ferrets. Arty explained, "Nadaroth's not the kind of guy who wants his enemy to walk right into the camp. He'd rather have the satisfaction of knowing he did it himself."

Iggy concurred. "Very true. You know how it is. Typical evil bad guy neurosis. Can't help himself. It's all part and partial to the evil status quo."

A few of them chuckled, including Taren. But then he looked at the two Guardians and said, "And speaking of evil. Now that it is apparent you two are no longer serving that purpose, can you please tell us what in the name of Imagia happened? Is there a good reason you almost got us all killed?"

Arty pointed at Enoch. "Hey now. None of that would have happened if Enoch would've gotten back in time to warn you. I dropped the key right by his hand so he could undo the rest of the locks. I told him to find you. It was all in his hands...er...so to speak."

Enoch grumbled. "Yes. Very clever," he replied sarcastically. "Except one minor detail. Every time I tried to hold your blasted tiny key, I kept dropping it. It took me forever just to reach the first lock. And as I was busy trying to escape your infernal chains, a group of those collectors wandered past me. I had to lie there and pretend to be trapped like some unintelligent beast. Do you two have any idea how intensely degrading that is?"

Iggy had jumped down from his perch atop Yetews and walked over to Enoch. The dragon looked down curiously at him, eyes squinted in agitation. Iggy pat him on his scaly shoulder and said, "Ah, yes. But what you call degrading, I call resourceful. We all learned something here, eh dragon?" Iggy smiled.

Enoch huffed, "Hmph..." he rolled his eyes, "I could still just as easily eat you, you know."

Iggy smiled again. "Nah. Wouldn't be worth the indigestion." He nudged Enoch while grinning and then turned to rejoin Arty.

Taren pinched the bridge of his nose and shook his head. "If you two are quite finished, could we get back to discussing the situation at hand? Do you or do you not know how we get to Nadaroth's fortress?"

Iggy nodded. "Sure thing. Apparently, *finding* his fortress isn't the hard part. It's trying to get *inside* his land that's the trick. Lucky for us, old Ognotz gave us the details."

"What kind of details?" Taren asked.

"The kind that will keep us from dyin', of course." Iggy shook his head and sighed.

Taren pulled his map from his pack. "This map doesn't show much beyond Southern Imagia, but perhaps you can give us a vague idea which way we need to head."

Iggy shook his head. "You won't be needin' a map. Like I said. Finding it's not the problem. Do you see that mountain in the west? The one covered in shadow?"

Everyone looked through the trees at the dark shape in the distance. Taren said, "Yes. I see it."

"Well, that would be his fortress."

Titus scoffed. "Not very impressive, is it?"

Arty answered, "I think that's the point. It looks like any other mountain, but it's his. No one ever goes to that mountain because it's always covered in a strange darkness."

Iggy interjected, "I suppose we shoulda known that was why you couldn't get close to it. He's made it almost inaccessible to unwanted guests. It sure explains why the mountain always looks engulfed in shadows; as if the sun has never touched it."

Sam thought back to how Nadaroth appeared in his dreams. He was the very essence of shadow. It would make sense that he'd live in a place that reflected his projected image.

Iggy continued, "Once you get there, you have to survive the fog that surrounds his lands. We were told that even some of his most skilled collectors get lost in the mist."

It didn't make sense to Sam. He couldn't understand how hard it could possibly be to walk through fog. He'd seen his parents drive

The Gateway to Imagia: The Tale of Sam Little

through fog on mornings after rain. "But isn't it just fog? Can't we just take a torch and walk through it?"

Though it seemed so obvious an answer to Sam, Iggy shook his head with certainty. "This isn't your ordinary fog, Sam. It's so thick you can barely see a hand in front of your face. It moves and twists around anyone who enters and disorientates them until they get lost or go insane. You can't fly over it or dig under it. It was created for the sole purpose of sensing any intrusion. Nadaroth would be fully prepared to attack if a breach is made. So you have to go inside *his* way or risk alerting every beast under his control."

Memories of the Impossible Way were swimming to the front of Sam's mind. It was a difficult task, trying to find a way through the dangerous depths of those waters. Something had to be imagined that would lead them through a clear path to safety on the opposite banks.

As he considered what new levels he'd have to put his mind to, he hoped that he would be just as successful. He wondered if there would be another ancient sentry bound to serve the misty entrance to Nadaroth's fortress. As frightening as it was to think about, there was still a small flame of excitement burning in him for what may await in the unknown.

Iggy and Arty explained to everyone about the route they must now take. All of them discussed how long it would take to reach their destination as well. It seemed simple enough in theory, but actually succeeding would be another story entirely.

According to the information that Arty and Iggy retrieved from Ognotz, there was a lone pathway where the mist wouldn't affect their course. The path would be on the southeast side of the dark mountain. Its single entrance was through a grove of bone-white, gnarled trees that no longer carried life in them. After finding the correct tree they'd find passage into the mist. Once inside the mist, it would allow a course into the shadowy lands at the base of the mountain fortress, providing one doesn't stray from the open path. A single wrong step off of the path would call upon the fog to consume its prey until they are no longer on the right road.

The greatest danger wasn't the eerie mist, but what lie waiting inside the dark lands beyond its borders. Creatures and marked beasts roamed the lands, prisoners to the mist until released into Imagia by their master. And no matter how many times the mountain fortress is circled, no visible entrance to it would be found. If he allows access, a door will morph into the side of the mountain. If not, then the best course of action would be to attempt safe passage back through the mist.

After an hour of disclosing all gathered information and discussing what their next move would be, it was becoming apparent that the list of dangers and complications was becoming more concerning. Nevertheless, it was also obvious to everyone that remaining so close to the recent battlegrounds would be less than wise. As Taren had pointed out, it was likely that Nadaroth would send other collectors or creatures for them. The last memory in Ognotz's mind would be the first place they'd search.

They quickly cleaned and bandaged their surface wounds courtesy of Sam. He imagined plenty of clean cloths for them to work with. Sam's wound had been the deepest but Taren did a great job mending him. He managed to stop the residual bleeding and wrap his shoulder up tightly to avoid any more damage to it.

Taren hadn't even tried to tend his own injuries. Now that Sam had imagined bandages, Taren was finishing up working on his shoulder. He wrapped the cloth around Sam's shoulder and split the loose end of it with a quick tear and tugged it tight before he tied up the two ends. "There. How does that feel, kid?"

Sam rolled his shoulder once, wincing quietly. He felt a little nauseous and swallowed hard. He rubbed it with his other hand and then wiped his sweaty hair away from his forehead. His hair had already grown some since arriving in Imagia. He had a fleeting thought about who might cut hair in this world before he answered Taren. "It's alright."

"Well, it's about the best you're going to get right now. We have to start moving." He pat Sam on his good shoulder reassuringly.

Yetews grumbled something to them and Titus replied before Sam had a chance to interpret. "He's right. We should find shelter and figure out our best course for reaching the mountain fortress."

Taren, his hand still perched on Sam's shoulder, agreed. "What do you say, Sam? That was a hard fall you took down the hole. You should probably get some rest." He glanced down the hole and frowned. "How you didn't see that hole in front of you is beyond me."

Sam shrugged and then winced at the sharp pain the movement

caused. "I don't know." He looked down the hole too. He hadn't realized how large it was until Taren mentioned it. It really was surprising that he had missed it.

"So, how about it? Ready for a rest?" Taren asked again.

He wasn't exactly thrilled with the idea of resting. It was likely that he'd connect with Nadaroth again and he wasn't sure that he was ready for another round of visions and nightmares. It seemed that sleeping might become even more dangerous now. One wrong thought in his state of in-between could very well put them all in danger of being found or attacked.

Sam was about to answer when he noticed three things simultaneously happen. Taren's eyes widened, all heads turned towards the trees behind him, and at least half of their party was growling.

Before Sam had even a moment's chance to ask what was happening, he was being shoved to the ground courtesy of Taren's hand.

"Get down, Sam!" Taren yelled as he pushed Sam out of the way. The breeze of an arrow barely missing him rustled the hair on the side of his head and missed the Protector by half an inch.

In less time that it took for him to take a breath, Taren retaliated. His bow was drawn and an arrow was flying straight and true to its intended target. Someone in the thick trees was howling in pain.

Arty shouted a warning. "It's a collector!"

"Take him down!" Iggy yelled.

Sam lifted his head enough that he could see a dark figure moving towards them through the weeds and grass. The figure barely dodged another of Taren's arrows by jumping behind an especially wide tree. Keesa was weaving stealthily through the trees to attack the collector from behind and as Sam watched her, he worried for her safety. So the next time the intruder peeked around the tree, he imagined a heavy, roped net falling from above.

It worked. As soon as Taren saw the collector was trapped, he joined Keesa with Titus and Enoch in short pursuit.

Yetews was doing everything he could to pull Sam to a safe place away from the commotion. Iggy and Arty were following, running on all fours behind them. Sam kept so close to Yetews that he could feel his Guardians hair rubbing against his face. It felt oddly warmer than usual. They finally came to a stop a good distance between them and the trapped collector.

Sam was panting and put his hands on his knees to catch his breath. The same warm sensation he'd felt earlier happened again, only this time it felt wet as well and the warmth was moving slowly down his cheek.

Confused, he wiped his face. His fingers smeared through what could only be blood. He didn't feel any pain. He couldn't understand why he was bleeding when he had no memory of being hit this time. He felt around his head and checked his arms for any signs of where the blood was spilling from when suddenly he felt something drip onto him.

His heart sank into the very pits of his stomach as the panic welled up inside of him. The warm sensation he'd felt made perfect sense and he looked up at Yetews. There, deeply embedded in his Guardian's shoulder was the collector's arrow. It had missed Sam – but not Yetews.

Yetews noticed Sam looking at him with a look of absolute horror. Yetews, favoring his arm now, sat down on his haunches and tried to shake the boy out of his stupor. He growled and grumbled until Sam understood that he was okay.

Sam felt dizzy from the shock of seeing his best friend hurt in such a way. By the time Yetews, Arty and Iggy had calmed him, the others had rejoined them, no worse for the wear.

While Sam regained his senses, Taren worked frantically on Yetews' shoulder. Now that the arrow was out, the wound was bleeding so much that Taren couldn't manage to get it under control. Worried, he looked up at Yetews and said, "I can't stop the bleeding."

They both looked at the wound and then hesitantly looked to Sam for help. Taren said, "I know you don't want to do this. But he's losing blood. There aren't any internal injuries. You're connected to him in a much more intimate way than you are with Keesa. You can fix him."

Sam looked nervously to Keesa. He didn't want to cause Yetews the same pain that he'd inflicted on her. He bit his bottom lip. But more than anything, he couldn't bare the thought of not trying to help and in turn losing his best friend. He looked into Yetews' gentle green eyes, silently pleading for reassurance that it was the right thing to do.

The Gateway to Imagia: The Tale of Sam Little

Yetews was getting weaker from the blood loss. He struggled to lie down on the ground so Sam could get a clear view of his wounded shoulder and firmly nodded once. He grumbled to Sam.

He swallowed loudly then said in a shaky voice, "I hope you're right. I don't want to hurt you too." Standing close to the Guardian, he examined the deep wound where the arrow once was. He gingerly moved the blood-soaked hair out of the way with his shaking hands and began to mend the flesh in his mind. He didn't want to admit it to the others, but he felt so tired. He knew he'd pushed himself too far already today with all he'd imagined. He could see the skin knitting back together in his mind as if an invisible needle was stitching it.

Sam opened his eyes to peak, but nothing was happening. He glanced towards Yetews' face and saw how worried he was. So he tried again. His best friend's life depended on it. He saw the skin knitting together again.

Yetews jerked as his skin shifted and it frightened Sam. He stopped suddenly and the wound reopened abruptly as if cut with a razor. Yetews grunted in pain as the wound tore back open, causing the bleeding to start back up with a vengeance.

Sam gasped as he saw what he did. He lost his confidence and his friend was paying the price. So Taren knelt beside Sam and watched as Sam battled with the belief in himself. He gently said, "Sam, Yetews needs you. Your bond with him is like nothing else. You must try again – for your Guardian."

Sam watched the apprehension in Yetews as he looked at his wound and then took his good arm up and reached out. He stroked the hair from Sam's forehead with a bended knuckle and smiled warmly.

He was so tired. But, it gave Sam the confidence he needed to try again. He concentrated all his efforts on imagining Yetews' healing. The wound invisibly began to stitch closed again. Yetews jerked again, but Sam ignored it. The bleeding slowed as the cut closed until it was no more than a rough scar.

Yetews moved his arm cautiously at first. Once he realized that there was no danger and that Sam's morphing was a complete success, he picked his boy up and hugged him tightly.

Iggy, amazed by what they all had just witnessed, said, "You get more and more intriguing. We were right to put our hope in you."

"I couldn't agree more, Iggy," said Arty.

Enoch beamed at him. "They are right. There is hope for us yet."

Taren, though silently beaming with pride for the boy, interrupted the moment. "Yes. But we can't linger here. That collector isn't going to be the last of our problems if we don't get to the mountain fortress soon. I'm afraid we can't wait any longer. If we don't get there ourselves, we might end up going as prisoners."

Titus huffed. "Or we might not get there at all," he added under his breath.

As harsh as Titus' words were, Taren knew that they were true. "Titus is right. Nadaroth will keep sending others to find us – to find *you*, Sam. Now that he knows what we are trying to do, we can't wait any longer. We know the way. Now we have to go."

Iggy looked west. The sun was still high, leaving plenty of daylight to travel in. The trees were too dense to clearly see the shadowy mountain where Nadaroth dwelled. But from the vantage point of the clearing they'd battled in, it was easy to see that it would be a long journey, either way they looked at it. "Every collector and evil beast of his world will be looking for us and it's at least a ten day journey." He sighed heavily.

Arty gazed westward too. "Iggy's right. We've already been attacked twice and the day's not done. This is hopeless. We're never going to make the walk there."

Arty's words ignited Sam like a rocket. His mind was moving faster than he could put into words. All he managed to get out before he started to run, was, "That's it!"

Everyone was entirely surprised by Sam's course of action. All seven rushed to follow him through the trees, back up the mountain. He was leading them straight back to the scene of the fight. Each of them protested as they followed.

Sam ran through the battleground, trying desperately not to look at the bodies scattered everywhere.

Before they knew it, they were all standing in the clearing, right behind Sam. He was smiling and staring up into the clear sky.

The combination of running and the confusion of the situation left Taren winded. As he tried to regain his composure, he frowned and barked his question to Sam. "What in the world are you thinking, coming back to this place?"

Sam, not taking his eyes off of the sky, saw what he was looking

The Gateway to Imagia: The Tale of Sam Little

for before he answered the baffled Protector. He grinned wider. He pointed to the answer. Three dark shapes, silhouetted against the white clouds in the sky, were growing larger by the second.

Taren put a hand over his eyes to shade them from the bright sun. The three figures were getting larger and more distinct. He looked at Sam nervously and his hand reached over his shoulder, ready to pull an arrow at a moment's notice. Wide-eyed and uncertain of what was approaching, Taren asked, "What's going on Sam?"

Turning around, he saw seven very wary faces anxiously watching both him and the shapes in the sky. Still lost in his own thoughts, all he said to reassure them, was. "See? We don't have to walk at all."

His hand still ready to arm himself, Taren tried to not sound agitated with Sam's vague response. "Make more sense, please. What *are* you talking about?"

Looking back at the three magnificent winged creatures that were now but a few wing beats away, he simply said. "We can fly."

Chapter Twenty-four: Into the Shadow

Sam was beaming as they flew over the beautiful mountains. Yetews kept a firm hand on the boy, despite his constant reassurance that the saddles he'd imagined kept them quite safe from falling. But as the magnificent beasts soared ever higher, Yetews tightened his hold for peace of mind.

It was serene in the sky. The flying beasts of burden that Sam had imagined to ease their journey to the mountain fortress were graceful and gentle. As they broke through the graying clouds, the welcoming sun shone brightly on them. The way the light hit the creatures, brought new life to their bronze feathers and hair. Their feathered wings easily expanded the same width as Enoch's. They soared through the sky effortlessly, their wings beating slow and steady.

The creatures were a sight of tranquility. Their bodies were a perfect meshing of bronze feathers that melted into long tawny hair. They had a strong neck that ended in a sleek and noble head. Their bottom jaws jutted out slightly under their bird-like beak, giving them a jovial appearance that left one wondering whether they might be smiling. Small, emerald eyes were nearly hidden under their plumes of hair and feathers that flowed elegantly as the wind blew across

The Gateway to Imagia: The Tale of Sam Little

their faces. Two strong legs helped guide them and give them balance combined with the two, clawed hands that were crossed and occasionally tucked beneath their chests.

The riders could feel the immense power of their mounts, however subtle it appeared. Taren looked over from his right side position to Sam. They shared an encouraging look and then he marveled at the beast he rode.

There were no outward similarities between these beasts and the sea turtles that Sam had imagined to cross the Impossible Way. But something in the way they moved and the gentleness of their demeanor was all too familiar. Their willingness to aid Sam with no question and their ability to understand his needs was fascinating. He couldn't help but to smile at Sam's creativity and tenderness involved in their creation.

He'd spent so much of their time together discouraging Sam from imagining such things in hopes of keeping low profile. But now that they were heading directly towards the one thing they'd been evading, there was no point in hiding. It seemed like it might be a good time to let Sam unleash his deeper talents.

Taren was surprised, at first, that Sam had enough strength left to imagine such amazing creatures. Before they'd gotten on their mounts, he strongly tried to sway them away from taking flight. He'd explained over and over how much more dangerous the skies would be compared to the camouflage of the land. But then several of their group pointed out that they'd been attacked so much on land already and that it couldn't hurt to give this a try now that they were so close to the far north.

Eventually Taren conceded and asked Enoch to keep watch in the open skies for danger. Enoch was on Taren's side for the matter. He explained that he was far from being the most deadly thing in the sky, but he agreed to help, nevertheless.

Taren smiled at the thought of Sam's creativity once more. Then his smile faded and his brow wrinkled with lines of worry. He silently hoped that he was not leading Sam to his demise. He couldn't help but to feel worry and fear for what they were about to embark on. Sam and Nadaroth were two beings so alike, yet completely different. He hid his doubt and stroked the neck of his mount. It purred loudly in response.

Taren turned to see Titus. He was panting nervously in the saddle behind him. Taren reassured him, "Sam did a really good job with these saddles. Don't worry, you won't fall off."

Titus shook his shaggy head anxiously. "Regardless...dogs were not meant to fly. If we were, we'd be birds!"

Taren laughed heartily.

On Sam's left, Keesa was riding in a deep Saddle that held her steady. She was about as comfortable with flight as Titus was. Though she tried to hide it, her three eyes were wider than usual, betraying her brave façade.

Enoch, glad to be freely flying again, weaved in and out of the clouds as he kept a close watchful eye on the dangerous skies.

Iggy and Arty had scurried up onto Yetews' hairy hump excitedly. Due to their small size, it didn't matter which mount they rode because they would be hardly a burden to bear. They were positively enjoying themselves and were daringly testing the limits of what they could do this high up in the air. It was very entertaining to Sam. But seeing as how they were using Yetews' horns as props to their daring feats, it only irritated the Guardian. He grumbled annoyingly.

Iggy stopped his acrobats long enough to ask Sam for a translation. "What was that he said?"

Sam told him, "He said you're going to fall off if you're not careful and wants to know what you'd do then?"

Iggy boasted, "As you pointed out yourself, we are perfectly safe."

Yetews rolled his eyes and shook his head subtly at the same time that the creature adjusted course.

Iggy, completely caught off guard, slipped from his perch on Yetews' spiraling horn and fell off of the flying creature. Yetews gasped and reached out too late to grab him as Arty yelled, "IGGY! NO!"

Iggy was yelling as well as he plummeted out of sight through the clouds below. Sam panicked for a moment. He came to his senses quickly and was about to tell the creature to dive to catch him when Enoch burst through the clouds under them, Iggy firmly clinging to the dragon's hand.

Enoch made sure that the others saw the ferret and placed him atop his head. Iggy grasped tightly to his horns. Once realization that he was safe dawned on him, he whooped and hollered, punching a free paw into the air with excitement. "Woo-hoo! Top that, Arty my friend!"

Enoch rolled his eyes with the others.

Arty clutched his heart and then angrily shook a fist at him. "You IDIOT! I thought you were dead for sure!"

"All part of the show, Artemus my friend! All part of the show!" Iggy winked. Brave façade or not, both of the ferrets kept quite still for the rest of the flight.

The journey was going quickly and they were covering a lot of ground quicker than thought possible. They only stopped once to rest the creatures' wings and recuperate with fresh water and food. They flew through the rest of the night without any trouble and straight through the morning. By midday they had reached their destination. They had seen the mist from a distance and landed a short walk away from it, hopeful of avoiding early conflict.

Sam thanked the tawny beasts for their aid. Taren and Yetews helped cut them loose of their saddles, freeing them of further burden. Everyone watched as they took flight and disappeared into the wild skies. It was if they were watching the sea turtles disappear into the depths of the Impossible Way again. Only this time their mounts didn't guide them through the danger, but rather towards it.

They quickly reached the twisted ivory trees that led to the sole entry to Nadaroth's living mist. Oddly enough, there was nothing outside the mountain's barrier that deterred them from entering. It could only mean one thing; that the true threats lie inside.

Taren watched Sam carefully. He was sure that the boy would be swaying from entering the one place everyone else in Imagia would undoubtedly circumvent. But there was no outward sign that he was about to run in the opposite direction. In fact, there was barely an emotion on his face. It worried him.

Sam stared into the trees and watched the mist as it hovered, perfectly still. There was no emotion on his face because he wasn't sure which emotion he would inescapably yield to. He couldn't tell if everyone was waiting for him to lead them on or if they were just as hesitant as he. If they were, then he hoped they'd understand that he wasn't sure if he could move his knees. It was as if he was staring directly into one of his nightmares and given the choice to sleep or wake. He'd come so far and survived so much. He had to move forward.

As Sam took his first step, Taren spoke up from behind and he about-faced. "We have to be sure to enter at the right tree. We only get one shot at this." He spoke to Iggy and Arty next. "Are you absolutely certain you know what tree we have to find?"

They both nodded in affirmation then Arty said, "We'll find it. Old Ognotz gave us a very vivid image." He tapped the temple of his head twice then added. "It's all up here."

Enoch huffed quietly and whispered sarcastically to Keesa under his breath so that Sam could hear too. "How incredibly reassuring."

Enoch's attempt at humor made Sam smile and the feeling it gave him pulled him out of his stupor – for the moment. He said, "I guess that means you two get to lead the way then."

The two ferrets looked around and saw all eyes waiting for their next move. They puffed out their small chests. Arty said, "Well then, off we go. You first, Ignatius?"

"Oh no, I insist we go together." As they both walked by Enoch, Arty raised his brow and quietly said, "And I'll have you know my mind is *entirely* reliable, dragon."

Enoch smiled slyly at Sam, winked, and followed the two. Sam wondered if those three were really as annoyed by each other as they let on. Though they tried very hard to mask any bond they might have developed in their time together, he had noticed subtle changes in them since their journey to find the collectors.

They wandered through the twisted, lifeless trees for a while until they reached a point where Arty held up a paw to stop them. They were standing in front of a tree that had especially large roots at its base. There were strange symbols etched into the dead wood.

Upon closer examination they realized that the symbols were so thick on the tree's trunk that it took on the appearance of aged bark. Sam cocked his head while he looked at them. "Huh. I wonder what they mean."

Surprisingly, Iggy had an answer. "They are marks of the collectors. Nadaroth created this code for collectors to understand. It's how he keeps in contact with them. The marks say that we enter to the right of this tree and continue through the mist directly northwest."

The Gateway to Imagia: The Tale of Sam Little

Taren wasn't the only one looking down at them in surprise. Iggy simply shrugged and said, "What? You think after hangin' out around collectors all these years that we wouldn't pick up a few of their tricks?"

Satisfied with his response, Taren said, "Okay then. Northwest. You said the path is not wide so we walk single file. I'll go first. Keesa, you take the back."

Keesa nodded. "Not a problem."

Iggy warned them once more before they stepped into the thick mist. "Remember what we said. If you see the mist moving around you then stop where you are. The more you move, the more confusing the mist becomes. We'll get our bearings and begin again."

With that said, Taren pulled his bow out and walked cautiously into the gray haziness. Titus was quickly on his heels followed by Enoch. Iggy and Arty were already sitting on Yetews again. But this time, they were not the only ones. Sam was sitting on Yetews' shoulders once more so that his Guardian could be sure where he was. Keesa was the last to enter as they left the pale trees behind.

The descriptions they heard of the mist couldn't have been more accurate. Not a one of them could see much more than the tail end of the one they were following and it was dead silent.

Sam felt Yetews stop suddenly. The mist was still calm so he wasn't sure what was happening. He couldn't see Enoch's tail from his perch. "Yetews, why did we stop?"

Yetews grumbled his response and pointed in front of him.

"Can you help me down? I can't see anything up here." Yetews pulled Sam down carefully and placed him right behind Enoch. It was a relief to see his tail. "Where's Taren?"

Taren heard him in the stillness and quietly called to him. "I'm right here. I stopped because Titus felt the mist moving."

Worry struck Sam for his friend. "Titus? Is he okay?"

"I'm fine, Sam. Taren pulled me back quick enough. But we have to find a way to not get separated. This mist is madness."

From behind Yetews, Keesa agreed. "I don't believe that this path was meant to be traveled in multiples. Anyone that comes through would either be leading or being led by chains."

"Hey!" Sam said a little too loudly which made Yetews jerk backwards slightly. "That's a great idea!"

Taren whispered harshly back, "Not so loud! Do you want an army waiting for us when we get through?"

"Sorry," he apologized quietly.

Keesa asked, "What is your idea, Sam?"

Sam went silent for a moment, causing Taren's curiosity to peak. "What is going on Sam?"

Sam imagined a long rope, about two inches thick. Yetews, being closest to him, perked his ears up and tousled Sam's hair. He grumbled to his boy. Sam handed him the looped end. "Thanks Yetews. Put this around Keesa's head for her." Then he turned and addressed the others. "I just imagined a long rope. If we tie it to ourselves in a row, then –"

Taren finished his thought. "Then we can't get separated. You know, I think you're getting smarter by the day, kid. Feed me the other end."

Yetews passed the rope to Enoch after tying another loop through it. After each one of them, save Iggy and Arty, had the rope securely tied around them, Sam looked up at the ferrets who were tightly clinging to each of Yetews' horns. He smiled crookedly and said, "No acrobats, k?"

"Not a problem," they both said in unison.

Sam finished securing his section of the rope around his waist much to Yetews' apprehension. He was nervous about Sam being on the path.

Taren began to move forward again. They kept the rope taught so as to not risk veering off course again. It was taking them longer than they thought it would to find their way through. They had to stop many times so Taren could find the right path and a couple of times to pull someone back in line before the mist confused them further.

The stillness of the mist made it almost impossible to know exactly how much time was passing while there. But Sam knew one thing for certain; his feet were sore, his scarred knee was starting to throb and his sides ached from the constant tugging of the rope around him. He longed to take it off. He was sure there would be rope burn across his tender ribs.

As he was considering releasing the tension and began to examine the knot, Enoch stopped. It caused Sam to trip as he stepped on the dragon's tail. Enoch let out a quiet growl in pain at the same

The Gateway to Imagia: The Tale of Sam Little

time that Sam fell into the mist. It began to violently swirl around him and he instantly felt lost. He had forgotten about the failsafe rope around him and began to panic. It was no longer quiet. Whispering voices filled his mind, confusing him all the more. He couldn't understand what they were saying making it all the more terrifying. He felt sweat bead on his forehead and he dug his palms into the ground to push himself up. The ground was ice cold and felt abnormal against his skin. He felt something moving around him in the mist and he was suddenly aware that he was not alone.

Sam's only response to the panic he felt was to run. He pushed hard again into the unstable ground to get to his feet, but his hands dug into the ground. The earth was too soft and he felt it move under his fingers. Things were slithering under his palms. His mind started swimming with visions. The slithering things took form in his mind and he saw his hands gripping piles of maggots in rotted flesh. He gasped loudly and rolled to his back to escape the horror of it. But the maggots were still on his hands and started to eat at his skin. His heart raced.

He started shaking his hands to knock off the horrible creatures and felt the panic begin to peak right as the tug of the rope jerked him back to safety. His hands were still shaking and his chest was heaving when he met eyes with Yetews. He shook his head nervously and with wide eyes, he said, "That was *not* cool."

Yetews responded only by pulling Sam closer and tightening the slack between them. Sam said that he felt like he'd gotten lost in that mist for several minutes, but Yetews told him he'd only just fallen a few seconds ago.

The party was still not moving. Sam quietly asked whoever could hear him, "Why did we stop?"

Enoch turned his long neck around and Sam could see his emerald head muddled in the fog. Whispering low, he answered. "Taren has reached the border of the mist. He's trying to see if there is any danger before we all reveal ourselves."

Suddenly, Sam felt hundreds of butterflies fill his stomach. A moment ago he'd have given anything just to leave this dreary mist. Now he felt that he wanted nothing more than to stay hidden inside it. But before he had a chance to think too long on the matter, he was being pulled forward once more.

One by one, each of them left the misty border behind. After removing the ropes, they cautiously traversed the dark grounds that lie between them and the base of Nadaroth's mountain fortress.

The land was darkened. It was as if the sun was trapped by shadows of the sky, like the clouds before an ominous storm. Crooked trees stood lonely amongst the rocky crags of the land, their twisted branches aching for the sun that wouldn't come. Though the sounds of creatures howling and snarling echoed off of everything from each direction, they could tell that nothing was too close to them.

Taren had warned them to stay as quiet as possible in hopes of reaching the mountain unnoticed. He kept himself well armed as a precaution. Sam watched him anxiously and hoped that Taren wouldn't need his weapons just yet. But he also knew that it was a really small chance that things would go smoothly. The closer they got to the mountain's base, the more difficult he found it to continue moving. Yetews actually had to nudge him a few times encouragingly to continue.

By the time they reached their destination, the lesser distance, it seemed, was between them and the unseen creatures that continued to call out. Eight sets of eyes now looked up at the massive black wall that blocked all access into the mountain fortress. The red glow of firelight blazed from ragged windows high above them, beyond the wall. There was no way to see inside and no visible door for entry.

Taren felt around the harsh stone and then backed away while looking upwards. He turned to Iggy and Arty. "Is there a gate or a door we have to find now?"

They looked at one another and then Arty said, "Nope. This is it. This is where we want to be."

Sam wasn't entirely sure what they meant. He didn't see anyone or anything that looked remotely like Nadaroth and he was positive that they were leaving out some key point to continuing onward. "I don't get it. Didn't that collector tell you where to go from here?"

Iggy and Arty exchanged an unsure look. Then Iggy said, "Not exactly."

Keesa huffed, "That foul beast must have given you some idea on how to get into the fortress. Otherwise no one would ever see Nadaroth. There simply has to be a way."

Iggy shook his head and examined the wall momentarily. He

rubbed the back of his head then said, "He was vague at best. He just said that if we want to see Nadaroth that we have to reach the wall and then…let him see us. Whatever that rubbish means."

Arty scoffed as well. "Yeah. I guess we could try yelling." He trotted over to the wall and pounded it with his small paws.

Sam watched as Taren suddenly became tense and then cautiously asked Arty, "What are you doing?"

Before Arty could answer, everyone realized only a moment too late what he was going to do. Before anyone could stop him, he yelled as loud as his small stature could manage, which ended up being rather impressive in the barren lands. "HEY, IN THERE! IS ANYONE HOME?"

Over half of them were holding a silencing hand out to Arty but their efforts were in vain. The damage had already been done. Arty's voice ricocheted loudly across the trees and rocks. And through the echo of his voice, the sound of the approaching danger was closing in on them with pristine precision.

Everyone turned to face the unknown danger as they backed closer to the wall. Yetews pulled Sam close to him, nearly hiding him completely from view. The only other sound was of Iggy, who had slapped Arty on the back of his head and furiously said, "You fool! What were you thinking?"

But beyond the growls of the creatures, Sam heard another sound. It was the familiar frightening laughter of his enemy. He didn't know if he was the only one who could hear it, but he swallowed hard. He felt the color draining from his cheeks as he stared at the moving shadows in the distance. He said, "He knows we're here."

Sam no longer needed Yetews to pull him further towards the safety of the wall. He was backing closer to it himself.

Taren watched him closely, seeing the horror in his eyes. As he anxiously turned back to face the approaching danger, he knew that he didn't have to ask Sam what it was he meant. There was only one 'he' that could cause so much fear in a person. However, he did ask another question. "How do you know that Nadaroth knows we're here?"

Through pale lips, he simply answered, "I can hear him laughing."

Taren furrowed his brow in confusion. He hadn't heard anything.

Though it seemed all creatures he'd met in Imagia had a way of growling, there was something familiar to Sam about the growls that were targeting them. His mind raced to place the specific sounds that were now only moments away from being seen. While he fretted, everyone began to take a defensive position.

Keesa was out in front, her hackles raised and baring her teeth. As Sam watched her and heard her returning growls, he suddenly remembered why it was so familiar to him. Before he could share his revelation, Keesa did it for him.

"Kupa cats!" she yelled.

Taren responded by pulling his bowstring taught. Without batting an eye, he asked Keesa, "How many?"

"A large pack. Ten…maybe twelve."

The kupa cats were in sight and closing in on them fast. They had nowhere to run but forward. Sam was momentarily shocked. He couldn't think clearly and didn't even try to imagine something to help them. Taren, on the other hand, had already fired a direct hit into the pack.

One kupa cat went tumbling out of control as the arrow fatally pierced a vital organ. Another cat tumbled head over heels as the dying creature fell in front of it. Two more arrows were fired before the pack began to slow. They were moving more cautiously now, circling their target. There were eleven, including the fallen one.

They were hopelessly trapped against the wall by the kupa cats. Taren pulled another arrow back and took aim at the largest. It was a male; nearly twice the size of Keesa and it dodged the arrow effortlessly. He shifted his aim at a smaller one that was dangerously close to Titus while Enoch burst into his larger form, pulling one of the larger cats into the air with him.

Sam, finally snapping out of his stupor, quickly imagined a defensive wall of spikes between them and the pack. The wooden spikes grew out of the ground like deadly roots of a tree and they grew in an angle towards the pack. But it wasn't enough to stop them. Half of them leapt gracefully over the spikes. Only one didn't entirely clear the obstacle and tagged its back leg on a spike in the effort. The smaller ones simply weaved through unharmed.

There was a terrified madness in their eyes as they closed the circle around Sam and the others. Enoch was flying in to grab another

The Gateway to Imagia: The Tale of Sam Little

one. Taren had just taken down one that had clawed him in the arm. He aimed another arrow at the next closest target. But then, the completely unexpected happened. Keesa jumped in front of him and yelled, "NO! They're my cubs!"

Taren didn't have enough warning to fully adjust his aim. It was impossible for him to anticipate Keesa's sudden move and the arrow grazed her shoulder. She howled in pain but didn't stand down. A brief confusion swept over the pack. Most of them backed away in a temporary puzzlement.

The events that followed happened in the blink of an eye.

The large pack leader turned his focus to Keesa. She had only an instant to retaliate but managed to dodge his first blow. Sam watched in horror as the male flipped around effortlessly while Keesa turned to face him. She bore her teeth to strike back but it was in vain. The male was already on her back, his saber teeth sunken deeply into her flesh, making any attempt at escape impossible.

Keesa yowled and Sam screamed as he watched the male throw her to the ground with a crushing blow to her previously injured side. Sam tried desperately to push through Yetews' strong arms. He was screaming for Keesa. "NO! KEESA GET UP!"

Taren was shooting at the male as he closed in for the kill. It dodged every arrow despite Taren's accuracy. Sam continued to fight his way to Keesa, but his Guardian's hold was too strong.

Keesa lay on the ground, struggling to move away from the pack leader. She dug her sharp claws into the ground and pulled her broken body with all the strength she could muster. She braced herself for the inevitable but it never came.

Three of the youngest kupa cats circled her. They sniffed her quickly and that was all it took. The madness that darkened their eyes dulled. They tightened the circle around her but this time it was in a move of protection. They challenged the male in Keesa's defense.

Sam stopped struggling. He, as well as the others, realized that when Keesa stopped Taren from firing earlier, she was protecting her lost cubs. And somehow, the tides had turned. The pack halted all attacks at Sam and the others. The three young ones pulled together and fought against the leader.

It was a short but violent fight. Once the remainder of the pack realized that the leader was in danger, they retreated leaving the four behind to finish the fight. Three against one was enough to bring down the pack leader. He was no longer a threat. With blood spattered everywhere and the only sound left being distant echoes, the three fell back to Keesa. They sniffed her and nudged her gingerly.

Sam pleaded with Yetews. He needed to go to Keesa. He had to help her before it was too late. "Please, Yetews. Let me go. I have to help her."

Yetews cast an unsure gaze to Taren, unsure what to do. Taren looked over at the remainder of the pack and saw that the madness in their eyes had somehow been tamed. He nodded to Yetews. "Let him go. I'll go with him."

Yetews released his hold and Sam burst forward, only slowing when the three cats turned and growled protectively at what they could only see as a potential threat to their defenseless mother.

Sam stopped and knew the only thing he could do was beg. The biggest of the three, a male, laid his ears back and growled another warning to the approaching humans. He was smaller than the pack leader but still impressively larger than Sam. In fact, Sam was surprised that they weren't babies. The way Keesa spoke of them, he was sure that they were still just helpless cubs. But they weren't babies and they certainly weren't helpless. Her son was bigger than *she* was.

Taren held his hands up in a peaceful gesture and Sam didn't hesitate to speak to them. He was certain that they would be able to speak back – just as their mother had when they'd first met. "Please let me see her. She's my friend and I can help." Sam's voice shook with worry as he pleaded with them.

Keesa's son cocked his head and blinked as he relaxed his ears. He moved slowly closer to Sam. He stopped a few short feet away and growled again, causing Taren to pull Sam back quickly.

Before anyone else could say or do anything else, there was an answering snarl to the young kupa cat's growl. Keesa was warning her son. Then the three young ones opened a path to her.

Sam hesitated for only a moment before running to Keesa. He knelt beside her, Taren crouching close by his side. They could see the blood flowing from her wounds and dripping from her nose. Taren examined the damage closely as Sam spoke to her. "Keesa, what do I do? Where are you hurt and…and how can I fix it?"

The Gateway to Imagia: The Tale of Sam Little

Keesa tried to move her head to look at Sam but winced in response. She was fighting to get air to her lungs as she spoke to the panicked boy. "You...can't heal me this time, Sam." Her words were barely more than a whisper.

Sam tried hard to swallow the lump in this throat. He knew that he had to try and help her. He refused to give up. He begged her to help him. "No. I can help. I did it before. I can do it again. Just tell me where you are hurt. I...I know I can do this, Keesa. You just have to help me..."

She smiled feebly up at the boy. "Sam," she whispered, "it's done. Please..." She gasped and winced again at the pain. "My cubs are *alive*." She smiled so genuinely that Sam knew she was happy to be reunited even in such grim conditions. "They will help you."

Sam closed his eyes to fight the burning tears that were sure to come. He stroked her head gently and despite her pain, she purred once and leaned her cheek into his small hands. "No...please Keesa. Let me try. I know I can..."

She stopped him before he could finish. "My dear Sam. They will help you now. Keep them...safe."

Sam looked up through the tears that fought to spill out and saw three triple-sets of eyes watching over them with equal concern. As hard as he wanted to help Keesa, the blood now flowing freely from her mouth somehow made him know that there were injuries too deep for even his best imagining. He blinked and the tears poured down his filthy cheeks.

When he looked back down at Keesa, she was smiling at him with the love of the world in her fading eyes. "You are – a good – cub." The words were becoming more broken. She used the strength she had left to lift her tail. She brushed it lovingly against Sam's cheek in the same way she had once before.

Sam threw his arms around her shaggy head and hugged her tightly. He sobbed into her tawny hair and whispered, "I love you, Keesa." He held tight to her, his mind racing desperately for a way to save her.

As he held tight, he fought against the idea of losing her. He'd never dealt with death before and he refused to believe it possible. He began to imagine Keesa's healing. His mind fought against the pain in his heart that ached through his core. But it was too much for him to control.

The next thing he felt was Taren's warm hand on his shoulder.

Taren pulled on him lightly. "Sam."

Sam pulled away from Keesa in answer to him. But he didn't need to hear the words that Taren fought to find. He looked into Keesa's face. The three crystal blue eyes that once gave him so much peace, had closed for the last time.

Sam now knew what his heart feared most. Keesa was gone.

Chapter Twenty-five: In Between

Only moments had passed since Keesa's death and things were already taking a turn for the worse. Taren was pulling Sam reluctantly away from her body when another attack began. Only this time, everyone else could hear the shrill laughter of the unseen enemy echoing through the air. Each of them turned nervously in every direction looking for the source that refused to show.

Sam's cheeks were still shining from the tears he couldn't hide. He wiped the remnants away with the back of his dirty hand and returned to his Guardian's side. There was only one thought that managed to hover in the front of his panicked mind: Nadaroth's vision from the nightmare was coming to pass.

He looked around nervously to each of his remaining comrades and wondered who would be the next target. The pack's attack had already left its mark on most everyone. Taren's arm was bleeding and nearly everyone else had wounds that needed nursed.

Taren was standing close to Sam. So close, in fact, that Sam could see the worry hidden in his eyes. There was no doubt in anyone's mind as to what was coming next. In the dreary sky, breaking through the foggy border that imprisoned them, dragons were approaching.

Taren whipped around and his eyes pleaded with Sam. "Now might be a good time to test your imagination, kid." Another frightening sound pierced the air, this time from ground level and Taren looked for the source along with the rest. He turned back to Sam, eyes still pleading. "Seven of us won't make good odds." He smiled feebly.

The faith Taren had showed in him helped Sam remember why he was here. Regardless, it didn't hide the unbridled fear that was quickly growing inside him. But when Yetews brought his head down to Sam's level and purred encouraging words into his ear, that fear was subdued momentarily.

"Thanks, Yetews," Sam said. He took two steps forward and tried to encompass every detail of the world around him. He closed his eyes and took a deep breath. He tried to remember what it was like before Imagia. Though it felt like an eternity ago, there was a time when he was able to imagine entire worlds in the blink of an eye.

But things had changed so much. *He* had changed so much. The harder he imagined, the more exhausted his mind became. With exhaustion came fleeting images that only remained corporal for a short time before fading from existence.

Every day Sam was pushing himself further, but he wondered how far he could stretch his mind this time. Certainly, he would have to try harder now than ever before.

Slowly, his mind began to weave an army of protection into the world around him. To the coming dragons, he imagined fifteen massive creatures of flight. Many of them were alike, but not one exactly the same as another. He knew, even through closed eyes, that his imagination was taking shape around him. The wind from fifteen sets of wings touched the back of his neck and ruffled his hair as they took flight.

Sam pushed his mind further. Three scaled creatures with a set of lethal horns circling their heads charged forward, uprooting trees as they tore across the land. They were followed by a variety of other beasts that charged the oncoming danger with blind loyalty to Sam. A group of creatures, all familiar reminders of his pre-Imagia days, stood as faithful sentries just in front of everyone. He had created them for one sole purpose – protection.

"Excellent Sam!" Taren called out.

Arty echoed the encouragement, "Amazing! Keep 'em coming!"

Sam stretched his imagination further and, with open eyes, he pictured a moat surrounding them. The ground quaked beneath them as it appeared.

Yetews squeezed the boy's shoulder lightly while Taren nodded in praise.

Sam stopped and looked out at the poor creatures he had imagined who were now fighting his battle. Though he had no direct connection to them, it felt strange to have created them simply to send them to their doom. For just a moment, he wondered if their fleeting creation was worth the price. He wondered if, by creating them for this purpose, it made him just like Nadaroth. But as the thought passed through his mind, he caught Yetews' eye. To be trapped in a world like this without the love and friendship of his Guardian, would be a fate he didn't know if he could bear.

Sam felt his limits setting in. He was having difficulty concentrating on any one thing. He was sure he had exhausted his mind. And as if he needed proof of this, the moat he'd imagined began to dry up and fade back into the land while two rock-like sentries quickly followed in its path.

"What happened?" Arty asked, confused. He hadn't been around long enough to understand Sam's limitations.

Taren tried to simultaneously build Sam's spirit and explain to the others what happened. "It's normal. His mind is powerful, but still young. He has limits to his imagination. He stretched his mind too far." He glanced over to Sam briefly and with understanding reflecting from his brown eyes, he said, "Don't push yourself. Rest up, kid."

But there was no time for rest.

Keesa's eldest cub laid his ears back and bared his teeth. "He has sent another pack of kupa cats!" He growled and his brother and sister flanked him on either side.

Taren squinted his eyes and searched for what the cubs' keen eyes could already see. "From which direction?"

Titus' heightened sense of smell picked up the scent and he answered for Keesa's son. "There. Beyond those rocky crags," he said as he looked in the same direction as the three cats.

One encounter with a pack of kupa cats was quite enough and Sam's fears became renewed. Nadaroth's vision flashed through his mind and he couldn't shake the thought that another of his friends' lives was in danger of being cut short. That fear fed his need to protect and he began to concentrate on the area of ground that surrounded them.

The earth in front of them rumbled. Thick, woody vines shattered the surface. They weaved and intertwined until they became a thorny wall at least five times the height of Enoch's full size. There was now a wall of protection between them and the looming threats.

Sam took a deep breath and he felt his knees buckle. It was the most he'd ever tried to imagine in such a short time. He bent over and grabbed his knees with shaking hands. He held them for support until the exhaustion passed. Yetews was already by his side lending a powerful shoulder to lean on.

The pack of kupa cats had reached Sam's wall. Through the natural gap of the vines, the beasts could be seen pacing and seeking a weak point to break through.

Sam watched Enoch land next to Taren, wings spread wide to keep his full size. He explained the situation, but Sam could only hear the last half of it through his hazy mind. Imagining had never left him so drained before. He strained to hear what Enoch said.

"- but it's hopeless. Nadaroth has sent every marked beast in this land. Our numbers are dwindling fast. His army isn't going to last at this rate."

Though Sam didn't have the energy to look up and see the look Taren had on his face, he heard the Protector reassuring Enoch. "They'll hold them back long enough. We need to concentrate on finding Nadaroth."

While Sam was still focusing on remaining conscious, he felt someone other than Yetews' presence suddenly beside him. It was Taren. He was kneeling. He helped Sam stand straight and braced his unsteadiness. There was true worry in his kind eyes.

Sam wondered how he must look to them. Weak? Helpless? Or perhaps he simply looked how he felt. Small. The same look of pleading in Taren's eyes made Sam wonder what he was about to ask next. It worried him. He wasn't entirely sure he had anything else to give.

But when Taren opened his mouth to speak, his first words weren't directed at him. "Arty and Iggy. What *exactly* did Ognotz say about finding Nadaroth? Don't leave out any details. We're going to need to figure this out. Now."

Both of the ferrets were already standing at Taren's feet when Arty answered. "We *did* tell you every detail."

The Gateway to Imagia: The Tale of Sam Little

Iggy put a paw facing up in front of him and counted on each clawed finger. "First there's the tree. Second – the mist. Third was finding the wall. And fourth is Nadaroth."

Taren rolled his eyes in agitation. "Yes, we got that part. But what exactly did he say about *finding* Nadaroth?"

Iggy snorted. "Look, we told you. The brainless collector's *exact* words were, 'if you want to see Nadaroth, then once you reach the wall, you have to let *him* see *you*.' I told you it sounded vague."

Arty scratched his head absentmindedly. "The big oaf probably never thought we'd make it this far on our own. Probably didn't feel like he needed to give us specifics."

Enoch grumbled low. It was obvious he was slightly annoyed. "And you two didn't think of this *before* we killed him?"

Sam cringed. He knew deep down that Ognotz was dead, but the idea of death reminded him too soon of the one he had just witnessed. He fought desperately against the urge to look back at Keesa's broken body.

"Look, dragon," Iggy defended, "in case you didn't notice, we were a bit busy worrying about everyone else's necks to think about the details! You asked us to get directions and we got them. End of story."

Sam was getting frustrated by the bickering and couldn't take it anymore. He was getting angry. "Stop fighting! Isn't there enough of that going on?" Everyone stopped, surprised by his sudden outburst. Once he had their attention, he asked, "What should I do now? How do I make him see me?"

There was a pause before Yetews started growling his best idea to them. Sam was so consumed by what was suggested that he forgot to translate to the others. As his Guardian spoke, he knew deep down that he was right and he felt his palms go sweaty at the thought of what he needed to do.

The others waited anxiously for Sam's translation that never came. Luckily, Titus was now nearly as efficient as Sam at understanding Yetews' strings of growls and grumbles.

"He suggests that Sam should fall asleep," Titus explained. "Sleep is the one place that Nadaroth is stronger than anyone else. Yetews thinks that Nadaroth will connect to anyone's in-between if they are at *this* wall." He paused to look at Sam. His heart instantly ached for his dear friend. He hesitated in the remainder of the translation. "He thinks...that Nadaroth wants to see Sam – or anyone for that matter – in their weakest state. Nadaroth's the only one who has the power to invade and control another's mind."

Taren closed his eyes briefly. He, as well as the others, knew that Yetews' assumption was accurate. He felt guilt and disgust for what he was about to ask Sam to do. Regardless of his reservations, he looked steadily at the boy. "Do you think you can do it? Can you fall asleep and, more importantly, can you keep some control of your mind like you did before?"

The nerves in his sweaty palms had shifted and focused on his stomach now. The butterflies he'd felt so often were now angry, stinging hornets that threatened to destroy him from the inside out. He'd avoided sleep so frequently for the very reason he was now expected to face full on. He was so exhausted that he knew falling asleep should come naturally. But the question wasn't whether or not he could, but rather whether or not he would let himself.

Now that he was here, Sam didn't want to do this. His stomach churned and before he had time to even think about the sensation, he doubled over and threw up. He was vaguely aware of everyone watching him, but felt too poorly to be embarrassed at the moment. He wanted to put his hands over his head and wake up from this nightmare, safe and sound in his bed.

Sam knew this wasn't in the realm of possibilities, so fought back the bitter taste in his mouth and concentrated on his hands that were now grasping the dirt beneath him. He felt Yetews' reassuring palm pat his back. He blinked and looked up.

Sam glanced around at the faces of his friends. They weren't judging him for his fear. In fact, the only look he saw was sadness. Whether for him or for the situation – it didn't really matter. As small as he felt, he knew that he didn't want to let them down now. They'd all come so far with their hopes so highly set in him.

His head weighed a ton as he tried to nod it. Somehow, through the fear and doubt, he managed to nod it twice. Then, as if nodding his head was the switch that put him to sleep, his body relaxed. His knees were no longer locked and he felt himself being held by Yetews' powerful arms. Before he knew what had happened, he found himself wandering through the vast expanse of his in-between.

The Gateway to Imagia: The Tale of Sam Little

Silently, Sam wondered if he had enough control of his own mind to willingly remain in this expanse. He wondered how long he could hold on before falling completely asleep and giving full control over to Nadaroth. He could still hear Taren's voice and Yetews' grumbling as they talked amongst themselves. Everyone was hopeful, yet wary of what this would accomplish.

As he listened to the voices, he tried to focus on them, remaining attached to his own semi-conscious mind. It helped him gain control of falling too far into his dreams.

He stared off into the expanses of his mind and waited for the one thing he dreaded. He could sense the edge that led to where his dreams waited. One more step would have him falling into the abyss that led him there.

He was so tired. Staring into the peaceful chasm of his thoughts only made him realize how exhausted he really was. Sam couldn't resist the pull on his mind to let go his conscious self.

It was too much and his will caved. He left the voices of his friends behind and leapt into the abyss. But just before his last semi-conscious thought, he sensed Nadaroth's dark shadows engulfing him.

Sam was asleep and he was not alone. It had worked.

Nadaroth was there.

No sunny forest welcomed Sam to his slumber. No tricks. No subtlety. There was only the dark and its never-ending dread. Some part of Sam knew what was happening. He understood the nightmare for what it truly was, but his knees still locked tight and his chest tightened, making it difficult for the air to reach his lungs.

Nadaroth wasted no time. His flaming eyes burned in the darkness as he hissed his warning. "Sam Little." The whisper of his voice blended effortlessly into a frightening laugh that mocked Sam's name. "You will lose everything."

The same vision that Sam had been forced to watch upon his last encounter with Nadaroth played once more through his mind. He tried to avert his eyes, but it was useless. So Sam tried to fight back with his words. "No! It won't happen!"

"It has already begun."

Sam gasped suddenly as the vision burst into another scene. The glow of the image was slightly warming and he couldn't help but be intrigued by what he saw. It was as though he was seeing his own memory played out like a television show. It flipped through images of his parents and his home briefly before changing yet again.

He now saw memories of his time in Imagia. The images were more vivid than his memories of home and they changed almost instantly. He saw flashes of Orga, Warg, Dolimus and various others he'd met along the way. But the most vivid image was of a memory that was all too fresh in his mind.

Sam was watching just moments before losing Keesa. No amount of effort could draw his eyes away. His heart pulsed harder as he reluctantly relived her death. Though he couldn't find the strength to move, he did manage to open his mouth. The hushed words passed over his white, trembling lips, "Keesa …no."

His knees gave way beneath him and he cupped his hands over his face. He'd never known pain such as this before and didn't believe that his heart could ache any more than it did at this moment.

As Sam grieved in the nightmare, Nadaroth was already changing the scene. This time, there was no sense of familiarity to what Sam was watching. Yetews was standing mere feet away. The Guardian was surrounded by all of his friends and they were standing watch over a small figure that was lumped on the ground. Sam could see the genuine concern in their eyes as they watched the motionless body.

Sam pulled himself to his feet and walked closer to the scene. As he neared his group of friends, he recognized what it was that held their interest.

It was him.

Sam blinked and he was suddenly no longer outward looking in. He was lying on the ground in his nightmare and looking up. Everyone watched him for a moment until they left from different directions. Yetews was the only one remaining and Sam had no idea where the others had gone.

Though he didn't know how, Sam was completely aware that he was still deep in his nightmare. And as he lay on the ground he could see what Nadaroth wanted him to see. A dark, winged beast was descending upon them from the sky. Before Sam had time to react, it snatched Yetews up and pulled him further away with every beat of its wings.

Sam was reaching out uselessly for his Guardian as he screamed. He watched Yetews get pulled further into shadow. At the last

The Gateway to Imagia: The Tale of Sam Little

moment, when he felt like his heart might beat out of his chest, Nadaroth appeared and hovered inches from him.

In a voice that sent a course of shivers through Sam's body, Nadaroth hissed, "Your Guardian will fall and you will all die. Imagia is mine!"

The chilling words were still echoing in Sam's mind as his eyes burst open. He was still lying on the ground, but he was no longer dreaming. The scene mirrored his nightmare. Sam felt himself breathing hard from what he'd just witnessed in his mind.

There wasn't even a split moment's time to think. The scene was already unfolding exactly the way Nadaroth had shown him. The difference was that the sounds of other creatures fighting around them filled the air.

The pack of kupa cats were fighting their way through as a massive beast with saw-like teeth aided them by shredding through the barrier that kept Nadaroth's army at bay.

Sam looked around and watched as each of his comrades took off in separate directions to fight. Taren was shooting flawlessly aimed arrows through the gaps in the barrier to keep back the approaching enemy. Enoch was taking on the saw-mouthed creature, while all the others were doing everything in their power to keep Sam safe.

Suddenly, Sam understood what he had missed in his nightmare. Everyone left his side just as Nadaroth planned. They were being distracted. The scene was nearly complete. He was up on his elbows and felt his heart leap into his throat as he heard a horrendous shriek from above. The sound caused every creature, friend and foe alike, to cease attacking momentarily.

Sam could hear every beat of his heart as he turned to look into the sky. There, as if cloned from his very thoughts, was the dark creature from his dream descending through Sam's imagined blockade. His imagined barrier had a weak spot and it was already too late to correct it. He'd imagined a wall, but left the sky open for Enoch to fly. The creature, nearly twice Enoch's size, was a wing's beat away. Sam looked one last time into his Guardian's innocent, green eyes. He managed to scream out as the beast wrapped its razor claws around Yetews' shoulders. "YETEWS!"

In an instant, Sam was on his feet and the others were rallying to his side. Yetews was being torn away from them, a look of shock and

326

horror on his face. Taren was firing arrows, testing for a weak point. Enoch, with Iggy and Arty firmly grasping his horns, circled back and attacked from behind. The two ferrets were crying out excitedly in the heat of battle.

The beast thrashed its thick tail and knocked Enoch away, slamming him into the wall around Nadaroth's mountain fortress. Stone shattered and rained down as Enoch fell. Arty and Iggy managed to hold on as Enoch's wings folded and he shrunk. Digging his sharp claws into the stony wall saved them from the fall.

Something caused the beast to shriek in pain. Taren was pointing to an arrow deeply embedded in the monsters chest and he shouted out, "SAM! His underbelly looks like the weak point!"

In the blink of an eye, Sam felt the power of his imagination double in size. His exhaustion no longer mattered. He barely had to concentrate on the wall that he'd created as he morphed it. The thorns on the vines of the wall grew out in every direction, closing the weak spot instantaneously. The thorns, thick as tree trunks and sharp as polished spears, shot across the opening at an impossible speed.

The thorns pierced the black beast in its softer underbelly in several places. The roar of pain only lasted for a moment before it gurgled out. Its claws went limp and Yetews was free falling from above.

Enoch took flight to catch his body as Sam watched in horror. He caught him a few yards before hitting the ground, but not before hitting several rocks on the way down.

Sam, seeing Yetews safely in Enoch's grasp, focused on the battle around him. For a moment, time seemed to slow down and he saw creatures and friends battling one another in every direction. Everyone he cared for was fighting to give him a chance. Everyone was willing to defend him. Everyone was willing to *die* for him. He looked back at Enoch carrying Yetews out of harm's way. His best friend – his Guardian – was hurting because of Nadaroth's evilness.

Suddenly…Sam was furious.

He flipped around and focused his mind on the fighting around him. For every beast or monstrosity that Nadaroth sent, Sam created a way to thwart them. The ravenous kupa cats were suddenly restrained with iron chains that pinned them to a wall of rock not there before. The saw-mouthed creature was trampled by a stampeding herd of two-headed beasts of burden. As quickly as enemies appeared, Sam created a way to equalize them.

Sam was so engrossed in the battle and set on protecting his friends, that it took Taren three times to get his attention. He placed a bloodied hand on Sam's shoulder and pulled him around. "Snap out of it, kid!" Once he had Sam's attention, he could see the pain and worry in his eyes. It was more than any child should ever have to bear. He started to say something else, "Sam –"

Taren didn't have a chance to finish. Something caught Sam's eye from fifty feet away. Enoch had put Yetews on the ground in the mountain's shadow and everyone was crowded around his body except Taren and him. Time seemed to slow down. Sam could hear nothing but his own breathing and frantic heartbeats. He looked at Taren's blood drenched hand upon his shoulder. His eyes went wide with fear.

It wasn't Taren's blood.

Sam was already running to his Guardian. He was ten feet away when he stopped cold in his tracks. He could see that something was wrong. Yetews wasn't moving.

He squinted his eyes and focused on his friend, too afraid to get closer. He watched for some sign of life. But visions of Keesa's motionless body bombarded his mind and the similarities couldn't be ignored. The sharp stab of pain in his heart ached twice as much as it did for Keesa. His worst fear was being realized.

Nadaroth's vision was coming to pass.

Yetews had fallen. He was gone.

Sam could hear someone calling to him, but he couldn't place from where or who. He suddenly found it hard to breathe steady and his will to stand nearly failed him. Darkness began to grow from behind him and he fought to find the will to turn and face what he knew was coming.

Taren ran to Sam and threw his arms around the boy's waist to pull him back from danger. "Get back!"

Titus was growling aside Keesa's sons and daughter and begging for Sam to retreat. "Come on, Sam!"

Iggy, panic in his pleas, yelled, "Run! It's him! It's Nadaroth!"

With those words, Sam looked up and saw the shadow taking shape. For the first time, Sam was looking upon his enemy in true form. He recognized the fiery gaze and smoky, cloaked figure. He was far more terrifying than in his nightmares.

Sam backed into the safety of Taren's chest and stopped resisting his protection. Taren turned Sam around to tell him something in haste. "Fight him. You have to try. Yetews —"

Before Taren could say another word, an invisible wall that cut Sam off from all of his friends suddenly silenced him as if he were in a bubble. He could see them, but he couldn't hear or reach them. They must've not been able to see or hear him as well, because everyone was franticly looking around everywhere but where Sam was standing.

A familiar chilling voice shattered through the silence and Sam knew he was alone in this fight.

Nadaroth hissed, "You suffer the pain of loneliness. You weakling. So sad and pathetic. Your Guardian has fallen and now…so will you."

The Gateway to Imagia: The Tale of Sam Little

Chapter Twenty-six: Nightmares

Sam's emotions were all over the place now. He'd never felt such anger toward anything in his life, but at the same time, he'd never been so hopelessly afraid or alone. He wanted to fight with every fiber of his being, but something forced its way into his mind. Nadaroth, though standing several feet from Sam, was somehow inside his thoughts.

Sam's head started to throb. He gasped at the sharp pain that spread to his temples. He rubbed his head with his eyes closed. Then, as quickly as the pain came, it was gone. He opened his eyes and Nadaroth had disappeared.

Sam was no longer standing in the battlefield, but rather in a void space. He stood there, a dull light coming from behind him and stretching only far enough to reach his feet. He didn't turn to see where the source of light came from, afraid that Nadaroth was lurking in the darkness before him. But footsteps from behind him sent a shiver up his spine. He held his breath. It sounded like the footsteps of a person.

"Sam?" It was Taren.

Sam spun, eyes wide. "Taren! How did you get in here?"

Taren looked around, his bow down to his side. "I don't know. One moment I was outside fighting and then, next thing I knew, I was in here. Where are we? What is this place?"

Sam shrugged.

Taren walked up to Sam. He put a hand on his shoulder as Sam looked around the dark room, waiting for Nadaroth to show himself again. He looked down at the kid and said, "Sam, things are bad out there. If I hadn't somehow ended up in here, I'd be dead too."

Sam's heart flipped. "Dead *too*? W-what do you mean? Like Keesa?" he said hopefully.

"No, Sam." He paused and dropped to one knee to look directly at the scared boy. "When you disappeared, we had no protection. We were overrun. Without you and Keesa, it was just the three of us against impossible odds. When Titus ran after you, the kupa cats tore through him like paper. Yetews was already gone and Enoch was taken by another one of those giant flying creatures. It broke his neck before I could help him. I was the last one fighting. And then...then I was here."

Sam's eyes went wide and he started to shake his head in disbelief. He couldn't believe what he was hearing. "No," he whispered. "No. *No.* It can't be true. Yetews...Enoch..." he paused and closed his eyes before continuing. "Titus. He wasn't even supposed to be here, and now he's...he's..."

"Dead. I know. I'm so sorry Sam. All hope is lost. We should get out while we still can."

Sam felt the tears burning his cheeks and he started to shake all over. "What about Iggy and Arty? Did they get away at least?"

Taren stared back at him, a blank expression on his face.

"Taren? What about Iggy and Arty?" When Taren still didn't respond, as if he had no idea what the question meant, Sam's brow furrowed. Something wasn't right. He looked closer at Taren's face and noticed that there was something different about his eyes. They weren't the right shade of brown. He also noticed how Taren's bow wasn't even ready for a fight like it always was in these situations. Sam suddenly felt himself taking two cautious steps back.

Taren noticed. "What's wrong Sam? Why do you look so frightened by me?" He reached his hand out, but Sam jerked away. "It's me. I'm not going to hurt you."

Sam turned around and looked into the darkness. He was shaking. He realized what was wrong. He'd never dreamed about Iggy and Arty before, so Nadaroth had no idea who they were. This Taren was an imposter. He got angry again. He flipped around to the imposter and shouted, "You're not Taren!" He then turned back to the darkness and yelled, "This isn't real! Sh-show yourself, Nadaroth! I know I'm dreaming, because Taren would *never* tell me to give up!"

Without warning, two arms grabbed him around the throat. Sam started gasping for air as the imposter Taren dragged him across the floor. Chilling laughter echoed all around him in the darkness as he felt himself being choked. The pressure on his windpipe was crushing down harder as the imposter began laughing maniacally. Sam felt his eyes close and began to believe that it wasn't really another nightmare. He blinked hard, concentrating desperately to wake up. The darkness was taking over his eyes as he gasped one last time, fear swallowing him whole. And then –

– his eyes were open and he could breathe again. He was lying on his back in the dirt, panting hard. The chilling laughter and imposter Taren were gone. It had been a nightmare. What Sam couldn't understand was how he'd fallen asleep and not known it.

Realizing his vulnerable state on the ground, he jumped up and looked around. He realized he was still where he was before the nightmare started. He was cut off from his friends, who were still very much alive and fighting. He couldn't see everyone, but that was the least of his worries at the moment.

Nadaroth tilted his head slightly. A long, shiny sliver of metal formed in mid-air right in front of his shadowy cloaks.

Sam squinted to see what it was. His eyes went wide when he realized it was a large dagger and that it was pointing directly at him. By the time he reacted, the dagger shot through the air. He didn't even have time to think about using his imagination to help, but rather jumped to the right in hopes of the dagger missing him.

It didn't. It grazed him on the side, right across the ribs. He threw his arm across his waist and winced as his hand came back bloody. It wasn't too deep, but enough that his shirt turned red and his ribs burned hot with pain. Sam had just enough sense to react by imagining a bandage around his waist in hopes of stopping, or at least slowing, the bleeding. He had a fleeting sense of gratefulness to Taren for all the training he'd given him. He regained focus on his enemy.

Nadaroth was still there. The silence was eerie as he hovered just above the ground. But three bolts of lightning, one right after another, struck the ground menacingly just a stone's throw away from Sam, shattering the silence. The force of it threw Sam backwards, violently knocking the wind out of him as he fell hard. His arms shook as he tried to push himself up off the ground. The all too familiar taste of blood filled his mouth again and his ears were ringing. He was so tired of hurting – so tired of the taste of blood.

He coughed as the dust cleared where the lightning hit. The thick air burned his lungs. He rubbed his eyes, not believing what he was seeing. It was a gateway. Through it, two dark beasts of burden dragged a cage with two people in it. They were bound, gagged, and blindfolded. They were also filthy, like they'd been dragged through the mud. The creatures had flames for eyes and horrific fanged under-bites. They roared as they approached their master. Nadaroth stroked one of the beasts with a single bony finger and pointed towards Sam.

The beasts warbled and obediently pulled the cage forward. The entire world seemed to be growing darker as Sam fought to see who the poor kids were that had been captured and dragged here in fear. As he looked closer, he realized that they weren't kids at all. They were adults.

They were his parents.

"NO!" Sam screamed. "Mom! Dad!" His parents, not knowing where they were or where Sam was, tried to shout out to him through their gags. But it only came out as a garbled mess. Sam didn't understand how this was even possible. He was terrified of what was going to happen next. "Let them go! They aren't supposed to be here! *Please!*" He begged to his enemy and ran towards the cage. The beasts of burden quickly hissed and snorted angrily, starting to charge him.

But Nadaroth hissed, "*No*. This victory is *mine*." With a mere flick of his wrist, the cage squealed and the bars bent to his will. He was morphing it. It toppled over and Sam's parents fell out. They squirmed until they were on their knees.

The first thing Sam did was start running to them, altogether forgetting his power to imagine. He didn't get more than a few feet when the ground began to tremble beneath him. He looked over to Nadaroth, who had his head bowed in deep concentration. As soon as the ground shook, there was a deafening cracking sound. The earth between Sam and his parents began opening. Rocks and dirt fell into

The gaping fissure, lost to the fiery glow below. Sam skidded to a halt just in time. He looked from the chasm to his parents in sheer terror. "NO!" he screamed. "Don't hurt them!"

That same horrific laughter filled the air again and Nadaroth pointed to Sam's parents. He cocked his head as if amused by Sam's fear. His finger twitched and the blindfolds and gags on his parents evaporated into wisps of smoke.

Sam's mom blinked when she saw her son. "Sam?"

"It's me mom! Don't move! I'm gonna help you!"

She had tears streaming down her dirty cheeks. "Where...where are we? What's happening?" There was panic in her voice.

His dad was looking frantically between them both. He could barely find a word. "Sam?"

"Dad! I'm so sorry!" It was all Sam could say. He looked again at Nadaroth and then remembered who he was now. He wasn't a completely helpless ten-year old boy.

Not here.

Not now.

He squinted in concentration for the briefest moment and a bridge formed as he began to run across the gap. He also formed a barrier between his parents and Nadaroth, blocking them from his enemy's line of sight.

But Nadaroth was more skilled at this game. As Sam started onto the bridge, a boulder appeared from above and fell across the stony pass, destroying it. Sam jumped back to the ground a split second before the whole thing collapsed into the chasm.

Sam got his bearings quickly. In the time it took him to blink, he imagined a giant eagle soaring down to grab his mom and dad.

But Nadaroth was too stealthy. He thwarted the eagle's path with a monstrous creature of flight that snatched the eagle out of the air as if it was catching a bug.

Sam was breathing hard. His head was throbbing. He was beyond his limits now. He looked down and realized he was on his knees and that Nadaroth was still mocking him. All he had left to do was beg. "Please," he barely squeaked out. "I don't understand how you got them here. I'll do anything you want me to. But, please don't hurt my mom and dad."

Nadaroth hesitated. He lowered his hand and Sam thought, for a moment, that his enemy was considering his plea. Instead, he spoke once more. "Understand this. The age of the Guardians is over. This world obeys *me* now."

The ground began to tremble again and Sam scrambled to his feet. He looked helplessly to his parents who looked at Nadaroth then back to their son, pleading silently for answers that they couldn't find questions for. The ground began to shatter before his parents. The fiery glow reflected in their eyes as they tried to back away, but the dark beasts behind them blocked their path.

His parents were teetering at the very edge of the chasm, the ground rumbling beneath them. Sam yelled out to them, "Mom! Dad!"

His mom cried out to him, "Get back, Sam! Run!"

His dad pleaded too. "Go, Sam!" His knee started to slip over the edge.

Sam tried to think of something…anything…to do to help. But Nadaroth interrupted his frantic thoughts. "Sam Little."

Sam, hearing his full name, turned his eyes to his enemy.

Nadaroth stretched one palm out towards his parents. He spoke one last time before closing his fist. "Imagia is *mine*." When his fist closed, the ground beneath his parents dropped like a carpet was being pulled from beneath them.

For one feeble moment, time seemed to stand still as Sam stood helpless and alone. His eyes connected with his mom's for a split second.

And then, they were gone.

Sam ran towards the chasm, dropped to his knees at the edge and began screaming. An unexpected familiar pair of hands grabbed him around the waist before the ground gave way beneath him. Nadaroth had dropped the invisible barrier between Sam and his friends just in time for Taren to see Sam's parents fall. He was dragging Sam back, kicking and screaming.

"Stop fighting me, kid! There's nothing you can do now," said Taren.

"No! NO! Let me go!" Sam fought to get out of Taren's strong grasp. He wiggled in just the right way and dropped to the ground. He was up and running towards Nadaroth before Taren could grab him again.

The Gateway to Imagia: The Tale of Sam Little

Fury filled Sam like nothing else ever had. He could hear Taren – his friend – coming up from behind again. He turned around for a fleeting second which was just enough time to imagine a barely visible wall between the Protector and him.

Taren stopped right before he ran into it. "Sam, what are you doing?" he yelled out.

Sam turned back to Nadaroth and his knees locked. Only this time, it wasn't for the sake of fear. He turned his thoughts to his friends, who were all fighting to find a way through his imagined invisible barrier to help him. He then thought of the needless loss of his friends' lives. His legs wouldn't budge. He could feel the ache of his scarred knee and the dull pain in his ribs, but he continued to stand in front of Nadaroth in utter defiance. He stood there for his friends who were fighting with him. He stood there for Keesa who'd lost her life for him. He stood there for Yetews – his best friend, unjustly taken from him.

But more than anything at this moment, he stood there for his mom and dad, brought here against their will – against the will of Imagia.

Silent tears fell through the new fury in his eyes.

Nadaroth laughed at the boy's sudden lack of fear and he began to imagine the already gaping ground falling into the molten depths below. Rocks were falling and the ground was slowly disappearing in front of Sam. A deafening roar overshadowed the rumbling of the shaking ground. A massive creature came into existence, some distance away, beside Sam. It was focused on the small boy.

Sam recognized the beast. It was the very same one Nadaroth had imagined that destroyed his own Guardian on that fateful day so many years ago. With nowhere to run, the creature would trample and kill him in seconds. He knew he should be terrified, but at that moment, he didn't care. There was already a dull ache in the front of his head, adding to all the pain he felt. But he had to push himself further. Because, seeing that creature made Sam understand what he had to do. He took a shaky breath.

Sam shook his head. He could hear Taren begging Sam to drop the wall while all of his friends were fighting to destroy it. He tried to block them out. Through his tired, tear stained eyes, he whispered, "For the Guardians that were." He blinked and focused his mind. His eyes flicked to a place just behind his enemy. Sam's anger didn't falter, but rather fueled his mind's eye.

Nadaroth twitched his arm and the beast behind Sam charged.

But Sam was prepared for this. He imagined the creature's equal running towards it. As the two charged one another, they fought and tumbled over the edge of the gaping ground. Sam jumped out of the way just in time to not fall with them.

He focused his concentration just in time to hear Nadaroth scream in fury again. Sam's head began to pound, but there was no more time left. He focused even harder and ten of the same creatures that had just fallen over the edge appeared, ready to charge Nadaroth.

Nadaroth laughed at Sam, mocking his strategy. "I fear nothing, child. Now, you will join your pathetic Guardian in death." He lifted his hand to focus on the ground in front of Sam. Nadaroth moved closer to him. His eyes burned brighter with insane rage. His shadow of darkness began to spread and he hissed, "No Guardians will survive this war. Like yours, they too will all fall. And now your friends will watch *you* die." Nadaroth's words lingered in the air.

But before he could imagine anything, Sam did something that confused his enemy and stopped him in his tracks.

Sam smiled. His gaze flicked once more just over Nadaroth's shoulder.

A white light glowed sweetly, slightly dulling the darkness. Nadaroth turned his own gaze behind him where Sam was looking. He shielded his eyes with a bony, shrouded hand as he faced the mysterious glow.

There, in all her beauty, stood the angel-like Guardian Sam had dreamed about so many times before. In the middle of the ring of beasts, stood the Guardian of Nadaroth's past. Sam had imagined Nadaroth's single weakness – his unhealed wound.

But he didn't stop with just her creation. He began to imagine the whole scene from the nightmares he'd witnessed. Around the Guardian, an entire forest appeared. Sam kept his focus. He needed to control everything about this moment, including the beautiful Guardian. He stayed connected with her and she opened her arms to Nadaroth, smiling sweetly.

Furious, Nadaroth threatened, "How *dare* you imagine her, boy!"

The beasts surrounding her roared angrily and Sam closed his eyes in a level of concentration he wasn't sure he could hold on to. His head was screaming in pain and he fell to his knees. Blood began to trickle from his nose.

With his eyes closed, he flashed through all he'd lost today, remembering everything in reverse. It all began with one, single pain. Sam whispered one last thing. "For Keesa." He opened his eyes and released the ten beasts.

The bane of Nadaroth's own past tore across the distance to kill, not him, but the defenseless angelic Guardian.

Nadaroth turned frantically to see the creatures that threatened his once lost Guardian. It was happening exactly as Sam had witnessed in Nadaroth's own mind, tenfold. The creatures would inevitably destroy the unsuspecting Guardian.

As the beast closed in, Nadaroth looked on in horror at what was about to happen. He then made a sound that was even more terrifying than his laugh.

He screamed.

"NO!" Nadaroth screamed again as his Guardian's joy turned to terror. In that instant, the nightmare Sam had witnessed once before changed completely. The unexpected was happening. In a blink, Nadaroth was standing between the stampede of creatures and his Guardian in a feeble attempt to save what was already lost to him.

Sam watched as the beasts trampled and tore at Nadaroth's now solid form, bypassing the Guardian in their wake. They dragged his limp body over the ground. All but two of the beasts plummeted with him into the fiery abyss, Nadaroth's screams fading quickly with them.

What Sam didn't plan for was the sudden change in the remaining beasts' intentions. With Sam's loss of focus, he had suddenly become the new target. With stealth, they leapt the abyss and began to charge him.

He fell backwards, not expecting this turn of events. He had braced himself for the same fate as his fallen enemy when four blurs of tawny fur and a flash of green amongst a rain of arrows shot past him. He watched the ambush happen and he couldn't help but to breathe a sigh of relief.

The barrier he'd imagined had fallen and Sam's friends were attacking the creatures in full force. With barely an ounce of strength left in him, the angelic imagined Guardian faded into nothingness leaving behind the broken bodies and barren landscape of the battle around him.

Nadaroth was gone.

As Sam watched his comrades scatter to fight against the remaining threats, he tried to get to his knees again. He turned his head to see Taren standing above him with an outstretched hand. He gratefully reached for it. Despite the look of pride and amazement on Taren's face, Sam couldn't hold back his pain any longer. He looked at Taren's gentle eyes, now filled with pity. His lip quivered. "Taren, he killed them." He shook his head. "My mom and dad. I don't know how, but…"

Taren interrupted him. "I know. I saw the whole thing. But they couldn't have been real. Nadaroth doesn't have the power to bring them here. He can't. He couldn't possibly…but…Sam…" he paused, uncertainty flooding his face. He wasn't sure enough to guarantee the boy. Sam was looking at him, tears streaming freely. He dropped to one knee and pulled Sam to his chest. Sam was in too much pain. Impossible or not, it was very real to him. "I'm so sorry, kid. I'm so sorry."

Sam held onto Taren and sobbed. "Keesa…Mom…Dad…" he paused to sob again and finished with a whisper, "Yetews."

Taren's eyes went wide. He hadn't realized that Sam didn't know already. He pushed Sam back just enough to look into his eyes. "Sam, Yetews isn't dead. He's hurt pretty bad, but he's still alive."

Sam's eyes went wide in disbelief. Without another word, he ran to Yetews and threw his arms over the unmoving, shaggy neck.

Through the sobs, he apologized to his unconscious Guardian. "I'm so sorry." Sam sniffed loudly. "Yetews. Please be okay. *Please.*"

Sam felt the all too familiar warmth of Taren's hand on his shoulder. "Sam, he's going to be okay."

He looked back at Taren, "He's not going to die, is he?"

He smiled down at him. "He might be limping for awhile, but I think he's going to be just fine, kid."

As Taren uttered those priceless words, Sam felt another familiar warm hand on his back. He turned to face Yetews' gentle, green eyes staring feebly back at him.

Yetews grumbled something low to his boy and struggled to give him a goofy smile but winced in the process. He then saw the pain in his boy's face. Though he had no idea what had taken place, he knew something terrible had happened. He looked up to Taren who shook his head slowly, confirming Yetews' fear. He didn't need to know what happened at this moment. He just knew his boy needed him more than ever and he pushed through the pain of his injuries and pulled Sam into his hairy chest. Sam threw his arms around his shaggy neck in response, burying his head in the long black fur, sobbing uncontrollably.

As Sam held tight to Yetews, he fought to stay conscious. The battle seemed to halt when Nadaroth fell. The remaining enemies scattered, leaving the worn group of friends alone in the barren land.

The nightmare may have been over, but the pain Sam felt was far from gone. Nadaroth had fallen this day, but being comforted by his Guardian – his friend – was all Sam cared about right now. He hurt too much to hide it away any longer. He closed his eyes, and let his emotions go.

The worst was over now. It was time to go home.

Chapter Twenty-seven: Unexpected Turn

Sam yawned loudly as he stared across the familiar aged table. He rubbed at his eyes and smiled. He was in the place that he'd never thought likely he'd see again. Returning to Orga's home seemed quite impossible months ago. But as he watched Warg contentedly sleeping next to Titus, he felt at peace.

Since the fall of Nadaroth, things had been complicated. Sam still had to be careful about where he went and Taren and Yetews insisted on staying by his side nearly all of the time. Taren had explained that even though Nadaroth was gone, it would take a long time before all of his collectors and followers would be controlled. And Sam, with the powers he had, apparently brought a high price for many of them. For the time being, things were just as dangerous for Guardians and children.

Sam had spent most of his time resting and healing from everything he'd been through. His physical wounds healed fairly quickly. But his mind was a different story. After the battle with Nadaroth, Sam's mind was incredibly worn out. It took him weeks before he could imagine something as small as a butterfly into existence. And even then, it faded quickly. Orga, of course, had a theory for that as well. He was certain that Sam pushed himself too far and that his mind, much like the physical wounds of his body, would take time to heal. He compared it to breaking a leg, but trying to run on it over and over again before the bone could mend itself.

But it wasn't just the imagining parts of his mind that needed time to heal. The emotional wounds he'd brought back with him were deep. They were the worst scars he'd carried since that day.

Sam spent the first month after the battle, fighting nightmares of his own. Each time he closed his eyes, he could see his parents and Keesa dying over and over again. Nadaroth may not have been able to give him nightmares any longer, but Sam still woke up screaming at night from time to time.

There had been many discussions on the events of that day, much to Sam's dismay. The general consensus was that Nadaroth could not have had the power to open a gateway of his own freewill. Taren, though not entirely convinced himself, tried to make Sam understand that the people he'd witnessed die that day were more than likely just another creation from Nadaroth's mind that was meant to do exactly what it had done: Scare and hurt Sam.

Sam tried to believe this with all of his heart. However hard he tried, he still couldn't stop reliving it in his mind. Over the past months, he'd started to accept their theory. The first time, when he'd missed his gateway, he had to say goodbye to his parents. It took him long enough to accept that much. Regardless of whether or not they were real, seeing them die and saying goodbye again, was almost unbearable.

In the end, they all realized that they'd never really know for sure. They settled for simply being understanding and sympathetic of Sam's experience. The hope that his parents might still be alive was what Sam clung to. But none of this was relevant to the other loss they had all suffered. Keesa's death left everyone with pain. Her attachment to Sam naturally made the loss much more significant for him.

Months later, things were starting to return to a certain level of normalcy. It had taken them quite a long time to return. Without Sam's ability to imagine, the trip home to southern Imagia was nearly as long and frustrating as it was to northern Imagia. Luckily, they'd had some help from previous friends to aide their journey, making it not nearly as treacherous.

Today, it was nearing the dusky part of evening that Sam so enjoyed. He wanted badly to leave the confines of Orga's home to see the forest. With his elbow propped up on the table, he leaned his cheek on his hand. Taren was having an in depth conversation with Garrett and Orga about the next steps to take against the mess that Nadaroth had left in the wake of his reign.

Garrett was very comfortable in Orga's home after spending so much time as his temporary appointed Protector. Sam was glad to have him around. He always brought a new light to the room whenever he visited.

Sam sighed and realized that it was louder than he intended it to be.

Taren noticed and stopped in mid-conversation. He raised an eyebrow at Sam as he considered to himself silently. Finally he said, "After all of the danger and crazy days you've spent while here, is it too much for you to simply relax? Or does the protection and guaranteed safety bore you?"

Sam grinned. He'd known Taren long enough to know when he was attempting humor. Yetews nudged him with a hairy elbow and smiled as well. Sam shrugged. "I just want to go out for a little bit. I haven't seen Enoch in weeks and I was kind of hoping to talk to him about the other dragons he is looking for."

Taren started to shake his head but then caught Orga's eye and stopped. Sam also noticed the look that Orga was giving and he knew it meant he'd get his way.

Orga smiled. His large jowl jiggled as he laughed quietly and then he said, "If you go out now Sam, then you will have to take everyone with you. Don't forget that you were attacked just last week."

"I know," Sam answered. "I remember. But we won't go far. I just want to talk to Enoch." He pleaded with his eyes the way only a child could.

Iggy and Arty had opted to stay with Sam in Orga's home as well. They were playing a game called Skiltch that involved tossing polished stones into three triangles. Upon hearing Sam's plea to see Enoch, Arty chimed in. "Actually, I could stand to get some fresh air myself. Been meaning to have a few words with that dragon anyhow."

"Yes," Iggy agreed. He rubbed his bottom jaw as he spoke,

"Blasted dragon owes us a fair bit from our last game."

"Dirty, rotten lizard," Arty scoffed. "Should have known better than to play the game with a dragon."

Sam rolled his eyes at Iggy and Arty. The jabs at Enoch weren't fooling him. He'd seen them together in the heat of battle and on their trek home. Despite the way they jeered each other, they were friends and had proven it time and again.

Taren tried to hide his grin. "Okay. We'll go out for a while. But as soon as you're done talking with Enoch, then it's straight back here. Agreed?" The truth was, that Taren was almost as eager for a change of scenery as Sam was.

Sam was beaming. He jumped up from the bench. He hollered back as he ran to his room, "Cool!" He hurried to put his shoes on and was back in the big room before anyone had a chance to move towards the door.

Sam had barely made it outside when he felt Yetews pick him up. He had situated himself comfortably on his favorite place on Yetews' shoulders by the time they reached the top of the slope to the clearing.

Garrett had remained with Orga back at the home. Orga didn't share Sam's enthusiasm for exploring the forest. He'd lived in Imagia far too long for it to hold his interest. But he did ask as they left to take Warg along. He was always ready to go for a walk and enjoyed going with Titus, who was very tolerant of the little creature's need to tag along.

As Sam looked around, he couldn't help but feel like things were normal again. They were very near where Enoch was staying for the time in the forest. They'd be reunited with him soon enough. It was almost exactly as it should have been, save one. His heart ached for a moment as he thought of Keesa. He missed her very much. Her children returned with them to Orga's home, but they left a week after arriving. They felt it was their duty to seek out rogue kupa cats in hopes of saving them from a life of servitude. It was the best way they could find to honor their fallen mother.

Sam understood for the most part, but not having them around made it even more difficult. He missed seeing the three crystalline eyes looking back at him. She was the closest to a mother figure he'd had since coming to Imagia. Remembering her always reminded him of his own mom and it was doubly painful. There were just too many painful memories when he traveled down this memory lane. He tried not to think about it anymore and concentrated on other things.

Taren had come to know the different looks that Sam had. He recognized this one all to well. He brought up a new subject to help him out. "So, kid. Orga wanted me to talk to you about your big day coming up."

Sam looked down, slightly confused. "What big day?"

"Well, it's been almost a full year since you first arrived in Imagia. You know what that means. You've got a birthday coming up. If you factor in life experiences, that would make you what? Twenty? Perhaps twenty-one?" He smiled and winked.

Sam laughed. "Woah. I guess I didn't even think about it. My eleventh birthday. Has it really been a whole year?" He sighed. It was a bitter-sweet thought.

Taren realized he may have chosen a sensitive subject, but tried to put a positive spin on it. "Yep. In about five weeks, it will be a year. So, Orga thinks we need to have a party. We can invite anyone you'd like. I know for a fact that Garrett already has a gift for you."

Sam smiled. "Cool!" What is it?"

Taren grinned back. "I guess you'll just have to wait and see. Besides, he just wants an excuse to compare battle scars with you. So does that mean I can tell Orga the party is good to go?"

"Yes! I hope someone here knows how to make cake. I miss cake."

Taren made a silent note of that to himself. He also noticed that Sam no longer looked as distressed. They all went back to silently looking for Enoch.

He wasn't hard to find if he was in the sky, but in his less impressive size and being green, he was difficult to spot in the forest. Luckily, Titus had a keen nose and before Enoch could announce himself, he was revealed.

He weaved through the large trees as he walked to them. "It's getting late. I wasn't expecting you tonight. Is there a problem?" Enoch asked in his smooth voice.

Taren jabbed a thumb up at Sam. It was explanation enough for the dragon. "Ah, I see," Enoch said. "What is it you would like to know about tonight, Sam?"

"I was wondering if you found any other dragons to help you free the marked ones?"

Enoch flicked a quick look to Taren who was still trying to hide his grin. Enoch masked his reptilian smile with false seriousness. Everyone, including him, was aware of Sam's consistent need for adventure. He was quite convincing in his earnestness. "Hmm. Well, there are a few that I'm tracking, but it's the same news as it was last time. It's looking very promising though."

Sam had really hoped to meet another dragon, so he was slightly disappointed. More than anything, he was glad to be out of the confines of the home, so he tried not to dwell on the lack of news.

Arty and Iggy were already trying to convince Enoch of a quick game of Skiltch. Taren's interest was peaked and he asked to play a round or two before they were to head back home. No one was really pushing to get back too quickly.

As he watched his friends, reunited again, he couldn't help but to smile. Iggy and Arty were constantly finding reasons to leave Orga's home. As much as he didn't miss the hardships of his past travels, he did miss being together with his friends. Since their return, everyone seemed to come and go so often.

Yetews leaned his back up against a rather large tree trunk and rested. Since his attack, he'd developed a slight limp on his back leg. It ached more the longer he was on it so he welcomed resting it for the time. Sam joined him and propped himself up against one of his hairy legs.

Titus was the only one not preoccupying himself. He was standing at alert a good distance away from the rest of them. Sam watched his old friend for a time and considered the changes that he'd seen. Titus, though still a loyal and exceptional friend, had become very serious about many things. Above all else, he took Sam's safety more seriously than most anything.

And Sam was eternally grateful for his protection. No one could disregard any concern he had. It was for this reason that Taren stopped playing the game and carefully watched Titus, for his ears had suddenly gone on the alert.

Titus began to move cautiously closer to the trees, smelling the air repetitively. By this time, Taren was already at his side.

"What is it?" Taren asked.

Titus sniffed the air again. "Do you smell that?"

Everyone stopped what they were doing and concentrated on Titus.

Taren put a hand on his bow and smelled the air. He shook his head. "I can't smell anything. What do you think it is?"

"I don't know, but there is something very…familiar about it."

A small gust of wind ruffled Sam's hair. He barely had a chance to feel the wind on his skin when Titus suddenly jumped forward. At the same time, Yetews sat up straight, nearly knocking Sam to the ground with his quick shift in position.

"Hey!" Sam said, catching himself with his elbows as he fell backwards. "What was the point of that?" He started to frown but quickly changed his demeanor when he saw the alert expression on Yetews' face. He had sensed something too and Sam could tell.

Yetews grumbled something to him and Sam translated to the others, slightly worried by what might be causing such alarm in his friends. "He says he can sense something too."

Titus was focused on a spot, beyond the trees in the thick of the forest. Without warning, he shot off into the deep woods.

Without an ounce of hesitation, Yetews swiped Sam off of his feet and followed him into the trees. Taren was already running after Titus, and Enoch tailed them from behind with Iggy and Arty in tow. Warg, despite his awkward waddle and plump body, was managing to keep up fairly well.

Sam wasn't sure if he should be scared, worried, or curious. So he settled on being all three. Titus was barely a russet blur as he weaved and darted through the trees and foliage of the forest. Sam watched from atop Yetews and wondered what could have caused his friend to take off so quickly with almost no warning.

Before he knew it, they came to a complete stop in the middle of what was obviously a small clearing in the trees. It was barely big enough to fit all of them comfortably. Sam was about to ask what was going on when Titus spoke first.

"It's here. There is something about this smell that I can't place. But it's right here in this clearing. It almost smells like –"

He was cut short. Something was happening to the trees before them. As they watched, the familiar sound of tinkling wind chimes filled the air. The sound sent shivers through Sam. He'd heard this sound only a few times in Imagia and it never ended well.

The Gateway to Imagia: The Tale of Sam Little

Taren held a steady hand on his bow and arrow as each of them witnessed the opening of a gateway. Slowly, almost everyone began to back away from it – everyone but Yetews. He stood his ground for a moment before starting to inch closer to the opening. Sam wrapped his fingers deeper into the thick hair on Yetews' neck and held tight. He was about to ask Yetews to move back when a flash of something caught his eye.

"Yetews," Sam said, "Put me down."

Taren, justifiably concerned, protested. "We shouldn't interfere with this. Let's back up and let this gateway's Guardian take over." But even as he was saying this, everyone noticed that the gateway's Guardian hadn't arrived yet.

Yetews, much to Taren's dismay, placed Sam on the ground. He grumbled something low and Sam nodded. "I know. I can see it." There was unmistakable wonderment in his voice as he inched closer to the gateway.

Sam squinted his eyes and looked out into the world beyond Imagia. His world. As he looked out into the star kissed morning of his world, he saw another glimpse of what caught his attention before.

There was someone moving in the distance. Across an uncared for field with grass waist high, there stood a fence. Through the fence, Sam could see someone pacing outside the door to a home. And as he looked harder, he caught everyone by surprise when he gasped loudly.

Taren had his bow aimed directly at the gateway. "What? What do you see?" he asked frantically.

Sam flipped around, disbelief and shock in his eyes. "My home! It's...it's my home! I can't believe it!"

Taren dropped his bow to his side and joined Sam. The others followed close in his footsteps out of curiosity.

Sam looked at Taren and Yetews. "B-but...I don't understand. This isn't where my gateway was before. But it's really my house out there. And I can see someone." He squinted, trying to make out who might be living in his old house now. He was still convinced his parents had died. "Maybe my aunt or uncle bought the house after my parents..." Sam's eyes went wide and he stepped back fast, running right into Yetews and nearly falling on Iggy.

His frantic retreat caused everyone alarm. Taren had his bow aimed again. "What happened? What did you see?"

Sam was shaking his head in denial. "No. I saw them die. It can't be them. It just can't be!"

"Your parents. You see your parents, don't you?" Taren asked.

Sam nodded, still unbelieving. All he could find to say was one word. "How?"

Yetews grumbled the obvious answer. Titus translated. "Taren and Orga were right. It was never your real parents that you watched die that day." He paused while Yetews growled something else, then translated for him again. "He says that Sam is getting a second chance to go home." When Titus got those words out, he sat down on his haunches and couldn't believe what he'd just heard.

Sam frowned. "But I missed my gateway. You only get one. It's the law of Imagia."

Taren thought about it and then answered, "That's right. You do only get one. This gateway isn't meant for you. It's just strange luck to see one that leads to nearly the same place. Sometimes it takes time for a Guardian to find their gateway and reach their child on the other side." He looked around nervously as if waiting for someone to spring a trap. He considered something else. "The laws of Imagia have been broken once before though. You *did* send Elizabeth out of your own gateway. Everything changed that day."

Sam stepped closer and watched the person pacing. "Taren. It's my mom. It's really her. She's alive!"

Taren stepped forward and concentrated on the scene. He was also never fully convinced that Sam's parents weren't the real ones when they died. As he was watching, Sam saw an odd look in Taren's eyes that he couldn't quite place. He wasn't sure what it meant and wondered what the Protector could be thinking. Sam was suddenly distracted when Yetews placed a hand on his shoulder.

When Sam looked up into Yetews' eyes, they were pleading with him. Yetews' job as a Guardian was to get him home, and against all odds, he was being given a second chance; A chance to redeem his failure at returning Sam home so long ago on that fateful day. He grumbled to Sam and gestured towards the gateway.

Sam frowned and then swallowed hard. He never thought that he would have to make this decision again. He hesitated for a moment. He looked out at his home towards his mom as she paced solemnly in the morning light. He was torn in two directions. "Yetews? I – I don't

The Gateway to Imagia: The Tale of Sam Little

know what to do. It's not even my gateway."

The joy he felt from seeing his mom alive was greater than any joy he'd felt in long time. But it had been so long since he'd been home. He'd already started to accept his parents as being gone forever. And as much as Sam wanted to run to his mother, he equally wanted to remain with Yetews. He'd accepted his choice to stay in Imagia and wasn't prepared for a chance to return home. It was all happening so suddenly and his stomach lurched at the idea of saying goodbye. He wished the decision would be taken out of his hands.

He realized that it wasn't just the idea of leaving Imagia behind that kept him from running through that gateway. He was genuinely afraid to go back. He didn't know what would happen if he did.

But Yetews growled again and his eyes softened. Taren, not needing to understand the complex strain of growls and grumbles, knew what the Guardian was trying to say. He kneeled down, face-to-face now with Sam. With understanding and sadness in his eyes, he said, "Yetews is right. I don't know how or why, but this is a second chance. You gotta go, kid. You did what you had to do and now with an unexpected turn of luck, you have a chance to go home. Your mom is alive. That's reason enough. You don't have to hurt any longer."

Titus sat at Sam's side and whined quietly. "Sam, we can go home now. Before this gateway's Guardian comes, we need to act. But it is your decision in the end. I will go wherever you go."

Sam slowly shook his head. "But...I'd be taking another kid's gateway. Isn't that wrong? It's not meant for me. Right?"

Iggy, in a bittersweet tone, said, "The chances of this happening are astronomical! Imagia must be smilin' on you today. If I were you, I'd high tail it out of here before that gateway slams in your face."

"Yes," Arty agreed with the same tone. Like everyone else, they had grown very fond of Sam and no one was eager to say farewell. But nevertheless, he said, "Look, no one wants to see you stay more than us. Without you, we'd still be scraping by on years of amnesty from old Ognotz and the lot. Though, I must admit, it'd be nice to have you hanging around and imagining up a nice place to stay and maybe some nifty new clothes for us. Do you know how hard it is to get clothes in this size? Yep. A kid with your talent would sure come in handy, if you don't mind me sayin'!" He winked at Sam.

Enoch, not wanting to remain without opinion, rolled his eyes at

Iggy and Arty. He said, "I think what these two are *trying* to say is that you *deserve* this chance, even if the gateway isn't yours to take."

Sam still looked torn on the matter. He looked at Taren. "I can do more for Imagia. You said yourself that the battle is far from over. And my imagination is just now starting to go back to normal."

Taren began to say something, but stopped. He started again, "Look, kid. What you've already done was way more than anyone could have ever expected out of you. You went through..." He stopped suddenly and looked down. He grabbed Sam by both shoulders this time and looked directly in his eyes. "You experienced more pain and suffering than any person should have to. And now you know for sure that part of that pain was an illusion. You don't have to hurt anymore for that. Your parents are alive! You deserve to have this. And somehow...I think that this gateway *is* meant for you. Perhaps Imagia believes you deserve this too. Go home, kid. Be happy. I know it's what I would do." He let go of Sam and backed away, bowing his head again.

Sam could see the feelings were unanimous. He swallowed the brick that was stuck in his throat. He could feel the burning in his eyes as he tried to decide what to do. Yetews pointed at Sam's mom and growled sadly.

Sam closed his eyes tight as he realized that Yetews was right. "I know she's sad." He tried to get the next words out of his mouth but his tongue felt swollen as he tried. He concentrated on moving his lips and whispered, "I guess then...I should go home." He continued to fight back the ache in his heart and the burning in his eyes that grew by the moment.

Taren still had his head slightly bowed as Sam walked past him towards Enoch. He didn't hesitate at all, but threw his arms around the dragon's scaly neck. Enoch wrapped one of his muscular arms around Sam and returned the embrace. "Thank you Sam. For everything."

Enoch smiled and then Sam let go and smiled back. "Good luck with the dragons. I wish I could have seen them."

Sam turned to Iggy and Arty who were both fidgeting.

Arty said, "Thanks for keeping us out of the dragon's belly. Best decision you ever made." He laughed shakily.

Iggy added, "And, uh...not to mention defeating Nadaroth and

The Gateway to Imagia: The Tale of Sam Little

saving our necks a few times. We owe ya one."

"Or two," Arty said.

"Maybe even three." Iggy was chuckling again.

Sam laughed too and concentrated on both of them for a moment. Both ferrets jumped back as they realized they were now wearing entirely new clothes. There were two brand new packs on the ground in front of them that appeared to be brimming full of stuff.

Iggy shouted, "Hey! Parting gifts!"

"Excellent!" Arty said excitedly.

Sam had turned to Taren. The Protector took a deep breath and then looked back at Sam. For the first time, Taren was at a complete loss for words. "I don't know what else to say. This is so sudden."

"I know." Sam couldn't have agreed more.

"I guess that birthday party isn't going to happen after all." He grinned feebly.

Sam laughed quietly. He looked down at his feet. He was looking forward to celebrating his birthday with his friends. It would have been the first birthday he'd ever have gotten to celebrate with actual friends. He didn't know what else to say.

Taren seemed to be nodding to himself for a moment while biting his bottom lip. Sam had never seen that look on him. Taren finally spoke again. "Hmm. Well, I suppose I could thank you or ask for a new set of clothes, but neither one is good enough. A new set of clothes won't replace you and 'thank you' doesn't even begin to cover it. The best thing I can do is give you some advice. I don't know what will happen when you leave. But be careful what you say to people – even to your parents. They won't believe you and that could be…dangerous for you. Good luck." He looked like he wanted to say something else, but instead he merely sighed and stuck out a hand for Sam to shake. "Imagia won't be the same without you, kid."

Sam looked at Taren's outstretched hand. He slowly moved to place his hand inside of the Protector's palm. As he did, Taren pulled him in quickly and hugged him tight. Sam couldn't help but to smile widely. He really was the brother that Sam never had. He wanted to tell him how much he meant to him and how much he'd miss him, but the words wouldn't come. It was just too hard to put into words. He squeezed his eyes closed tight and sniffed loudly.

Sam imagined a new bow and set of arrows for Taren. It was

352

perfect in every way with carvings of vines and leaves that intertwined and weaved over its flawless arc. Sam said, "I'll miss you Taren. Please," he choked up as he said the words, "protect Yetews."

Sam wasn't sure, but he thought he saw tears in the mighty Protector's eyes as he firmly grasped the bow in his hands and nodded. "You have my word."

Finally, he'd come to Yetews. He stood in front of his Guardian and stared down at his shoes. There were no words that could make this moment easier. Saying goodbye to him was the hardest. He tried to get the words out but was afraid to look at him. "Yetews, I – I…"

As he fought to get the right words out, he felt a large, warm finger touch under his chin. Yetews pulled his chin up so that they were looking at each other.

Sam looked at the gateway and then back at Yetews. He whispered. "I'm scared."

The Guardian nodded. He understood what Sam was afraid of. He was scared too. Through the sorrow in his gentle, green eyes, he managed to give his goofy smile. He grumbled something and then tousled Sam's overgrown hair lovingly.

Sam smiled back and said, "Yeah. It *was* a pretty good adventure, wasn't it?" They chuckled together for a moment and then Sam stuttered through his next words. "I'll m-miss you…s-so much."

With that, Yetews pulled Sam to his hairy chest and wrapped his massive arms tight around the boy. That was all it took for Sam, and he sobbed into Yetews' chest. Yetews grumbled something and Sam answered, "I love you too."

Yetews gently stroked his boy's back. As he blinked, two large tears fell onto Sam's head.

When they let go, Yetews wiped away Sam's tears with his finger and then smiled tenderly at him.

Sam reached into his pocket and pulled out the tattered photo he'd imagined of his parents and him. He unfolded it carefully and then concentrated on it. It morphed in his hand. The creases and folds smoothed out. Then the image changed. It no longer was a photo of his family, but rather a perfect image of him and Yetews together. He imagined a second copy of the photo and a leather pouch in his other hand.

He handed one picture and the pouch to Yetews and then folded

The Gateway to Imagia: The Tale of Sam Little

the other one up and put it back in his pocket. He sniffed loudly and said, "I'll always carry it, ok?"

Yetews nodded. He put the photo in the pouch and hung it around his neck. He put a protective hand over the pouch as it hung close to his heart.

Sam couldn't believe that his days of imagining were about to end. It was hard to think that he had an amazing power that he was so quickly going to lose. So he imagined one last thing. The same flower that he'd imagined so many times before, appeared mere feet from the gateway. Then Titus joined him at his side.

Warg ran up to Sam as he nervously stared at the gateway and he slobbered on the boy's open hand. He grinned down at him and scratched behind his ear holes. "Say goodbye to Orga for me, k?" He looked back to Taren and added, "Will you say goodbye to Garrett for me too? Tell him I wish I could have compared scars again and see what he got me for my birthday."

Taren nodded firmly. "I will, kid. I promise." He smiled bitter-sweetly.

Sam looked around and smiled weakly at his friends. He wanted to say so much more, but he couldn't manage to find the words. He turned with Titus close on his heels. He closed his eyes and tried to step through the gateway but couldn't find the will to make his feet move.

As he struggled with his internal battle, someone came to his side to help him find the way. Yetews scooped him up one last time, placed him on his shoulders, and walked him through the gateway. When they were through, he gently placed him on the ground and hugged Sam tightly once more.

They looked at each other. Yetews grumbled something sincerely and Sam sniffed loudly before saying, "I will be. You be safe too, k?" Yetews smiled, nodded, and wiped one more tear from Sam's cheek before turning to go back through the gateway. As he turned, Sam asked, "Wait! What if I get scared again? What if something goes wrong?"

Yetews looked back. He smiled crookedly and grumbled. He winked and pointed at Sam's home. Sam nodded, smiled back and turned to look towards his backyard.

Sam could feel the early warmth of the light from the new day on his skin and said, "Yeah, I guess, but..." He turned back around to finish talking to his Guardian, only to see Yetews crossing back through the gateway. He felt panic as he realized what he'd just done. Suddenly he didn't want to go home anymore. He didn't want to say goodbye. Panic and fear flooded his thoughts. He spun on his heel to start following Yetews back. But before he could take two steps, he saw the image of his friends begin to fade as they waved to him.

He was too late.

And then – just like that – they were gone.

Now he was standing in the forest with only Titus by his side.

It was early morning there and Sam took a deep breath as he took his first step back home. As he emerged from the forest, he saw his mom. She was now sitting on the back step of his house gazing into the trees.

She must have seen him because she stood up and slowly walked away from the house. As soon as she made eye contact with Sam, she shouted something that he couldn't understand. Seeing her run to him, made him remember how much he'd missed his parents. All of a sudden, he couldn't remember why he was so afraid of this moment. He picked up his feet and began to run through the tall grass towards the back gate. It was wide open.

He realized that she must have shouted for his dad, because he was running out of the back door and close on his mom's heels.

They met him half way, screaming his name the whole time. When they reached each other, Sam's parents hugged him tight and he smiled. Despite all he'd been through and however long he'd been gone, the impossible happened. Through her heavy sobs of joy, his mom asked, "Where have you been all this time?" She kept running her eyes over him and patting his arms and face as if checking for injuries.

Sam looked for an answer that he could give her, but after a minute of silence, she hugged him tighter and said, "Oh, never mind! All that matters is that you are safe at home again."

His Dad pulled them all closer together and kissed his messy, overgrown hair. "Yes. Home at last."

He smiled and tightened his arms around his parents. He wasn't sure what he'd say to them when they asked again, but it didn't matter at the moment. After a few minutes of hectic questions and joyful

The Gateway to Imagia: The Tale of Sam Little

tears of reunion, they turned to walk across the yard.

His dad held a steady arm around Sam's shoulder and Titus fell into step at his friend's side. Sam's dad asked a question so quietly that it was as if he was talking to himself, "Where on *Earth* have you been for so long and how did you get back?" Sam looked down at Titus who was already looking up at him and grinning his doggish smile. Titus winked and Sam suddenly knew that things would never be the same after all he'd been through.

As they slowly made their way into the house, Sam took one last look over his shoulder at the forest behind him. Quietly, so that no one would hear him, he whispered, "Bye, Yetews."

He stepped inside. He was home.

* * * * * * * * *

Before Sam knew it, the day had passed and he was already lying in his own bed, staring out the window of his home. His cat, Cooper, was curled up at the end of his bed and purring loudly while Titus was sitting close to him on the floor. Seeing Cooper made him smile. His thoughts strayed to Keesa.

His parents finally shut the door after checking in on him for the eleventh time in an hour. He tried to pretend to be sleeping, but he wasn't tired at all.

Now that the door was shut, he whispered to Titus. "It feels weird to be back."

Titus looked at the door and turned back to Sam. In a very low voice, he answered back, "Yes. Very strange. I will miss them."

Sam thought about it. He already missed Taren and his other friends and vowed to never forget them. But most of all, he missed Yetews. Life in the normal world would never feel complete without his Guardian there to protect and watch over him. But despite what anyone told him, he was hopeful that he'd be reunited with his friends in Imagia again one day.

Titus saw the look of longing in Sam's eyes as he gazed out the open window. He whispered again, "I'm so sorry, Sam. I know you wish there was a way we could see them again someday."

Sam smiled. It suddenly dawned on him that Titus was still speaking to him. He hadn't noticed before this moment because he'd grown so accustomed to it over the past year. The rules of Imagia had somehow changed. He scratched behind Titus' ears as he thought quietly to himself. Then he said, "Don't worry. We'll see them again."

Cocking his head, he asked, "What do you mean? How?"

Sam continued to grin widely as he pulled his folded copy of the picture he'd imagined out of his pajama pocket. He looked at the picture for a moment before answering. If Imagia had found a way to send him home against all odds, then there was a chance Imagia could take him back. "I don't know for sure." He paused, and then added, "But I imagine I'll find a way."

As he drifted off to sleep, Sam's thoughts were of Yetews and his friends. He knew that if there were a way to get back to Imagia, he'd find it. At the moment, he simply wanted to dream peacefully in the comfort of his own bed.

He'd had one of the greatest adventures of his life. But for now, he was home.

Author's Note

Thanks for reading *The Gateway to Imagia: The Tale of Sam Little*. This is my first book and I am currently working on the second book in the series. I appreciate your time and interest!

Be looking for Sam to return in part two of the Imagia Triogy:

"*The Gateway to Imagia: The Gathering*"

If you enjoyed my book, please like and share my page on Facebook.

www.facebook.com/TheGatewayToImagia

Leave me a comment. I'd love to hear what you thought of it.

For those with access to e-readers, after 100 sales of my book, I'll put a free copy of the first chapter (unedited) to book two up for e-readers!

Thanks for reading!

And remember – keep on imagining!

Made in the USA
San Bernardino, CA
30 May 2014